The
WIND
WHISTLING
in the
CRANES

The

WIND
WHISTLING

in the

CRANES

A Novel

LÍDIA JORGE

Translated from the Portuguese by Margaret Jull Costa and Annie McDermott

LIVERIGHT PUBLISHING CORPORATION
A Division of W. W. Norton & Company
Independent Publishers Since 1923

The world is a very long story,
but we are the ones who weave the plot,
be it small or large. For all those who spoke to me of their enigmas,
for sharing this same thought.

And for the person who wrote on a wall
in the Avenida the following words:
Come alone and bring the Stars.

For Jean Stein,
who knew Faulkner's work so well,
and yet who listened patiently to Milene's story
when it was still just a dizzy dream.

And above all for my dear family,
who have always put up with me living other lives.

The hand that whirls the water in the pool
Stirs the quicksand; that ropes the blowing wind
Hauls my shroud sail.
And I am dumb to tell the hanging man
How of my clay is made the hangman's lime.

—Dylan Thomas

Translators' Introduction

THE NOVEL BEGINS ON A BAKING-HOT AUGUST AFTERNOON in 1994, with Milene Leandro standing at the gates of her family's old canning factory in the Algarve. She is seeking answers: Days before, her grandmother escaped from the ambulance that should have been taking her to a nursing home, wandered off into the night, and was later found dead outside the factory entrance. Milene shouts through the gates, but no one responds. Even the landscape—the sand, the gravel, the disused railway line, and the occasional fallen tree—seems willfully silent, and Milene imagines yelling at her surroundings: "Speak, you sneaky things, you cretins, you fools!" They don't obey her, of course, but in another sense they do: *The Wind Whistling in the Cranes* is the story of what the factory has seen ever since it was built on this empty stretch of coastline almost ninety years before. This story, in turn, is closely entwined with another: the story of Portugal's changing fortunes throughout the twentieth century.

The factory was founded in 1908 by Milene's bushy-mustached great-grandfather, José Joaquim Leandro. A paternalistic figure, he is cast by Milene's uncles as a great benefactor, employing "girls as young as seven, whose productivity would have been less than zero, just to give their families a helping hand," and paying for their uniforms himself. The factory went from strength to strength, as did the Portuguese canning industry as a whole, and profits soared during the Second World War: Portuguese factories sold canned goods to both England and Germany at inflated prices, despite widespread hunger among the population at home. And yes, Milene's uncles concede, José Joaquim Leandro may have made a fortune sending shipments over the border falsely labeled "Surplus from Portugal." However, they emphasize, he wasn't like other industrialists at the time: he never printed swastikas on the lids of his cans, or smoked thousand-escudo notes wrapped around his Cuban cigars.

By April 25, 1974, when the largely peaceful Carnation Revolution marked the end of almost fifty years of dictatorship in Portugal, the factory had been passed down to José Joaquim Leandro's idealistic grandson, José Carlos. In the aftermath of the uprising, workers seized control of factories, farms, and other workplaces in order to run them as cooperatives, and slogans like "Down with the exploiters" began to appear on the cannery walls. Not wanting to stand in the way of history, José Carlos handed the factory over to a group of workers, presenting them with the keys on a velvet cushion. The keys were returned to the family ten years later on the same velvet cushion, with the factory now an empty shell, the business in ruins, and the machinery all sold off. "Did we win?" Milene, a child at this point, asked her aunts and uncles as the last few workers sped away on their mopeds. Her relatives did not answer.

The Carnation Revolution also put an end to the Portuguese Colonial War, a thirteen-year conflict between the Portuguese military and the growing nationalist movements in the country's African territories. One such territory was Cape Verde, an archipelago off the west coast of Africa that was uninhabited when the Portuguese landed in the 1460s—more than three decades before Columbus reached the Americas—and which became the first European colony in the tropics and a major staging post in the transatlantic slave trade. Cape Verde, along with the other Luso-

African colonies, including Angola and Mozambique, gained independence in 1975. The decades that followed saw mass immigration from Lusophone Africa to Portugal, and it is a family of Cape Verdean immigrants, the Matas, who became tenants in the now-empty canning factory, paying a small amount of rent and maintaining the buildings in return.

However, the Matas' days in the factory are numbered: tourism is booming in the Algarve and the factory is sitting on prime real estate. The Leandro family sell the building off to a Dutch corporation that plans to build a luxury resort on the site, despite the environmental destruction this will entail. The developer's claims—"We won't disturb so much as the root of a palm tree. Quite the contrary. The palm trees will actually like what we do"—are as familiar as they are untrue. In this globalized world, even the events of the novel morph into marketing materials: we learn much of the story of the factory, for example, from an extended sales pitch delivered by Milene's uncles during a dinner with the Dutch developers. The Matas, too, are packaged up for publicity purposes: when flying over the factory in a helicopter, the Dutch developer is enchanted by the picturesque *Out of Africa* feel they lend to the landscape, though he is equally pleased to hear they can be swiftly evicted.

The romance that develops between members of the Leandro and Mata families throws into relief Portugal's troubled relationship with its colonial past. The discourse of multiculturalism and tolerance that became widespread in Portugal in the 1990s has been linked to "lusotropicalism," the contested notion that the intermixing of Portuguese colonizers with their colonized subjects created a uniquely hybrid, open-minded society.* Felícia

---

* For a fuller discussion of this in relation to *The Wind Whistling in the Cranes*, see Ana Paula Ferreira, "Lusotropicalist Entanglements: Colonial Racisms in the Postcolonial Metropolis," *Gender, Empire, and Postcolony: Luso-Afro-Brazilian Intersections*, edited by Hilary Owen and Anna M. Klobucka (New York: Palgrave Macmillan, 2014), pp. 49–68.

Mata's freckles and green eyes, however, are the result not of a fruitful cultural exchange but of the betrayal of her great-great-grandmother by a duplicitous French sailor. The behavior of Milene's image-conscious uncles and aunts also exposes this discourse of tolerance as a façade. They may be squeamish about the overtly racist language used by their brother-in-law Dom Silvestre, who lived for some time in apartheid-era South Africa, but some of their cruelest actions arise from an unspoken complicity with his views. In the love story at the center of the book, however, there exists the hope of a more progressive, equal society emerging in the future.

As Milene stands outside the factory at the beginning of the novel, fanning herself with her sun hat, she stares in frustration at her surroundings: "those silent things, mere passive witnesses, Nature's mute figures who, of course, had knowledge and memory, but who, when it came to it, never spoke." Lídia Jorge is interested in silent observers: she has said that her aim as a writer is "to be a witness to a time," charting the changes taking place in Portugal and the world and the ways people shape and are shaped by them.* This is what *The Wind Whistling in the Cranes* achieves so brilliantly: it tells the story of a country by telling the story of a single building, which is also the story of landlords, workers, revolutionaries, immigrants, precarious tenants, property developers, and even the flocks of birds that roost in the palm trees outside the gates.

---

* Mauro Dunder, "Entrevista com Lídia Jorge: 'A literatura tem um poder lento, mas é um poder seguro,'" *Revista Desassossego* no. 8, December 2012, pp. 9–10.

The
WIND
WHISTLING
in the
CRANES

Ceremony

ON THAT HOT AUGUST AFTERNOON, THE LONG BODY OF THE Old Factory still lay stretched out in the sun. Not quite intact, because the greenish roof bulged and bowed as if it were a continuation of the sea's undulating waves. And growing on some of the window ledges were bouquets of slender weeds like heads of hair, drawing the ledges down into the earth. Even the sign on the front, *Fábrica de Conservas Leandro 1908*, had lost nearly all its letters, and, from a distance, the only ones you could make out were *servas* and *908*, like a Kabbalistic message inscribed on the white wall. Not that any of this mattered. Milene was standing outside the old building simply because she was waiting for the gates to open and for someone to come out and talk to her.

Milene had a beach bag slung over one shoulder, so her hands were free, but whenever she tried to clasp them together, they slithered apart as if covered in some sort of sticky ointment; this was because, since half past eleven that morning, she had been back and forth across the muddy, slurry-filled field, following what seemed to be a footpath, until that path joined the metal tracks, the two parallel lines where she had stopped. The three o'clock sun cast the very briefest of shadows on the ground, and her hair was stuck to her forehead, glued there by her straw hat. Seeing her right now in my mind's eye, though, perhaps Milene had taken off her hat and was fanning herself with it, as she stood before the seemingly endless body of the Old Factory.

It really was a very hot day.

The Clio that she had parked at a slight angle on the shoulder of the road sat baking in the hot sun. Not a leaf stirred on the eleven palm trees flanking the walls, as though the leaves were made of green metal. Not a single car drove down the narrow street, as if a long Spanish siesta had descended upon the seashore. Milene had positioned herself facing the main gates, hoping to summon someone who could explain what had happened the previous Thursday night. That's why she'd so carefully rehearsed her words, until she knew them by heart. *Hey, is anyone there? Factory people, is there anyone who can explain what happened last Thursday?* There would be no need to repeat the question. She felt very pleased with herself, because this was exactly the right question to ask. As she walked tentatively toward the building, she took a handkerchief from her bag to wipe the sweat from her brow, but as soon as she stepped onto the tarmac, she hesitated. She still wasn't sure.

She needed to think.

On second thought, calling out to someone at that hour, the hottest time of the day, when not even the birds seemed to be awake, would be like bringing to a complete halt the search she'd begun by walking back and forth along that path. And this would mean abandoning all hope of discovering a clue she could take back to her aunts and uncles. Something very private and secret, to be shared only with the closest members of her family. If she started shouting—*Hey, is anyone there?*—that would be a sign that she'd given up trying to find, by her own means, the necessary words to explain what had happened to Grandma Regina during the night of the fourteenth of August, or a sign that she needed other people's words to construct her own version of the facts. When her aunts and uncles got back, she wanted to start by telling them: *Dear aunts and uncles, at around midday on Friday, I was at home listening to* Simple Minds, *when someone knocked on the door, and two policemen asked if I knew where Grandma Regina was. And then, just like that, they looked away and told me the news . . .* That's what she wanted to say.

She wanted to explain everything that had happened in her own words, because she wanted to be mistress of a situation that had more to do with her than with anyone else. But she intended to tell the story with the confidence befitting the grown-up she was, and not like the sort of grown-up child they all took her for. She wasn't a ten- or twelve-year-old, or even a twenty-year-old, she was a responsible adult, and the proof was that she had walked back and forth along that path, looking for some trace of her grandmother, a footprint, a hair, a handkerchief, a tube, a bottle, or even a crushed leaf or twig, anything to explain or at least confirm what had happened. She had carried out a detailed search, but had found nothing, even though she knew better than anyone that her grandmother had gone this way. The bare, arid landscape and its various objects knew this too. Yes, there was no doubt about it, they knew this as well as she did. But the sand, gravel, and slurry, along with the occasional old fallen tree, and the railway lines along which the wagons used to carry timber, were all part of the stubborn silence maintained by those silent things, mere passive witnesses, Nature's mute figures who, of course, had knowledge and memory, but who, when it came to it, never spoke. However many questions you asked, they remained hidden away, secret, silent. That was their response—silence. Milene almost felt like turning around and saying out loud—*Speak, you sneaky things, you cretins, you fools!*

Except that in the middle of that empty space, she couldn't start berating the world's objects as if *she* were an imbecile. Or as if she were only ten years old. All she had to do was imagine that these silent objects were deliberately conspiring to cover up what had happened on Thursday so that she wouldn't know what to tell her aunts and uncles. Milene stood there, fanning herself and staring angrily at the dumb creatures that made up the landscape, knowing that she would never get anything out of them.

You idiots, you fools, speak . . .

That's why she'd spent all morning searching. If it had been just her, she wouldn't have bothered, because she had more than enough facts and didn't need any more. Indeed, over the last few days, she'd gathered enough information to reconstruct the night when her grandma Regina had given the ambulance men the slip. And Milene had done this purely because she wanted to. Right there, in that very place, beneath the baking three o'clock sun, she could close her eyes and, with no effort at all, she could see her grandma Regina in her nightdress, filling the whole landscape, her body and nightdress occupying every inch of that black-and-white Thursday night. Right there, whenever she wanted, Milene could rewind the images, like rewinding a video on the TV screen, and the atmosphere of that afternoon would appear before her with utter clarity, along with the vaporous red clouds of sunset sliding over the plain, followed by the gloom of dusk descending on the service station, and growing still denser along the path taken by her grandma Regina. She could see her grandma Regina as clearly as if she'd been there with her, could see the marks left by her bare feet on the earth track. She could imagine her stumbling, stubborn, unstoppable steps as she made her way to the place she wanted to get to, and that place was the *Fábrica de Conservas Leandro 1908*, the factory, that heap of masonry, half-way down Mar de Prainhas, and which the family secretly called the Diamond. And she could imagine her grandmother's hands too, gnarled and ringless, her bare bent neck unadorned by gold chains or necklaces, her white hair which, lately, seemed to be getting shorter and shorter, as if someone, for some reason, were determined to deprive her face of its frame.

But it was one thing seeing and accompanying her grandmother in her imagination, and, still in her imagination, knowing for certain what had happened: that her grandmother had walked there alone, without anyone helping her along that beaten track, as far as the main gates of the factory, where she would have sat down to rest. It was quite another thing producing actual proof. That's why Milene had decided to revisit, yet again, the places where the weed-free path would have been soft enough to retain a footprint that would allow her to say to her aunts and uncles— *Yes, I'm quite sure no one carried her, she walked there entirely alone, all the way to the Diamond. She ran away from the ambulance when it stopped at the gas station. She set off on her own, I even found a footprint . . .* And that would be proof enough that her grandmother had passed that way. Milene, however, had lost count of the number of times she'd crouched down to study the sparse sand and the mud, to no avail, which is why something was telling her now that there was no point going back and trying yet again. She had decided. She would abandon her searches among the mud and slurry.

She would go back to her car.

Between thinking and acting, though, there is an atom inhabited by someone else, a swift stranger, an unexpectable, as João Paulo used to say. And so, instead of returning to her car and setting off to Praia Pequena, where her friend Violante was waiting for her, having served coffee all morning behind the bar, Milene strode over to the factory, shouting: "Hey! Is anyone there . . . ?"

She started shouting loudly, throwing all her energy into it, surprised to hear her slight, fragile voice on that hot afternoon, and surprised that it sounded the way it did, reverberating importantly in the air. Hearing her words spreading and multiplying around her as if they were increasing in size and volume. Excited, Milene again filled her all-powerful lungs with air before shouting—"Listen . . . Please . . . Is anyone there?"

No answer came from inside the long building. The red-brick chimney rose up above the roof like a clenched fist. The image of a gigantic raised fist, emerging from the decaying reality of the factory, in defiance of something invisible to the eye, but which hung in the air like a threat. A security tower, the Diamond's own personal security tower. So Milene continued to shout, until her voice gave out completely, and sounded to her like the ridiculous quacking of a duck—"Can anyone hear me?"

"Is anyone there?"

At that moment, a truck laden with salt appeared from the direction of Bairro dos Espelhos, grinding along, and the driver, enthroned in his seat and looking straight ahead, leaning slightly toward the windshield, his eyes fixed on the road, as if all he had to do in life was carry behind him that mountain of salt, passed her by without even seeing her. Milene waited for the great open-top trailer to head off down the road and disappear into the distance. Then she stared at the factory gates, beneath the intense three o'clock light, which neither retreated nor withdrew, and she accepted the facts as they were: If someone *was* hunkered down in there, they were either deaf or deliberately refusing to answer. No use to her at all. And so she didn't know what to tell her aunts and uncles.

As often happened, she had all the right elements lined up in her mind, and even though she knew what she wanted to say, she couldn't. Cousin João Paulo had always been of the view that, if a person didn't have words of their own to explain something, then they should use other people's. And she did sometimes think such a strategy both good and useful, helpful to those who lacked the necessary arguments to explain important thoughts. The more important the thought, the more likely people were to lack the right words. People like her. So she needed to think very carefully before deciding whether she had enough words to explain what had happened on that Thursday night.

She had certainly tried hard enough to find them.

Only the day before, Sunday the seventeenth, between eleven in the morning and three in the afternoon, Milene had sat in the Church of São Francisco, waiting for someone to come through the gates and talk to her, and it had been a long wait. She had waited until she'd exhausted her entire store of good thoughts, which included memories of *Star Wars* and U2, and other movies and records, boat rides and road trips, sitting with her cousins, next to João Paulo. Then, at one point, feeling too alone beneath that white vault, in the shadow of those saints who seemed to have been sleeping for whole eternities with their eyes wide open, Milene had looked around and managed to decipher a few important words on the white walls, in between the various other ornaments. Among others, she had read—Alms Box, *Pax Domini*, *Introibo ad Altarem Dei*, and then, getting to her feet and standing in the middle of the transept, it occurred to Milene that she might be able to make use of them. Putting them all together, one by one, she could perhaps say to her aunts and uncles—*Dear aunts and uncles, no need to worry about me. They brought Grandma Regina into the church and I spent a few hours next to the Alms Box and the Totus Tuus, and because Grandma Regina was still there at that point, I felt I was in company, and thought about nice things to pass the time . . .*

Yes, she might have begun by saying that, but she soon changed her mind. On further thought, she realized that it wasn't enough to explain why she hadn't felt alone, because her aunts and uncles certainly wouldn't be concerned about the hours she'd spent alone in the church with Grandma Regina. By then it would all be over, and she herself was still alive. Her aunts and uncles would want to know the circumstances in which her grandmother had died, and other people's words couldn't help her then.

Milene continued to think as she stood before the eleven palm trees.

The Clio was still baking in the sun, and Milene was thinking about the return of her aunts and uncles. Imagining them, one by one, opening the doors of their cars, the engines still running, flinging wide the doors and emerging from their air-conditioned interiors just to ask—*Milene, how do you explain this, eh? . . .* She could see her aunts and uncles as they each, one by one, removed their dark glasses so as to look her in the eye, the car doors opening and closing one after the other, and Uncle Rui Ludovice's chauffeur looking at her while pretending to be studying the ground—*How do you explain it, eh?* And, standing there before them, she might begin by saying that it had all been a terrible coincidence, various coincidences, for which she even had proof if they insisted. No problem at all.

Then, if her aunts and uncles cared to consult their diaries, they would see that Friday, the fifteenth of August, had been the first day of that holiday weekend, which is why there was no one to be found in offices and so on or in any of the other places you'd normally expect them to be, it was why the roads were swarming with cars beeping and honking crazily. Houses that were usually inhabited stood empty, while those that stood empty all year were occupied, with the outside lights on. The houses on either side of Villa Regina, for example, were all closed up, with no one at home. And Milene could prove this, or perhaps find someone who would back her up, but as for the phone calls she'd made to the houses of her aunts and uncles, the phones ringing and ringing with no one answering, she had no proof of that at all.

Yes, she'd made dozens of phone calls. When there was no answer, she'd gone around to their houses, and only then did she learn, from Aunt Gininha's gardener, that not one of them was in Valmares that weekend. Finally, on the morning of Saturday the sixteenth, she'd gone to the council offices, in the hope that, in Uncle Rui's absence, someone would be on duty. And the front door had been open, revealing a spacious lobby furnished with two large metal desks, behind which someone should have been sitting, except no one was. No one. The only sign of another human presence was Uncle Rui's giant face staring down at her from above his neat white collar on which was printed the slogan: *Others Make Promises, We Take Action*, words that appeared beneath the photo in two wavy lines, as if they were part of a poem. That had been Uncle Rui's campaign poster, when he'd won the election a year and a half before, and it was still there—unjustifiably, some might say. At the time, though, these details were unimportant. What mattered was that Uncle Rui, at least, had not disappeared completely. Then Milene had called out, imagining that if there *was* anyone there, they would hear her and realize the gravity of the situation—"Hello? Can anyone hear me? It's just to say that the mayor's mother-in-law has been found dead outside the Old Factory . . . She's dead . . ." Milene's voice had echoed around the vast hallway of what, three centuries before, had been home to a company of discalced nuns. But no one answered. There was no doubt about it, the solemn edifice where Aunt Ângela Margarida's husband was mayor was completely deserted. In the courtyard, where, at ten in the morning, the sun was already beating fiercely down as if intent on melting or cracking the paving stones, there was not a soul to be seen. In the streets of Santa Maria de Valmares, groups of foreigners were wandering about, looking vaguely alarmed beneath the peaks of their baseball caps, and stopping to wonder at the white houses, as if they were gazing upon the dried-up bed of the River Nile. Milene had made eye contact with a few nice people, who even smiled at her as they passed, but none of them had anything to do with her life, let alone the lives of her aunts and uncles. She certainly wasn't going to stop them on the sidewalk and tell them what had happened.

She hadn't even told the waiter in the café, where she'd sat down on the terrace to eat ice cream. At one point, the waiter had come over to her unasked. He'd leaned on the table and said—"Excuse me, but that's your fifth ice cream. All that ice cream could make you sick . . ."

"Yes, five ice creams."

And she could easily have explained what had happened, but was afraid that mixing up her family life with the number of ice creams she'd consumed might open the door to an endless conversation she wasn't ready to begin. So all she said was that she hadn't been counting. Besides, it was getting late. Only then did she notice how the shade from the awning had shifted, how the boldest of the pigeons were gathering around her table, picking up crumbs scattered on the ground, even right next to her sandals. From the harbor came a rich smell, at once putrid and salty.

It reminded her of the great Ocean, of which it must be a part. It reminded her of Mar de Prainhas. Why hadn't she gone swimming with Violante, hand-in-hand, in the gentle waves of Praia Pequena? Why? For the simple reason that she couldn't bring herself to announce to her aunts and uncles when they arrived—*Since I didn't know quite where Grandma Regina was, I decided to go for a swim* . . .

Milene had asked the waiter—"Did I really eat five ice creams? Well, if I did, I didn't realize . . ."

And, feeling distinctly stupid, sitting there all alone, apart from a few plump pigeons, with the waters of the Ria gently advancing and retreating, insinuating themselves into Santa Maria de Valmares and perfuming the town with the odor of shellfish and mud, she'd decided to go home. For at that moment—it was already late afternoon on Saturday the sixteenth—she felt it was her duty to find certain items belonging to her grandmother, and take them to her. Clothes, scarves, even her grandmother's favorite walking stick, which must be lost somewhere among the winter umbrellas, inside one of the many deep wardrobes to be found in Villa Regina. Yes, that's what she would do. Having made this decision, Milene left the waiter a fat tip for allowing her to sit there while he served her ice cream after ice cream. Now she really was going to put body and soul into collecting those items of clothing, however long it took. And so she left the table and hurried off to the house.

In her memory of that night, however, the past and present became completely interwoven, which is why it had taken her so long to separate out the sort of clothes her grandmother was still wearing at the time of her death from the sort she used to wear twenty-five years before, when Milene was a little girl. It was hard to tell. With all the lights on and the wardrobe doors flung wide, she had scoured every room on the two floors of Villa

Regina, searching out objects in every corner of that rather large house. And without her even noticing, Sunday the seventeenth of August dawned, yes, in the midst of all those open drawers it was a brand-new day. No matter. After that frenzy of activity, Milene would be able to choose what was most important. Just how she would explain what had happened, though, she didn't know. And that was when she remembered her cousin João Paulo.

She had just found her grandmother's silver-tipped walking stick, and with it still tucked under her arm, Milene walked over to the phone. To dial or not to dial? Normally it was Grandma Regina who dialed the number, and even stayed to listen to the conversation, to observe and record, then report back to her son Afonso what Milene and João Paulo had talked about. Now that her grandmother was going to be shut up in that *thing* forever, Milene would have to dial the number herself.

She dialed the number.

It wasn't long before she heard her cousin's voice on the answering machine speaking softly and in English. *"João Paulo?"*—Milene spoke equally softly into the mouthpiece, that is, into her cousin's answering machine, linked to the same current, coming from the other side of the Atlantic—*"João Paulo? Grandma has died . . ."* The word *died* suddenly seemed inappropriate—*"Passed away, I mean."* The house turned upside down, the lights blazing. No answer from the other side. She hung up. Then she saw that it was six o'clock on a Sunday morning. In Massachusetts it would only be one or two a.m. On this side of the Ocean, the sun was coming up above the tops of the olive trees. And it was then that she recalled João Paulo saying to her five years ago, one autumn morning, right there in Villa Regina—*"Don't be silly, Milene, there's no reason why you shouldn't make use of someone else's words when you need to. What are other people's words for if not for us to make use of them? . . . When you think about it, none of the words we pronounce are actually ours. Someone created them before we came along . . . Nothing belongs to us . . ."* Remembering these words, it felt as if João Paulo were about to come into Grandma Regina's living room, as if he were about to walk over to the table and say, right there and then—*"Did you hear me, Milene? Nothing belongs to us. We're the ones obsessed with owning things . . ."*

Nothing belongs to us, she thought as she chose a pair of shoes, and folded up a dress her grandmother had bought on her trip to London, along with a handkerchief and a Liberty scarf with a bold poppy print. If nothing belongs to us, then a person should get her duties done as quickly as possible, in order to be free of them. So Milene again rushed down the road, laden with all kinds of possessions, and arrived swiftly and efficiently beside the *thing,* only to find that, hours before, someone had already wrapped her grandmother first in a white cloth and then in a black one, thus obliging Milene to deposit the clothes and everything else she had brought next to Regina Leandro, as if they weren't an important part of her attire: the hat, the gloves, the silver-tipped walking stick, and even the wedge-heel shoes she liked so much. Relegated, as if they didn't even belong to her.

This was another detail that would be hard to explain to her absent aunts and uncles, which is why, when she arrived at the church, she had remained standing, hoping that someone would come in and say something to her so that she could use their words. Meanwhile, she'd stayed there, thinking. At around midday, once she'd exhausted all her nice thoughts, and all the others too, the silence had begun to rise up before her like a provocative, needling remark. She couldn't remain in that expectant state for much longer. Her grandmother was covered now by the wooden lid, while Milene stood listening for any footsteps approaching from beyond the thick walls, people walking past the church, then heading off toward the beach. She waited with bated breath for anything happening outside, however insignificant—*I'm sure someone's going to come into the church now. Yes, something good is about to happen. Something very good . . .*

And it did.

It had announced itself from some way off. A voice suddenly interrupted the silence. Then someone came in, but it wasn't her aunts or uncles. It was a priest in his white cassock entering through the side door, walking across the tiled floor, following the stream of sunlight bathing the floral wreaths, and he wasn't alone. He was accompanied by another, similarly dressed figure, and a woman whose heavy footsteps brought with them a pair of sturdy legs with powerful, square calf muscles. Yes, finally, three people, three officials, had entered, forming a kind of crowd, and when the priest addressed her, since she was the only person there, apart, that is, from Grandma Regina, Milene realized that this was her big chance to hear the words of a trustworthy person. The words that the priest enunciated so very clearly, with the help of some impeccably white teeth and two raised eyebrows that kept moving together and apart, forming circumflexes on his face. She wanted to hear the words that emerged from his person and from his surplice so as to be able to say to her aunts and uncles—*Dear aunts and uncles, this is what happened . . .* She wanted to memorize his words and repeat them. The only problem was, would she be able to transform them into things that would be useful? That was her great worry.

Milene's eyes fell on the gleaming Christ that the carpenter had nailed to the coffin, a Christ made out of thick metal, his back so arched that he appeared to be hollow, and rather resembled an insect trying to wrench itself free from the wood, and, in the meantime, she could hear the booming words that the priest was hurling forth at that unseemly hour on a Sunday, as if he wanted to hit someone, as if he were throwing stones, although she retained only the very loudest, words like *iniquity, pride, arrogance, a rumor that passes by, a ship that sails through the billowy water, a bird that flies through the air, while we were consumed in our wickedness* . . . And many more. But all she could retain were those few disparate words and phrases hurled by the priest at the walls of the empty church. That priest, whom, for reasons that escaped her, she had never seen before, continued to speak in that over-loud voice, as if he were preaching to someone she couldn't see, and Milene felt a kind of fear, the fear that perhaps might have been felt by the person or multitude he was addressing, only there was no one there. She felt afraid for herself too, afraid she wouldn't be able to explain how she had accompanied her grandma Regina imprisoned in that *thing*. Afraid of being alone and hearing those words, unable to retain a single one that could be useful to her, of the many proffered by the priest at that strange hour. Until finally that whole business stopped, although she couldn't have said quite how.

Because, as she would recall later, the last part happened very quickly.

It went like this.

The priest's words were still rebounding off the saints, when a large car reversed its way toward the church, as if intent on actually driving into the building. Then everything went into rewind, and the external walls swallowed up the soothing gloom she'd been inhabiting since eleven o'clock that morning. The saints slithered away. Everything changed its appearance. She too was being carried off by that enormous car. She was sure of it. Milene closed her eyes, felt an engine throbbing beneath her seat, while around her the flowers filled all the available space, pressing up against the windows and shifting about as if they were living animals about to take a breath and make themselves comfortable, changing place and shape, gardenias on top of gladioli, and she could see the calm, very solid, white landscape of Rua de São Francisco through the smoked glass that protected her eyes from the intense afternoon brightness, as if the whole car were a giant pair of sunglasses. The dogs lying in the street scrambled to their feet to allow the heavy vehicle to pass, with Milene seated inside, as if on a throne, her eyes almost open, almost closed.

When she opened her eyes, some men with close-cropped hair were removing the flowers from the car and piling them up beside the open grave, into which six pairs of hands would place that *thing*, with her grandmother inside it. As it was being lowered in, Milene felt a kind of horror at the sheer brutality of the dug earth, but once the earth closed up again, she experienced a sense of relief, certain that Regina Leandro wasn't there, and that she would be able to say as much to her aunts and uncles, even if she didn't know where her grandmother actually was. Or, more precisely, where she, Milene, had left her. This surprising thought kept her rooted to the spot. *No, she's not here. She's somewhere else instead . . .* Milene would have said if the priest hadn't been present. But he was.

The priest had positioned himself on a slightly higher piece of ground, and his shadow was as clearly delineated as if it had been drawn in charcoal. Apart from that, his forehead and cheeks were dripping with sweat. Milene saw him beckon to the woman with the square calf muscles, who, to judge by her headgear, must have been a nun, and the two stood talking in low voices. The priest descended from his elevated spot and asked Milene—"Do you feel all right?

"Are you feeling ill?

"Do you feel unwell?"

Milene wanted to answer there and then, which is why she

allowed her eyes to drift around a little, this way and that, over small piles of earth, little marble houses, innumerable gold-painted names and dates, and then, once she'd reeled her eyes in again, she had nothing to say. Yes, she felt fine, especially after the priest's unexpected question, his kindness in coming over to her and repeating the question, and that's why she began to smile, only a little at first, then more and more broadly, a silent thank-you to the person asking the question, a way of demonstrating that she felt fine. She was smiling to show her gratitude to him for having spoken at such length in the church about Grandma Regina, when there was no one else there, apart from her and her grandmother and those official people. So many thoughts rushed into her head that she couldn't say anything.

"As I said, Father Honório, she's the mayor's niece. His niece by marriage . . ." These words were spoken by the woman whose legs had appeared in the light of the church and which were there now planted on the dug soil, fleshy and strong with their distinctive calf muscles. "But God is great . . ." she added. And she beckoned to the man accompanying them. The three, their heads close together as they walked down the path, began to speak to each other as if they were sharing a secret. Then they walked away.

"God can do all . . ." the woman said.

The three of them, still keeping very close together, waited for Milene, who came stumbling over clods of earth and stones, over the faded flowers scattered along the narrow paths between the little houses. Then the four—because for a while all four had walked along together—drove down into town in the priest's car, stopping at the church. The brief, intense shadows at the foot of the walls also appeared to have been outlined in black ink. But then she got into her Clio, where she had left it earlier that morning, and the three of them, including the priest, stood watching her, utterly still, as if they were three angels with wings furled, come down from the tops of those small stone houses to take a closer look at her. No one said a word.

Milene wished she knew why they were looking at her like that, because they seemed to be waiting for her to start the engine, as if wanting to be sure she could actually drive, for they all waved exuberantly when she drove off. Even when she was some way away, she could still see them in the rearview mirror, still watching. They seemed pleased, and Milene, in order to reassure them that she was perfectly at ease behind the wheel and was in complete control of the engine and the clutch, stopped at the top of the hill, performed a rather striking U-turn, then headed serenely down São Francisco de Valmares. They had stood there watching, doubtless feeling very satisfied with her. Or with her driving. But not even after that encounter, which had gone reasonably well, had she managed to find so much as two useful words. That is, words that could properly explain what had happened that day, up to the point when the grave was filled in. She still didn't know what had happened between the gas station and the factory. And everything depended on her finding that out. What would her aunts and uncles say? Especially her aunts. She was very fond of her aunts.

She was asking herself this question as she stood before the eleven palm trees, whose shadows remained utterly still and upright, never stirring. She knew it. There was sure to be a confrontation. With her straw hat on her head and her bag over her shoulder, she once again thought that, as João Paulo had put it, between thinking and acting there is an atom inhabited by someone else.

The fact was she didn't know what had happened, she'd merely reconstructed it in her imagination, based on the summary provided by the policemen and the scenes described in detail by the young man at the gas station, as eyewitness. That's all she knew. The policemen themselves had taken her to the gas station on the Friday afternoon, and one of them had said—"Hey, you, stop working for a moment, will you? The girl's a bit confused, and has no idea what happened . . ." And they'd left her alone with him.

Then the young man at the pumps, who was dressed from head to toe in yellow, repeated everything he'd already told the police officers, listing the facts in order, one by one, as if testifying were a matter of making the events happen all over again. Standing there near the gas pumps, he told how, the previous night, at around twenty-one hundred hours, an ambulance had appeared at the crossroads, scattering beams of blue light, beams of light that, in his account of events, had moved the way his arms were moving, whirling about his body. Blinding lights that would have lit up the final onset of dusk in vivid blue. Blue lights. Bright blue. These lights had obviously made a big impression on him, an impression he was making a point of passing on to Milene.

The young man described how the ambulance, lights flashing, had approached very tentatively and kept stopping, first at one house, then at another, until it came to a halt just short of the gas station. He pointed to the exact spot. The female ambulance driver and the male nurse with her had climbed out of the vehicle, both at the same time, and opened the two rear doors, so that anyone who wanted could peer inside. That's what he said. He also said that he'd seen the driver and the nurse repeat this operation more than once since they'd stopped at the bend in the road by the Frame Store, and that certain passersby had gathered around and even leaned into the back of the ambulance to see what was happening. He'd done the same. But all he could see was a white shadow wrapped in a white sheet. And just as he leaned in, the ambulance driver had unceremoniously shone her flashlight at the face of the shadow lying on the white and blue rectangle of the stretcher. Feeling slightly confused himself, he asked if the shadow was a man or a woman, and the nurse, still trying hard to make sense of an address he had written on a piece of paper, had replied rather rudely—"Can't you see it's a woman?"

"Is she alive?" someone else had asked, leaning right inside the ambulance and tugging at the white sheet.

And the nurse, rather irritably, raised his voice loud enough to be heard all around the gas station—"Do you really think we'd be returning someone to her family if she was dead? Good grief, if stupidity was a tune, you'd be an entire concerto . . ." Angrily brandishing the incomprehensible piece of paper.

The young man, however, thought such rudeness perfectly understandable. It seemed to him that both the nurse and the ambulance driver wanted to be rid of that shadow, along with all the other shadows filling the beds in the local hospitals, because of the likely carnage on the roads that holiday weekend, and even more so because, by the time they reached the gas station, they'd already spent more than two hours looking for Kilometer 44, which was the address on the piece of paper they'd been given. And yet it would seem that, up until then, no one had been able to tell them where that particular kilometer was, or who the woman was that they were taking there. He himself didn't know. And of all the people gathered beneath the whirling blue lights, not one of them knew the address or the name, and no one recognized the person inside. Only an emigrant newly returned from America, a middle-aged man, who had leaned in when the nurse again directed his flashlight at the patient, thought he recognized something about the woman's heavy-lidded eyes, which he recalled seeing on the face of a woman he'd known when he was just a boy. But he couldn't remember who she was.

"Do try to remember, please. We've been going around the houses for Lord knows how long," the driver had said.

"I'm trying, but I just can't," the returnee had said. And he was truly sorry not to be able to help, and kept staring at those heavy-lidded eyes, over which the beam from the flashlight passed again and again. But it was no use, he couldn't remember. Then, feeling angrier still and beginning to get desperate, the nurse and the driver had begun to search the immediate vicinity, crossing the road and going down the side streets, knocking on doors behind which only the deaf appeared to be dining, even going into gardens when the streets were blocked by new buildings that had sprung up. When they finally returned to the ambulance, determined to resolve the situation once and for all, and with an idea now of where Kilometer 44 was, and just as they were about to jump back into their seats, they discovered that the shadow had vanished. The shadow wasn't lying where they had left her.

The shadow was gone.

Right there, by the pumps, the young man had described the effect of seeing the ambulance devoid now of any shadow. How both nurse and driver had searched the roadside and the grass shoulder. How they'd made endless calls by phone and walkie-talkie, desperately traipsing up and down, around the ambulance and along the road, until, at last, they'd left, closing the two rear doors, which, in the darkness, resembled two wings. He himself had seen the doors close. He'd been an eyewitness, and could still feel the effect of that strange scene. The big empty ambulance. But beyond that, he could tell her nothing, apart from saying that, meanwhile, the cluster of people had tired of waiting beside the ambulance and left. During that time, he too had been busy serving customers, and all he knew was that the blue lights continued to turn like the lights on a lighthouse, on and on, with no one else around. Who would have thought it? And the young man, eyes wide and moist, held out his arms to demonstrate his innocence. Yes, he, as eyewitness, had told her all he knew. He hated to say this, but the person he'd seen inside the ambulance, lying on the stretcher, seemed more lifeless even than the sheet covering her. How had she managed to walk? How had she managed to disappear? How had she crossed those roads full of speeding cars? How?—Then, seeing Milene's face, he had changed the subject.

"I'm sorry. Now that I look at you . . ."

He could see now that she was a member of the shadow's family, she had the same heavy-lidded eyes, the same arched eyebrows. He actually used the word *shadow*. And he regarded her very seriously, because he had recognized those eyes, while the cars at the pumps were beginning to form the kind of long line you always get on a holiday weekend and his colleagues kept calling him over to help. And yet he continued to talk, still with his arms raised, still imitating the whirring blue light, the light that had brought that brief story to a roadside gas station, where nothing normally happened apart from the opening and closing of gas-guzzling tanks.

"Yes, I can see now that you must be her daughter. Well, daughter or granddaughter . . ." he said, heading over to the pumps where his colleagues were now urgently calling for him. "All right, I'm coming . . .

"Really, that's all I saw . . ."

And with that they parted.

Which meant that, as far as that particular witness was concerned, she would have no problem. Milene retained, word for word, everything the young man had said, but she still didn't know what had happened afterward. That was the missing piece.

But what if everything she didn't know about what had happened afterward got in the way of her remembering what had happened before? The past immediately preceding that. The final moments as witnessed by the young man at the pumps? Milene started brushing the dust off her legs, bare beneath her short skirt, she had again taken off her hat and was fanning herself, disturbing the short hair framing her face in a kind of threatening vortex. Something dangerous.

Everything was getting muddled up.

Standing before the eleven palm trees, so lush it seemed as if their tall trunks must be sucking up energy from some invisible spring deep beneath the earth, Milene wasn't just aware of her hair moving in the air as she fanned herself with her hat. She also felt that her mind was full of faces, of nights, of those last four nights, of gas pumps, wooden boxes, fleshy flowers, crisscrossing roads, cars setting off in different directions, names, addresses, open graves, Mar de Prainhas, which she could just glimpse beyond the factory building and the sand dunes, nightshirts with no hem or placket, ambulances, drivers, high-sounding words from the priest's Bible, everything she had collected over the last four days, all useful stuff to tell her aunts and uncles, to show them and offer to them as a gift she could be proud of. But there, in the heat that continued to beat down with perverse rigor, she felt she wouldn't be able to keep intact for much longer the basket of facts inside her head. Those facts would all begin to disintegrate, to escape like freed ions, would be strewn along the sandbanks, along the whole coast of Mar de Prainhas, throughout the waters of the Atlantic, until her head was completely empty, and then, when her aunts and uncles arrived, she would have nothing to tell them. When they asked her—*What happened, Milene?* she would have no answer. She would have nothing to say.

———

They might ask her—*How could such a thing happen? You neglected Grandma Regina and can't even tell us what happened. Far worse than letting her die is the fact that you can't even explain how she came to die . . .* She could hear her aunt Ângela Margarida saying this, and Uncle Rui Ludovice, her husband, listening and nodding, they who were so powerful, who made such a handsome couple, who knew so much, who had won elections under the unbeatable slogan *Others Make Promises, We Take Action,* and now they would be demanding explanations from her, and she had nothing to say. She felt that everything she had accumulated, far from making sense, was about to disappear.—*Tell me, Milene, how do you explain this: We left your grandmother in the new nursing home, paying two hundred thousand escudos each—and that was just the registration fee, mind you—so that we could go off on vacation in peace, because we weren't happy about leaving her alone with you in Villa Regina, and, when we left Portugal, she was perfectly safe there, with everything she could possibly need, even a pair of tennis shoes if she fancied taking a walk around the swimming pool, and yet two weeks later, she was found dead, abandoned, outside the Old Factory. How do you explain that?*

Yes, how could Milene explain why she hadn't waited for them before letting her grandmother be buried like that? Why hadn't she made sure her grandmother had been heaped with all the flowers and all the honors she so richly deserved? Why hadn't she taken personal care of the body? Why hadn't she stopped all those people, the police, the doctor, the men in black, the priest? Why? If she'd waited just a few days, Uncle Rui Ludovice might even have been able to arrange for two horses from the National Guard to follow clip-clopping behind the hearse, there could have been a sermon in the church, someone could have brought along a couple of guitars, one in each hand, and sung to her grandmother, celebrating her long life, her many qualities, that woman who, long ago, had been the driving force behind the *Fábrica de Conservas Leandro 1908*, who had been kind to everyone—indeed, entire generations were indebted to her—and yet her own granddaughter hadn't been able to wait. To understand the full significance of what had happened, Milene didn't need to count using her fingers, because she wasn't a ten-year-old or a fiftcen-year-old or even a twenty-year-old. She counted anyway, just to be sure, counting off all the most important absences, one by one.

Aunt Ângela Margarida hadn't been there at Grandma Regina's side, nor had Uncle Rui Ludovice, with all the gravitas that his presence would have implied. Nor had their daughters, her cousins Joana and Sabina. Nor had Uncle Afonso Leandro, or either of his most recent wives, not even the first, Aunt Alda Maria, the mother of his two sons, Milene's cousins Danilo and João Paulo. Not even Aunt Gininha or her husband Dom Silvestre, or the little ones her grandmother had so doted on, Bruno José and baby Artemisa. Nor any of the more distant members of the family. Nor had any of Grandma Regina's former employees, who were still pretty much at her beck and call. Nor any of her grandmother's lady friends with whom she used to get together to eat cake—slices cut from one of those tall cakes with a hole in the middle—nor any of the servants who had remained close to her and used to bring her cabbages and eggs in baskets filled with straw, just the way she liked them. Nor the old grocer, or her godson Barbosa, the owner of the restaurant Mãos Largas. No, none of them had been there, it had all been a most unfortunate mistake, the result of a terrible coincidence: everyone away, offices closed, hospitals full to bursting, endless road accidents creating a whole series of pileups, care homes fully booked. Her grandmother had died in the midst of that extraordinary confluence of events, and she, Milene, wouldn't be able to explain why. It wasn't just what had happened between her grandmother leaving the ambulance and arriving at the factory that she'd be unable to explain, it was far more than that. Far more serious. Between what she did know and didn't know, all the words had disappeared, vanished, which is why, when everyone arrived, she would have nothing to say. She would be as empty as a dry, dead conch shell. While pondering this vacuum, the vast vacuum making her heart sink, Milene began to walk toward the factory gates, toward the Diamond.

"Hey! Is anyone there?" she called.

No, not even a startled bird.

The gates appeared to be held shut only by a latch. It would feel so good just to go somewhere far away, to follow those thoughts rapidly dissolving into the water, the earth, the air. But this was impossible, because, as she stood outside the gates, feet firmly planted, she was conscious of one thing only, of an entirely different solution with but one goal, a solution that was heading in her direction. A good solution. Without further ado, Milene did as those thoughts were telling her. She went up to the wooden sill where the two gates met rather unevenly and, keeping her chubby knees together and her heels apart, gave the middle of the gates an almighty shove, then, pushing harder still, managed to force the latch, so that the leaves of the gates flew open with a clatter, which surprised both her and the birds, startling them from their sleep. Milene stood for a moment in the space cleared by the open gates, listening to the rustling of the birds. Only then did she go in. There she saw the courtyard with its tall, redundant red chimney. That was the only thing she recognized.

The courtyard seemed rather small, as if the surrounding buildings had grown inward, and there were some new red-brick buildings that did, in fact, jut out from the original surfaces. A small gray house, the color of cement, protruded like a nodule. Sealing off the area was a new wall, on which hung a huge coiled hose. Connecting these new surfaces were various clotheslines propped up on poles and draped with white summer clothes and bright bedsheets printed with huge roses, which hung there like a fabric forest. One of those clotheslines swayed, and from between the sheets emerged two animals: a huge guard dog, which opened its mouth to bark when it saw her, then immediately lay down on the ground and rolled around, before getting up again and lifting its leg for a pee, while a small gray poodle, its fur unclipped, was tethered by a chain that should have belonged to the guard dog. At first the poodle barked frantically, as if activated by batteries. Then it too threw itself on the ground, setting its chain clanking, before licking itself and jumping about as best it could, landing feet first in the water trough, spilling the last drop of water. The dogs fell silent when they realized that nothing of importance was about to happen because of this new human presence, and Milene came to her own realization that, although the court-yard was closed off—for she had gone back and pushed the gates shut—it still left her too exposed, too visible.

The doors of the buildings inside the courtyard, the ones that opened onto that enclosure, were locked, and between a pot of geraniums and a sack of dog food stood a small pile of folding chairs. She could take one. She did. With a chair under her arm, Milene looked for a spot among the washing. She was sure to find a good hiding place behind one of those clotheslines. Not behind the first one or the second, but behind the third, which was draped with larger sheets, the ones with the lilac roses, along with bath towels and tablecloths. Yes, there was some pleasant shade among the sheets. She rested her cheek on the washing, certain that she'd found a place where her aunts wouldn't be able to find her, neither then, nor later, when she had nothing left in her head to tell them. They would never find her. Never. Knees together, her bag on her lap, and her hat resting on the bag. Hugging her own body, with that bundle of things on her lap. There, in the cool of the courtyard, on Monday, the eighteenth of August, Milene was hidden away inside the Diamond.

But other people came up with very different versions.

Some said that Milene had been found wandering near the golf course, without her bag or her hat. Others swore they'd spotted her walking briskly in the direction of Bairro dos Espelhos. Still others that she must have spent those five days at the beach, eating raw fish and sleeping out in the open. They probably said these things with the intention of belittling her life, marring her mysteries, with the intention of propelling her into the domain of insignificance and obscurity, that place where everything is eventually lost and annulled. But we didn't let them.

MILENE'S
BOOK

I

THAT WAS WHEN THE MATAS, RIDING IN THEIR THREE VANS, left the main road and headed into Bairro dos Espelhos.

Bairro dos Espelhos—the Neighborhood of Mirrors—was no more than a low, level cluster of houses, unnamed on the map, and so called because, at five in the afternoon, the aluminum sheeting and panes of glass together produced thousands of reflections, like the twinkling panels of a space station built to resemble the eye of a fly.

This reflective effect was most common in spring and autumn, after it had rained, when the surfaces were washed clean and the sun was at its mid-point in the sky. At those times of year, for the fishermen of Mar de Prainhas, the neighborhood served as a kind of afternoon lighthouse. Perhaps surprisingly, it was in summer that the fewest fires were recorded, not because there was any less in the way of scattered debris and scraps of paper, rags, fruit and vegetable peels, bits of wood, and other flammable materials, but because the dust lay undisturbed on the windows and window frames in a thick, heavy layer. During high season, it could be said, there were almost no mirrors in the Neighborhood of Mirrors. The dust churned up by the passing cars wasn't a problem: indeed, it protected the houses, contributing to the safety and general upkeep of the area. Sometimes a bucket of water was spilled on the ground between one wall and another, and sometimes far more than a bucket. Now and then whole barrels were accidentally overturned, their contents forming glass eyes at the center of thin muddy rings. But the residents would never wash a door or window with the water that flowed, between six and nine each morning, from two taps at the entrance to the square. It would have been wrong to put that precious substance to such frivolous use. This principle, for them, was an important law that did not need to be written down.

Why should it be?

Most of the residents of Bairro dos Espelhos came from lands in the maritime area of the Sahel: torn-off pieces of Africa, islands in the Atlantic that, after the last glacial period, had expelled all their rain and swallowed all their rivers, with only the odd stream left here and there as a memento—streams that dribbled along, disoriented, then ran dry for years on end. For these people, a tap that worked with cosmic regularity, between this hour and that, was itself a plentiful stream, and once they grew accustomed to this new reality, any trickle of running water began to feel like a river. Two intermittent rivers for an entire neighborhood. There were, however, luckier people, people who had left Bairro dos Espelhos and now had three rivers inside their own home, all for a single family of no more than nineteen people. A river in the kitchen, a river in the toilet, a river on the roof of a hut from which water ran down, sometimes as a single jet, and sometimes as tiny droplets like rain. Even the leaks from the showers and washbasin, little brooks that puddled together in the courtyard, gained the status of rivers. The younger family members soon adjusted to this new reality, forgot all about it, thought water was water, there for drinking or wasting, as natural as the air they breathed, but for the older ones it was different. Whenever a tap was turned on and water came out, they knew they had the mouth of a river at their fingertips, the bed of an endless stream—at least, this was how the older Mata women saw it. Until five years ago, the Matas had lived in Bairro dos Espelhos. Now they didn't go there very often. Only the men did, on Sunday afternoons, to drink lukewarm beer and play cards. When they did play cards.

But that day, the day our cousin Milene hid in the courtyard of the Diamond, before evening set in, the Matas' three vans had turned off the tarmac road and down the dirt track, arriving in the neighborhood in a cloud of dust. As the cloud approached, some children had burst through their doorways, others had jumped straight out of the windows onto the street, and in less than a second, gathering and circling like a swarm, they had surrounded the three vans, blocking their path. The three vans stopped. This is precisely why they had come: to be stopped in their tracks.

"The Matas are here!" the children shouted into the houses.

The first van, metallic blue in color, was driven by the eldest brother, Domingos Mata. Pulling into the square at full speed, the van got one wheel stuck in a puddle, sending up a shower of fat brown drops. As it struggled to free itself, the engine gave a guttural roar. Conceição Mata, Domingos's wife, covered her ears with her hands. The two boys sleeping slumped against the window woke up. Aunt Dilecta, sitting in the backseat, dozing among the various packages, her forehead resting on the glass, also began to stir. When the van stopped growling and jolting back and forth, everyone inside it seemed taller, even the boys, João and Aloísio. But it wasn't this van, an ancient Mercedes, that all the neighborhood children went racing toward. Nor was it the second.

The second was red and newly serviced, and the dust that clung to it made more of an impact. Even so, it was recognizable from a long way off, in part because of its color and shape, but most of all because painted on one side was a likeness of the youngest Mata brother, Janina Mata King, the singer. Next to the likeness was a guitar, and below it, in black letters against an arc of yellow brushstrokes, were the words *Black Power*, like a caricature of some distant, dated thing, a solitary sticker from an old album that suddenly peeled off and entered our lives again with renewed energy. The dark shape at the top of the image, representing Janina Mata King's hair, fused with the B of *Black* and the *r* of *Power*, to form a kind of upper rim. Between that rim and the base of the yellow arc, two brushstrokes suggested the singer's features in high contrast, and from between his teeth and lips, spreading across the whole van, floated treble clefs and quavers shaped vaguely like axes. It was an extraordinary vehicle. Unlike the metallic blue van, the dusty red one had stopped on a dry patch of earth and was crammed full of so much stuff there was barely room for the various people inside, all of whom were dazed from the journey. They were the driver, Heitor Junior, and his wife, Claudina Mata, along with his father Heitor Senior, his wife Germana Mata and her mother, and their two daughters, Sissi and Belisa, who were still sound asleep, despite the sudden interruption.

But it was the gray van, a metallic Mitsubishi, driven by the young guy in black, that the neighborhood children all thronged toward. They knew. This was what they'd been waiting for. When that van finally came to a halt, glittering in the sun, the kids had shouted in frenzied anticipation: "Look, look, Antonino Mata's arrived!"

Yes, he had arrived.

Antonino Mata, his black shirt unbuttoned, had taken off his baseball cap and flung wide the van door, revealing himself from head to toe. But he couldn't manage to make himself heard.

The children, pressed up against the third van, had begun to clamor at the top of their lungs—"Pringles! Pringles!" By then, the young man in black was clutching an armful of tubes to his chest, which he started to throw, two and three at a time. Practiced at catching objects in midair, the children leapt so nimbly that not a single cardboard tube hit the ground, and even before they had all been given out the children were crunching on the chips, making a noise like hyperactive rodents. "Pringles!" they shouted again. Antonino turned, scooped up the remaining tubes, and began throwing these as well, but the children, their hands full, were now heading them like soccer players, scattering the ground with cardboard containers that got crushed and buried in the dust. Meanwhile, some powerfully built women had emerged from doorways too narrow for their hips and were approaching the vans, dodging the fights over the fallen chips packets. One woman strode straight through the middle of the scrum, kicking at the children as she went, and then threw up her arms and yelled with delight: "The Matas have arrived! Oh, glory be! Quick, tell us everything . . ." But since the Matas still in the vans seemed to have puffed up like dough after the hot, stuffy journey, the happy woman added: "No, don't say anything, we already know. It was just incredible in Lisbon, we saw it all on TV . . ."

Felícia Mata, the family matriarch, leaned out of the window, hugging herself, letting her chest lift and fill like a tire, before crying out at last, exultant: "Oh, you'll never believe it . . . Janina stayed on afterwards . . . Everyone loved him . . . There's no one like him in the world. What can I say? . . . It was just wonderful . . ." Felícia was hanging out of the window now, and happiness sang in her voice.

Another woman, brushing up against the dusty vehicle, wanted to know: "Isn't Janina coming back, then?"

For two seconds, the singer's mother held the triumph in her chest. Then out it came: "Only he knows that now. We just know that we took him there, and left him to do his thing. As for whether he's coming back, we don't know . . . He stayed on with his brother."

"Good Lord!" the woman said, more loudly. "And your other boy, Gabriel, does he sing too?" Not waiting for an answer, the woman turned away and began to dance. She was sturdily built, but as she danced, it was as if her neck and waist were made of separate rotating parts. She spun away, then back, always moving and dancing, her arms above her head. Still dancing, she said: "Oh my, you people produce nothing but singers. Oh my . . ."

Felícia Mata, chest swelling, laughed merrily. Her voice had become deeper, more velvety and mellifluous since her son's success, a success recognized by everyone who came rushing from the doorways of Bairro dos Espelhos to see the Matas. Leaning all the way out of the vehicle, she was almost singing herself: "No, not him. Gaby just went to support his brother. Well, they always were practically joined at the hip, weren't they . . . ?"

Inside the third van with Antonino and Felícia Mata were Emanuel, Cirino, and Quirino, Antonino's three sons, and almost hidden behind the cardboard boxes and packages sat the oldest of all the women, Ana Mata. She was sitting across from her daughter Felícia, and another woman was making her way toward her, a tiny woman, around the same age as Ana Mata, and also originally from Santiago Island. Well wrapped up, despite the August heat blasting the neighborhood's low walls, the thin old woman, as thin and as old as Ana Mata herself, had approached the window where the latter was sitting, laid one hand on the edge of the glass that was rolled right down, and asked in their language: "Are you happy, Ana Mata?" If the gray van pulled away, the woman would be carried along with it. Ana Mata was smiling too much to respond.

"Are you really happy?"

The two women, both very thin, very old, and very dark-skinned, looked at one another, chuckling. The vans all at a stop now. "What a question . . ." Ana Mata answered at last, also in their language. "What do you think? My father had that voice, you remember, my brothers had that voice, my sons, they all had that voice too. Now they're all gone, and that voice, the voice that belonged to all of them, is in my grandson Janina's throat . . . Janina has brought them all back to life . . ." Ana Mata shut her eyes to feel the fullness of her joy. The sun beat down. "And you ask me if I'm happy. Ha! What a question, woman . . ."

"So you're very happy, then . . ."

"Of course! Very, very happy, my dear. When Janina sings, all the men in my family sing. The moment he starts tuning up, all my male relatives are there with him. Sometimes I tell him he doesn't own it. That his voice belongs to all those other people too, but he's not interested. He sings like it's his alone . . ."—This was Ana Mata throwing a wrench in the works of her immense happiness. Calling up a slight imperfection so the happiness could roll on as it should. All said in their own language.

"There's no harm in that, Ana Mata. Look, if you're happy, I'm happy too. Our people . . ." The old woman was still holding on to the window as she said this, her two hands gripping the edge. "Our people are also . . ."

But then Domingos Mata, Felícia's eldest son and the driver of the first van, which was parked on the other side of the puddle, grew impatient. "Are we going or not?"

"Yes, yes, we're going."

The engines, in neutral until then, started up, the dust billowing into the air again and the wheels turning once more. All the women, the sturdy and the slim, including the very slim and the very old, bound together by the sheer force of the good news, standing together on the dusty patch of earth that connected the houses, had started to dance. Their flesh trembled in the swirling dust. It was as if the hot earth itself were glad. The children, the same ones, were still munching on the chips, shouting— "Pringles! Pringles!" And then the three vans, turning away from Bairro dos Espelhos and all that had recently taken place there, left the dust and the jolts behind them and joined the tarmac road, making for home.

Yes, the Matas' three vans had sped down the road.

The red one between the other two, as if under their protection, and all three in a line, gliding swiftly along. Glory contained in the very movement of the vans. The landscape around, neglected, speckled with piles of rubble, seeming to need them as they passed. Glory in life, in action. Once achieved by a single member of a family, glory can nourish past and future generations, bestowing on them a meaning they would otherwise lack. At last, the three dusty vans approached the sprawling shadow of the house, like the shadow of an old locomotive that had ground to a halt there. A long train with windows in which the darkness was still darker. Melancholic, sometimes, as the sun went down. But at that moment, the row of three vehicles, next to the mound bristling with grass, turned that strip of gloomy earth into a sliver of peaceful repose. "We're here"—Domingos had said, as if it needed to be spoken to be known.

"We're here!"—said Felícia Mata, her deep voice ever more velvety. "Phew, time to stretch these legs . . ." Getting out with some difficulty, shaded by the palms.

Because thank the Lord that Gaby had stayed on with his younger brother. Thank the Lord the entire Coliseu had applauded Janina, as soon as he sang that opening line—"*Carpeting the sea, carpeting the sea, with my handkerchief . . .*" And thank the Lord they lived there, in the nice building standing before them, where, as well as nonstop streams of water in three different locations, there were at least ten plug sockets providing electric current day and night, which blossomed into light, movement, heating, ventilation, refrigeration, sound, and images. So much good fortune. Janina's triumph onstage, the Matas' triumph with that building, their house. Indeed, Felícia Mata had a sense that one was a consequence of the other, and setting aside how they fit together in time, she couldn't even have said which came first—whether that solid bricks-and-mortar house, or Janina's voice. All she knew was to be thankful, because both of them had come.

"Thank the Lord!"

Heitor Senior also climbed out very cautiously, holding Heitor Junior's hand. Only then did the others follow. One by one, they squeezed around huge boxes that contained a whole world of tech, electronics, and IT, the newest and most compact on the market. Objects from Korea, Japan, the United States of America, and who knows where else. Things from a vast array of countries, originating in far-flung locations and then hitching a ride through the air, to save time, marvelous machines that came from everywhere. Put more simply, you could even describe these marvelous things as children of the whole world. And now here they were. The things. From inside the vans came stoves, barbecues, vacuum cleaners, drills, televisions, Nintendo and Game Boy games for the children, music equipment for people of any age, all with their magical possibilities. And the Matas were unloading thing after thing, their souls brimming with happiness, talking loudly outside the forty windows, most of which were clouded, cracked, and overgrown with weeds, in the shade of the eleven palm trees where the birds, woken from their sleep, now hummed and chirruped. But just six windows, six, in what was left of the Fábrica de Conservas Leandro, had sealed and painted frames, and these, along with the relevant portion of roof and some of the old factory walls, were home. The Matas' home. To which they themselves had added the necessary rooms.

"Ah! At last . . ."—said Felícia Mata for the tenth time, stretching out her arms on which glory had landed. A fifty-five-year-old woman getting out of a Mitsubishi van, so very happy, so very slow.

But old Ana Mata, after a journey spent trapped between large boxes in her grandson Antonino's van, had hopped out and, despite taking tiny steps, as if her body had somehow seized up, was moving very quickly. While her daughter Felícia was still taking off her shoes, Ana Mata was shuffling toward the gates on her frail, crooked legs, holding her purse wide open and searching among the tissues for the big metal key. She found it eventually, but, as it happened, she wasn't going to need it. Ana Mata had already put the key in the lock and even begun to turn it before she looked around and announced with many a loud cry that the gates were already open.

"Open?" That was impossible.

Domingos put down a box he'd been carrying on his shoulder, sprang to the gates, stood motionless in front of its two misshapen halves, staring at those leaves that never quite met, and only then made a shushing sign at the other family members, kicked aside a kind of broken pot, felt around in the dirt, and produced a knife.

In no time, Felícia Mata's eldest son had rolled up his sleeves, spat on his hands, tucked the knife in his belt, and stepped into the courtyard, as if it were a mysterious wasteland where danger could lurk even in the air. Domingos searched the whole space, his back to the walls, moving among the buildings. He inspected hidden corners, the doors of the makeshift houses, the opening at the base of the big red chimney, the battered entrance to the old salting house, and the other rooms, all of which took several long, frightening minutes. Only then did he return to the main gates and declare that the coast was clear. There was no sign of anyone after all. Next he had to examine the handle and the lock. Yes, the wire catch was unhooked, the latch unfastened, and the wooden bolt dangling loose. Someone had pushed the gates open. And standing in front of him, an incredulous Ana Mata was clutching the key, waving it helplessly around—"Oh no! Who knows what they'll have stolen?"

Still hesitant, the six Mata women made their way across the courtyard as a group, followed by their children, with the eerie sensation of entering a violated space. They nervously looked in every corner, expecting to find things missing or disturbed. But Domingos was right. Everything was as it should be, intact. Jugs, clothes, folding chairs, sun loungers, barbecues, water bowls, and even the pair of television screens standing calmly under the lean-to, waiting for someone to switch them on. Nothing unusual. No sign of a burglary. All exactly as they had left it. Just the two dogs whining and rolling about on the ground, sniffing the ladies' feet, the guard dog whimpering like a little mouse, the poodle trying to wriggle free from its heavy guard-dog chain. Their various bowls completely empty, after all those days. No, nothing had been stolen. Domingos Mata, irritated after checking and double-checking each of the unused areas in turn, ended up losing his temper and blurting out his theory. He knew he was right. It had been none other than their grandmother who had left the gates unlocked before they went out. And it must have been because Ana Mata still couldn't help wanting to be everyone's mother. To be the one to lock up behind them, and to let them back in, the one to give all the orders, when these days she didn't even know how to follow, let alone how to lead. So that was the last time Grandma Ana Mata would be in charge of turning the key before they set off, and the last time she'd be allowed to go to the gates before anyone else when they came home. *The last time, the last time*, Domingos Mata said, his tone resolute, as he carried boxes of domestic appliances and fancy gadgets into the factory, turning the courtyard into a kind of unloading dock for techno-logical progress itself. It had been a real shock, and for no reason. A needless scare. Still, all they had to do now was jump in the shower, lay out dinner, and sit down to eat while it was still light. A leisurely dinner, the table piled high, after Janina's triumph and the pleasant journey back. A beautiful dinner.

But that wasn't what would happen.

Conceição was Domingos' wife, and Claudina Mata was the wife of Heitor Filho. Two young women should be like two hands, each hand washing the other, before coming together to rinse the face. On entering the courtyard, Conceição took charge of the two youngest children. Heitor's wife began folding the laundry, which had stiffened and crisped in the sun. She took it down piece by piece, shook it out, and stowed it at the bottom of the plastic basket. It was quite difficult to fold, because after four days on the line at the hottest time of year, some sheets were as hard as iron. Sweating, Claudina Mata shook and pulled, stretched and piled. Then suddenly she froze, and began to shout—"Heitor! Heitor!" But it was her cousin, Domingos Mata, who got there first, and with his knife in his hand. There was no need to say anything else. Domingos realized right away that they had found the explanation for the open factory gates. The explanation was right there. Behind the washing, partly hidden by the sheets that Heitor's wife was still holding aloft, too taken aback to lower her arms, sat a white girl.

Domingos had placed himself, himself and the knife, between Claudina and the girl. Only then did Heitor appear, followed by Antonino and the other women. Yes, it was true, a white girl really was sitting behind the washing, looking at them, laughing at them, not saying a word. And the Matas, equally silent, unable to believe their eyes, were looking back at her. Speechless. Except for Heitor's dad, still some way behind, dragging himself along on his crutches and shouting—"Have you caught him? Have you caught him?" Imagining the presence of a genuine thief. The others, all silent. Nothing had prepared them for this. There was something about the white person they had just found, something tragic or comic, they couldn't tell which, but whose meaning they urgently needed to unravel. Something as yet undefined, blocking the path of the Matas' success that weekend. Something comical, perhaps. So they thought.

Yes, at first the discovery had been such a surprise that the comedy of it merged with the glory. Not to overturn it or destroy the comedy, of course, but merely to diminish it. Perhaps only to threaten it. There was something comical about that pale, intrusive thing there before them, all hunched over, with frightened eyes and parted lips, smiling or even laughing—a defensive laugh, the laugh of someone caught just before committing a crime, or at least some other kind of mischief. That person huddled up in a strange position, clutching her belongings, looking at once defenseless and menacing, entrenched among the washing lines. But what most set off the comedy was the presence of a countervailing force. Claudina Mata. Now, with Heitor pinning down her arms, she went on letting out little uncontrollable shrieks, while the thing continued to laugh. The thing, sitting on the plastic chair with a beach bag in its lap, its round knees pressed very tightly together, its thin neck very thin indeed, its short hair all disheveled, its gaze fixed on the Matas. Laughing. The comedy gaining ground, taking over their space, when all they wanted that evening was the sweet smell of success. Domingos had put the knife away, but, having led them in that surprise discovery, he now led the interrogation, asking repeatedly who the person was and what she was doing there, settled in behind the washing.

At that point, however, Felícia took over. In a loud voice, a voice still swelling with glory, projected all the way to where Milene was sitting, she said: "Now then, tell us. Who are you?" And to be sure the girl had understood the question, she took a step forward. That was when she noticed the girl's dirt-smeared face. Felícia opened her arms, moved closer still—"Oh! You're all dirty. Is something wrong? What's the matter with you?"

Milene's feet, sandals, and what could be seen of her legs, thanks to her very short skirt and seated position, were caked in dust. Her clothes seemed to have been wet and then dried again on her body.

"Can't you speak?"

"Where have you been? Your legs are all muddy . . ."

Felícia looked at her sisters, Dilecta and Germana, then all three of them stared, stunned, at the white girl. "The poor thing, she can't speak . . . Hold on, Domingos, look, she can't speak . . ."

But Milene said that yes, she could, and as proof had begun to stammer out words in the direction of those fifteen or so people who were studying her intently, and she recognized them too as the ones her family called the "third batch," and who rented or borrowed part of the Old Factory. These were the people she had been searching for since morning. But searching for people and finding them was one thing, and being found was quite another, when no one had found her in such a long time, not even her own uncles and aunts. Now there she was, in front of all those people, unable to remember what she had to say. Or rather, having nothing to say. As if those muddled, confusing days still had her in their clutches, instead of speaking calmly with one or two people she found herself in the awkward position of confronting fifteen or twenty, all of whom were staring at her as if she were a caterpillar to be flicked away. Yes, they were surprised, but no more than she was. Now the Matas drew a little closer. Cautiously. Felícia, meanwhile, leaning slightly toward Milene, was jubilant: "Look, she can speak, the girl can speak . . ." Then, encouraging, bending closer: "Tell me, now. Why are you here? Do you know who we are? Do you?"

Yes, she knew that too. It was very simple: they were the "third batch," the "third wave," and they were there to guard the Old Factory, to polish the Diamond, to hide it, guard it, keep it warm until it hatched and multiplied by a thousand. Yes, she knew, but she wasn't going to say any of that.

"Who are we, then? Who are we?"

By that point, Felícia was very close to Milene. As the others stood by, terrified and immobile, Felícia had been inching toward her, with the delicate cunning of someone attempting to catch a nervous cat with her bare hands: "Who? Who are we?"

Milene looked back and forth between Felícia and the other Matas, who were bunched together, forming a barrier between her, the wall, and the washing, and she knew that their name, the name of the third batch, or third wave, was very short, very simple, very easy to pronounce, just a syllable or two, but in that moment she couldn't remember. It would be the same when her aunts and uncles came home: she would be unable to hide from them, and unable to speak with them. Inside her head she felt a spiraling cloud, a merry-go-round of facts, of details near and far, all jumbled together, from which she failed to extract even the most basic information, while those faces encircled her, waiting for words that didn't come—then she thought she could try being quick. Sometimes she managed to get beyond that spinning carousel of cloud, that circular space like a fish-eye where everything looked close and equidistant, moving quickly enough to burst out the other side. Her cousin João Paulo, who knew her better than anyone, had given her that advice. To practice being quick, not thinking about what she was going to say, or the effect it would have, but just to practice saying everything really quickly, all in one go, racing to the end, leaving no gap between her thoughts and her lips. And now those people had found her and were even being extraordinarily patient with her. So why not be quick? For those people around her, one of whom was armed with a knife, the time she spent struggling for words must have seemed like a never-ending nightmare. All the Matas, even the children, arranged in a semicircle, staring at her as one, a row of simultaneous gazes rooting her to the spot. Imprisoned by all those eyes, and a hidden knife, Milene didn't move.

But the young man in the black shirt, who had some frightened children clinging to his trouser legs, took a step forward. He bent closer—"It's not that she's stupid, it's that she's completely shocked . . ." And moving closer still, he asked—"What's wrong, why are you in a state of shock?

"Why?"

As the young man in black examined her more closely, Milene let the expression *state of shock* ring inside her head, feeling oddly satisfied to be hearing, again and again, how that person had described her. Because, yes, that might just be it, she must be in a state of shock. *My God, it's that I'm in a state of shock. Maybe I've been in a state of shock for a long time, ever since I was born . . .* And Milene smiled, feeling, at that moment, a great sense of gratitude for that phrase the third-wave people were proffering, out of the blue, because it could explain much or even all of her life. Yes, this was no time for thinking about the past, but at least when it came to the present moment, it was surely the right expression. She was very possibly in a state of shock. That sounded good to her, and reasonable, or at least it put her in a good position. As if the expression *state of shock* could help her shake something loose that had been lodged in her head and around which everything else swirled, as if around the blades of a blender. Milene began telling them, at top speed.

She began telling them how she was sitting peacefully at home, watching *Raiders of the Lost Ark* while at the same time listening to an old Simple Minds record, and how she had suddenly found out, just like that, that Grandma Regina had died. She told them how she was the only family member at home, and how all her aunts, uncles, and cousins had left Valmares and she didn't know where they were. And she told them what she had done next, how she had spent four hours in the Church of São Francisco. She said all this at a breakneck pace, her eyes never leaving the Matas. And then, finally, she explained how Grandma Regina had collapsed right there, outside the factory gates, the previous Thursday night. And last of all, she said—"I don't know, I didn't speak to Grandma Regina, but I think she wanted to come in here and think about her past. Honestly, I think—"

"Come in where?"—asked Felícia Mata, not relating those factory gates to *their* factory gates.

"Here, into the Old Factory," Milene said.

The three sisters frowned at one another, not really following. Since Milene had broken off her tragic account, still sitting there, Felícia, incredulous, wanted to know more—"You mean this woman, the woman you're talking about, ended up here, outside our gates? Keep going, girl, keep going, and let's see if we can get this straight."

Fidgeting in the chair and still hugging her bag, Milene confessed—"Well, that's just the problem. She died and I can't explain why she died." She said this while looking at the Matas, as if the faces of those people were a vast, implacable landscape. And the Matas leaning in, trying to decipher what they were hearing, as if they had found an oracle, an offering from another world. Felícia moved her face close to Milene's and reached out a hand to the girl.

"Wait a second . . . Explain this to me. You're here, and you're Dona Regina Leandro's granddaughter, and you're saying Dona Regina has passed away . . . First things first . . . Why are you here?"

"I came to see if someone could explain what happened to Grandma Regina"—answered the white girl.

The Matas burst out laughing. Domingos laughed too, then, dismissing the comical moment that had overshadowed the Matas' well-deserved happiness and plenty, he said very loudly—"Right, there's our explanation. She's got a screw loose, she's here saying crazy things and we're wasting our time listening to her, with all there is left to do . . . You'd better phone up the landlady, Ma, and say one of her daughters or granddaughters has turned up at our house. Who knows who she is? Maybe she's nothing to do with her . . ."

Milene spotted the flaw in this.

"There's no point phoning, she won't pick up. I just told you, she's passed away . . ."

The more Milene persevered with the words she was saying, the thinner they became, the less substantial, and the less they seemed to make sense. Soon not even she sounded very sure whether the person in question was dead or alive.

Claudina couldn't believe what was happening. She laughed too, tickled by the way the girl before them interpreted and responded to the world: "Have you ever seen a dead person answer a telephone? Well, have you?" It was all very funny. Yes, as things stood, the Matas would truly have liked to be respectful toward that person sitting all crumpled up on one of the chairs in their courtyard, but they just couldn't help themselves. The Matas had begun to laugh openly, happily, each doubling up with mirth. The Matas laughing.

They laughed and didn't stop, as if they were still in the Coliseu dos Recreios and seeing the funny side of their great triumph. But what was happening here and now was entirely different. The girl was rather lost and overwhelmed, which was very sad, but they, the Matas, couldn't step outside their hard-won happiness, couldn't and wouldn't, and so the situation didn't interest them at all, and as a result they drew back from that person, laughing among themselves. And Milene, hearing them laugh, laughed too.

But then, without getting up, still held in the chair's plastic embrace, Milene opened her bag, rummaged inside it, found a paper tissue that she used to wipe her face and neck, and only then started to cry. It was so long since she'd cried. Thinking about it, she hadn't cried since her cousin João Paulo had left. Such a long time ago. And why shouldn't she cry now, in front of these third-wave people, if she wanted to so much? So she did. She cried silently into the open tissue, covering her eyes completely and drying her teary face. The tissue grew grubby and tore in half. She moved on to another, which got damp and tore as well. She cried like a child into shreds of tissue that fell apart in her hands, sticking to her fingers in soggy clumps. Seeing this, the Mata women began to move closer. Silence fell in the courtyard. Milene's crying wasn't noisy, but it melted something around it.

It melted the comedy and in an odd way it reinforced the glory. For the Matas, at that moment, sadness was other people's business, a strange excrescence there in their home that had nothing to do with them, although they all knew that anyone happy who sees other people suffering has an irrefutable duty to be kind to those people. Felícia Mata saw all this from a long way off, with the swift logic of a winner. This was it—someone was in serious trouble who had come to their house seeking refuge, seeking the Matas' help, and welcoming that person as good hosts might even shore up their rights and status, heightening their moment of happiness. Felícia Mata, between her sister Germana and her sister Dilecta, crouching right in front of the girl and offering her handkerchiefs, suddenly patient, addressed her in a velvety voice.

"There, there, my dear. There, there. We never dreamed it would be something like that . . . Come to think of it, you do look like your family. We didn't even notice. And, of course, your grandmother's our landlady. Tell us, dear, tell us how it all happened. We won't laugh, we'll just listen . . ."

And Milene, again hurling herself at the words, told the whole story one more time, developing a detail here, a detail there, in response to their questions, articulating facts about the past few days as if gathering them from the depths of a distant lake. Telling it with no mention of time or space, invoking her absent family members scattered across the tourist resorts of the world, and her apprehensions about their return. And since she seemed to be describing a dream, and not a real situation, they all felt, as they listened, strangely removed from the world, from life's structures and laws, still propelled as they were by the glow of that crowd in the Coliseu dos Recreios, where the Matas had been sitting in the third row, with Janina singing, from that seemingly infinite stage, *Carpeting the sea, carpeting the red sea, with my foreigner's handkerchief* . . . Driven on by the wild applause that reverberated from the stalls up to the balconies, and which they could still hear in their ears, as well as that joyous return home, so joyous they hadn't even noticed the white Clio parked outside. And since their joy had now run up against tragedy, and since the tragedy belonged not to the Matas but to that girl who didn't know how to speak, and who was almost certainly making things up—because surely no one in the state Grandma Regina had apparently been in could have escaped from inside an ambulance and ended up there, without anybody's help—Felícia, her voice rising higher, as if a pair of sharp tweezers had picked it up and was holding it high above her head, said—"You poor dear thing, you really are shocked . . ." Looking Milene in the face and doubting her words. All the Matas felt the same. Surely the girl was describing some make-believe fantasy, while Felícia repeated—"You must be very shocked, very shocked indeed . . . What did you say your name was?"

But a group of people has its own logic of defense and attack, like a shoal, like a flock. Shoals and flocks are mysterious things, at least as mysterious as their individual members. Domingos, who had gone back to unloading and unpacking boxes by then, building a pyramid of paper and plastic in one corner, suddenly grew frustrated and shouted from the door—"Antonino, go to the gas station and see what's going on, it's time we got to the bottom of all this. And hurry . . ."

The young man in black buttoned up his shirt and headed toward the gray van. His three small children followed him, tumbling along in a single mass and getting under his feet. The three children strapped into the back as if embarking on a long journey. But it didn't even take half an hour. Then they were climbing out of the van again, all four now tangled together. Antonino shook himself free of his children and confirmed everything—it was true. No one at the gas station could tell him much, and they weren't even sure who he was talking about, except for one young guy who had just finished his shift and came forward with what he knew. And if he was to be believed, everything had happened exactly as that white girl had described it. It seemed Dona Regina Leandro really had been found right there, outside the gates they were always going in and out of. She had been found by some amateur cyclists out training early that holiday morning. It was the cyclists who had forced their way in, thinking she was someone from the house. Only then were the police called. By the cyclists. After that, no one could tell him anything else; the events had changed hands and continued elsewhere.

"So it's all true . . ." said Antonino Mata, standing by the open gates, taking off his cap. His eyes on the gates. Everyone's eyes on the gates. The Matas had left Milene sitting back there, and now they weren't looking at her but at the gates, transfixed by that stone step where their landlady had ended her days.

"So it's true?"

They looked through the two gates at the gentle, white-mottled hills far beyond them, walls running through a distant grove of trees and trickling toward them like a dull, gravelly mixture, and then the barren land next door, a yellow and auburn expanse, where the remains of unidentifiable trees lay forgotten like thorny skeletons, all this together, in the reddish light of sunset. In the foreground the potholed road, and then, right in front of that, the gates. No one said anything. Death was there with them, it had left its mark inside the building and outside it, with the gates, like a double-edged sword, dividing their past and future lives. And the white girl, still back there behind the washing, was its messenger. Now the Matas looked at Milene, surprised and alarmed, as if she were the first letter of a long sentence yet to be read. They moved nearer. And since night was falling, hot and thick with mosquitoes, and no one was switching on the lights, the Matas gathered uneasily by the gates. Ana Mata shuffled up and down, bewildered, not knowing what to think, pushing her plastic arm-chair with her. How was it possible? They all asked. Yes, how was it possible that on the same day they set off from Lisbon, cross-ing the bridge, the sun beating down on the river and making it glitter like their islands in the Cape Verdean light, yes, how was it possible that on the same day as their heads were full of won-derful thoughts, they had returned to the news of their landlady dying on their doorstep? What to do? What to think? It was like a bereavement. Dilecta even thought of fetching a chaplet and saying some Paternosters and Hail Marys for their dead landlady, as if it had only just taken place.

But Felícia didn't let her.

The more the light waned, the more incapable the Matas seemed of doing anything, drifting about in a silent daze, but she saw things clearly. Yes, it was all very clear, very simple, for Felícia Mata. Because you needed your wits about you in this life, even when it came to death. And, standing in the middle of the court-yard, giving out contradictory orders, she began telling her family to pull themselves together, because the process of death was part of life, of the life after death that God gave us, and not some dark specter that came along and snapped a person in two. Whoever had come up with that?

And as for Dona Regina having died on their doorstep, that seemed perfectly clear to her too. The way she saw it, the landlady had been fond of the Matas, and with her own family's where-abouts unknown, the woman had looked for some respectable people she'd be safe with. After all, Dona Regina knew full well that the Matas had never shirked their duties, paying ten thousand escudos for that space at the beginning of each month, as well as pulling up the weeds, replacing the fallen roof tiles, scaring away the wild animals, and making sure no local tramps moved in. Yes, Dona Regina knew; she was the one who had invited them to live there. And at first, she'd been the one who came to collect the rent and have a look around. Keeping an eye on things. The last time had been about two years ago. Felícia could still see her getting out of the taxi and walking toward the main gates, with her lilac-dyed hair, dark glasses, and a layer of beige and brown powder on her face. Of course she remembered.

Dona Regina had come to check that the factory was clean and tidy, and to pass the time of day. Standing very erect, fingers laden with rings, chatting away with Ana Mata, chatting with all the women. She remembered it so well. They'd had a cold drink together just over there. She could still see her, pointing her cane at some scraps of paper blowing along the ground, then saying goodbye and heading back to her taxi, which had waited for her outside. And she could see her moving off down the road, sitting stiffly in her seat like a queen mother, on the very first day they spoke. That was before, perhaps five years ago. They all remembered it. Yes, five years ago, the Matas having lunch by chance under those palm trees and Dona Regina striking up a conversation, offering them the use of the house. She hadn't wanted much in return, and the Matas had made just one request—that she switch on the electricity and water right away. Yes, they remembered that June afternoon. A bright, sunny afternoon. A younger Dona Regina in another taxi, and them on the mound, the terms agreed. Dona Regina's hair, fuller then, gleaming behind the taxi window, and the taxi gliding away down the road. Yes, they remembered. A great day, a great afternoon. Why spoil those memories now with prayers, rosaries and other such things? "Shoo, shoo, sad thoughts, go away . . .

"Go, go . . ."

Felícia telling the sad night thoughts to be gone, in a firm, mellifluous voice. Standing by the gates. All of them standing by the gates, through which they saw the Clio opposite, parked on the shoulder. The darkness closing in on the slender trunks of the palm trees. They heard Ana Mata's muffled sobs, as she sat alone in her plastic armchair, talking to her landlady's absence. Sighing so loudly that Felícia said—"Stop, Ma, that's enough. What are you crying for? Watch some TV, think about something else . . ." But suddenly, in the middle of the thoroughly sensible words Felícia was spreading around, an important idea had arisen. An idea whose sheer enormity had her wiping the sweat from her hands and face and vigorously rubbing her eyes. Her chest filled with air, her voice shook. And she asked the girl—"Is there anyone waiting for you back home?"

Milene was heading for her Clio. The Matas looking at the gates and then at her.

"No one?"

"And in that case, where are you going to sleep tonight?" Felícia asked Milene, almost shouting. And in the darkness descending around them, Felícia's idea took shape—"Now, look, if you don't have anyone at home, we Matas are good Christian folk. You can stay here with us; your grandmother would thank us, wherever she is. Go and get cleaned up, then you can have dinner here, you must be starving, and you can sleep in my musician sons' bedroom, then tomorrow we'll see, because you're in no fit state to go home like this, after such a shock. I bet you're actually very smart, very intelligent, you're just shocked by this whole upsetting business . . ."

The Matas looking at the wide-open gates, at the dark plain where even the white car was vanishing as if it were made of earth. And Felícia giving orders—"Conceição, Claudina, put some clean sheets on the little bed in the musicians' room. Both of you, it'll be quicker. Chop-chop, or dinner will be late. Hurry up, come on. We won't have any crying here. It's a special day, too special for tears. Did you hear that, Ma? Get your *cautcha* and go and sit down, but over there, by your rivers, and meanwhile stop all that moaning. Come on, come on . . ." Felícia clapping her hands. The hands whose clapping had served her so well the night before, and which were now chasing out the gloom, cutting short any sadness, and driving the rotten memories away. "Shoo, shoo, bad memory. Good memory, make yourself at home . . ."

And she said no more, because it would have seemed inappropriate, but as she set everyone in motion around the courtyard, Felícia felt an urge to sing Janina's winning song, to sing it as a woman and as the mother of a singer, in her beautiful contralto. If it wouldn't have looked bad, she'd even have sung for Dona Regina, for the happy memories she had given the Matas, as well as the factory itself. She would have sung "Carpeting the Sea" in full church style, as if it were the Gloria Patri. But she didn't, because not even her own family would understand how she could sing at a time of mourning. Instead of bursting into song, Felícia strode up and down, issuing orders—"Quickly, hurry . . . Clean sheets on the bed, so the girl can sleep . . . Chop-chop . . ."

"Do you want to spend the night in our house or don't you? Yes or no?"

Yes, Milene did. Our cousin hadn't so much as set foot on the dark, shadowy road. She was hungry and thirsty, tired and afraid. Her ankles stung, as if she had been bitten by insects or scratched by spikes of dry grass. The night seemed to her like a house of infinite dimensions where she would almost certainly get lost, and meanwhile someone back there had given her the key to those days, perhaps the key to her entire life. Or rather, when she least expected it, other people's words had come to her, full of meaning and explaining everything—*Yes, me in a state of shock since Friday, me in a state of shock for years and years, ever since João Paulo took me out in Guinote's boat and started to say those words. I was in a state of shock even then. A person in a state of shock, alone, tired, driving her car in the middle of the night? Out of the question . . .* And they looked at her and she looked at them. She turned back.

Which was how Milene came to spend that night, the night of the eighteenth of August, in one of the buildings of the Diamond. A tiny act of volition deciding the course of her life. But it wasn't true that the Matas had found her a long way from the Clio, on the road to Bairro dos Espelhos, with dust all around her and no bag or hat. Let alone that the Matas had called her over and taken her with them, crammed in, presumably, among supermarket boxes, sweaty passengers, and other odds and ends. Milene was the one who hid behind the washing, the one who accepted the invitation, and the one who walked back into the courtyard, of her own perfectly free will.

But we wouldn't learn all that until later.

II

YES, OF HER OWN FREE WILL, IN WHICH HER TIREDNESS would also play a part.

The truth is that, after being discovered behind the washing line, and once night had descended over Mar de Prainhas, all Milene wanted was to be able to sleep in the bed offered to her by the woman with the strident voice, who seemed to have known Grandma Regina quite well. To be able to spend the night among people who shared her perplexity about what had happened, to sleep among people who continued to speak directly to Grandma Regina, people like Ana Mata sitting in her plastic armchair in one corner of the courtyard. To stay with these otherwise speech-less people, who even told their children to be quiet. Close to that young man who had first appeared wielding a knife, but who, now that he was unarmed, seemed to do nothing but stare at the factory gates. That other man, all in black, who'd said she was in a state of shock, and who kept pacing around, looking for some-thing he couldn't find. In accepting Felícia's invitation, Milene, our cousin Milene, had, as she herself would say later, felt com-forted. That night, at least, she wouldn't have to think about the police or phoning her aunts and uncles, nor about the streets she'd walked, nor about that *thing*, nor about the priest's long speech,

nor about the woman with the square calf muscles, or the flowers shifting around inside the black car, or even about the search
she'd carried out during that same long day, until she found those
third-wave people who had welcomed her so serenely. Milene
didn't resist. She didn't even need to speak.

Compared with driving back home in the dark, all of this seemed
very good indeed.

The bed they gave her for the night was in what appeared to be
a recording studio, where there was a little of everything, and
which felt extraordinarily cozy. She felt very at ease among all
that musical stuff, keyboards, stringed instruments and drums,
various piles of records alongside bits of equipment on which
to play them. She felt so good that, right then, she didn't want
to think about anything else. Her only task was to fit into that
tiny bed, crammed in between two larger beds, in the middle of
that room transformed into a red bazaar. At one point, Claudina Mata had left, taking with her the two curly-haired teenagers, Sissi and Belisa. Then Conceição had appeared. All four
of them had taken a good look at her before vanishing. Closing the door behind them very carefully, almost silently. Finally,
Felícia had come in to tell her that she could leave the light
on, the lamp placed beside her tiny bed in between more piles
of records. A relative silence had descended then. Outside, the
only sounds were Ana Mata crying in the small gray house, and
one of her grandsons complaining because he could hear her.
Felícia calling for silence—"That's enough crying and bickering,
be quiet now . . ." After a morning of walking up and down in
that muddy field, and a whole afternoon spent hiding behind
the laundry, Milene didn't need to speak; she felt safe. Given
the circumstances, it was good that she didn't have to go home.

Then Milene closed her eyes and thought of the happy times she'd spent there in the Diamond, immediately after the second wave had given up and gone.

She couldn't say exactly when it had been, nor did she want to, but as for where, it had happened in that very place, when the factory was still known as the *Fábrica de Conservas Leandro 1908*. It had been an amazing time. After washing her face and legs in cold water, and with the light from the courtyard sifting in through the curtain, Milene lay on the bed recalling the encampment they'd set up during the three months that João Paulo used to call *the best summer of our lives*. Aunt Gininha with her long hair was still unmarried and went everywhere with her boyfriend. And the three inseparable cousins spent all their time running about in that wide-open space, right there, in front of that tall chimney. Milene remembered all this, reliving the good times they'd had there. She didn't need to remember anything else.

She didn't need to remember the five workers from the "second wave" handing back the keys on a velvet cushion and mouthing phrases so typical of 1985, when workers had been obliged to return any properties illegally occupied in the wake of the 1974 Revolution. She didn't need to remember the slogans we ourselves would repeat ad nauseam, sneering and making fun of the workers—"No more treachery. We're returning this piece of shit exactly as it was given to us . . . We buried our bones here, and for nothing . . . Here are the keys, returned to you on the very same velvet cushion, so that you can't say that we kept back so much as one tiny crumb of this great swindle . . ." No, Milene didn't need to remember those words or the five workers staring into the middle distance, as tense and nervous as if they were about to kill us. The one female in the group, with cropped hair, had added—"It's pure thievery, that's what is . . ." At this, Grandma

Regina had frozen. The whole family too, as if they were prepared to stand their ground and be stoned to death without so much as flinching. All very dignified. Grandma Regina with her wedge heels firmly together, as if she were a general. Her lips as if sewn shut, her heavily lidded eyes looking heavier than usual when she heard the word *thievery*. The four men turning their backs on us like someone signing a letter of capitulation in a battle. Then the four men had left, and the woman with the almost shaven head, the most uptight of the five, the most outraged, had started heaping insults on Humanity in general, on thieving Humanity. The corners of her mouth were turned down, as if they'd learned their shape from the crescent moon. And after picking up the last of their belongings, a few papers and files, they all left on noisy mopeds that went roaring flatulently down the road. The woman was riding a scooter, her skirt tucked into her panties, her helmet behind her on the luggage rack. Policeman-like, with her almost shaven head bare to the winds. The five disappearing off down the road. To the end of the road. Yes, it had been a very awkward moment, but Milene didn't need to relive that just then. Lying on the little bed, all she remembered was spending the entire sum-mer camped out there and waking up very early in the morning, borrowing Guinote's fishing boat, and heading off down the Ria, the drowned river valley.

And yet, Milene had, like us, been present at that handover.

Indeed, at the time, Milene couldn't contain herself, and had said in a very loud voice—"God, that was scary! Did we win?"

Aunt Ângela Margarida had shot her a glance telling her to be quiet, then continued walking along arm-in-arm with Grandma Regina, kicking aside the fishy, salty boxes and crates lying in their path, past the cans piled high around the conveyor belt, the overturned canisters, and the patches of spilled oil. No one said anything. Only João Paulo, who responded—"Given the way they looked at us, as if they were ten Rasputins, I reckon we've all lost . . ." The eyes of the whole family, including Aunt Gininha, were all fixed on João Paulo then, like steel ball bearings. And in the ensuing silence, amid the sounds of footsteps and boxes and crates being kicked aside, the three of us had hung back, trying to stifle our laughter. The walls were daubed with foul language and threatening slogans, which we'd had to have removed in order to live in peace. The grass on the hillside, where a murder had taken place, had been mown. The buildings had been swept and sluiced out. Because when the second wave left, we would occupy that large space, and spend the summer of 1985 there, *the best summer of our lives.* Milene would have remembered that. Three whole months spent camped in the factory. But Uncle Afonso had never referred to us as a wave.

The idea of waves would only surface with the third wave, which was this one, made up of the people who had taken her in and given her that tiny bed, where she could now stretch out at her ease without thinking about anything, apart from life's good times. Like, for example, we three cousins sitting in Guinote's boat, slipping along the waters of the Ria, and Milene protected from the sun by her cousin's shirt and holding on to the bucket. At the time, João Paulo still had the long, slender legs of an adolescent, but was already coming out with alarming questions— "Listen, girls, do you reckon that light is actually the spirit of fire?" Then Milene had sprung to her feet, almost capsizing the boat— "Don't tell me the water's going to catch fire . . ."

He had managed to steady the boat, and everything settled down again. He made her sit in the prow, put her straw hat back on her head, then draped his shirt over her. João Paulo swore that we three would never be parted—"We'll always be together, always united, never separated, for the rest of our days. Okay?" Peace reigned over the waters of the Ria. She was thinking all this, but she didn't need to say the word *peace*, to say the word *ria*. These realities existed independently of words. On this particular night, the eighteenth of August, Milene was a girl wearing a borrowed shirt and wrapped in good thoughts, only good thoughts, lying on a tiny bed, then falling deep asleep until she woke the next morning, when the people of the third wave were beginning to move around.

Milene didn't need to say the words *good morning*, either. The reality was there to be seen.

Long before the sun rose, Felícia Mata began to move about in the dark courtyard, spreading life and energy. The dogs that followed her, equally full of energy, frolicked at her heels, wagging their tails and nipping at each other, sharing with her the rudder of life. As soon as it began to grow light, Felícia had picked up a broom, and with a great bristle and bustle, got to work sweeping litter into one corner, working from the center of the courtyard toward the main gates that had been such a source of alarm to everyone the previous night. This was her happy, fortunate life as the mother of Janina Mata King, and she wasn't going to allow anything, not even the dead body of one of the owning classes, to make her deviate one inch from the path of her happiness. With her muscular arms, Felícia had dragged two pots of rather stunted geraniums over to the door. Dragging the pots and various crates had made almost as much noise as a delivery truck, but no one seemed to have woken up, not even Ana Mata, in her little gray house. Felícia dragging the pots, the dog and the poodle scampering madly about, the three of them announcing the coming of morning, as if the previous night hadn't existed. And walking past the room usually inhabited by her musician sons, Felícia called out—"Dona Milene, are you awake?"

Then, standing very close to the red curtains, she had called again—"Listen, if you're not awake, then wake up now. I have something important to tell you . . ."

Then Felícia had gone over to one of the windows in the building opposite, saying in a loud voice—"Domingos, get up!"

Domingos Mata would soon be crossing the courtyard, a bundle of clothes under his arm, before disappearing behind a wall. Inside the lean-to, a tap was turned on and the water from a shower began to flood the flagstones in the courtyard. Domingos was already returning, washed and dressed, when Felícia said— "Hurry up, Domingos, you're the one who's going to take the girl back to her family . . ." At that moment, however, her second son, Antonino Mata, appeared, first in the other window, then framed in another doorway. Looking distinctly glum in the coming light of morning, he too crossed the courtyard with a bundle of clothes under his arm. When he returned from the shower, he was dressed all in black, as he had been the previous day. The two brothers met outside the lean-to, their hair wet. Felícia caught up with them. She seemed about to speak to Domingos again, but changed direction at the last moment, closed her eyes, and pointed at Antonino—"No, on second thought, you can take her home, not Domingos." Felícia was pointing at her second son now, her eyes still closed, as if her decision came from another place or another person and she had only to raise her finger to pass on an order issued by a superior power—"You can go because you're quicker on the uptake and a better talker. No, no buts, you're the one who's going to deliver the girl to her family, and that's that . . ." They were all gathered around the table now. No one was saying a word. Felícia again explained the reason for her choice, still with her finger pointing at Antonino—

"No ifs, no buts. It's decided, and I'll tell you why. Domingos may be older, but Antonino is quicker on the uptake and better at explaining. Now, the person who delivers the girl is going to have to explain several things at once, he's going to have to be quick . . ." And since her sons were pretending to ignore her, she described the nature of those "several things" herself— "No, *many* things . . . The person who takes her is going to have to explain that we knew nothing about what happened, that the girl came here of her own accord, that we didn't go looking for her. And he'll have to say that we only offered her a bed and food because of the state she was in. And that she slept in Janina's room, in the room of Janina Mata King. Yes, he'll have to say that as well . . ." Felícia still had her eyes closed and her finger raised—"The problem is, all this is so close to the truth that it could sound horribly like a lie. In matters of defense, the truth is very dangerous. The truth can easily resemble a false-hood, much more easily than an actual lie. So when you deliver the girl, you must be very careful with the truth. Heitor could go, I suppose, but he's just a brother-in-law, and less of a family member . . ."

The three men were eating standing up. Antonino was eating and looking at his watch, as if, while he paid no heed to the con-versation, the watch itself were sending him messages. Felícia, her finger still raised, said—"And stop looking at your watch! There's no point, you don't stand to win or lose anything."

Antonino still kept looking at his watch.

Irritated, Felícia said—"So what if you lose an hour or two hours or three, you'll just have to lose whatever you have to lose. Our Lord Jesus Christ lost much more, he lost his life for the whole of humanity, and he only complained once. And at most you'll lose an hour and a half. What's that in an entire lifetime?" Brimming with energy, Felícia strode out into the courtyard again, stood next to the red-curtained window, and called in a singsong voice—"Young lady? Dona Milene? Are you awake? Listen, my son Antonino is going to take you back to your family. He's happy to do that, so there's no problem. That way, you won't arrive unaccompanied. What would your relatives think if you did?"

Felícia standing outside by the curtain—"No, you won't go alone, we wouldn't allow that. If you're afraid of your aunts and uncles, you need someone there to explain what happened . . ." Felícia spoke again in a graver tone—"Get up, dear. You just need to tell us the address. Preferably the address of one of your uncles. Do you hear?" Outside the factory, Domingos's metallic blue van was already setting off. Only Antonino was still there in the courtyard. And although Felícia had finally lowered her finger, her voice remained the same—"You're not going to lose much time. Our Lord lost much more, and never a word of complaint. You'll see. The girl's a bit slow, but she won't be long . . ."

"Are you there, dear?"

Antonino had started pacing again like a caged beast. When Milene eventually appeared, with her hair still dripping, to show how hurriedly she'd washed and dressed, she strode through the main gates toward the palm trees, without saying a word. Antonino had meanwhile climbed into the gray van, and she had gotten into the Clio parked on the other side of the road. But while Antonino prepared to set off, Milene didn't move. She was still settling into her car, not yet putting the key in the ignition, instead adjusting her seat as if it were someone else's car, then feeling for something on the dashboard that wasn't there, until Antonino Mata, after waiting for what seemed like an age, shouted—"Hey, you there in your stopped car. Do you actually know how to drive?"

When she heard this, she looked up, but still didn't turn the key in the ignition. Then Antonino performed a rapid U-turn and drew alongside the Clio, where Milene was still fiddling about with something or other. Seeing him there, she finally started the car, and Antonino took the opportunity to clarify a few matters, raising his voice above the sound of their engines.

"Do you want to go first or shall I?" he asked, checking his watch for the umpteenth time as she came up alongside his van. "Which way do you want to go?"

"Via the gas station," said Milene, equally loudly, still adjusting her seat. "Then take the highway as far as the crossroads at the Estrada das Brisas . . ."

He couldn't believe it. He shook his head in disbelief. "That's a very long way around. If we went via Bairro dos Espelhos, we'd be there in a flash . . ." And feeling, despite everything, slightly reassured—for it seemed that the girl did, after all, know how to drive—Antonino advised her, still in a very loud voice, to follow him and watch out for the traffic lights. Then he backtracked. In his haste, he'd forgotten something vital—"Where is it exactly I'm supposed to take you?"

Milene began to explain that it could be the crossroads near the Hotel Miramar, or, more precisely, Kilometer 44 on the Estrada das Brisas. She said this quickly, so that their conversation would be over just as quickly, since he was clearly in a hurry. And also because, at that precise moment, she too was being unusually quick. Extremely quick. Yet he still didn't feel he had enough information, and wanted to know more—"So who's going to be there to receive you? Do you know?"

"Oh, there'll be someone."

This was too evasive an answer. Antonino, who was again ready to set off, got out of his van and spoke to her patiently and deliberately, as if explaining a very important matter to someone very stupid. A brief, practical chat so that they could get on their way. With a lot of explanatory gestures, he bellowed—"Are you listening?" Yes, she was listening. "Really?" Milene was watching him standing there, all in black, his shadow sprawled on the ground. He looked rather frightening. Yes, she was definitely listening—"Right, let's get this straight. I'm here to take you back to your family. Correct? And you're with me so that you won't have to go alone. Correct? I know exactly what I have to say, but the question you need to ask yourself is: Are you or are you not in a state of shock? And you are, aren't you? Correct? A person in a state of shock needs to go and see her other family members. In your case, when you see your family, all you have to say is that your grandmother, their mother, died, and that you don't know how or why. That you were only called in to identify her body. Since they weren't around, you had to deal with everything on your own, which is why you're in the state you're in. And that's why you came to seek shelter in our house. Do you understand? Otherwise, say nothing, because, the way I see it, there's nothing more to explain. So where shall I take you?"

It was as if he hadn't spoken, because Milene, still fiddling around with things on the dashboard, said—"Like I told you, Kilometer Forty-Four . . ."

There was nothing more he could do. Faced with the inevitable, Antonino showed admirable patience. Patient impatience. He rolled his eyes in despair, and she saw this. Then he turned his back on her—"All right, follow me. We'll take a right, and if we keep straight on through Bairro dos Espelhos, that will be quickest."

Then Antonino Mata again headed east, and both cars set off first along the potholed tarmac road, then along the dirt track, where the metal bodies of their cars were immediately enveloped in the cloud of dust churned up by the wheels. And then he noticed that Milene had wound up her windows and hit the brakes. And quite right too, because as they crossed the dull gray square in Bairro dos Espelhos, Antonino's van was intercepted by two men who stepped out from behind a kind of gate. One of them, wearing a wide-brimmed hat, like a Mexican sombrero, stood right in the van's path, laughing and coming much too close, arms spread wide, as if quite prepared to be knocked down.

"Now, tell me something, will you? Is it true that you left Janina the singer in Lisbon with your brother Gabriel? And that Janina has quit high school for good?"

Antonino had not allowed for such an encounter in his tight schedule, but he stopped nonetheless to say that he couldn't talk just then because he was in a hurry. And he further explained that the girl driving the car behind his had been found sheltering in their house, and that he was on his way to take her back to her family.

The two men looked at Milene. Both the van and the Clio continued to rev their engines, throwing up little spirals of dust. Antonino's haste was in marked contrast with the laid-back attitude of the two men. They planted themselves in front of the van, blocking the road—"You found her in your house? And you're going to take her home? Well, I wouldn't do that if I was you . . . Who is she, anyway?"

Antonino gave a hasty explanation, saying that she was the granddaughter of Dona Regina, the owner of the Old Factory, who had apparently gone there to die at the factory gates. That's why he was in such a hurry, he was on a mission. Then the man in the sombrero had a light-bulb moment, and, taking off his hat and placing it on the windshield, he yelled—"Wait there, man, don't move!" Holding one hand in front of him and the other up in the air, as signalmen used to do in the old days, he boldly barred the way, calling—"Flora! Flora, come here!" A woman in a white silk bathrobe immediately appeared at the door to her house. The man's voice grew shriller—"Guess who's in that car?"

With the hem of her robe dragging in the dust, the woman, filled with curiosity, came out into the street.

"It's the granddaughter of that person who died all alone and had no one at her funeral. The mayor's mother-in-law."

"Just a moment," said the woman, hurrying across the yard toward the Clio. Once there, the person called Flora let her robe fall open and, pressing her two hands on the window, she slid them all along the side of the car, examining it from every angle. She was very thorough. She wanted to be quite sure this coincidence was real, and once she was quite certain, she became like a woman possessed. It was just amazing. Drumming her two hands on the glass, letting the hem of her robe drag in the brown dust, she asked one question after the other, as if she'd prepared them beforehand—"Open the window, girl! Were you really the only one at the funeral? And were all your aunts and uncles on vacation in Japan? Come on, open up so we can have a chat . . ." Milene remained locked inside. "Is it true your grandmother was all covered in ants? If it is, there's no need to be ashamed, it could happen to anyone . . ."

The two men had gone over to the Clio too, as if they weren't the least bit interested now in Antonino Mata. And Antonino, in turn, had climbed out of his gray van, determined to stop what was about to happen. "Let's be clear," he said. "I was just told to take her home. Once I've done that, you can call her house and ask the people there what happened. It's none of my business, and I'm in one hell of a hurry, all right?"

Flora clutched her robe about her and began to laugh—"Phone *where*? No need, it was all in yesterday's *O Comércio*. It was there in letters this size—*Great Scandal as Mayor's Mother-in-Law Dies*

Alone . . ." So said Flora, tapping herself on the chest, unprotected now by the frilled edges of her robe. "I read that with the eyes God gave me. What I didn't know was that it all happened outside your front door . . ." And, turning again to Milene, she shouted—"Unlock the door, dear, wind down the window. What's your name? Marlene? No, Milene Leandro. That's it. The paper said it was you who told them everything. It was all there—*People shocked to hear that the mayor and his family, on vacation in Japan, left a close relative to arrange the funeral, with no medical help and no family present . . .*" And they say it was this same Milene Leandro who spilled the beans. I'm not sure if it was Japan or China, because the person who wrote the article didn't know either. It seems even the Town Hall knew nothing about it. No one knew. Come on, open up . . ."

Antonino was standing right by the window now and wouldn't let Milene wind it down. They needed to get going, but the woman was still so entranced by this extraordinary coincidence that he thought it best to address the men instead, who were now standing around the car as well—"You have to understand, the poor girl's in a state of shock and doesn't want to talk. I just have to take her home. You know what the newspapers are like, full of lies. In fact, all they ever do is tell lies. Nothing they say ever has much to do with reality anyway . . . Now, would you please get out of the way?"

Antonino Mata pushed them roughly aside. Then, getting back in his van, having removed the sombrero from the windshield and tossed it over to its owner, he set off, gradually picking up speed along the dirt road. Milene followed behind, her windows still firmly closed. In the rearview mirror, she could still see Flora, her robe wrapped around her, standing between those two men, who had been joined now by a few new arrivals. Soon, though, the dust on the windows and the mirrors blended with the dust thrown up by their cars, and, a few seconds later, everything, reflections and reality, was dust.

The journey to Villa Regina would be a short one.

The gray van had crossed a sandy track before heading down another road full of bends and yet more bends, past places where the makeshift shacks looked more like kennels, where the sides of the road were cluttered with abandoned water troughs and pigeon lofts, where the roofs were made of this and that, and dismantled cardboard boxes served as stepping-stones between muddy paths and asphalt, and then suddenly, without warning, they had reached the main road. Antonino announced the change in direction well in advance, stopping and putting his hand out the window, waiting some time, and only then setting off down the empty road. They drove for almost a mile, as far as the Hotel Miramar, a perpendicular block rising up like a traffic light at the crossroads. They had arrived. He moved aside, allowing her to pass and drive up to the door of the house. On the wall separating the old buildings from the streets, someone had painted, in rather wonky letters *Km 44*. Behind the wall, half-covered in ivy that, in some places, threatened to grow up as far as the eaves, was another sign: *Villa Regina*. A huge roof-high walnut tree with crinkled leaves rose out of a clump of greenery. To the east, the terrazzo-clad façades of the other 1950s houses looked distinctly tatty, while to the west, another had been half demolished to allow the river of asphalt to pass close by, and in the morning light the amputated remains resembled a disemboweled steam iron. They could easily still have been in Bairro dos Espelhos, for while the quality of the buildings was different, the mental territory the place occupied seemed much the same. Milene, though, was thinking only that she was home. Unlike the previous night, she felt glad to be back. In contrast to the scorched roadsides, the green garden with its microclimate felt like a paradise. It was there, when standing in the shade of the walnut tree the previous day before heading off to Praia Pequena, that she'd had the idea of going to investigate the muddy path in order to have something to tell her aunts and uncles. A pointless exercise, as it turned out. At least now, though, that young man all in black could finally leave. There he was, in front of his van, checking his watch. She checked hers too; it was only half past eight, so he hadn't wasted that much time. At most twenty minutes. But instead of rushing off to wherever he was supposed to be, Antonino was now walking toward her, asking her to call someone so that he could safely hand her over.

"Preferably a man, one of your uncles," he said.

They remained standing by the front door of Villa Regina. Outside, everything was exactly as she'd left it, which meant there was no one in the house he could talk to. Milene intended being very brisk and efficient, and didn't want a repetition of what had happened in Bairro dos Espelhos. She said—"Listen, there's no one here now, but there wasn't anyone here before, so it doesn't matter. You go and get on with your own business. After all, I'm home now."

Antonino got annoyed. "Look, I'm supposed to hand you over to someone, so how *can* I go and get on with my own business?" He turned his back on her, as if he needed to do so in order to grasp exactly what was going on. When he turned back around, he looked quite desperate. A line of acacias belonging to the house next door cast a long shadow across the yard. Clapping one hand to his head, like someone who has just made a decision or been obliged to accept someone else's, he said sourly—"I might have known you were going to bring me to an empty house. Just tell me where your relatives live, will you, so I can hand you over to them."

Milene had begun to feel troubled by the direction the conversation was taking. She even thought that if she ran into the house and locked the door behind her, the situation would be resolved, to her advantage and to his, but his voice was stronger than hers and held her glued to the spot—"Don't you understand? I need to hand you over, person-to-person, face-to-face."

Yes, she did understand. She even rather liked the idea of arriving at the house of one of her aunts and uncles accompanied by someone else—someone who, more to the point, had said that all this had come about because she'd been in a state of shock. And in her head, she repeated the words *state of shock* and smiled gratefully at Antonino. She even imagined herself there, in Villa Regina, and her aunts and uncles arriving, and her saying to them—*I was in a total state of shock. As for those first dreadful days, all I remember are Totus Tuus, the Alms Box, and Introibo ad Altarem Dei, nothing more* . . . She was thinking all this and feeling grateful to the young man, smiling contentedly at him, even though he continued to address her in that rather brusque manner. He spoke to her, arms akimbo, his watch on his left wrist, its second hand constantly jerking forward, the whole of him waiting, like an iron bar determined not to move. Yes, she would give in. She thought it would only waste more time, but, yes, she would give in. She wouldn't shout at him or use the rude words that she knew and was perfectly capable of using if anyone bothered her. That wasn't what was happening here. She owed him a lot. *State of shock.* That's why she would give in. Milene said—"Let's go to Aunt Gininha's house, then. It's a long way, in Amurada . . ." All the while thinking to herself that it would be better if he just gave up and they each went about their own lives.

The same idea had occurred to Antonino, to just abandon the girl and leave her there. Indeed, he'd even gone back to his gray van fully intending to do just that, but then he saw her standing by the Clio, smiling at him, her hair still wet. Her face scrubbed clean, the strap of her hat looped over her arm, and her bag slung around her neck. She had a slender neck, and her eyes were smiling at him. She was the girl they'd found. What should he do? Behind her lay all of Felícia Mata's orders—*You're the one who's going to take her, to explain where we found her, and how we took her in, and, more importantly, that we had nothing to do with Dona Regina's tragic end . . .* And all the rest. So he had no choice but to do as he'd been told. He got back into his car, shouting—"Let's go to your aunt's house, then. Quinta da Amurada, you say?"

"Yes, Quinta da Amurada," she replied. "I know the way, so I can go in front."

But he again took the lead, joining the broad highway where, at that hour, a swift-flowing river of traffic was traveling along like some metallic creature. Taking care to indicate any changes in direction, he headed off toward their destination. When she overtook him, to show him the exact route, it was ten past nine. By the time he came back, it would be past ten o'clock. She would have liked to say—*Why don't you just go, it's broad daylight now, I can get there alone.* But she knew this wasn't his intention. On the contrary, the more clearly he saw his unreachable goal, the more determined he was to reach it and the more important the goal became. This could also be called stubbornness. She knew it from João Paulo. A glance in her rearview mirror was confirmation enough. Milene began to feel afraid of his accumulated bad temper, and could see that he was getting angrier simply by the way he drove, the front wheels of his Mitsubishi van almost grazing the back wheels of her Clio as if he were trying to propel her along, until finally they both came to a halt outside Aunt

Gininha's house, where a gold sign announced—*Vivenda Dom Silvestre*. He leapt out of his van.

"Is this it? Ring the bell, then . . ."

For Milene, this was a repeat of what had happened on Friday. Not quite a repeat, because this time the gardener wasn't there. The sprinkler was sending out regular pulses of water, the lawn glittering in the sunlight as if each blade contained specks of golden glass, but all the doors of that house bursting with cornices and verandas were locked. Lovely lines, lovely open areas, and ample, spacious interiors, cozy nests in which to rest. She knew it well. That was the best spot to sit and read, and over there was the perfect place for a nap, while the stone bench was ideal for listening to music in the moonlight. Lovely, just lovely. But no one was home. She rang the bell again. Then Antonino Mata took off his sunglasses and rang the bell himself. He pressed hard, keeping his finger on the buzzer—gold like the plaque bearing the name of the house—pressing and pressing as if his finger were glued there. He rang and rang. No answer.

"You knew no one would be in, didn't you?" he said furiously.

Milene gave a noncommittal shrug.

It was as if he'd been struck by an arrow.

"Don't you dare do that again. You know perfectly well that I have to hand you over to someone, so who? Tell me, who?"

Milene saw the danger. She realized how very unwise she had been bringing him here. She leaned against the white door above which hung the sign bearing the name of the house—Vivenda Dom Silvestre. She wasn't going to say anything. Motionless, arms folded. But Antonino had shifted the peak of his cap to one side—"I'm not letting you stay here, no way. Not if it's the last thing I do. You obviously don't know me. I'm going to hand you over to someone whether you like it or not . . ." He consulted his watch and tapped its face. "Come on," he said. "You go ahead in your car, and I'll follow behind, and you're going to take me someplace where there *will* be someone to receive you. Do you understand?" Still leaning against the snow-white door, clinging to the wooden frame, Milene had no intention of leaving. He came closer, his eyes glittering in his otherwise neutral face, the whites of his eyes larger now than his dark pupils. The shadow he cast on the ground made her afraid. She understood then that there was no point clinging to the doorframe. He was insisting that she find someone. He talked on and on, and all she heard was *someone, someone.* Frankly, life was very stupid. The very person who had offered her such sensible, suitable words, including the expression *state of shock,* was now insisting that she find someone who didn't exist. *Keep calm,* she thought. They got back in their vehicles.

Her in front, at the wheel of the Clio. Him behind.

While it had been easy enough to get into Amurada, it proved much harder to leave. Vivenda Dom Silvestre was part of a kind of paradise of lawns and luxury homes. Some had walls like ornate lace, as if they'd been brought from some Asian temple, with swimming pools the color of sapphires and emeralds. A perfect urban domain. This is why all the streets heading north appeared to be dead ends, for they headed to the sea. Inside that perfect world, Milene went around and around, checking in her rearview mirror that Antonino was following behind, as if their two cars were attached by an invisible cord, the gray van obediently making the same turns as she made in the Clio. Why was this happening to her?

Milene stopped. The van stopped. He got out and, showing her his watch and tapping its face again and again, asked if she knew what a labyrinth was. Because his life had become a labyrinth. Telling her that her appearance that morning was all it had taken for the labyrinth to slam shut, with him inside. They had stopped beside a wall separating the road from the sea. You couldn't see the beach from there, only the vast expanse of sea as far as the horizon, its smooth surface sparkling in the morning sun, as if speckled with gold and silver. He clearly saw none of this. He had unbuttoned his shirt to the waist before saying— "Look, it's getting late. This is what we're going to do, we're going to get out of here and go straight to my work so I can show you to my foreman and explain what I'm doing. He'll mark me down as absent, but at least he'll know I'm telling the truth. Do you understand?"

When he said *you*, his voice took on a steely, aggressive tone. *You.*

The only thing to do was to go back the way they had come.

They finally managed to escape from the labyrinth and rejoin the main road, heading in the other direction, with the Clio behind and the gray van in front, until Antonino turned off down a sandy road flanked by wire fences, at the end of which, beyond the pine trees, in a vast hollow, the foundations of a kind of city began to emerge, rising up out of the sand, out of nothing. Nothing comes of nothing, João Paulo used to say, that much was clear. Everything came from nothing and returned to nothing, she thought, and for the first time, this idea didn't sap her vital forces. Antonino Mata jumped out of the van and shouted—"Stay there, where they can see you, so the foreman will know I'm telling the truth." And then, in an angry voice, he went on—"If tomorrow or later on my kids get sick, do you think he's going to give me time off?" Arguing with her as if, in that future scenario, she'd been responsible for his children falling ill. Issuing orders—"Stay there, but get out of the car so they can see you. Don't get back in the car. Stay outside. And keep looking . . .

"Keep looking . . ."

He set off without a backward glance. When he did turn around, she was still standing in exactly the same spot at the edge of the crater. He continued on down, getting dust on his black sneakers, on his black trousers, his black shirt flapping about him and his cap on straight now, until he disappeared, then reappeared in the middle of that construction site. The foreman, or whoever, was talking to him. Both men consulted their watches. Antonino waved to her from below, put on a yellow hard hat, and vanished in among other men wearing the same yellow hats. She waited. Beside her, his van stood with the driver's door open. But she couldn't leave. She could see him moving about in the depths, along with a lot of other men. No, she couldn't leave. Then she saw him driving back and forth in a small vehicle bearing the name *Bobcat*. How much longer would this go on? It was half past twelve. Standing with her hat on her head, stock-still so that the foreman would see her, Milene passed the time by thinking, by looking for the words to explain what she would soon have to explain, imagining how she would phrase things to her aunts and uncles—*Dear Aunts and Uncles, it was like this. This is how my grandmother disappeared from my life . . .* The intense sun beating down on her. *"Except that she didn't disappear, she's just hiding somewhere . . .* The scalding sun on her bare legs, her bare back, on the beachwear she'd put on the previous morning, before she'd been gripped by the desire to find some trace of her grandmother along that path, so that she could tell her aunts and uncles. And all for nothing. He'd said—*Stay there where they can see you, so they know I'm telling the truth . . .* That's why she wouldn't move, but she did think it was time something good happened, just one good thing. *Just one, just one . . .* And as she was thinking this, Antonino finally came staggering up the slope and said, almost panting—"I worked for an hour and half, and the foreman said he'd put me down as having worked all day. He told me to write the word *bereavement* on my worksheet . . . The devil must be asleep. Yep, he must have taken a really strong sleeping pill. *Bereavement . . .*" And, turning to look down at the shapeless cement- and earth-colored crater, full of piles of building materials, he added, as if a part of himself had made peace with her—"You know, it's a shame, really. If it hadn't been for you, the man driving that Lieb-herr today would have been me . . ." And he pointed at a crane, which at that moment was very sedately turning from one end of the site to the middle, depositing some gray planks at the center of a slab in front of a group of men. Very slowly at first, then more quickly, the jib slid across the sky. All the other cranes were motionless.

"But then you turned up . . ." he said, adding: "Anyway, I now have the whole afternoon to hand you over in peace. Let's go . . . Give me the address of someone I can return you to, even if it's far away, we'll just fill up with gas and off we go . . ."

But before getting back in his van, he turned around again.

"If you hadn't shown up . . ."

He stood there in the middle of the scorched grass.

"No, on second thought, I'd better take you to the Town Hall. If your uncle isn't in, there'll be someone else in his place, some-one who can take care of you, and that'll be that. All signed, sealed, and delivered. You'll stay with whoever that person is and then they'll be in charge of handing you over to a relative, and I can go home with a clear conscience."

Once more they drove off in their respective cars. The van in front, the Clio behind, both of them bumping over the uneven track. Now they were heading down the road looking for somewhere to stop and have something to eat. They went into a café with a large red awning, a long eyelid casting a deep shadow. The name of the café was Hollywood. In the shade of the awning, Antonino seemed quite different. Now that he had the rest of the day free, he appeared relaxed and at ease. He put on a pair of mirrored sunglasses, so she couldn't see his eyes. And he didn't particularly want to be seen by her. When their order of hot dogs and cold drinks came, he was sitting facing away from her, staring at the endless line of cars. He ate without once looking at her. He had the nonchalant manner of someone about to complete a task and who can already feel the relief of having done his duty. And he had been rewarded twice over. The foreman must have gone mad. Antonino had never known such generosity. He said out loud—"Yes, the devil must have taken a siesta yesterday afternoon and not yet woken up . . ." But still he didn't look at her.

This was partly because almost opposite them, in a metal rack, weighed down at one end by a load of women's magazines, he had spotted a banner headline. He suddenly stood up and went over to the rack, from which he took a broadsheet newspaper, the *Novo Metrópole*. With much rustling, he opened it and began to read, holding it up so that the large pages stood between them. For a while, a long while. Then he put the paper down, looked at her, and asked—"What's your name? It's Milene, isn't it?"

"Well, Milene, you're toast. That woman in Bairro dos Espelhos was quite right. It says exactly what she said. And much more. It also says it was you who spoke to them. You know how to read? Well, read that and see if I'm wrong . . ."

In the shade of the red awning, Milene read.

She read, but couldn't understand how things she had never said could have been attributed to her. What she found most surprising, though, was how truths and lies could be so skilfully woven into what appeared to be the truth. Yes, her grandmother really had been found by cyclists, and yes, none of her aunts and uncles had been home, and she had indeed bought flowers and traveled alone in the car along with the wreaths and that *thing*, and so on and so forth, but she had never told this to anyone, still less made a *statement*. No one had asked her anything. It was as if her thoughts had been burgled. And now all her worst fears were confirmed. The problem would no longer be having to explain to her aunts and uncles how her grandmother had died, it would be proving to them that she, Milene Lino Leandro, hadn't said anything, hadn't complained to anyone about anything, had told neither truths nor lies. Milene felt like hiding away in the depths somewhere. In some dark place, with no light. But one must be careful of such places, she thought. *Abyssus abyssum invocat*, as João Paulo used to say.

Yes, be careful, very careful, Milene.

The young man with her had once again placed his mirrored sunglasses between him and the world, the world in which she was sitting, but this time his face was quite serene, or so it seemed beneath his brown skin, under whose surface the blood flowed unseen. The young man said—"I don't think we should go to the Town Hall. You're not up to facing a situation like that. It's your decision, but if I was you, I wouldn't do that . . ."

Antonino Mata, face hidden beneath the peak of his cap, his black shirt buttoned up now and stained white with sweat on his chest and back, was looking straight ahead, apparently absorbed in his own thoughts, but saying to her—"If I were you, Milene, I'd come back to our house and stay there and see what happens. It's up to them to come looking for you . . ."

Ex nihilo nihil. She couldn't now remember what those words meant, something much more complicated than nothingness, or the nothingness of nothing, or nothingness for nothingness's sake, or nothing comes of nothing, which is why there must always have been something, or whatever. The kind of thing João Paulo used to come out with. The only thing that filled her head with good thoughts was repeating softly to herself, *God of Truth, Totus Tuus, Alms Box. Call me, call me. Other people's words.* Saying to herself as she got into the Clio, *With gas, without gas. What did I do wrong?* But she could hear João Paulo saying—We didn't do anything wrong, Milene. Someone did it for us, long before we even existed, and even if they didn't, they left us with the memory of that wrong. Our only option is to fend for ourselves. That's how it is, Milene. That's why you must be very careful with the abyss. It's all around us, we just have to open the door of our life to it. Don't put so much as one toe on the edge. The abyss is so easy, so pleasant, so simple, all we need is to close our eyes and let ourselves go. It's there waiting for us. Nothing could be simpler. The hard thing is learning to resist. That's very hard. *Abyssus abyssum invocat.* You might one day have to fend for yourself, but only if we're not there with you. That would never be for long, though, hardly any time at all. But you know that even when we're apart, the three of us are as one, and we'll never leave you on your own. Never, never ever. And never, never ever means *while we're still alive* . . . Things, however, took a rather different turn. This was all very well as long as we, her two cousins, didn't have our own lives to lead, didn't fill in application forms headed London International College, Georgetown University, University of Massachusetts, and so on, and even long before that our lives had already begun to draw apart. Until it got to the point where Milene was phoning one of us and, day after day, always getting the same response—*Hi, you've reached five-seven-three-seven-nine-three-one-zero* . . . *If you want to leave a message for Lavinia or João Paulo, please do so after the tone. Thanks. 'Bye.* As if João Paulo had died too, leaving that functional message instead of a grave.

Please, let's go back now to the Old Factory, on the fifth day of this confrontation with the disorder of the World.

III

YES, THEY WENT BACK DOWN THE ROAD TO MAR DE PRAINHAS.
Milene followed the Mitsubishi van, and as they drove through
the open countryside, remnants of all she had seen since the
morning rose up before her, among which the figures of Flora
and her two attendants stood out, milling around in the dust of
Bairro dos Espelhos. But they were nothing but stray silhouettes
of shifting people, meaningless messengers, shadows with no plot
or substance.

What she saw, and saw repeatedly, as if all the world's energy
were concentrated there and the rest was just a vague landscape
through which her car was gliding, were her aunts and uncles' faces
as they came walking toward her, asking again and again—*What
did you tell those newspaper people, those professional gossip-mongers,
paid to spread gossip? Why did you do it? Couldn't you have kept what
happened to Grandma Regina to yourself?*—That was what she saw
and heard. And then, on returning to the mound, where only the
dusty red van was parked, the one belonging to Janina Mata King,
Black Power, dotted with musical notes shaped like axes, all she saw
was the mound and all she saw were the gates and all she saw was
the shadow of the palm trees, and all she saw was Antonino Mata,
jumping out of the van and saying—"Here we are, back again." And
then the course of events passed, in its entirety, into Felícia's hands.

———

Because at that moment, the whole thing began to look very different. It was as if someone had said—*The key person is here.*

Felícia Mata was talking on the phone when she saw them, and at first she couldn't believe it. For a moment she thought Milene had just come back to collect something she'd forgotten. Only when her son told her what had happened did Felícia understand the situation, and then she was at a loss for words.

At that hour of the afternoon, she was wearing a floral dress that showed off her breasts, where beads of sweat were so pronounced they trembled as she walked. Felícia pressed her hands to her chest in astonishment: How was it possible? Had Dona Milene's family still not come back? And was the newspaper really full of lies? True lies? False truths? She was lost for words. In a voice of sympathetic understanding, and yet also unshakable determination, the same voice with which she had ended her interrupted phone call, saying, *Yes, Janina, dear, onward and upward, keep at it, we're all behind you. 'Bye, now, lots of love,* in that same voice, Felícia Mata spoke to Milene, before Antonino had finished explaining—"Don't worry, Dona Milene. No need to stand there shaking like a leaf. No need at all. Listen, you're not alone, you're with the Matas. All these people you see around you, they're your family now. All these people are your people too . . . What more can I say?"

Everyone lost for words.

When Ana Mata, sitting in the plastic armchair by the streams that ran from the showers, peeling potatoes into her lap, saw Dona Regina's granddaughter return, she tried to make sense of the phantom delivery her grandson Antonino had failed to make. The knife frozen in midair. And when she looked once more at the girl's eyes, with their eyelids that resembled Dona Regina's, she resumed her lament. How had Dona Regina made it all the way there, in the middle of the night, without the help of a taxi? And why? What had Dona Regina wanted to tell her, Ana Mata?—she wondered in her own language. Heitor Senior, leaning on his crutches, also still shaken by their landlady's death, was asking himself similar questions. Even Antonino's three sons, sleeping slumped in the laps of their aunts Dilecta and Germana, had woken up. Only Domingos's children and Heitor Junior's two daughters, busy watching the two televisions, were oblivious to what was going on. But their mothers, Conceição and Claudina, had they been present at the time, rather than away working at supermarket checkouts, would surely have been lost for words as well. Felícia Mata, wrapped in floral fabric, swelled with righteous indignation. She, who had found that house for her family one spring afternoon, and who was the mother of Janina Mata King, the singer who could be heard on the radio every day, was shocked.

"Sit down, Dona Milene. Now, let's see. What day did the tragedy with your grandmother happen?"—Milene sitting down, facing them all, just like the day before. "It was on Thursday, and today's Tuesday, the nineteenth, and so far no one's come. Right?"

They were speaking in the courtyard, around the small square tables that could be pushed together or separated as needed. That afternoon, the tables were all pushed together into one. Felícia shocked, Dilecta and Germana shocked as well, and their mother, with deep sighs in her chest and tears in her eyes, talking of the twists and turns of fate. What were they going to do? It was a very delicate moment. Of course, Antonino had done the Matas proud. He had brought back the girl and the newspaper full of lies, true lies, and now the girl wouldn't be abandoned on the

doorstep of some empty house like an unwanted cabbage. Felícia would never have dreamed of leaving someone alone like
that. But as for what to do, in practical terms, no one was quite
sure. Since Milene couldn't decide either, Felícia reached for the
phone and held it out—"Here, Dona Milene, call whoever you
like. We can't leave you with no one to look after you . . ." But
then she amended her gesture, turning the phone to face herself,
as if it were an intelligent object with whom she was discussing
an important next step. She decided—"In fact, I'll get in touch
with your aunts and uncles myself . . . You watch." And Felícia
got ready to make the call, from halfway down the long table, for
everyone to hear. Milene could tell her the numbers for all her
relatives. Then Milene could listen as she left messages for them
all. This was how it would go—"Is anyone there? No? Well, then
I'll leave a message . . ."

And, looking at Milene all the while, Felícia left messages in a
very loud voice, speaking on her feet, imperious as a high school
teacher, with everyone listening, in the middle of the courtyard. Are you there? No? Messages, messages for them all. They
were to come and collect the girl who had turned up there in a
state of shock, hidden behind the laundry. They were to come as
soon as they were back from vacation. They were to make their
way, without delay, to the Mata family's house. In the *Fábrica de
Conservas Leandro 1908*. End of message. They'd know perfectly
well where she meant, since they were the immediate heirs, the
factory owners. Felícia, loudly holding forth about injustice and
indifference, on her feet, at the center of the table. "The girl's
been in our house two days now, and not a peep from her aunts
and uncles. Unbelievable . . ."—yelled Felícia to one family member's gardener, who had answered the phone while cleaning the
swimming pool, the only living voice that responded and with
which she could have a conversation in real time. Deciding—

"No, no, the girl's not going home alone. We're Christians in this house, do you understand, Mr. Gardener? She'd be happy to, but we won't let the girl go back to her grandmother's house unaccompanied, not after such a big shock . . . You see, Mr. Portuguese Gardener, we're Matas in this house, Cape Verdean *badios* born and bred, honest folk with good hearts . . ." Felícia, one arm in the air, the other at her ear, talking into the phone. Leaving that message. An embarrassing message to receive. And to Milene, sitting at the big white table made out of many small ones, she said—"Be brave!

"Be brave, dear. They should have come a long time ago. The day after tomorrow ought to be your grandmother's seventh-day mass, and I bet there isn't even a remembrance mass booked in. I feel sorry for Dona Regina, really I do. Thank God a good, respectable woman like her won't have any trouble at Heaven's gates . . ." Felícia with the phone flipped shut. Surprised—"And yet there you are laughing, with all this going on. You're laughing because you're so upset, but you've got real character, you're very brave . . ." This was Felícia Mata, standing among them, back at the helm, the prow of the ship. At the very forefront of life.

Antonino had sat down as well, listening to the phone calls. He'd put a cold fizzy drink on the table and took the occasional sip. His mirrored sunglasses tucked into his black shirt. His baseball cap pulled firmly down on his head, peak forward. Feeling restored after that long day. The decisions he had made too had been good ones. It wasn't right to go from door to door trying to deliver a person as if she were a bundle of clothes; a person who deserved respect, and, what's more, who was going through a difficult time. Looking at the girl sitting there now, he was even reminded of himself, two years before, when he'd had his own days of rage.

"You know what I mean by days of rage, don't you?"—said

Antonino, addressing Milene, spacing out the words, as if she were deaf, or a very young child, and he were keen to get his message across. "Don't think you're the only one, it happens to us all. At least once in your life, rage comes crashing down on your head. No one knows who sends it, or why, or what for, but there you are, minding your own business, and then it hits you. Day after day, you're barely out of bed before you've run slap-bang into life's wall of shit . . . And then suddenly it's gone again, but it takes part of you with it and never gives it back . . ."—Antonino sitting opposite, as if speaking only to her. And these, she noticed, were the sort of words that normally went by quickly, but he was making an effort to say them slowly, as if he wanted to slot them into her understanding in a way that had less to do with what he was saying than with what he would perhaps have liked to say. Still, what he was telling her, and what she was hearing, seemed perfectly comprehensible. She knew all about terrible days.

When Antonino finished, Felícia said—"Leave it, son, that'll do."

"I know"—said Antonino. "I'm just reminding her that we all have days like this. Anyway, I'm off . . ."

And, leaving the drink can on the table, he went to the source of the water, the stream, the river, that ran from the shower. The river ran for a long time. Then Felícia's son was crossing the courtyard, shirt buttoned, cap gone, smelling of aftershave, in a rush again, all agitated again, as he had been several times already that day. Hurrying off somewhere, no doubt making the most of his free afternoon. Antonino's sons, in front of the televisions, were snoozing in their cousins' laps now and didn't notice a thing. Meanwhile, everyone still there was insisting that they had no words to describe that troubling situation. But Felícia, unfazed, went on thinking good things, doing good things, addressing the urgent and practical questions of life, because now, with Milene back to stay for who knew how long, she was going to put her up permanently in the music room. And not only that. Since there was no word from Milene's family, and other people were slandering her unfairly, Felícia was going to show what goodness really meant, offering her not the tiny bed, or even Gabriel's bed, but the bed of her son Janina, the singer, who now lived permanently in Lisbon.

"Over here, come on . . . Look, Dona Milene, this is where you're going to sleep . . ."

Now she could see it with her own eyes, taking her time. The old building where they used to make the cans really had been painted black, with poppy-red curtains hanging down from the ceiling like in a TV studio, and between the neatly made beds along the walls were instruments on stands or propped against folding chairs. Everywhere there were wires, plugs, handlamps, piles of records, soul and African American music, pictures of Louis Armstrong and Jimi Hendrix when they were young. Photos of Janina and his band on the four walls. Around a poster of Terence Trent D'Arby, his face half hidden behind his braids, someone had written—*LITTLE BRO*. Yes, Milene had slept there the night before, but without really noticing all that stuff. Now, however, realizing the significance of that space, she wasn't sure she should accept Janina's bed. Milene would rather have had the tiny bed. Although really, if she was honest with herself, she wouldn't rather anything at all. She felt, at that moment, very close to the other moment, the day before, which had made her want to hide behind the washing. When her head had felt as empty as a dead conch shell. But Felícia Mata, bursting with kindness, and pride too, at the marvelous sentiments moving her, such as Beauty and Goodness, insisted that Milene take the big bed—"You'll get a good night's sleep in Janina's bed, I promise you that.

"Girls! Do me a favor, bring some sheets for Janina's bed. The big sheets, the checkered ones."

Yes, that empty room belonged to her musician sons, musicians and singers, though it was only Janina who really sang. A lucky room. Felícia explaining about her sons' success, spreading the sheets over Janina's bed, shaking out the duvet, plumping up the pillows, bringing the inanimate objects to life. The objects coming to life. The phone ringing in her pocket—"Not now, Janina, something unexpected has happened . . . The girl's here again . . . In your room, son . . . Yes, listen, in your bed. You don't mind, do you? I knew you wouldn't, you've got a heart of gold, you really do . . . Onward and upward, son, keep at it . . . Bye-bye. Big hug . . ." Felícia folding the phone shut, tenderly, as if the phone itself were part of Janina.

But just before she put the phone away, Felícia seemed to startle herself. She reconsidered—"Silly me. I never gave you the phone. Here you go . . . Before you get settled in your room, phone whoever you want, phone calls will do you good. Speak all you like. We understand your situation. A rich family, a lawyer, an important businessman, a mayor, them and their wives all off gallivanting on the other side of the world, without a thought for anyone else. Honest to God! Go on, dear, speak to whoever you like . . ."

Milene still hesitant, standing before Janina's bed.

She wasn't sure whether or not to accept. This was a big problem. But the really big, really serious problem involved putting her toe on the edge of the abyss. The abyss was so easy, so pleasant, so simple, you just had to close your eyes and let go. It's been waiting for us with open arms since the day the World began. Nothing could be simpler. The hardest thing was learning to resist. It's really, really hard. Maybe one day you'll have to fend for yourself. *In that case, do whatever you need to do, whatever it takes to survive* . . . Milene thanked Felícia Mata, took the phone, and left the following message on João Paulo's answer machine—"*João Paulo? Listen, this is just to say that I'm feeling very alone. I'm staying with the Mata family* . . ." And she was going to say *the third-batch* or *third-wave people*, but she didn't. Felícia, her sisters, Ana Mata, Heitor Senior, the teenagers, along with the Mata children, had abandoned the televisions and gathered outside the musicians' room. She wasn't going to stand there and call them what her aunts and uncles called them at home. She looked at them all and said—"*But I'm very happy because I've found these people, and they're being very nice to me* . . ." Everyone's eyes on her. "*But I can't talk now because it's too expensive* . . ." Everyone laughing at her, and her laughing back. Ana Mata not moving her potato peeler, Heitor Senior not moving his crutches. The children watching her, their TV programs forgotten. Because the white girl, who had come back because she had no family, was right there in front of them, in their uncles' room, and apparently she didn't even know how to use a telephone. Milene added—"*Anyway, João Paulo, this was just to say that I'm very happy. Bye-bye* . . ."

"Dona Milene, don't you want to make any more calls?"

Felícia paced up and down the middle of the music room. Seeing Milene still hesitating to put her things on Janina's bed, she thought the shadow of her aunts and uncles must be hovering over it. Her aunts and uncles who could punish her and cause problems for them, the Matas. But Felícia wasn't afraid. She spoke in that loud voice precisely because she wasn't afraid, of the Leandros or any of their relatives. And she explained what she was thinking.

Milene needn't worry. As things stood, the Matas were up-

93

to-date with their rent, had done everything they should have done, and didn't owe anything to anyone. Any problems were for the landlords themselves to solve. As for the Matas' obligations, the transfer was made before the eighth of each month, without fail, sometimes by Heitor, sometimes by Antonino, sometimes by Domingos, taking it in turns, so it wasn't always the same one who missed work. The payment was made out to Dona Regina Leandro, ten thousand escudos per month, and they had the bank receipts to prove it. All in hand. And if they hadn't white-washed the outer wall of the factory that year, it was only because the Leandros hadn't brought any whitewash. There was no white-wash left, only paint, and they hadn't sent any more paint either. The Leandros were the ones in debt—in debt to the factory walls, to their own mother, to society at large. She wasn't afraid. After all, they were the ones who had moved their own mother from her rightful place, without so much as telling their niece. They were the ones who had snuck her out of her house. And they were the ones who had missed their own mother's funeral, just like the newspaper said.

Milene had nothing to worry about.

A simple, sensitive girl like her shouldn't fret about things that weren't her fault. Now, listen, at least get a good night's sleep. Wake up whenever you like. All these people, all these children will get out of your way. I'll close the door nice and softly, so you can go to sleep in your own place. After all, you're a landlady too. You must own, what, a twentieth of this house? In fact, as the granddaughter, the only child of one of Dona Regina's children, and her with five children, you must own more like a fifth. Now, dear, have a good sleep. No one can stop you. What's yours is yours. You'll wake up and fall asleep in your own home. If they let you choose part of it one day, take the part where we live, where my sons' room is, Janina and Gaby's room. The music room. It's yours whenever you need it. Now get some sleep, in your very own home. Goodbye, goodbye, good night.

"You'll wake up under your own roof. Okay?"

Then Felícia was gone from her life. Milene slept all through the night. The abyss didn't enter the room.

Sissi and Belisa did, though, as did Domingos' sons, João and Aloísio, and Antonino's sons too. All seven children peering at her, in the early morning light. Laughing at her from the doorway. Jostling in and out, tripping over each other. Even Antonino Mata's children, who laughed so rarely, laughing. Even the littlest, gloomiest one, showing his tiny white teeth. Carrying on and on. Endless fun.—"Wakey-wakey, Snow White . . . Pink as a piece of bacon, we should fry you up and eat you for our Sunday *frigi-nato* . . . Off you go, into the forest. Quick. The squire has orders to kill you . . . Bam! Just like that."

Waking up for the second time in the red-curtained room, Milene thought—*Maybe my days of rage, my muddled, confusing days, are over. I'm going to be a happy person again.*

Because that new day had nothing to do with the previous one.

It was late morning for the second time, and the men had gone to work long ago. Felícia yelled—"So you want to peel potatoes like Ana Mata? With an apron and a little bowl like her? Next to her rivers? Don't, your hands will get filthy, woman. But if you really want to, Belisa will get you a proper knife. Belisa!"

Thinking about good things again. Forgetting the horrible things— men dressed in black, those fleshy flowers, the woman with square calf muscles, the sun beating down on little houses with stone angels on top . . .

———

Felícia went on—"Hey, Dona Milene, want to cut up some chicken? You don't have to. My sisters Dilecta and Germana here will do a perfect job of it. They'll be done in no time. If you could just hold the legs. Hold on, then, hold on tight . . ."

Remembering when the priest thought Milene couldn't drive a car, and Milene got into the Clio and showed how well she handled the clutch and accelerated away . . . It was her great triumph over them. My triumph over that look from the woman with square calf muscles who didn't believe in me, whispering away in the priest's ear . . .

Life was going to change, she could feel it.

And then, on the afternoon of Wednesday the twentieth, Felícia said—"Boxes, boxes everywhere. It's so tiresome taking the boxes apart. I throw them out just like that, all open, jumbled together. But if you like, Dona Milene, you can move the dogs out of the way—they're always sleeping inside them—and the children as well—and start piling all the cardboard up. If you really want something to do, that is. The children will help with the dogs. The children really love you . . . Never in my life have I seen boxes tidied the way Dona Milene does it. Getting it all in order . . . Your house must be neat as a pin, eh?"

Let my aunts and uncles turn up whenever they like, it doesn't bother me. I'll go back to Kilometer 44 alone, without them. My days of rage are over. My happy days are going to come back . . .

Yes, it was chicken and potatoes for dinner. The table very long again, made out of several smaller ones, and everyone sitting around it, even Antonino Mata, with his three children clustered together. Eighteen people at the table, including her. Felícia ate a lot, and so did her sisters, Dilecta and Germana. Ana Mata ate very little. Domingos, the one with the knife, addressed Milene for the first time—"Hey, Dona Milene, aren't you going to eat anything? Do you want to be wise forever like Grandma Ana Mata? Our grandma thinks that if she doesn't eat, the pipes of wisdom will never get blocked up. She thinks she's going to die wise . . ." Heitor Junior laughing and helping himself to more chicken and potatoes, in the wavering light—"If she ever does die, that is . . . Right, Grandma?"

Everyone laughing and looking at Ana Mata, such a long way from her plastic *cautcha*, with her hair in a perfect bun on top of her head, which was slightly elongated at the back like a football, her small eyes set deep within it, deep and alive, shining, her legs crossed, her elbows raised, perched at the table like a mosquito, feeding on nothing at all. No, you're never going to die, Ma. To drive the topic away, Felícia sang—"*Carpeting the sea, carpeting the sea . . .* Hey, Dona Milene, don't you know that song? It's one of Janina's. Domingos, go and put Janina's record on the new machine. The one you bought in Lisbon . . ."

The record turning, Janina's voice rising, from the very first track, and the courtyard beginning to tremble. "This is the track he won with at the Coliseu dos Recreios. Did you know that?"— Felícia said very loudly, her triumphant voice leaping over the music itself. "Sing along, Dona Milene. Sing along. Forget death, forget lies and loss. Dance with us. Can you dance?

"Wow, you can even dance. That's it, that's right . . . We need to scare death away from the dead. The dead like seeing us dance. They like us happy, dancing and singing, and thinking about them. It means they can be happy too . . . For every person who sings here in this world, a whole crowd is singing in the next. It's a shock to begin with, because we miss the dead person, but that doesn't last. We get on with our lives. And if the dead are good people, they're glad for us. They enjoy it all the more when they look down at us from Heaven . . . Oh! Here we go again . . . Now play the third track, that one's just right for dancing . . ."— The music filling the courtyard, making the seats of the chairs vibrate. All the chairs. All the tables. Then the adults, the children and Milene. Felícia delighted with her handiwork, her creation: Milene unwinding, Milene happy at last. Felícia on her feet, making the most of the moment.

"Now, that's what I call dancing. You're a lovely-looking girl, Dona Milene, even the way your knees turn in has a certain charm. You might seem a bit lost sometimes, but I bet you're not really. And you can certainly dance . . ."—In front of the space guarded by the geraniums, the Mata children dancing, and Milene, wearing Judite and Claudina's clothes, dancing too. Death wasn't there anymore. Neither was fear.—"Well, dear, if you want something to do, do whatever you like, make phone calls, wash the dishes, dance, read magazines, sing Janina's songs. Don't just stand there, leaning against the wall and laughing. Whatever's in your soul, let it out."

It was midday on Thursday, the twenty-first of August, inside the Diamond. Milene was leaning against a wall. From there she could see Felícia's red fingernails, covered in white chips like tiny holes. She had nothing to do. She could do that. What was it João Paulo used to say?—*Abyssus abyssum invocat.* No, no. Yes, yes, she could. Milene laughing loudly. "Felícia, ma'am, I could fix your nails, if you like. Do you have a bottle of nail polish and some polish remover?"—asked Milene.

Felícia taken aback, lying on the white plastic lounge chair, in the factory chimney's never-ending shadow. Felícia beaming, thoroughly amused. Of course she did, but Dona Milene wasn't really going to do her nails, was she?

"Yes, I am. I've done it before, loads of times. You'll see. I just need a stool, a bowl, some nail varnish remover, some nail varnish and cotton . . ."—said Milene.

She burst out laughing again. The sole of her right shoe drawing back from the abyss. Back toward safe, solid, friendly ground. *Good, at last I'm going to do something useful, I'm going to collaborate with the world again, as João Paulo used to say.*—Felícia holding out her hands to Milene. Ana Mata looking on from her armchair, her spindly feet crossed, where the three rivers from the showers all met. Milene removing the red marks from Felícia's nails, discarding the cotton, shaking the bottle so the teenagers, Sissi and Belisa, could see. Did they want theirs done too? No, they couldn't want that, they had to obey their father. Heitor wanted the girls' hair in braids until they were grown, he didn't want painted nails, he didn't want them looking like whores. But Felícia was a grandmother, so there was no problem there, or with the Leandros, or with anyone else in the world. She wasn't harming anyone. So why shouldn't she accept the girl's offer, when it took her an hour to go all the way to the salon and back? No, Felícia saw no harm in accepting. And when Milene said, more loudly than usual, "*Now, Dona Felícia, ma'am, time for your feet . . .*" Felícia again said no, but a moment later, in a fit of madness, she went to wash them and then presented them to Milene with a great gleeful whoop. Big, leathery feet, with a crease where the leg met the instep, the mark of a full life. A great belly laugh from Felícia. Milene laughing too. And when evening came, in the middle of the courtyard, Felícia danced barefoot, so that everyone could see those twenty nails painted by Dona Milene.

Felícia had even dreamed, the night before, of a bowl full of pomegranate seeds. Which, in fact, weren't pomegranate seeds at all, but the painted nails that lay in store for her. And the bowl wasn't a bowl either. It was the kind heart of Dona Milene, that lovely girl who had turned up in their house. The things dreams could tell you, it was quite incredible. It had been the same with Janina. Every night leading up to his triumph at the Coliseu, she had dreamed of a wave that, instead of foam, flung pieces of gold at her feet. She hadn't wanted to wake up. Her whole body glittering with expensive jewels. And it turned out the sea was the Coliseu, and the jewels were the applauding hands. Now the bowl was Milene. The pomegranate seeds were the twenty nails painted for all the world to see—"Dreams are the damnedest things . . ."

Go away, go away, abyss. Away to your hole, far away from my life. Don't come back here, you're not wanted here.

Was it a different day now, a different afternoon? Another morning? Felícia hadn't even noticed—"What a blessing that you came, dear. That Antonino brought you back. It's been wonderful getting to know you. And you're actually really intelligent, a really nice girl, really amazing . . ."—said Felícia. "I'm saying this because your aunts and uncles will probably be here soon. By now, wherever they are, they will have heard what's going on in Valmares. But be brave, Dona Milene, and don't let them bring you down, if they start accusing you, I mean. They're the ones in the wrong . . ."—Felícia displaying her ten painted fingernails. Her ten toenails that matched her patterned dress. "Our Lady of Guidance will watch over you. Okay? Because we've decided what we're going to do. We're going to send a signed letter, recorded delivery, so they know we followed the law. Now, Dona Milene, you just focus on your own life. Be brave. Be very brave . . ."— Eventually Felícia began to doze on the white sun lounger, under the lean-to. But first she advised Milene—"And see if you can sleep, and dream as well. The secret is to get more sleep than you need. The rest will be dreams. It does us so much good . . ."

———

Milene was expecting to dream about Felícia's happiness, and her painted nails, and how pleased she was to have painted them, but that's not what happened.

It was late on Thursday. Milene was sleeping in Janina's bed for the fourth time. By that hour of the night, she didn't know if it was still the same day, or if the next day had already begun. She felt very tired. Or rather, half of her was tired, unable to lift an arm, or move a finger, an eyelid, or open her lips a little more to breathe, and that part of her, the part experiencing that crushing fatigue, merged with the life she had lived there, in that very place, with her uncles and aunts, all younger then, Aunt Gininha with her gorgeous hair, her string of boyfriends, odds and ends of memory, which included, against her will, visions of velvet, the velvet cushion for the keys with the word *Leandros* embroidered on it, and the five members of the second wave roaring away on their mopeds. And then the high, smooth walls, scrubbed clean of obscene words and photographed by her uncles and aunts. And her and her two cousins, with João Paulo in front, sailing Guinote's boat, gliding down the tributaries of the Ria. These were images from the *best summer of our lives*, as João Paulo used to call it, and which always made her happy. But that night, to her surprise, they left her too tired to move.

Because a second part of her was fighting against that frail, depleted part, and these two opposing forces were locked together around the same axis, like greased bodies in a wrestling match. This second force, the second part of her, was all-powerful, all-knowing, and even had opinions about other people, and it was always on the move, making for where those other people were. Fearless and weightless, it flew toward them. And, assessing these two forces, Milene saw in them the unmistakable mark of Life and Death, in big letters. But Milene was able to think and at the same time say to herself—"You're not clever enough to come up with thoughts like that. Someone's breathing those words onto your lips, and you're just repeating them back . . ." This was the stillness weighing down the movement, making it bow and droop and fall still. Milene went on struggling within herself, divided, like two wrestlers, separated at the arms but joined at their slippery chests. Eventually, however, the more agile part managed to break the heavy part in two, splintering it like chopped wood. And when this happened, her heart was pounding, like the heart of a racehorse crossing the finish line, drenched in sweat. She thought—*It's all fine, I remember everything, I'm ready.*

She was sure.

That is, Milene has her own version of events, her own words, and she's very well prepared for her test. She deserves a good mark . . . —thought Milene, her heartbeat slowing. Because, as João Paulo used to say, between sleep and wakefulness there are only your eyelids. What difference was there between being asleep and being awake? Her cousin João Paulo knew a lot about life. But at that moment, she was still lying in bed, inside the Diamond. It was still too early to get up. In the courtyard, the poodle wasn't yet nipping at the guard dog, as it usually did. It was another day, and that day, she felt sure, something was going to happen. She prepared herself.

Slowly.

IV

VERY, VERY SLOWLY. COMPLETELY PREPARED. ACCORDING TO Felícia Mata's wall calendar it was Friday, August 22, 1994. Everything was going according to plan. At ten o'clock in the morning, the muffled sound of a car engine could be heard approaching the entrance. Milene walked over to the gates. There was no mistaking the sound—it was Uncle Rui Ludovice's car come to fetch her.

Just as she expected, it was parked in the shade of the palm trees, and one of its doors was held open by Senhor Frutuoso. There was really no point in him standing there, though, because she fully intended taking her time. She was wearing Claudina's orange Bermuda shorts, and all she had of her own was the beach bag slung over one shoulder, her straw hat under one arm, and her heart quietly beating away in her chest. Beating so very quietly she couldn't even feel it. She didn't look back either, although she knew Felícia and Ana Mata would be watching her walk over to her uncle's car. Felícia would doubtless be saying some of those words she herself now knew by heart. And yet she wouldn't turn around to wave goodbye. She didn't want to lose one iota of concentration.

Senhor Frutuoso even bowed slightly when he said good morning, but she didn't say a word. She didn't feel like talking to that man who usually looked at her in rearview mirrors, peering inside her as if he had a fishhook in each eye and wanted to draw up to the surface things she didn't want to show him. Besides, before they purred silently off, Senhor Frutuoso had even said—"Oh dear, your car's still here, and I'm not sure we'll have time later on to come back . . ." He was rustling around in some papers and consulting his road map. "It's a shame to leave your little Clio baking in the sun like that, Miss Milene, you might want to move it into the shade . . ."—This was Senhor Frutuoso trying to make conversation, trying to creep in through the cracks of her private life, as he always did. She, however, was prepared now to confront a far more serious situation and merely gestured to him to drive on.

Then her uncle's car took flight, though keeping low to the ground, and Milene only had time to stitch the facts together in their final order, the facts she would present to "them." She was utterly focused. The fields were still dry and parched, and the faded yellow straw around the base of the trees or by the walls had already taken on a silvery tone, and on either side of the road there were signs of stubble-burning, which, in some places, had affected the trees as well. In this white landscape, large stretches of scorched pasture adorned the bends in the road. It felt that all it would take was a single lit match to burn down the whole of Valmares. The driver continued talking to himself—"Dreadful road, appalling . . ."

No, Milene would not respond.

If she did, it would only be to say what she had managed to find out, supported, of course, by the words of others and by her own certainties. Words and facts. Although what first came into her head were words. She closed her eyes so as not to lose concentration. She squeezed them shut tight. Talking to herself. *This is how it was, dear aunts and uncles*—Introibo ad Altarem Dei,

Pax Domini, Totus Tuus, Alms Box. What hath pride profited us? Or what advantage hath the boasting of riches brought us? All those things are passed away like a shadow . . . And we, our eyes closed, look all around ourselves in order to remember the words we need to say to our aunts and uncles . . . But facts first.

Reviewing those facts one by one, this is what had happened. First the police had come to knock at her door, and a gentleman in black had come to ask her for money. Then there had been that to-and-fro of decisions, yes and no, in white houses and before marble tables, from which they had all been absent. She herself had cried out, on the landing of one of those staircases, also made of marble, that she didn't want them to carry out an autopsy, that she didn't want her grandmother to be cut up, and she had cried out in the name of her powerful, unreachable uncle, and had achieved what she wanted thanks to him, the uncontactable one. But apart from her, everyone, including the powerful uncle, had been absent. That's why, now that she was going to meet them, there would be no *Abyssus abyssum invocat* for her, only for them. The facts, which, days before, had all spilled out of her head, had now been gathered up and strung together so that she could sum them up very precisely in two key words. Two. That's why her heart was beating so quietly that she couldn't even feel it. When they reached Kilometer 44, Senhor Frutuoso ran to open the car door for her, and she got out without saying a word. She felt very good. She was calm. She was prepared.

But nothing would happen as she had imagined it would. Neither as she had imagined nor as she had wanted.

Indeed, when she went into Villa Regina, her heart was no longer beating fast. It didn't need to. And initially, everything seemed to be intact. The coatrack in the hall still held Grandma Regina's three hats in its embrace, and the mirror her grandmother usually looked in before going out still seemed ready to reflect her lilac-colored hair. The same dark outlines framed the blank spaces on the walls left by paintings that had been removed. Not only was the red stair carpet in its usual place, fixed to the wooden runners by a row of hooks, but it still offered the same soft cushion that delicately absorbed the sound of footsteps, just as her grandmother wanted. Milene had walked up the stairs, making scarcely any noise, as if everything really were intact. As she advanced, she could imagine her family sitting around the cherrywood table like a frieze, waiting for her. She could see them all together, each with their questions cocked and ready to fire. A scheduled shooting practice. But when she reached the room, which her grandmother usually referred to as "the living room," using the English expression, it was as if no one were there. Only her two aunts were present, sitting in the two places formerly occupied exclusively by Grandma Regina—The armchair on the left, from where she could see the garden, and the armchair on the right, from where she could watch television. It had been like that for twenty years. And the aunts knew this, and yet there they were, the two of them comfortably ensconced in her grandmother's armchairs. It really was quite shocking. Milene had been prepared to reveal everything she knew, but not to just two people, and especially not when they were sitting in chairs that weren't theirs. Upset by what she saw, Milene thought—*They're going to have to get out of those chairs. When they see me, they're going to have to get up. Then, once they've done that, I'll be able to explain what happened* . . .

And Milene remained standing in the doorway, without going in, so that they would understand and jump up, full of apologies, as soon as they saw her. However, her aunts, at that moment, were not her two aunts, they were merely two seated sorrows.

They wouldn't be able to understand the message she was sending them. On the far side of the room, her aunts were sitting opposite each other, uttering occasional nasally sounding words, as if behind their faces there were nothing but unwitting, weary tears. Two griefs that had taken on human form. Milene wasn't ten or fifteen, or even twenty, and this, she felt, was not a good moment to tell them they were sitting in the wrong chairs. Milene knew what their lives were like. She felt sorry for them.

No, she wouldn't provoke them.

Besides, Aunt Gininha had seen her now and was calling to her, and so, rising to the occasion, her heart serene, Milene entered the room, and Gininha held out her hand to her, speaking to her very softly, as if she herself barely existed, as if she were merely a shadow of a person with the long hair of a young girl— "Oh, my dear, dear niece . . ."

They kissed. Or, rather, Aunt Gininha stroked her cheek with one hand and then silently held her close for a long time, leaving damp patches on Milene's face and clothes, before finally stammering out—"You were the only witness . . ." Then she began sobbing again. It was a very difficult moment. But Milene was prepared. And her anxiety about being prepared and her desire to be useful distracted her from the outflow of love and sorrow she felt for her aunts' grief, especially for Aunt Gininha, of whom she was very fond. She pressed her knees together, hard. Eyes closed. Yes, she was completely prepared. Like a rumor that passes by, like a ship that sails through the billowy water. *Actually, when they arrived I was listening to Simple Minds'* Live in the City of Light . . . No, she wasn't going to launch into an account of the facts. Very softly, so as not to upset her aunts, Milene said simply—"I can tell you everything you want to know. I remember perfectly every step taken. I have it all here inside my head . . ."

Aunt Ângela Margarida, leaning back in the chair, simply asked—"How was such a thing possible, Milene? How?"

The voice of Grandma Regina's oldest daughter also sounded slightly damp, but in a different way, coarser, stronger, as if steeped in some denser liquid. It would, though, be hard to respond to her aunts' questions, because they didn't really dovetail. Milene didn't even have time to ask them to get up from those armchairs, because their grief had rendered them so very feeble. Ângela Margarida, who, despite it all, was more energetic than Gininha, had said to her—"You can tell us everything when the time is right . . ." Aunt Ângela Margarida, with one eye puffier than the other. A slight swelling on her left eyelid. Her aunt went on to say—"It's all very sad, very sobering . . . Sit down, Milene." Then, shadow-like, she herself stood up.

No, Milene's moment had not yet come.

As if connected to some electric current generated by the shock, Aunt Gininha had begun to speak gloomily about how unfair it all was, about how they, Grandma Regina's two daughters, had always been so close to their mother, had always taken a real interest in her health, always phoned her from wherever they happened to be to make sure she was all right, only for this to happen when, by pure coincidence, they had both been out of town. And, aghast at the sheer unpredictability of life, the younger aunt had also stood up, thus leaving the two armchairs free, arms wide open, as if waiting for Grandma Regina to come in. The two armchairs remained unoccupied while the two aunts, both now on their feet, compared the good death we all deserve with the grotesque death that had befallen their mother. Her two distraught aunts pacing up and down the room, as weightless as if they were spacewalking, as if they were lost in a desert, repeating to each other that they had never experienced anything like this in their entire lives. The two aunts. One tall, the other short. One almost dark, the other almost blond, a difference they had always taken great pains to emphasize at their respective hairdressers. A difference that made no difference, though, for they were both almost beautiful, especially Aunt Gininha, and each was thinking how her whole life had been turned upside down by this earthquake. Unable to comprehend how life could have ambushed them like this. And the two aunts continued to walk around and around, muttering disconnected phrases. When the word *ambush* appeared, however, Aunt Ângela Margarida stopped crying. She didn't agree. It hadn't been just one ambush, it had been several.

"Several ambushes, brought about by specific people, some of them with particular objectives, persecutory, personal, even political . . ." In her view, the family must react and take action against those responsible.

"What kind of action?" asked Gininha.

But their minds were not fully focused. They flew over the photographs filling the sideboard. Photographs of Grandma Regina, from when she was a tender child to shortly before she started having her hair dyed lilac. With her husband on their wedding day, with her father-in-law beside the Chrysler. With her three oldest children, with all five children, including the girls, the two younger ones, the five grouped around their mother, then minus one, then minus two. Each moment of her life frozen in its own silver-plated rectangle. Grandma Regina, her face now lined, with just three children. Grandma Regina with her grandchildren. Grandma Regina alone in front of the factory. The whole panoply of a life. Yes, they must do something. And doing something meant taking at least four separate entities to court. A lawsuit against the nursing home that had mutilated their mother's name, calling her plain Maria Soares instead of Regina Maria Soares Leandro. How would anyone have known who she was? Unbelievable. That was the first lawsuit. Another against the hospital, which had turned a bedridden person out onto the street, not even checking the state she was in. Another against the two paramedics who had allowed her to escape. And still another against the two newspapers that had published those sordid lies. Grandma Regina's oldest daughter counted them off on her fingers—"Six altogether. Six lawsuits, not four."

But what would such actions achieve?

Aunt Gininha had sat down on the big, soft sofa, into which she sank so deeply that her knees came almost up to her chin. Across from her, Ângela Margarida was counting on her fingers—"Six, possibly more."

"And what about her traipsing all that way across the sand to the factory gates? How do you explain that? Who would you sue for that?"

The two aunts had reached an impasse.

When they thought of their mother in her hospital gown, dragging herself along the railway tracks to the factory, and everything else that had followed, they felt utterly at a loss. Pondering these grim details as they sat facing each other, the two aunts were as one, immersed in the dim greenish light of the house. Perplexed. Filial love turned into horror. The actual images of that death entering through their eyes, offering them a bitter, obscene cup to drink. The aunts felt cut to their very souls by this derisive, mocking gesture from life. This was the second time they had talked together. The first had been the previous night, when they had returned from their vacations, but they always stopped short at those terrifying images of their mother lying outside the factory gates. And they stopped because both suspected that their mother's death was like a parable of her life, a story told backward, as their mother used to say about their father, but they didn't yet know how to read the parable life had thrown at them. At that moment, all they wanted was to understand why some nameless being had rained down these arrows on them. And, sitting in the middle of the room, the two aunts remained utterly consumed by their own disorientation, while Milene continued to wait for her moment.

Besides, her aunts didn't even seem to notice her presence. It was as if the events they were discussing and the future they were apparently already planning had nothing to do with anything Milene might say. As if there were no relationship between her aunts' lives and what she had witnessed and kept inside her head. In fact, Aunt Ângela Margarida, with her puffy eyelids, one much puffier than the other, didn't even look at Milene. The two aunts were so distraught they barely looked at each other. Then Milene checked her watch, took a handkerchief out of her bag, and loudly blew her nose. The moment had come to say what she had to say, and she was prepared, full of confidence and courage. Folding up her handkerchief and putting it away, Milene said—"I can tell you what happened. I didn't see everything, but I know a lot. To begin at the beginning, I was sitting right where I'm sitting now, listening to Simple Minds, when the police knocked at the door . . ."

Her aunts both turned and stared at her in amazement, as if they were returning from somewhere far away and seeing her for the first time. Outside, at that precise moment, another car was approaching Kilometer 44.

Milene was unable to go on.

Yes, another car had stopped outside just by the acacias. They heard the car door slam. It was Afonso Leandro, who had flown in from Heathrow that very morning, his plane arriving four hours late. A four-hour delay in what used to be the home of punctuality and promptness. He was coming down the corridor, and they could already hear him giving this explanation. On hearing his voice, the two sisters had embraced. The arrival of someone who had not yet shared in their grief only revived the intensity of their feelings. Standing there, arms around each other, it seemed they were expecting him to embrace them too, so that the three of them could merge into one shared grief. However, the vacationer who appeared, arms raised as if holding up the doorframe, would never have been mistaken for a man in deep mourning. His glossy hair and deep tan were in marked contrast with his white clothes, and, when he came in, all he did was rant on about those wasted hours. Four whole hours. His two sisters waited, still with their arms around each other. He then declared his outrage in no uncertain terms—"So what the fuck happened here?"

The two sisters emerged from their embrace. Suddenly walls and furniture disappeared. Afonso Leandro, in his white clothes, filled the entire room, repeating the same blunt question, demanding to be told what had happened, as if he didn't already know. Feeling justifiably offended, Ângela Margarida confronted her brother.

"You mean our mother died a week ago and you've only just found out?"

"How the fuck was I supposed to know? I was in Cyprus with Isabel." And he took a big step forward, like an equestrian on his horse. "How was I supposed to know, eh?"

His sister retreated slightly.

"Look, no one's saying you should have known. We only arrived yesterday ourselves, although we'd heard the news days before. But there were no flights. Not for us from Cancún or even for Gininha from the Canaries, and that's practically next door. In both cases, there simply weren't any flights. These travel agents always claim they've thought of everything, but at the first emergency, it's back to the Stone Age. Sorry, there aren't any flights. And you were in Cyprus—"

"But how did it happen?" Afonso insisted, brushing aside the matter of flights and, like his sisters, beginning to pace the living room, up and down, up and down, bumping into an agitated Aunt Ângela Margarida on the way. Gininha was also on her feet. The two sisters feeling shocked at his shock.

"Do you really not know what happened? Well, Mama fell ill and was taken to the hospital, where she got better, but instead of returning her to the nursing home, the hospital sent her back here, except that they didn't have the correct address and couldn't find the house. They just drove around, completely lost. While they were parked near the gas station—because by then it was dark—they left the rear doors of the ambulance open, and because they left the doors open, that's how it happened . . ."

"They left them open?"

"Yes."

"So how did Mama get to the factory?"

"No one knows."

"But that's just unbelievable . . ." said Afonso Leandro, moving around among the furniture. "Who took her there?"

"She apparently walked the mile and a bit on her own. Do you understand? She walked there. No one took her."

"She walked?" Afonso stopped pacing. "No, someone must have taken her. She couldn't have got there on her own, all the way from the gas station to the factory . . . If she'd had a stroke, how could she have walked there?" And he recommenced his pacing. "I bet the Matas took her. Yes, it must have been them. I had a very strange message from them, very strange indeed . . ." Afonso felt for the piece of paper in the pocket of his white shirt and found it. "I learned about my mother's death from this wretched letter which that fool Páscoa left on my bed, worried I might not see it otherwise. I'd just come home with Isabel, for the first time. And there was this bit of paper . . . They must be behind it, that third-wave scum . . ."

"No, not at all. They were in Lisbon, at the Coliseu, they were even seen on television. There was no one there that night. Our niece must have had the same idea as you, because three days later she went to the factory, but they still weren't back. She hid behind some clotheslines until they returned . . . You clearly don't know anything . . ." Ângela Margarida added wearily—"Why don't you read what the tabloids have to say? It's full of lies, but you'll get a rough idea of what happened, and then we won't have to tell you . . ." Then she said, in a faint, desperate voice—"Especially that business about the ants, which is just horrific. Unbelievable and horrific, and they emblazoned it across the front pages. Just horrible . . ."

Uncle Afonso placed one hand on the armchair on the left, then turned around and placed that same hand on the arm-chair on the right. "Ants?"—No, he didn't sit down on Grandma Regina's armchairs. Her uncle's small eyes gleamed in his broad face like two matches that flare up, then instantly go out. "No, surely not."

"Yes, it's true"—said Ângela Margarida. "If you must know, Mama was found outside the factory the following day, covered in the creatures. Black with them. That's the truth of the matter."

"What do you mean?"—Afonso was about to sit down in the armchair on the right, but instead swerved slightly and directed his hips—as slender as a young man's—onto the larger sofa. And, noisily opening first one newspaper then the other, he began running his eyes over the reports. When he looked up, he rested those eyes on Milene.

"So was it you, Milene, who told those bastards all these vile lies?"

Milene was about to respond. She was prepared. Quicker than a rumor that passes by, than an arrow shot at a target, *Totus Tuus, Introibo ad Altarem Dei,* you're a very intelligent girl, a very good person, believe me, an amazing person, you've got to defend yourself, and so on, Milene gripping the handle of her bag, absolutely ready to respond, her memory open in her head like a carnation, but she wouldn't have time. Her aunts responded for her.

"No, no, it wasn't Milene"—said Gininha, emerging from her state of tear-stained shock. "They're all fools, liars. Milene didn't speak to anyone. Our niece was quite lost, with none of us here, not a soul around. Nevertheless, she covered our mother's coffin with flowers, and put each of our names on a separate wreath. Yes, all our names were there, which was really thoughtful of her. Not everyone would have been so thoughtful. But those wretches took advantage of the situation in the most sordid way. They even used the poor girl's name . . ."

Afonso was looking at Milene with his piercing eyes, then reading and rereading the reports as if the newspapers' lies were the best possible source of information. They contained facts he couldn't obtain in any other way at that moment. Finally, he folded up the papers, looked around, and announced to his sisters, as if beginning a new phase of his life—"Well, frankly, our mother's to blame. I knew she'd do something like this. She was never one for making other people's lives easier. At least with our father, it was just a glass of wine one December morning out in the garden. The glass fell to the ground and he followed. A nice, clean death, and all over in an instant. But not her. I knew it. She wanted to make us look bad. Bad children, dreadful children . . ."

"Don't shout . . ."—said Ângela Margarida, shouting as well.—
"This is just the way things are, Afonso. First off, there are at least
six court cases we need to bring—now. Because it's a political
matter too. Six . . ." The siblings sashayed past each other in the
room, as if they were dancing.

"Count me out," said Afonso. "She was to blame. And it wasn't
me she was punishing, because I hardly ever saw her. I hardly even
came to this house. It was you. She wanted to show *urbi et orbi*
how you abandoned her in the middle of August. Bad daughters.
Do you see? She might not have thought it through, she just did
it instinctively. To punish you. In that little head of hers, she was
thinking—one's in Cancún and the other one's in the Canaries,
so I'm going to play a trick on them . . . Six court cases? Count
me out. The only purpose those cases would serve would be to . . .
No, enough foul language. Besides, it's just like her to come up
with that business with the ants. It was all the work of her imagination. She thought of everything. She knew . . ."

The large living room, with its heavy furnishings, had vanished.
Instead of people, there were only passions. Feelings pitted against
feelings. Aunt Gininha was gazing incredulously at her brother.
The way she saw it, his words revealed a base, malicious inter-
pretation of the facts. There was no way she could accept what
he had just said. Her respect for her mother remained unaltered.
Ângela Margarida, on the other hand, could see where Afonso
was coming from. Walking between the two armchairs and placing one hand on the back of each, as if they were someone's shoulders, she was more conciliatory—"I wouldn't go that far, but it
was always Mama's excessive energy that brought us down, that's
true . . ." She looked straight ahead. The three siblings cautiously
looking for an answer. Milene, behind them, waiting for a different answer herself. They were all immersed in thoughts that had

nothing to do with the truth. Weren't any of them interested in what she, Milene, knew?

No, no one was interested.

Outside, the walnut tree was curling its branches and reaching up to the eaves. It filled the garden with a musty smell that rose up from the dead leaves at its base, leaves that had remained unraked for days, and from the automatic sprinklers that came on at set times, randomly watering places that shouldn't be watered. Yes, it was a woodland mustiness. Invisible mushrooms, tubers, buried rhizomes, a patch of fertile soil in the midst of those desert lands. Earth transforming into lush leaves, petals decomposing into earth, substances metamorphosing into the essence of other substances, a brief senseless cycle that her aunts and uncle were only now beginning to notice, and it left a very bitter taste. That's what it was. Life for them had suddenly emptied of all meaning. Or any apparent meaning had been destroyed. And while the three of them sat there, each absorbed in his or her own personal state of shock, Milene looked at her watch and saw that it was already two o'clock, and she was just as prepared as she had been at ten o'clock. *Totus Tuus, Verbum Carum.* Her aunts and uncle sat silently on. She remained silent too, guarding her grandmother's armchair with her eyes. Eventually Uncle Afonso stood up, glanced at his watch, and asked—"What about the others? What are we waiting for? Aren't they coming? Where are Dom and Rui?" And he got up from the big sofa and sat down in his mother's armchair, the one on the left from which she always used to keep watch on the ever-evolving garden. And with his slender, youthful hips, in his youthful newlywed's clothes, he curled up in the seat. Milene was prepared for everything except that. *Ah, no, he's going to sit in Grandma's armchair . . .* she thought several times. Should she scream? In the midst of the surrounding silence? If not, what should she do instead? Physically drag him out of the chair? Milene couldn't take her eyes off that large body curled up in an armchair that had been made for her grandmother's body, not his. Sitting in an armchair that wasn't his.

Milene clutched her bag with both hands.

Be brave, very brave, and remember that you're a very intelligent, very special young woman. It's just that you're in a state of shock. Do you know what that means? Yes, she did, and she was going to scream at her uncle to get out of that chair. Any second. Then Aunt Ângela Margarida looked at her and said, far too abruptly for someone who was getting ready to scream—"Why don't you tell us what happened, Milene? Unfortunately, everything we know has come to us in a very distorted form. We've only heard from people who didn't actually see anything . . ." And perhaps because of the abrupt way in which Aunt Ângela Margarida spoke, no one heard the sound of another car, announcing the arrival of Uncle Rui Ludovice. Yes, it was definitely him, and by now, he was coming up the steps. Uncle Afonso got to his feet. Uncle Rui burst into the room, greeting his brother-in-law, clapping him on the back. The rest was silence. All they could hear was the faint sound made by Uncle Rui clapping Uncle Afonso on the back.

"What a very tiresome business . . ."

Her aunts sitting very erect, shoulder to shoulder on the sofa. Grasping their damp, crumpled handkerchiefs, their tears in their hands, not in their eyes. Their tears in their handkerchiefs. And Uncle Rui saying—"It's just so tedious. Just inexplicable really . . ." *Verbum Carum, Pax Domini, as when a bird flies through the air, as when an arrow is shot at a target, the air, thus divided, comes together at once, so that no one knows its pathway.* Now, finally, something is going to happen. Yes, Uncle Rui Ludovice had entered the room.

Tall and lithe, he was wearing a beige linen suit, brown shirt, and a glossy dark brown silk tie, his long wavy hair brushing his collar. He had arrived. Grandma Regina's large living room, in which, until then, they had each been immersed in their own tortuous thoughts, had suddenly become filled with another substance, pushing aside what had been there before. For Rui Ludovice had been obliged to return from abroad sooner than expected, and was already, on that first day back at work, feeling the pressures of bureaucracy, the hustle and bustle in the streets, the importance of the vast public square in which real things happened, social, palpable, measurable, tangible things. Perhaps that's why he couldn't help smiling at the troubled state in which he found Grandma Regina's offspring. He embraced the two dis-tressed women equally, not even singling out his own wife. He embraced Milene. He swept in from the air, from the street, from life itself, and, noticing what Milene was wearing, and despite the general atmosphere of tears and sighs, he said—"Dressed for the beach, I see. Ready for a dip, eh?" And Milene looked down at her-self. It was true, she was wearing Claudina's Bermuda shorts, not that she was going to say whose they were. This wasn't what she was prepared for, she hadn't sat in the back of the BMW driven by Senhor Frutuoso just to talk about her clothes. Nor was this what her uncle was interested in. And the proof was that he immedi-ately withdrew his gaze from her orange shorts and asked—"So, Milene, who did you speak to that day? Come on, tell us."

Milene felt her heart thumping. At last, it was her turn to speak. Yes, finally. But she had to focus on *that day* and *who did you speak to*. She gazed up at the ceiling to concentrate, fixed her eyes on the stucco, and tried to think. She thought about that day. She thought about the undertakers, the young man at the gas station, about the doctor, the nun, the priest, about what the priest had said, just for her benefit, *like a rumor that passes by, like a ship that sails through the billowy water,* and so on, proof that she was still prepared, that she could remember everything. She lowered her gaze and smiled at her uncle. She was about to speak, about to tell him what she knew. He answered for her.

"I know, you're going to tell me you didn't speak to anyone . . ."

She said—"But I did." And she smiled at him, at her aunts, and at Uncle Afonso too.

The new arrival loosened his tie a little. "All right, all right. No one spoke to anyone, okay. We know that . . ." he said. "Journalists feed off the misfortunes of others the way mites feed off dust. It's the same everywhere. Leave them be, poor things. No one really understands how they know what they know. They live in their own invisible world . . . It doesn't matter. If anything goes wrong, never fear, Rui is here to take it on the chin, but Rui can fend for himself, what's more, he has very broad shoulders . . . They can hit me as hard as they like, and the harder they hit me, the tougher I get. They'll be sorry, though . . ." Uncle Rui was standing in the middle of Grandma Regina's living room and talking at his usual rapid pace. He had taken off his jacket, and when he walked past Aunt Ângela Margarida for the first time, he gave it to her to hold. Rui Ludovice's broad, muscular shoulders appeared in all their glory. "Let's get down to facts."

"What facts, Uncle?"

Milene wanted to speak. Did her powerful uncle not want to listen?

He did not respond. Jacketless, he went over to the doors that opened into the garden and the walnut tree and flung them wide. And the blazing two o'clock sun pierced the leaves and branches and alighted on the cherrywood furniture, on the white china, on the red carpets and the gilt picture frames, as if suddenly everything were up for sale. He kicked the doors right open, pulling aside the curtains with his large, nimble fingers, opening up the folds full of cobwebs, which he hastily brushed off. Then he gave a final kick to the draft stopper, releasing a few crumbling dry leaves. The street entering the house. The house swept clean. And inside, everything moved, everything stirred into action. Indeed, it wasn't so much Uncle Rui Ludovice who had arrived, but Action itself. *Others Make Promises, We Take Action*. Action, however, then stepped out into the garden's microclimate—where the odors of dust and leaves mingled, filling the air with a smell like dung—and looked coolly around him like a realtor preparing to buy or sell. There was no need for him to say anything, the way he moved his eyes said it all. Somewhere between affectionate and distrustful. Like the gaze of a man evaluating a woman's naked body. That's how he was looking at the façade of the house, with a Levantine eye, leaving the doors open to the microclimate. His back was slightly damp with sweat, as he said from out in the garden—"I thought Dom was supposed to be coming. We need him . . ." And since Afonso was still in a kind of stupor, leaning against one faded wall, Uncle Rui came back up the two steps into the living room and said to his brother-in-law, as if announcing a hopeless economic tragedy—"We need to see what Dom has to say, but in my view, as a house, it's worthless. Lovely building, terrible location. End of story. It's that wretched road out there. The work of my ignorant fool of a predecessor . . ." And he drummed his fingers on the windowsill. Milene was looking at Uncle Rui's hands, at the furniture, at her aunts' legs, at the sofa in which they were sunk, far away from the armchairs. Everything and everyone exposed to the glare of the light.

Then the subject changed.

Now she was the one exposed to the glare. "And what about the girl?" asked Uncle Rui, as if "the girl" weren't there.

A silence fell. Action deactivated. Mute inaction. Silence in the living room of Villa Regina. Silence. You could hear a leaf from the walnut tree fall to the ground making a tinny sound. No one was looking at Milene.

"I'm not sure she should stay," said Gininha at last. "I think we should take her away from here . . ."

"Yes, take her away," said Ângela Margarida. It was all happening very fast.

"But where?" asked Gininha.

"After this terrible business . . ."—said her sister, her almost blond hair gleaming in the potent, dazzling light flooding the house.

"One moment." Rui Ludovice was in a hurry. His quick, perfect mind devoid of the sentiments binding the others to inaction. "One moment. There's every reason in the world, and more, for Milene to stay here. She needs to take responsibility for herself. To maintain her emotional stability. To stay in the house where she's always lived. She needs independence and a job of her own. Above all, she needs regularity and continuity in her life. That's what I would decide, if we had to decide, and if she was my blood relation . . ."

"Yes, but Mama asked us never to abandon her"—Gininha pushed back her long hair, so long that it sometimes fell across her face like a curtain.

"Well, Mama isn't here anymore to stop our niece from looking after herself. What qualifications does she have?"

As if Milene weren't there, Ângela Margarida answered for her—"In ninth grade, she only did science and art."

"And what does she like doing?"

Ângela Margarida asked Milene—"What would you like to do? Be a waitress? Look after children?"

"Your grandmother would never have allowed that"—Uncle

Rui said, interrupting. "But we will. Now you can have your own timetable, your own money, you can work with other people. After all, you drive your own car, go shopping, do the cooking, you're an independent person. We'll find a way for you to do whatever it is you want. You can work when you want to, come home when you want to, choose how much you want to do. You'll earn your own wages. It'll be great." He looked at his watch. Twenty past two. A lunch appointment. But Action was action. Who could give his niece a job? Who? Who? *Oh, I know.* He consulted his address book, tapped in a number, and said very loudly—"Barbosa? We have a problem. I assume you've heard about your godmother? Yes, she passed away. Yes, the thing is, we need you to help out our niece . . ." He turned. On Action's back, the sweat was forming a still darker brown stain. He was speaking softly now. He ended the call, then folded his phone shut. *Click-clack.* He looked at Milene and said—"All sorted. You can begin whenever you like. For a trial period initially, of course. So that's that."

"What do you mean, 'that's that'"?—asked Aunt Gininha. "If *we* don't even know who you were speaking to, how do you expect *her* to know?"

Then Uncle Rui Ludovice placed both hands on the back of the armchair on the left—he didn't sit down, though, Uncle Rui never sat down on either of Grandma Regina's armchairs—and repeated the conversation he'd just had with the owner of the Restaurante Mãos Largas. She could start whenever she liked. Tomorrow, even. In response, Milene was thinking that while she was perfectly prepared to tell them everything that had happened during the last five days, from the fourteenth to the eighteenth of August, she couldn't possibly just say yes or no to what was being proposed to her now. And her aunts asked her—"Yes or no, Milene? Yes or no?" Her aunts smiling at her, and her smiling at them, all of them standing up now, with no one sitting in the armchairs, no one sitting on the sofas, no elbows on the tables, Uncle Afonso all in white standing right in front of her. No, she wouldn't say anything. They weren't going to force her to give an answer to a question she wasn't prepared for. She smiled at them, but didn't answer.

"Have you nothing to say?"

And Uncle Rui Ludovice looked her up and down, as if approving of her refusal to answer—"You're quite right not to make a decision straightaway. Your grandmother probably never let you carry a tray in your life. We'll talk about it later . . ."

Uncle Rui must have been feeling grateful to her for remembering the flowers. Instead of confronting her with all the vile things the newspapers had printed, he was thanking her for having so thoughtfully placed a wreath on the coffin bearing his name, the mayor's name. On his behalf. Her uncle guarding the two armchairs, now with a hand on the wing of each chair, preventing the others from sitting in them. And for that reason alone, she felt grateful to Uncle Rui, whose arrival had changed everything. Her aunts were no longer crying, Uncle Afonso was not using the kind of foul language banned by Grandma Regina, and instead stood alone and silent, staring down at the tips of his white shoes. Uncle Rui Ludovice, the sweat stain on his shirt now a still deeper brown, receiving his beige jacket from the hands of Aunt Ângela Margarida and putting it on over his brown shirt, and Milene still wanting to explain, because she was still ready and prepared, exactly what had happened at the Town Hall, how no one had been there, not on the Friday or the Saturday morning, and how that's where she'd had the idea of ordering a wreath bearing her uncle's name and that of the Town Hall. Because he'd shown some interest in her, she wanted to repeat, at least to him, all those other people's words she'd stored away, *Pax Domini, Introibo ad Altarem Dei*, like the arrow, like the bird, like the smoke, etc., yes, Uncle, I spent several days inside the Diamond, etc., it's just that I couldn't say anything until you gave me permission. He came over to her and said—"Don't you worry, Milene, you can stay here in Villa Regina with your aunts and uncles . . . Now I have to go. Senhor Frutuoso will be getting antsy." Action in motion hurriedly saying goodbye to Aunt Ângela Margarida. They would talk later, there were a million things to sort out. Now, though, he was in a hurry. He had so much to do. He looked for his sunglasses, which he couldn't find anywhere—"Bury the dead and take care of the living, eh?" he said, still looking for his glasses. Uncle Afonso blocked his exit.

"Hang on a minute, Rui. You breeze in, say your piece, then vanish. I think it's all a bit more complicated than that. I foresee some real problems. For example, who exactly is going to keep the girl company? Just so we're clear."

Uncle Rui, who was about to leave the room, sat down again— "Where's the cleaning lady? What's her name? Juliana? Where's her number?"

The phone flipped open again in his large hand. He keyed in a number—"Dona Juliana? It's the mayor speaking. Shouldn't you be here at my mother-in-law's house? Didn't you know she'd died? Oh, I see, you were on vacation. Are you still on vacation? Well, look, you either come now or we get someone else in. My niece can't be left alone. Do you understand? You can't do any more hours? You're not sure. Well, if you can't, just say, and we'll find someone else. You can't. Oh, you can. Then come as soon as you're free and sort things out with my niece. Yes, we're all here. If you can't manage to come earlier, then be here by five at the latest. You can arrange it with my niece . . ." Action closed his phone with a click. Sorted. "Anything else?"—No, no one could think of anything else. They all felt as if they'd received a sharp blow to the head. Ah, there were his sunglasses. All in white, hands on narrow hips, his brother-in-law was still barring the way, but Rui Ludovice didn't speak to him, he spoke to Milene. It was clear that Action was thinking elliptically, performing mental leaps. Making synopses in order to get things done more quickly. Leaping from the brother-in-law to Juliana, from Juliana to Milene—"Later on, you must give me a blow-by-blow account of exactly who you spoke to. We'll sort all this out ourselves, no court cases. Whose idea was that anyway?" He was doubtless referring to Aunt Ângela Margarida's suggestion, but in order to be as quick and efficient as possible, he didn't mention her name.

Uncle Rui Ludovice had his jacket now, as well as his sunglasses, his phone, and his address book; he patted his trouser pockets, his jacket pockets, his shirt pocket, his long, honed body fresh from exercising in some far-off swimming pool, so far off that he wasn't going to name it, so that it didn't get confused with Japan or China—how absurd, when they'd been on the opposite side of the world, in Cancún—smoothing his long curly hair glossy with coconut oil, smoothing down Action itself, both physical and mental, and then he left, leaving the living room in Villa Regina wide open, sunny and green, and leaving the two aunts and the other uncle feeling lost and dizzy. Especially the aunts. But Uncle Afonso Leandro too, to a certain extent. It was nearly three o'clock. "'Bye, Angelita"—said Uncle Rui Ludovice as he was about to leave, adding—"And no more talk of court cases, all right? There are other means. In politics, alas, there are only other means. Milene will talk when she's ready. It'll just take a little tact and time. She'll talk . . ."

But the mourning period wasn't over yet.

———

The aunts closed the windows, lowered the blinds, any cobwebs or bits of leaf now disappearing from view, any stains on the china fading to white, any marks on the paintwork merging with the plaster, letting the shadows creep quietly in on their many feet. Grief bloomed anew. The three siblings came together in a kind of somnolence, where mourning took the form of a painful pleasure. None of them felt hungry or thirsty. Repeating the words they'd started with, flights, court cases, ants, news, newspapers, the seventh-day mass that would never happen. But Milene was certain that if they were all to leave, the house would be a cleaner place. Now that she knew she wouldn't have a chance to explain anything, she just wanted them to go.

Her aunts, however, were delaying their departure, wandering around among the furniture, opening drawers, looking at linen, studying tablecloths, and their hands kept rummaging around, moving everything, but taking nothing out. "Mama had *such* good taste . . ."—Gininha was saying, her long hair falling over her face.—"You don't see hem stitching like that anymore . . ." Ângela Margarida was saying, having apparently forgotten Afonso's suspicions about their mother, and too absorbed now in the linen chests, in which she found a reflection of her mother's soul. And Gininha felt as if she'd found a piece of their mother's soul itself when she stumbled upon the fans she used to use, the faint breeze like a breath, her mother's sturdy wrist, the soft tinkle of her bracelets, the age spots freckling her hands, and both daughters heard that breath as they looked at the fan, and both wept, while their older brother, Afonso Leandro, regarded them with a scowl. But he could hear his mother's hands moving too, a feminine intuition that took him by surprise, touching a nerve in his male self that was sensitive to fans and linen. What could have happened? He appeared to have abandoned his theory that their mother had conspired against her children, especially her daughters. Now, saying nothing, he allowed himself to feel surprised. And suddenly, just as Aunt Gininha was glimpsing another piece of her mother's soul in the Chinese porcelain rice bowls she was looking at, but only looking, mind, only touching them with her fingertips, saying only, *So beautifully preserved,* Aunt Ângela Margarida had just discovered some bundles of letters tied up with ribbons, which she held aloft as if they were biographies. *Put them back where they were, Aunts, put them back.* There were her aunts, both of them, touching Grandma Regina's untouchable things. And then Afonso Leandro, as if emerging from years of mourning, got to his feet, looked at his watch, picked up his phone, and began tapping in a number.

While he was doing this, he turned his powerful back and walked on springy agile legs toward the door opening out onto the garden-cum-microclimate, but instead of his lower body transporting his upper body through the French doors, as might be expected, it turned, and when the person at the other end answered, he sat down on one of his mother's armchairs. He shuffled around, making himself comfortable, ran one hand along the arm, the arm of the chair where Grandma Regina would sit to watch television, and as if he'd just caught some sought-after, airy thing, he said very loudly—"Ah, Isabel!" Shouting. "Yes, I'm still here . . ." And instead of getting up, he leaned right back in Grandma Regina's armchair.

"Yes, still . . ."

He leaned back with his whole body, upper and lower, letting his head roll from side to side between the two wings of the chair, as if the whole thing belonged to him, had surrendered to him, obliterating Grandma Regina's shadow. And Milene felt an opaque substance blinding her to everything but the body of that older son curled up in the chair, practically in a fetal position, and she shouted so loudly that Afonso Leandro, startled, ended the call and leapt to his feet, looking behind him at the chair—"What did I do?"

"Get out of there, get out!"

Restrained by her aunts, Milene was standing on tiptoe, heels apart and knees together, shouting—"Get out of that chair this minute . . . It belongs to Grandma Regina, do you understand? Do you understand what I'm saying? Get your skirt-chasing ass out of there . . ."

She knew her eyes were full of hatred as she stared at her uncle. And he, a mature man from the neck up, a mere youth below, stood frozen, dumbstruck. He hadn't slept all night. Four hours spent hanging around in that frantic hellhole called Heathrow. Four hours. He froze. The contrary of Action in action, instead Inaction in inaction. And this man, who had once been a commando and, on weekends, was one of the best riders at the riding club, as well as being a brilliant lawyer with an office right next to the court, now stood dumbstruck before his niece.

Milene tried to shake off her aunts, who were holding her by the elbows—one elbow per aunt—telling them to go away, to leave the house as it was, that they had no right to mess with Grandma Regina's things, they could look at them, but that was all. And her aunts, Gininha and Ângela Margarida, avoiding her jabbing elbows, simply didn't recognize their niece, this was the first time they'd ever seen her so angry, unless it was just bad manners, one or the other. But anger was one thing, bad manners quite another. Although they still for the moment put it down to anger.—"Milene?"

"Calm down, Milene, no one's going to hurt you . . ."

They again cautiously approached Milene's elbows, like someone approaching a pet cat that has suddenly turned vicious. Forgiving her, calming her, telling her that, of course, no one would touch any of the sacred places that had once been Grandma Regina's. The desire to smooth things over flowing through their veins and appearing on their faces. The three siblings united, fearfully keeping their distance. Milene keeping her distance too, feeling very worked up, hearing inside her, *You're a very bright girl, amazing, if they bother you, don't let yourself be browbeaten . . . Defend yourself, defend yourself. Totus Tuus, Introibo ad Altarem Dei, Misereatur Tui,* other people's words, like a bird that flies, a rumor that passes by, smoke dispersed before the wind, passages from the Book of Wisdom. She's the mayor's niece. Courage. Get out of my sight.

No one was going to get the better of Milene—"Go home, all of you. I wish the afternoon would just swallow you up. Just go, okay?" In a thread of a voice—"Yes, I wish the afternoon would just swallow you up, you and your fucking lives . . ."

V

YES, THE AFTERNOON SWALLOWED UP HER UNCLES AND aunts, their cars and their hair, and their several sorrows. The afternoon carried them with it down the road, toward the roofs of the Frame Store and the Big Market, leaving, in the place of their tears and sighs, a kind of silent shadow that was something like peace. Her aunts had even said—"Time to get some rest."

And since she was still guarding the door behind which her grandmother's armchairs, along with her television and her footstool, now stood undisturbed, Afonso Leandro had shouted— "Is this the kind of person José Carlos left us with? Is this what he brought to us in a bundle of laundry and never took back? Is this his legacy to his long-suffering siblings? This ludicrous person . . . ?"—Uncle Afonso had said, pointing at Milene with his equestrian arm, his whole body tired from the night flight between Cyprus and Athens, plus those four wasted hours at Heathrow Airport, and all for nothing. Exhausted. Completely wiped out after reading the gutter press, the headlines on the front pages and the full stories on page three, tired of searching his soul for polite words to express thoughts that were nothing of the sort. "It was that ludicrous person . . ."—her uncle had said, as her aunts led him away, one on either side, like two caryatids, propelling him through the garden microclimate toward his convertible. "José Carlos left us this rude, uneducated person who's poisoned our lives. And nothing else . . ."

"Shush, Afonso, this isn't the time. Calm down . . . We could all do with some rest. Then we'll reconvene this evening. The main thing is to keep calm . . ." said Aunt Gininha, almost bumping into the coatrack as she passed. Aunt Ângela Margarida's heavy eyelids were swollen. One far more swollen than the other, because of the insect bite acquired in Cancún. Utterly focused, Milene's aunt continued to guide him by the arm, directing him down the steps outside the house, pushing him from behind. Her two aunts steering her uncle beyond the ivy-covered wall, through the iron gate that bore the name *Villa Regina*. Even from there, you could hear Uncle Afonso braying—"That person who quite simply makes my blood boil . . ."

This was when the afternoon carried her three relatives in their three cars away down the road, with puffy eyes and clothes crumpled by the long, long journeys back from their interrupted vacations.

Her aunts had said—"Come on, let's get a bit of rest . . ."

Milene needed rest too.

She really did. Until they set off, she had stayed on the doorstep, to be absolutely certain they were leaving, and her hands resting on the doorframe had trembled. This was because Milene knew full well what Uncle Afonso really meant when he started shouting. But then why hadn't Uncle Afonso gotten straight to the point, as he usually did when he lost his temper with her? Why hadn't he come right out and said that her father José Carlos had been a total waste of space? A fool and a hopeless romantic, to the point of falling head-over-heels for that air hostess, who even before giving him a daughter had cheated on him a thousand times? Why hadn't he been more direct, why hadn't he said all that, word for word, as he had once before when João Paulo was there? That day, Uncle Afonso had said, in front of João Paulo— *Listen, son, she was just about to have Milene and even then she was sleeping around, leaving him with cuckold-horns the size of TV antennae . . .* Straight out, like that? Uncle Afonso could easily come back and repeat those insults again. He could come back and say that José Carlos should never have shown up at his own mother's house, on Christmas Eve of all days, clutching a frilly carry-cot with a newborn baby inside. An ugly little red-faced thing with a soap-opera name, a name chosen by the air hostess. *Milene.* And *she* was Milene. Yes, why wasn't he saying that? Instead of just calling her *that ludicrous person*, why wasn't he saying all the rest, as he had done countless times before? Why wasn't he shaking off his two sisters and storming straight back, to vent all his frustrated vacationer's energies on her? Yes, let him come back and tell her again, to her face, that José Carlos had done the same thing with his life as he had with the Old Factory. Accusing him for the thousandth time of throwing the family jewels down the drain. That was what he wanted to say to her, she was sure.

She knew her uncle very well.

As she watched him approach the convertible, squeezed into those tight-fitting clothes, she remembered all the things he used to say to her. And then there he was, pinned between her two aunts, stumbling, obedient, letting himself be led, presumably because he was just exhausted. But if he hadn't obeyed them, if he hadn't given in, he would have turned around to remind her, as he so often did, of the day in 1975 when her father had handed the factory keys to the workers on a velvet cushion. He would speak for the hundredth time of the cushion on which Grandma Regina used to rest her elbow when she tried on jewelry or gloves. The cushion bearing the name *LEANDRO* in gold stitching, and which José Carlos had been idiotic enough to take from the house and give to a gang of common thieves, like a king surrendering his castle keys to a vassal. And he'd recall another scene too, the reverse of the first, from 1985, when the same thieves had returned the keys, by then rusted and filthy, on that same cushion, which was now filthy as well. Without once mentioning how they'd camped out in the factory during *the best summer of our lives*. Uncle Afonso no longer cared about that. What he cared about was remembering how stupid the once-dignified, intelligent José Carlos had been, and how he had ended up destroying himself, fathering a child with some slutty air hostess, then stealing it away so she'd be forced to follow, counting on maternal instincts that his air whore quite simply didn't have, since she never once came looking. That child was her, Milene. That's what Uncle Afonso wanted to say, and if he didn't it was only because those grubby white clothes, brought back all the way from Cyprus, seemed to be turning him into a total coward.

Otherwise, he wouldn't even have left the living room. He would have stayed there, yelling, reminding her how, a few years later, José Carlos, not content with the great failure of his marriage, had, of his own free will, gone to Lisbon to look for the air hostess, and how on a long straight road in the Alentejo— so straight, so straight you didn't even need your hands on the wheel—the car had overturned with the two of them inside it. Uncle Afonso would actually laugh when he told the story, and say that, to look on the bright side, so as not to be entirely negative, he liked to imagine that his brother had let go of the wheel because he and the air hostess had patched things up and spent the whole journey canoodling, this being the only flower that could possibly be laid on the heap of metal that had once been José Carlos's Porsche, in that flat, silent landscape, with a few birds flying past overhead, completely oblivious. And the end product of all that was her, Milene, their only daughter, who could have been a nice, normal little girl, a good student, a good niece, but who had, instead, gradually shown herself to be that ludicrous person.

Yes, surely that was what, deep down, Uncle Afonso would have wanted to say, while being led away by her two aunts, toward the open-top car, like a kind of voluntary prisoner. But if he felt like getting all that off his chest one more time, why didn't he shake off her aunts and turn back? Why didn't he come up the steps and tell her what he'd told her so many times before? *It was thanks to your Dad, Milene, that we missed out on state intervention in the Old Factory. If he hadn't given the keys to that gang of lowlifes, our family would have pocketed three million escudos like everyone else, which we could have shared out between the five of us and been just fine. And now we're not fine at all, and what's more we're stuck with a ludicrous person like you. Do you hear?* That's what Uncle Afonso could have said. In fact, even then, he still had time to get out of his convertible and retrace his steps, and she was still waiting on the threshold of Villa Regina, so that, if he really did come back, she could do something about it. Shut the door and then, after shutting it, say, in her thin, reedy voice, as only she could—*Don't come back, okay?* She wished her uncle and aunts would go away and rest forever. After all, she was feeling just fine, home alone, wearing Claudina's orange Bermuda shorts. She had everything she needed.

You're the ones who should rest.

"I, Milene Lino Leandro, don't need to rest . . ."—she said, as the glaring afternoon light swallowed up Uncle Afonso and her aunts, their cars and their hair, their shared and secret thoughts, the ones she did and didn't know about, and above all, as the afternoon carried away their respective posteriors, which she would never again allow to sink into Grandma Regina's armchairs. Never again would she let them touch anything that belonged to their mother. They'd helped themselves to quite enough already. As she watched them disappear down the road, all Milene felt like saying was—"Phew! Off they go. Yes, go away, go away . . ."

She turned back to make absolutely sure—Had they really left?

Because now, she decided, she was actually going to list the things they had already helped themselves to. They were shameless. It had been two years since her uncle and aunts had started taking furniture and other knickknacks from the house, with Grandma Regina turning a blind eye. Often Milene entirely forgot about objects and possessions and the like, and even when she thought about them they left her fairly indifferent, but suddenly, after that encounter, she found herself remembering everything they had gradually taken away.

She didn't even have to try. It was a real disgrace. The evidence was plain to see all over Villa Regina. Right there, next to the coatrack, where her grandmother's three hats still hung, a bright, medallion-shaped mark in the hallway's green paint recalled the oval frame from which her great-grandfather, José Joaquim Leandro, with his bushy mustache and rather irate expression, had, for decades, kept an eye on everyone entering and leaving the house. The photograph belonged to that wall, but Uncle Afonso had taken it, temporarily, saying it would do him good to keep that visionary gaze close by. He had hung it in his office. He had never brought it back.

On the way into the living room too, the oak dresser with big drawers and barley-twist columns had left a huge dark square on the wall, over which an Indian tapestry had hastily been hung. That was Aunt Ângela Margarida's doing. The glass-fronted bookcase and wooden stepladder, along with the leather-bound books, had also been taken, and the two aunts had dragged one of the little sofas into the empty space, where it now hovered rather forlornly between two vases. They had also taken a wooden chest with a rounded lid, an antique that Aunt Ângela Margarida thought dated back to the Portuguese Discoveries, but they had left undisturbed anything they considered Art Nouveau, the statuettes and furniture that Aunt Gininha and Aunt Ângela Margarida both hated, and which had been there since Grandma Regina's youth. Luckily for Grandma Regina. From the wall on the stairs leading up to the first floor, a large painting of a battle between the French and the Dutch had vanished, along with one of a Turkish armada on the seas of the Orient, both by a French artist. The only paintings left showed the Bay of Naples, with Vesuvius in the background, and Venice, with St. Mark's Square a fluttering mass of pigeons. Her grandmother had said she didn't mind. When it came to the living room, however, they hadn't been brave enough to take the cherrywood table with its three carved tripod legs, or the beveled mirror that reflected it. Or the linen chest, or the bookshelf on which sat the Capuchin Bible and the *Great Portuguese and Brazilian Encyclopedia*. Milene examined what was left. Paying particular attention to the stool where Regina Leandro used to rest her feet, and the television, and the record player where her grandma often listened to classical music and strange albums like *Caminito Mío* or *La Violetera*, and the two upholstered blue armchairs, one on the left and one on the right. From that day on, they weren't going to take anything else. It all belonged to Grandma Regina.

You all belong to Grandma Regina.

So it was just as well that she'd shouted at them—"Go away and don't come back, not today, not tomorrow, not the day after that, not ever. Go away, go on . . . You can plonk your asses down wherever you like, but in your own homes, not here, okay? Are you listening to me?" she'd said, standing on the threshold, arms outstretched and hands gripping the doorframe. And meanwhile, the hot afternoon was taking her uncle and aunts away down the road, taking the three cars, the three sorrows and the three wearinesses, and their three separate states of unease. Taking them all, first her uncle, then her aunts.

Good. Milene alone at last, in Villa Regina.

She had it all planned out. Before night fell, she'd turn on the living room lights and raise the blinds, and the only reason she wouldn't open the windows would be to stop the geckos, the mosquitoes, and the evening dust from getting in. Anyway, her aunts and uncles had left, and she hadn't even told them the two basic ideas she had prepared during the days she had spent in a state of shock, as a guest inside the Diamond. So, that was that. And now Uncle Afonso, who had been unreachable, in Cyprus, as uncontactable as Aunt Gininha and the others, each of them uncontactable in a different part of the World, each believing the others were contactable, they were now calling *her* a ludicrous person. She needed to tell her cousin João Paulo right away.

João Paulo?

The telephone that Grandma Regina kept by the armchair on the left was still in the same place. Milene dialed the long line of numbers. Things were beginning to come together.

First of all, it did her good to hear the greeting—*Hi, you've reached five-seven-three-seven* . . . She waited. But when the recording was over, she didn't, after all, describe everything that had happened. Instead, as if part of what she was feeling had relaxed because it knew she was about to speak to him, and that she would be safe in the world when she heard his voice, Milene hesitated, kept quiet, and then simply said—"*João Paulo? I'm back at home now. Your dad and your aunts were here this afternoon. Then they went home to have a rest. I'm resting too, in our house. There's no one around. All the neighbors are on holiday. How about you? Are you on holiday as well? Call me. Goodbye, see you . . .*" She didn't hang up. She carried on speaking—"*Actually, don't call for a few hours because I might not hear . . . Yes, I'm going to rest for a bit now. I'm going to close my eyes, like the three of us used to. The road will rest, the shadows will rest, and Claudina Mata's beach clothes, which I'm wearing right now, but which I'm going to take off, they'll rest too. And Grandma Regina's furniture, all around the house, will rest. Everything will rest . . . Call me later. I'm going to sleep now, so you can call early in the morning, which will be around midnight where you live . . . 'Bye.*"

VI

AFTERWARD, PEOPLE SAID THAT, FOR AN ENTIRE WEEK, Milene remained holed up in Villa Regina listening to Cyndi Lauper's *Twelve Deadly Cyns*, without eating or drinking, and that she only went to the Pomodoro when the hunger pangs really got to her. People also said that it had been the Matas, when they brought back her Clio, who had saved her from starving to death, that they found her lying unconscious among the hydrangeas in that garden-cum-microclimate, which wasn't true at all. But people enjoy imagining grotesque events in other people's lives to feel safe in their own supposed normality. To be able to think— *Ah, I'm so much more intelligent, my behavior almost entirely beyond reproach. I get up every morning, regular as clockwork. People can rely on me having a coffee at the local café, sorting out business, signing checks. No one in my family died young, no one fell seriously ill, no one committed suicide. My solid house is solidly built, and built by me. It's so good being a decent person with an orderly life, day after identical day. My relatives all have a bright future ahead of them. Unlike Dona Regina's granddaughter, poor thing. When she finally dragged herself over to the Italian restaurant at the Miramar crossroads, she could scarcely utter the word pizza. Everyone had forgotten all about her.* That's what some people said had happened.

But that isn't what happened at all. As we would find out later on. It was confirmed that her family didn't abandon her. Contrary to rumor, no one cast our cousin aside as if she were a piece of detritus. On the contrary.

The proof is that, the following day, Milene ran to the window and saw two cars drawing up beneath the acacia trees, and out stepped her aunts and her uncle. She had left the lights on in the house all night, and now, at eleven o'clock in the morning, they were still on. Milene thought it wise to turn them off before taking up a position on the balcony. Why had they come back?—she wondered as she stood there, chewing gum. After all, hadn't she sent them packing the previous day? Hadn't she told them never to return?

It had been a long, hot night, but not long enough to salve the pain they had caused her. She was standing well back on the balcony, watching them, the front door locked. She knew they all had a key and could get in whenever they wanted. Normally, though, they never came in without asking Grandma Regina's permission. Would they just march straight in? Meanwhile, the three of them were already crossing the street, advancing very circumspectly, casting shadows on the tarmac. Uncle Afonso was staring off into the distance, as if he were much more interested in something on the far horizon than in the house he was about to enter. Her aunts kept close together. All highly suspicious. The gate creaked open and shut. Already halfway up the garden path, they stopped, and Gininha, taking a few delicate, almost tremulous steps forward, began calling up at the balcony. Milene? Milene? From inside, the voice of Cyndi Lauper, expanded and amplified by the speakers, was creating a serious barrier to that call. Milene ran and switched off the music, then returned to the balcony and leaned out.

"Milene? Look!"

Yes, Aunt Gininha was calling her. She was holding a brown paper bag in one hand and waving it about. Still brandishing the bag, she called again:

"Will you let us in?"

Milene knew that Uncle Afonso would only have to find the right key on his key ring, then turn the key in the lock, but he didn't, he was still staring off into the distance, as if he were urgently needed elsewhere. Aunt Ângela Margarida had stepped forward much more confidently and was standing, arms folded, as if ready for a fight that had not yet begun. Only Gininha continued to call up to the balcony.

"Open up, sweetheart, open the door . . ."

Her aunt's supplicant voice seemed genuine enough, but what really prevented Milene from going down and opening the door to them was that brown paper bag, which doubtless contained fresh food and which Gininha was waving around as if she'd brought a supply of nuts to feed a monkey at the zoo. Yes, that's what it was. Milene hated feeling that they were treating her as if she were still eight or nine years old, even when it was Aunt Gininha making her feel like that. She hated it. Perhaps that's why she still hadn't decided what to do, since they were currently respecting the usual rules that governed entry into Villa Regina. Her uncle even stooped down to remove a pebble he'd spotted among the couch grass, and still didn't produce the key that must be there in his pocket. No one produced a key. Aunt Gininha came closer still.—"Listen, Milene. If you don't want to open the door, we'll go away. We'll hang the bag on the door handle and leave. It's up to you . . ." Then her aunt turned around. They all seemed prepared to do as Aunt Gininha said. All three of them turned their backs on the house, as if about to leave.

Milene hadn't just switched off the music, she had also discarded her chewing gum. "No, it's all right"—she said, leaning over the balcony railing. "I'll open the door. I won't be a moment."

And, taken by surprise, with no time to reflect, she hurried down the stairs. When she reached the door, aunts and uncle were waiting outside for her in a meek, submissive line. Even so, Milene made a point of looking at them one by one, fixing them with a hard stare through the crack in the door which she opened very, very slowly, keeping one hand on the key, and remaining safely behind the door, ready to close it again as soon as the three had gone into Grandma Regina's living room. She was astonished. A radical change seemed to have taken place since the previous day. Uncle Afonso walked past her like someone walking past a wall, and Ângela Margarida barely raised a hand in greeting, while Aunt Gininha, also en route to the living room, continued to chat amiably away.

"Before you get on with whatever you were going to do, here's something to eat. And don't worry, we're not going to sit over there, no, we won't sit on Grandma Regina's armchairs. Why would we? There are other places to sit. Let's sit here . . ."

And the three siblings, doubtless to make clear that their actions matched their words, had all sat around the cherrywood table, on which they placed a few bundles of papers. "Rest assured, Milene, I swear, as we all do, that we won't sit anywhere we shouldn't. We just need to talk . . ." This was Aunt Gininha carefully trying to reassure her. "Do you understand, Milene? This is a matter for us siblings, but if you want to stay, then by all means do . . ." Aunt Ângela Margarida, her left eye still quite swollen, was staring anxiously at Uncle Afonso's glossy head of hair, which looked a slightly lighter shade of brown against his black silk shirt. Uncle Afonso, still studiously pretending he wasn't there, gazed up at the ceiling. Whatever her motive, it was good of Aunt Gininha to insist on that.—"If you want to sit down, then sit here with us, sweetheart . . ." And she offered her a chair.

No, she wouldn't sit down.

She wasn't going to abuse the trust they were suddenly placing in her. She accepted this absolutely. Since they asked so nicely, they could stay for as long as they liked. And in order that they might appreciate how generous she was being, she wouldn't even respond to that offer, she would simply withdraw, pulling her nightdress modestly down over her knees, and closing the door behind her so that they could talk more freely. Feeling almost happy, almost consoled, she even felt disposed to accept the bag of fresh food held out to her by Aunt Gininha. Now they knew who gave the orders in that house and knew too that they could only use the house with her permission. And back in the kitchen, drinking the hot coffee her aunts had brought her, and biting into the yellow cream of a large bun, she felt the pain inside her dissolving or at least changing to a duller pain. After all, whatever happened, they were her family, her aunts and uncle.

And they must be extremely tired.

Proof of this was the silent way in which the meeting in the living room proceeded. For almost an hour, not a word was heard. They must be going over what had happened, discussing the six court cases, pondering the nursing home's treacherous behavior, the account given by the young man at the gas station, the fact that the *thing* containing Grandma Regina had been placed in an ordinary grave, because, what with the heat and everything, Milene had completely forgotten that the family owned one of those little stone houses with an angel on top. Out of respect for her aunts and uncle, Milene didn't even put the music on in her room again. Once washed and dressed, she merely sat on the stairs humming snatches of the Cyndi Lauper album, sensing the peace and harmony emanating from the three siblings as they serenely, wearily came to some agreement over all those facts. Later, however, at around midday, everything changed. She was singing "Stone, the world is stone," very quietly so as not to bother them, when she began to hear the sound of wooden or metal objects falling to the floor, sometimes very loudly, other times muffled by the rug, along with the sound of paper being torn up and the clang of metal on metal. Immediately after this, utter discord must have broken out among the siblings.

It was Saturday, the twenty-third of August, and in Grandma Regina's living room, the siblings had, alas, fallen out dramatically. Even if Milene had tried, she couldn't have ignored the fact that her aunts and uncle were addressing each other in raised voices. Milene was particularly aware of Aunt Ângela Margarida's booming tones. The hours were passing, and they hadn't eaten, hadn't drunk, hadn't used the toilet, hadn't come out of the room. Too angry and upset. At one point, Afonso spoke particularly loudly. And Aunt Ângela Margarida, in her best matronly voice, shouted him down. Milene feared that no one would emerge alive from that confrontation. She had even gone out into the garden to peer in, but every window was like a barred cage. They had lowered all the blinds, and inside, the knives were out. The siblings were eating each other alive. When the door finally opened, it felt as if a dam had burst. Her uncle was the first to come out, spitting feathers. It was clear, though, that the sparse fringe of hair around his bald pate, although disheveled, remained intact, his powerful torso unchanged, and his legs still moved with the same gymnastic vigor.—No, the siblings hadn't killed each other, but her uncle's eyes were no longer visible beneath their heavy lids. She saw him flash past, a folder in his hand. Milene didn't recall him having arrived carrying such a folder. However, so turbocharged was he by the dispute that he literally leapt into his convertible, which instantly swallowed him up and sped like an arrow down the road.

Then it was Aunt Ângela Margarida's turn.

No, she wasn't sitting in either armchair, but on a sofa, and there she was, legs crossed, making a phone call, her back to the door. Taxi? Yes, she wanted a taxi. She wasn't talking to Aunt Gininha. Gininha was on the other side of the room, equally absorbed in her own thoughts. Between the phone call and the arrival of the taxi, no one spoke. When the taxi arrived, Aunt Ângela Margarida left, clattering down the stairs in her high heels, then down the garden path and through the iron gate, which again creaked open and shut. She was leaving. Only then did Aunt Gininha call out to Milene.

She called very gently—"Milene?"

A good half hour had elapsed since the battle, and even so it was clear that the siblings had inflicted deep wounds on each other. Aunt Gininha, kindly Aunt Gininha, was still quite breathless. Her long hair was electric, and when she ran her hand over her head, dark threads fluttered and crackled in the wake of her fingers. Yet she, the most badly battered by the quarrel, was the one who had stayed behind to talk to Milene, calling to her, almost in a whisper—"Milene? Come here . . ." Then she put her arm around her niece's waist, drawing her closer, so that her head was resting on her breast. Finally, she said—"These things happen . . ." Presumably referring to the quarrel. "It's just to let you know, Milene, that we opened the will, and I'm to be your executor. Grandma Regina wanted me to represent you, to look after your money and your revenues, well, your life, really . . ." Aunt Gininha holding her niece close. Milene, surprised, sitting pressed against her Aunt Gininha's perfumed shoulder, on which fell a thick mass of hair dyed burgundy brown, just like Grandma Regina's hair many years ago. Milene almost sitting on her aunt's lap.

"Have you nothing to say?"

The room plunged in silence. Gravity trailing its wings. The facts taking on substance. The future rising up like a vast mist through which they would have to trace an uncertain path. The two women clinging to each other, about to set off on a journey, which seemed already to have begun, without their knowing why or when or where they were going. Their hands clasped. The past like a wave, its foaming waters pricked with fear. At a certain point, though, Aunt Gininha, her chest barely rising and falling, as if the argument with her siblings were preventing her from breathing, added—"There's another thing. Apart from the matter of the inheritance, there's something else I need to talk to you about . . ." It was clear that Aunt Gininha, her almost flat chest hardly moving, was having difficulty formulating her idea. Yes, that much was clear. Ah, poor Aunt Gininha, how thin she had become. Then Grandma Regina's youngest daughter summoned up the necessary courage.—"It's like this, Milene. We've agreed to share you out in the following manner: you will continue to live in Villa Regina as you always have done, and carry on with your normal life, and we will take turns to be here with you at night. A kind of rotation, you see. I'll give you an example. Let's suppose that today, Saturday, it's my turn to keep you company. Tomorrow, Sunday, it would be Aunt Ângela Margarida. Then, on Monday, it would be Uncle Afonso. Tuesday, it would be me again; Wednesday, Aunt Ângela Margarida; Thursday, Uncle Afonso; and then me; and so on and so forth, every night for the rest of your life . . ." Gininha, a bundle of papers in her lap and a diary in her hand, counting off the days, as if the three siblings had been conferring with the angel Lucifer on the path down into Hell.

Her aunt saying—"We'll start a month from now, when the days are getting shorter and the nights colder. It would be rather sad then for you to be here all alone . . ." Her aunt running her hand over Milene's hair, stroking her back, as she explained this "perpetual calendar," and Aunt Gininha, fearing that her niece might not understand, even got up and went to fetch the calendar from the kitchen to show her how the days would be shared out.

"Do you understand?"

Yes, Milene understood. She was looking at those rows of squares, following one after the other, imagining each day filled either by one of her aunts or by her uncle, and it wasn't hard to conclude that, were they to keep to that rotation, the days of the week would never have any regularity. It also occurred to her that it would be quite a sacrifice for them. Which meant that they hadn't even been able to agree on a fair distribution of days. They could simply have decided—Mondays and Thursdays, Aunt Gininha; Tuesdays and Fridays, Aunt Ângela Margarida; Wednesdays and Saturdays, Uncle Afonso; and so on until the end of days. But that's where they must have come up against a major obstacle. There was one more day in the week, and they had probably argued over how to share out the Sundays, then descended into discord. They hadn't shared her out by weeks or months. No, they'd done it day by day, like being condemned to Hell. They had fallen out because of her. That, at least, is what she understood while staring down at the calendar that her aunt Gininha had placed on the cherrywood table.

"Don't you have anything to say, Milene?" asked her aunt.

That future measured out in squares was so complicated, so rigid, and at the same time so problematic, that she didn't know what to say. "We'll see . . . we'll see . . ."—said her aunt. And then, as if she had suddenly started to breathe normally again, she added—"Goodness, it's late . . ." Yes, Milene had understood.

They had removed the encyclopedias concealing the green safe fitted into the wall, which they had then opened and closed again. Several volumes of the encyclopedia still lay higgledy-piggledy on the shelves. Had they found that rotation in there too? No, Milene wouldn't ask. Inside the iron safe—a kind of umbilical nodule that had always intrigued her—there might be all kinds of enigmatic things guaranteed to provoke arguments, but they themselves had invented that rotation. She was sure of that.

"Have you nothing to say?" asked her aunt, all dressed in black and white, and suddenly in a tremendous hurry, as she kept announcing to left and right—"I'm sorry, I'm sorry, but I have things to do . . ." And without further delay, she was already heading out the door, already going down the stairs, crossing the garden-cum-microclimate, and leaving by the creaky wrought-iron gate bearing the name *Villa Regina*. Just like Aunt Ângela Margarida before her, and only then, as kindly Aunt Gininha—hurrying to get back to her baby, little Artemisa—was about to climb into her silver Honda, by which time it was about four o'clock in the afternoon, only then did Milene notice the coincidence. There were phrases that ran in the family genes, as distinctive as those heavy-lidded eyes. In fact, this was the second time someone close to her had promised—*Forever and ever, for as long as you live.* She couldn't believe it.

Aunt Gininha herself had said—"It will be a kind of perpetual calendar, for the rest of your life . . ."

In any other situation, Milene would have responded, as she was perfectly capable of doing, to the person proposing such a plan, but it hadn't been the right moment. They were all suffering for one reason or another, and the siblings had even fallen out because of her. Perhaps, she thought, she'd been rather unfair to them, her poor aunts and uncle, who now asked permission to enter the house and promised not to sit in the forbidden places. Perhaps, the day before, she'd had nothing of any real importance to tell them anyway. After all, she only had two rather insignificant ideas, created inside her own head, with the sole aim of getting free of them. Did she really have anything so very urgent to tell them? Not really. First, that she didn't know how her grandmother had died, but she had helped to bury that *thing*. Second, she hadn't spoken to the newspapers, who had reached their own conclusions. And she could have added a third idea, although she wasn't sure how valid it was. The sense that Grandma Regina hadn't stayed in the cemetery. When the earth had closed over her, and the surplus earth, forming a shape rather like a madeleine, had been heaped with the flowers, Grandma Regina was no longer there. But they mustn't ask if her grandmother had somehow escaped on the way to the cemetery or had evaporated at that precise moment. Because she knew this had happened, but not how or when. And that's all she would have wanted to say, which was very little and extremely vague. Such trifles, though, wouldn't have justified her aunts and uncle giving her more space at that family meeting. She had memorized all the words that had come her way during those last few days, as easily as she used to learn by heart the things João Paulo said. And because of her, her aunts and uncle had come up with that terrible plan—until the end of days. No, she wouldn't allow them to set off along that path.

She wouldn't allow it.

The following morning, Milene—washed and dressed and wearing five bracelets on each arm—picked up the phone and said— "*João Paulo? I waited all night, and you didn't call me back . . . This is just to say that my aunts and uncle were here again. They have a plan for me and for them which is supposed to last for the rest of my life . . . Do you remember how we had a plan too, but ours was really good, and just thinking about their plan makes me feel quite sick . . . it makes me feel like throwing up right now, for their sake and for mine . . . Anyway, I'll tell you about it later . . . 'Bye."* Milene had put on a CD at the far end of the room, so that she could make that phone call. In the intervals between her words, the voice of Cyndi Lauper could again be heard, as if she were singing from some hiding place beneath the floorboards. Milene waited a moment before adding—*"Did you go to Miami with Lavinia?"* Silence. *"Do you know who's singing? Guess. It's her. Twelve Deadly Cyns . . . Go on, call me back . . . I'm really going to say goodbye now. Call me . . . 'Bye."* Milene put the phone down very gently. The click the phone made on disconnecting did not depend on the human hand, the phone itself decided what sound to make. The phone was in charge. It wasn't a good sound. But no matter. She knew her cousin João Paulo would call back soon, saying, as he always did, that the three inseparable cousins would never be separated. And regardless of where they were, the separation would only be brief. Milene sat down near the phone. She waited. It was then that things began to move very fast.

João Paulo used to say that freedom lay in us, but that fate lay in circumstances, which we, being ignorant, imagined to be gods. Circumstances were the almost absolute monarchs of our lives. In this case, they *were* absolute, if we bear in mind what Milene was living through, and which would only be revealed two years later.

So Milene waited with the music still playing. She was in no hurry, she could wait.

A few days later, she again had the music blasting, while outside, someone was furiously sounding a car horn. It was a beautiful late afternoon in Kilometer 44. The neighboring houses were empty. Milene went over to one of the windows and saw a gray van and a man standing next to it. It was Felícia Mata's widowed son. There he was, in the middle of the street, insistently sounding his horn, with the driver's door open and his three children sitting in the back. Yes, it was him, the perennially agitated Antonino Mata. When he saw her, he couldn't help showing her how irritated he was. He jabbed his finger at her—"I've been standing out here for ages sounding my horn, while you're in there with the music on full-blast. You couldn't even hear me, could you?"

His voice sounded exactly as it had when, on another occasion, he'd suddenly turned the peak of his baseball cap to one side. A strong voice, but a bit hoarse, with a slight catch in it. Perhaps irritated by his own voice, he said—"You up there with that racket, and me down here, honking and honking . . ." She remembered the moment when he'd gone down into the crater of that construction site and told her not to move so that his foreman could see her. That's how he was speaking to her now. Milene hurried to the gate and clanged it shut behind her.

He shouted—"Have you got your car key?"

Yes, she had.

"Get in"—he said. "Show me the key. Anyone would think you wanted to leave your car outside our door just to cause trouble. Do you know how long it's been since you abandoned it there? I bet you don't. Six days, nearly a week . . ."

When she didn't respond, he accelerated so hard that the children in the back were thrown against their seats. She grabbed the door handle, and although he did check to see that the kids were all right, he didn't slow down. The van continued to race down the road, and he kept grumbling about her not having heard the horn, and especially about the time ticking past on his wrist, for he kept glancing at his watch as if he had another important appointment to keep. An important commitment. When he came to the turn that led to the shortcut through Bairro dos Espelhos, he hesitated. At the last moment, though, almost at the beginning of that dirt road, he swerved and headed instead in the direction of the gas station. Twenty minutes later, they were outside the Old Factory. Even before he stopped, however, he honked his horn several times and only then did he jump out and help his tearful, sleepy children out too. Milene headed straight for the Clio. He shouted—"Now, don't play that trick on me. The people here want to see you . . ."

And it was true.

The blue glow of Mar de Prainhas was still visible, but all around, it was rapidly growing dark. The shapes of the palm trees stood out against the vaulted world of dusk, and some melancholy thing had alighted on their branches and now stretched out as far as the eye could see. Milene felt that this same melancholy had somehow penetrated her very being, as if she were nothing and the world was everything. However, that sense that she didn't exist, that she was of no use to anyone, lasted only an instant; the Matas were already coming toward her, those people of the third wave, calling her by name. Children and women all eager to talk to her. Wounded by Milene's silence, Felícia addressed her in loud, injured tones—"Dona Milene! Why not even a phone call to tell me how it went with your aunts and uncle? Were they nice to you?" And she answered her own question—Of course they were, Dona Milene had been worrying about nothing. And Felícia also wanted to know if they'd been impressed that she'd slept in Janina's bed. No? Oh well, one day they would be. Meanwhile, how had she managed without her Clio? Did she have another car? No? So how had she coped? When Felícia learned that Grandma Regina's granddaughter had walked for thirty

minutes along a busy road to get a pizza, she was horrified—
"But there was no need, Dona Milene! Why spend hours walking down a dangerous road when you had your car here? You
obviously wanted to make life harder for yourself. But why? Why
struggle when you don't have to? It's quite wrong. Keep that for
when you have no choice but to struggle, okay? Keep your feet for
when you don't have any other form of transport. Your car was
here and all you had to do was phone, one of my sons would have
come to fetch you . . ."

Did Milene not want to come in? To eat? To chat? Well, then,
when would she be back? Soon? For example, she could come on
the day Janina was going to be on television. It was supposed to
be quite soon, but they didn't yet know the exact date, let alone
the time. They were all surrounding her, with only Ana Mata and
Heitor's dad still standing by the gates, near the scene of Grandma
Regina's tragic death. Along with the two flowerpots and those
puny geraniums. Well, if Dona Milene wanted to get back home,
that was fine. They were all friends again. Felícia embracing her,
and the younger women, Claudina and Conceição, saying that
the orange Bermuda shorts were a present and she didn't need
to return anything. We're all friends here, come back soon. *Ciao.*
'Bye, now, and remember, you're a very intelligent young woman,
very kind, and quite simply fabulous. A real gem. Come back
soon. We don't want to phone you or go to your house because we
don't want to bother you, so you must come to us when Janina's
on television. All right? *Ciao, ciao.* 'Bye. Lots of love. Milene got
into her car, smiling, her many bracelets tinkling. Her bag getting in the way, whether she wore it at the front or the back. She
was suddenly feeling pleased with life again, now that night had
fallen, a good night. But then the Clio wouldn't start.

"Won't it start?"

No, it wouldn't. The women and the children gathered around

the car. Perhaps it's out of water, or oil, perhaps it's because it's been standing there all this time in the broiling sun. The same thing happens sometimes with Janina's van. We push it, but it still doesn't go. Then we push it again, and it does. Who knows why? Everyone looking at her. Even Ana Mata. Felícia leaning into the Clio—"What do you think's wrong?"

"Antonino, come and take a look at Dona Milene's car!" she shouted.

Antonino was already there. He had appeared in the doorway dressed quite differently. He didn't look his usual self at all. No baseball cap, and wearing white trainers and a light-colored shirt. It was as if he'd decided to cast off his mourning, right at the very moment when she came to fetch her car. The whole of him glowing in the shadowy night. In a flash, she saw everything. This was an important day in Antonino's life, but there she was again, that wretched, needy, rather dim-witted girl, who, in the past, had been carried off in a bundle of laundry, with the name Milene already written on her forehead, but who meant nothing to him, nothing at all, yes, there she was, their paths crossing yet again. Antonino was standing, hands on hips, looking at her. As if he couldn't believe what he was seeing—"What's the matter now?"

"Antonino, please!" Felícia said beseechingly. "I know you're all dressed up and smelling nice, but there's no other man around at the moment. You've got to take a look at this engine, or she'll never be able to get home . . ."

Antonino turned away in despair.

"Oh, don't be mean. Just for once, let go of your anger. Come and take a look . . ." Felícia said.

Antonino slouched reluctantly over to his van and returned with a flashlight. He opened the hood of the Clio to inspect it, fiddled around with some vital part, and reached in to switch on the engine. Then, half turning, he bent over the dashboard and said—"It's nearly out of gas. You'll have to drive to the gas station, but be careful, because you might run out on the way there."

"But what if she does break down halfway there? In the same sad places where her grandmother got lost? Just the sight of them must make Dona Milene's heart sink."

Antonino jumped into his gray van and yelled—"Come on, then, you go ahead of me. This is getting to be a habit . . ." The Clio in front, and the van behind. Driving down the potholed road, with no streetlights until they reached the gas station, and there, suddenly, the fluorescent lighting in the canopy served as a reminder of the circumstances that had led to an ambulance, its rear doors wide open, heralding the start of her grandmother's extraordinary escapade. Not that Milene or anyone else could have known that. But circumstances—the absolute rulers of our lives, according to João Paulo—were once again about to weave their webs.

Milene had filled her tank in the self-service area, with her back to Antonino, assuming that he would have continued on his way, but when she turned around, he was still there. Antonino was watching from a distance, suspecting that she hadn't come out with enough money. And he was right to be suspicious, because instead of going straight over to the cashier to pay, Milene was ferreting around inside the car. She then got out, jumped up and down and shook herself, scanning the ground where the thing she was looking for might have fallen, then opening her bag again and again. Finally, she crawled into the backseat and emerged with her credit card, on which she bestowed a grateful kiss. And beneath the fluorescent lights of the gas station, Milene continued to kiss her credit card, with really smacking kisses, her eyes sometimes open, sometimes closed. Antonino burst out of his van.

"What the hell are you doing?"

Milene was now rubbing her card on her sleeve.—"This silly idiot had hidden itself away in the back of the car." And as if the card, in those circumstances, represented an inexplicable victory over the web of dependency that bound her to that man, who really should have left by now, she again kissed her card and, without turning around, ran over to the shop to pay. And, still without turning around, she said—"You can go now. I'll be fine . . ."

Out of caution, he still didn't leave.

You could never be sure with an unpredictable person like her. Who knew what to expect from someone who parked her car just anywhere and forgot about it and who kissed credit cards lost and found? Antonino was parked on the roadside, waiting to see if she drove off in the right direction. She did. He could safely let her go. He still hesitated, though, then followed her down the highway. Following behind her Clio until they reached Villa Regina, as if he doubted she could find her way home. However, when they reached Kilometer 44, Antonino didn't just stop, he was so intrigued that he got out of the car. He had already reached the conclusion that following this girl was like boarding a ghost train, full of surprises. This only proved it.

"What's that? A spaceship?" he asked.

"What?" said Milene.

"That."

He was referring to Villa Regina with all its lights on.

The light from the open windows spilled out over the dark surroundings, like a string of bright quadrangular objects fallen from who knows where. The highway was pointing all its signposts in the other direction, and the deserted houses all around were absent and opaque. It was as if Villa Regina were not quite connected to the earth. The top half of the walnut tree was all lit up and its leaves glowed green and rubbery. At first Antonino didn't know what to think, apart from it being a terrible waste of electricity. Then he took a few steps toward the gate and said—"You mean you're going to live here all alone? You're not, you can't . . ."

Antonino was not only wearing a light-colored shirt and white shoes, he was also wearing a lot of aftershave. He had obviously taken a shower after work, because his skin gleamed. His head gleamed, his cheeks gleamed. And Milene wasn't sure whether or not to respond to that man who could change, from one moment to the next, into someone in a terrible hurry, so abrupt and rude. She knew him now. She knew how he could turn the peak of his baseball cap to one side, and yet even when he was yelling at her, his voice took on a softer, almost feminine note. He didn't appear to be in quite such a hurry now, and, standing outside Villa Regina, he asked—"You're not, are you?" She explained that, no, she wouldn't be living there alone, that soon, every night, she would have the company of a family member. And Milene told him about the perpetual calendar and a little about what had happened. The bare minimum. Antonino stood before that brightly lit house, listening in silence. Asking her very short questions that demanded much longer answers than she wanted to give. No, he wasn't in a hurry at all. Or else that hurry was now less pressing. When Milene told him about the calendar, that plan, like an endless diary, just to hear what someone else might think, he said—"No way . . ."

"What's your name again? Milene? Well, Milene, I'm not saying they're lying to you, I'm not saying that, but, in practice, it's simply unsustainable . . ."

"Unsustainable?"—she said, and her bracelets tinkled.

"Unworkable, unviable, yes, unsustainable. Right? I'd give the whole thing a week at most. They'll soon forget all about it. It's just impossible . . ."—He spoke slowly so that she could understand. Spacing out his words. It wasn't really necessary, but that's how he spoke. His way of speaking at odds with his actions, because he was clearly still in a tremendous hurry. Circumstance alone was covering up his desire for action and speed. A temporary conceal-ment. At that moment, he wasn't looking at his watch, and had even begun zigzagging his way back to his van. He got in, leaving the door open. He was waiting. In no hurry. "Go in"—he said. "Go into the house, and I'll wait here . . ." The dark night, which had settled now on that old road, was swallowing him up. She could see his light-colored shirt, waiting inside the van, as she went up the brilliantly lit stairs inside, past the wide-open win-dows, from where she looked out at him, his van still waiting with the driver's door open, then closed, motionless, enveloped by the dark. Then setting off, gliding away down the road. Disappearing into the darkness.

VII

WITH JULIANA, MILENE WOULD DEVELOP A RATHER PARADOX-
ical relationship. An ambiguous relationship, the kind that forms
between someone who has always been ordered around and knows
only the pathways of obedience, and someone who doesn't know
how to give orders and yet needs to exert authority, however fleetingly. A mutual distrust, a double humiliation, settling in between
them. Two weaknesses in one. An inevitable farce. The maid
was barely through the door before she asked unceremoniously—
"What do you want me to do, then?" Without so much as a hello.
Not that it mattered. Milene was already trotting through the
house, leading the way, showing the woman what just needed a
quick wipe-down and what needed a thorough clean, which cloths
she should use, and which equipment, speaking very loudly, trying to sound like Grandma Regina. Don't do that, do this—"See
those armchairs over there? Just remember they belong to her, and
you're never to sit in them. Never in your life, do you understand?"

Juliana didn't say yes or no. She glanced at her watch, shaking it so that it slipped from her wrist to her hand, then holding
it tight in her palm as if it were a grenade—"Look, I got here at
three on the dot, okay?" And she went into the kitchen, put down
her bag and her helmet, and asked—"What's all this about me
sitting in Dona Regina's armchairs? Have I ever sat there before?

Honestly . . ." Then she launched into some questions of her own, fixing her eyes on Milene—"But why are you so cheerful? And what's with all the cleaning? All the high spirits? Isn't this house meant to be in mourning?"

In response, Milene turned up the volume on the stereo that contained various CDs, five at a time. Sick of Cyndi Lauper, with her red hat and sultry, dead-sheep eyes, she had gone back to Simple Minds, the tracks "Ghostdancing" and "Big Sleep" ricocheting off the walls. Next up were the Waterboys, whose sighs, keys, strings, and rumbling drums spread through the whole house. Milene could barely make herself heard. She yelled over the music, in the direction of the kitchen—"Open all the blinds, Juliana. And the windows too, please. Then I'll close them when it gets dark. Okay?"

Juliana, who was around forty years old, checked her watch and said—"Oh Lord, she's going to come back down to earth with a bump, and how . . . What on earth am I doing here?" But she went from window to window and opened the blinds all the way. Light gushed in, eviscerating the house. Her hands on her hips—"I'm not sure if I'll do everything you tell me to. Now that Grandma Regina's not here anymore to give orders . . . This is all going to end in tears, I can tell. Have you had lunch yet? Do you have anything for dinner?" asked Juliana, surrounded by brooms and other cleaning materials. Milene didn't hear, still wandering around, with Mike Scott and Jim Kerr keeping her company, spinning away unseen inside the stereo, so alive, a live recording speaking to her, to her directly, spreading happiness into every crevice of the house.

"It's six o'clock," said Juliana, when it wasn't far off.

"Six o'clock already? Okay, you can go."

Juliana was speaking too loudly as well—"Don't forget to write down my hours . . ." Suspecting that Milene wasn't paying atten-

tion, she went into the kitchen herself and, in her crooked, sloping hand, wrote, *Three Hours*, in the box for Thursday. "Now,
take care of yourself, okay? Here all alone, you're going to get
very mixed up . . ." And Juliana, rushed and brusque, already out
in the courtyard in her jacket and helmet, got onto her motorbike and screeched away down the road. *Three Hours*, don't forget. I'll do more hours tomorrow. How many? Juliana didn't mind
the work. But she'd only keep coming as long as the girl, home
alone and out of control, didn't have a total meltdown, which
she thought might happen any day. Milene, meanwhile, all kinky
hair and heavy eyelids, was waving out of one of the first-floor
windows, wearing her very short shorts, the dangly earrings that
Grandma Regina used to like, and lots of bracelets on each wrist.
"Take care, watch out for thieves and burglars!" Juliana advised
her before setting off. It wasn't clear if Juliana only ever saw dangers, if this was the finer stuff of her imagination, through which
she filtered the reality of her world. Nonetheless, once Juliana had
gone, all that stood between Milene and the dangers, known and
unknown, were the windows. The windows separating her from
intruders, from dust and the sound of the motorway that passed
just a few hundred yards from the house, rising and curving, a
tightly wound intersection shaped like a snake.

But in between too there were the phone calls from her aunts.

The clamor of the telephone filled the house, making Milene jump.
No, it wasn't João Paulo, it was Aunt Gininha, whom Grandma
Regina had made her executor, and she was, it seemed, speaking
in that capacity, still absorbed in that flurry of grief-stricken pacing, promising to read the will, mentioning sums of money, buying and selling, abstract notions, and repeating, *Milene, Milene*, as
if her niece's name were the new chorus of some ubiquitous bal-

lad. Milene replied—"Aunt Gininha? It's fine, I don't want to go to your house. Relax . . ." On the other end, Aunt Gininha was silent, and all the noises in the world of Valmares had stopped. Two white clouds up above, suspended and still. And then Aunt Gininha, caught off guard, surprised and not knowing what to say—"Any day, any day, Milene, any day . . ." But there was no need for her aunt to continue the song much longer. Everyone knew that Aunt Gininha was tragically unhappy, to borrow an expression from Grandma Regina. Everyone knew too that part of Aunt Gininha no longer belonged to her. For years, a percentage of her aunt had been the property of Uncle Dom Silvestre. When her aunt said, *Milene, Milene*, even Milene knew what the words concealed. Behind that tremulous repetition lay the story of Aunt Gininha's love affairs.

And suddenly Aunt Gininha was phoning her, as if the underlying situation had been turned on its head—"Milene? Come over . . ."

How could she possibly go there? Milene was completely taken aback. She knew enough about her aunt's past and present life not to believe the invitation. As regards the present, she knew that Uncle Dom would be at the Amurada house, and that was quite enough. And as for the past, she knew that Aunt Gininha's husband had been just one of her many boyfriends, the final one, and although that didn't explain everything, it certainly explained a lot.

Yes, between the ages of fourteen and thirty she'd had hundreds of boyfriends. During the summer of 1985 alone, after the Old Factory was given back, in the space of just two months Aunt Gininha had turned up with two different boyfriends, each of whom appeared to be "the one."

The first was a taciturn and rather sleepy pilot, so sleepy that no one understood how he could fly Boeings through the sky without accidentally dozing off. Then there had been a natural sciences professor who wore a magnifying glass around his neck, which he used to examine pieces of bivalve mollusk shells. Things hadn't worked out with either of them. She had broken up with the first for being so sleepy. It was as if the pilot, a handsome man in his forties—who, when he was awake, even sang romantic songs while resting his head on her aunt's shoulder—had been infected by the somnolence of the clouds. Milene's aunt was right. If they had ever lived together, what with all the flights and naps, would there have been any energy left for the couple's private world? What would have belonged to her? One day, after the pair had eaten lunch together, she had left him snoozing alone in a seaside restaurant, with a note written on a napkin asking him not to contact her again. As for the second, a somewhat pedestrian soul, Aunt Gininha had left him when she realized she'd spend the rest of her life traipsing along behind him, up and down the length of Mar de Prainhas, an area of the planet where this modern-day Darwin was convinced he would find ancient and long-disappeared species. The professor collected oyster shells, particularly pink pearl oysters, and on that final vacation he spent half his time following Gininha around like a second shadow, and half of it stooped down over the surf, foam swilling around him, bottom in the air like a flamingo. By the time *the best summer of our lives* had come to an end, Gininha had washed her hands of both boyfriends.

Which didn't seem to matter at all.

"Milene? Are you coming?"—her aunt kept asking that afternoon, on the other end of the phone, sounding desperate. But why was her aunt so desperate?

———

By the summer of 1985, people had begun to think that Aunt Gininha was searching for something she would never find in the men she endlessly fell in and out of love with. What her aunt wanted—that nonexistent figure or unnameable reality—seemed to be hidden away in some impossible place. A fantasy that existed only for her. This, at least, was what João Paulo had said that summer, when he saw their aunt glowing as she said her goodbyes to the natural sciences professor, still kissing him on the mouth, and handing him a little bag of mother-of-pearl shells. All the same, her classmates went on calling her the Mermaid because of her long, slender waist, everyone behaving as if she'd be twenty forever, and her future, whichever way you looked at it, seemed assured. Meanwhile, her nieces and nephews adored her and the Ô by Lancôme that emanated from her clothes, and most of all they loved the way she hugged them. She was free again, Aunt Gininha, at the end of the summer of 1985. But that was when two events, unexpected and interlinked, had thrown her completely off balance.

"Milene? Milene, sweetheart, come over. I'm at home, waiting for you . . ."

Two events: The first had taken place in Joseldo's hair salon. Aunt Gininha had just spent three consecutive months in the open air, stretched out in the sun beside her two boyfriends, running, swimming, relaxing, and on returning to Valmares, looking more svelte and tanned than ever, she had given herself over to the attentions of the hairdresser on the marina. But the assistant who tied on her cape had a nasty surprise, because suddenly, unmistakably, all over Aunt Gininha's head, white hairs had appeared as if they'd sprouted up like seeds. What had happened?

A shocked Joseldo had shared his staff's astonishment, examining the head in question and making emphatic pronouncements. A big event. So that everyone could take a look, the hairdresser had held Aunt Gininha's long hair up above her, bringing over a lamp so she could see the damage for herself, and, as if the whole thing brought him some secret satisfaction, Joseldo the hairdresser had begun giving orders, raising his voice, as if enthusiastically unveiling a monument to his own work. It was declared that from that day on, every other week, it would be necessary to dye Aunt Gininha's lovely hair. Quick, a bowl, a spatula, some black foam, all mixed and mixed some more, and then the resulting syrupy concoction was poured, for the first time, onto Aunt Gininha's head. And that was that. Joseldo bouncing up and down, rubbing his hands—*Here you are, you've made it, I didn't expect you so soon. And now you'll always come back* . . . Meanwhile, Gininha, looking very pale in front of the mirror, her soul longing to be living on the other side of her image. You'll be back, you'll be back. It was then, during that change-laden autumn, that she sank into a long depression, interspersed with bouts of flu brought on by the warm, wet easterly wind.

This was the beginning of an event that would have endless repercussions.

"Come quick . . ."—said Aunt Gininha, for the fifth time that afternoon. Milene hesitating. Would she go? Or wouldn't she?

The name of the second event was Domitílio Silvestre, but he played out in a rather different way. He was in a separate category altogether. In three stages.

First, word had reached Villa Regina, from the family's lawyer, that someone recently returned from South Africa was interested in buying some land that Grandma Regina owned in

Lentiscal, next to an abandoned quarry. Then Grandma Regina had received a phone call from a voice with an English accent, and soon after that a man of medium height, with dark hair and small, lively eyes, had rung the doorbell at Kilometer 44. It was Domitílio Silvestre, the buyer. Even then, Domitílio Silvestre drove a powerful car, with an enormous wolf-like dog asleep on the backseat. It was a warm, flucy winter, and Aunt Gininha was at the height of her depression about her hair. When the buyer arrived to discuss the purchase, mournful strains of Chopin were pouring into the living room and collecting around Aunt Gininha. No, they needn't go to any trouble, the buyer would be very quick, he just wanted to know about the patch of land in Lentiscal. Would she sell it or not? Yes, Grandma Regina said, she would, it was just a matter of agreeing on a price, though she was still wondering how useful a patch of rocky ground would be in a place like that, a scrap of wasteland next to an abandoned quarry. What did Gininha think?

Gininha hadn't left the living room, but she had considerably reduced the volume of the music, those droplets of sound assailing her senses like drafts of mandrake tea. With her fingers in her hair, Gininha had been listening to the negotiation, sitting up very straight. And Dom Silvestre had shaken his head—"Disused? Oh, ma'am, please!" *Ma'am*, as if he were still in South Africa. It wasn't disused at all. Faced with the word *disused, a disused quarry*, even his eyes seemed to laugh, darting back and forth between mother and daughter. "It's only disused, ma'am, until somebody uses it . . ." And what's more, he was very knowledgeable. Domitílio Silvestre spoke with an English accent and slipped English words into his sentences, with all the technical mining terms in English as well, and, as it happened, Gininha taught that very language. At that point, the sad music had stopped.

"Name your price. What do you say?"

———

But nothing would happen between them until one month later, when Domitílio Silvestre came to show the five-year renewable license that would allow him to exploit the Lentiscal Quarry, which had previously been placed under seal. On the document were the words *PORTUGUESE REPUBLIC*, with the watermark and national coat of arms. That day, Domitílio Silvestre's intensely dark eyes had shone with happiness, revealing an energy that made even the stillest parts of Grandma Regina's living room tremble. He had come to ask whether or not they would sell him the land. And the returnee from South Africa was so honest that, in light of this permit, he was now offering far more money for the patch of rocky ground. Not double, but almost—"What do you say?" For a moment, Grandma Regina grew thoughtful. Then, seized by generosity and resolving to meet the situation head-on, Regina Leandro sold the land to that man for the original price. And she didn't even object to her daughter Gininha going out for a two-hour drive in that car with the wolf-like dog dozing in the back.

"Come on, even the garden's waiting for you . . ." Gininha said insistently into the telephone, on that hot September afternoon. "I'm making us some dinner."

And so, outside Villa Regina, the dog had growled and circled around on the backseat of the powerful car, before sitting down at the sound of Domitílio Silvestre's commanding voice saying in English—"Sit, Buggy, sit . . ." It was another mild winter afternoon and the pair had installed themselves in the lounge of the Luxor Hotel, among the heavy-hanging drapes. Then, growing restless, the buyer had taken her to look at the quarry, a long, deep crater of terraced earth, in which he saw a kind of biblical grandeur, and so, with some effort, did she. Next they visited the Amurada site, where Domitílio had begun building a house that would bear his name. Some gray walls stood among the beeches and low plane trees, wrapped in protective plastic sheeting. He put the dog on the leash, and the animal bounded along by his side—"Sit, sit, Buggy! On the ground . . ." And then, two months later, they were married.

Everyone heard about it.

Grandma Regina, however, had disapproved of such haste. It was one thing for a girl to go for a drive on a winter afternoon because she was depressed, but quite another to get married, just like that, to someone who talked about business ventures that sounded suspiciously vague. Most of all, Grandma Regina thought it a bad omen that her daughter's relationship with that man had emerged from the fraudulent text on a paid-for permit, a piece of paper obtained through a bribe. Yes, of that she was certain. Months later, when it became clear that her son-in-law was never at home, never ate, never slept, and almost never spoke to Aunt Gininha, in either Portuguese or English, because he was always out doing business, multiplying, proliferating, Grandma Regina felt vindicated and began to call him various things, among them a sly fox. When discussing the matter, Grandma Regina spoke loudly, placing her daughter's situation within universal laws of compensation that she herself had formulated. She said it had taken her youngest daughter until the age of thirty to find a soul coarse enough to balance out the beauty and sensitivity that Nature had given her. The way she saw it, those two attributes were fatal traits that would always end up attracting unpleasantness, superior qualities that had led to her daughter Gininha's sudden infatuation with someone so diametrically opposed. It was the ancestral yearning of beauty for chaos. The incurable attraction of goodness to the dark. When it came to her daughter's husband, chaos and darkness combined to make him a sly fox. In the early days of their marriage, there were rumors of dreadful conjugal scenes. Rumors that the family were ordered never to repeat. Ever.

Grandma Regina's deep disdain for Aunt Gininha's husband had only wavered when, years later, in a family argument about Grandma Regina's decision to hand the *Fábrica de Conservas Leandro 1908* over to the third-wave people, he had been the only one to take her side. True, Regina Leandro had handed it over for unmentionable reasons, but Dom Silvestre saw in his mother-in-law's actions a pragmatic, long-term vision. They were sitting around the table, discussing the Matas, and as he poured himself another drink, he had said—"You did well to let them stay there, Dona Regina, ma'am. Left empty, the place would go to ruin in no time. Even the ground it stands on would be worthless. And listen, if you ask me, those hard little rocks underneath could be worth a pretty penny if we put in the work . . ."

And why not?—Domitílio Silvestre had come from South Africa, he had made the journey from Namibia to Lundo, he knew the region well, having crossed it in a Jeep, he knew all about rocks, their properties, and where they could be sold. He addressed his brother- and sister-in-law, clarifying, enlightening— "You people might as well be blind! Can't you see? It's right under your noses . . . Dona Regina knew what she was doing when she let them use that building. I'd have done the same in her position . . ." That day, Grandma Regina had decided he was an intelligent man. But she soon changed her mind again.

"Come on, please, before it gets dark . . ."—her aunt said into the phone.

Domitílio Silvestre's first lucky break had come thanks to a business card, before he got permission to exploit the Lentiscal

Quarry, and even before he met Aunt Gininha. His full name was too old-fashioned and too long, and, on returning from South Africa, he had asked the printer to shorten it as much as possible, to make the business card he needed look nice and simple. Or better still, practical. So that people knew exactly who he was the moment he pulled out his card. He let the printer think it over. Two days later, there was a beige rectangle on the print-shop counter with just two words in the center— *Dom Silvestre*. It was an inspired move. Everyone said so. By the winter after the summer of 1985, when Domitílio Silvestre had offered Aunt Gininha a gin and tonic in the Luxor lounge, the buyer already went by his abbreviated name. The hotel manager already addressed him familiarly as Dom, and his company was to be called Dom Silvestre Development and Extractive Industries. Meaning that Aunt Gininha would never know him as Domitílio. Only as Dom. And she herself would be referred to, from then on, by friends and acquaintances, as the wife of Dom the quarry guy.

"You can let yourself in. I'll leave the gate open. You can even park your car right outside the garage tonight . . ." said her aunt, on the other end of the line.

Once the family had cut its ties with the Old Factory, and before Uncle Rui Ludovice had been elected mayor, there were people who knew Grandma Regina only as Dom Silvestre's mother-in-law. The less noteworthy family members, including Milene, were known for being related to him. With just one important caveat— that from the very beginning, Uncle Dom had disapproved of Milene. He felt an intense dislike for her, less because of who she was than because of the accumulation of mistakes he thought the family had made with her, as if Milene were the result of some faulty accounting, and this drove him mad. In Uncle Dom's opinion, Milene would have been perfectly normal if she'd had a proper education. And once he was on the subject, he would effusively praise South African schools that had modeled themselves on correction facilities. Schools that were run like prisons.

Things had come to a head, however, during the last vacation João Paulo had spent in Valmares. The family were all at the Amurada house, sitting around the table under the awning, by the pool, with Dom talking about how to educate problematic people by dropping them in the middle of the jungle at dawn and making them find their way back to the starting point, navigating by the sun alone, and other similar techniques—a whole program, where there was sometimes even a suggestion of fasting and beatings—when Milene, taking advantage of a momentary silence, had burst out—"*Oh! Oh! I know a Dom, he's the baker's grandson . . . I know a Dom . . .*"

It had been a very embarrassing moment. Milene said one inappropriate thing after another, and everyone there, stock-still around the table like a frieze of statues, remained silent. Aunt Gininha didn't even blink. Grandma Regina was chewing something, a bundle of wrinkles meeting at the center of her lips and moving in a circle, as if her lips had been sewn together with a needle and thread. Caught in that silence, Milene had asked— "And all the Silvestres went off to work in the mines, in South Africa . . . Right, João Paulo?" Milene looked at Grandma Regina, who continued to maneuver that tough morsel around in her mouth, not looking at anyone. No one looking at anyone. The natural order reversed, strength ambushed by weakness. Just like that, with no word of warning. What's more, it was Uncle Dom's birthday, which was why they were all there at Vivenda Dom Silvestre. And then this had happened. Her uncle's eyes so very small, so very alive, shining in his face like two glowing embers.

Dom Silvestre had thrown his napkin down on his plate—"It's her or me, it's her or me . . ." Again and again, like a scratched record that somehow gathered force with every repetition. His arm outstretched, pointing—"It's her or me, it's her or me . . ." Then Milene had turned and fled from the table, and her uncle, exhausted by his own rage, had sat down. And then stood back up. That day, Uncle Dom didn't return to the table.

"Come on, I'm waiting for you on the terrace, playing with the baby. Are you sure you don't want to come?"—said Gininha on the other end. "Hurry, before it gets dark . . ."

At that time, Gininha and Dom Silvestre barely spoke to one another. Sometimes she needed to, but he didn't have time. There was a patch of rocky ground somewhere on Earth just waiting to be multiplied into millions, and he wouldn't rest until he found it. He knew the great multiplication would come one day. But when? They generally didn't go out together. Grandma Regina used to say that dogs were Uncle Dom's ideal driving companions, because they just growled and didn't ask questions or meddle in his life. As for Aunt Gininha, she tended not to travel in Dom Silvestre's cars. She taught her classes, and went there and back in her own vehicle and had told her sister more than once that Dom Silvestre spoke a kind of Soweto English. Nonetheless, every now and then they did appear in public together, and even after all that time, there were people who still called Dom's wife the Mermaid. The pair would attend drinks receptions at the Yacht Club, side by side, her tall, willowy, attractive, and him very alive and almost small. They went on vacation together too. When they came home, they seemed closer, and Gininha spoke about him more fondly. The part of her that was vulnerable to him somehow replenished. Everyone knew.

———

But that afternoon the telephone didn't stop ringing and it was always Aunt Gininha's voice on the other end—"What are you waiting for? Come over!" Her aunt's voice excited, as if she weren't in mourning, as if she were back in the summer of 1985. And yet, what Aunt Gininha really meant was something else. Something more like—*Come over, because Uncle Dom isn't here tonight, thank goodness* . . . Milene had taken the initiative of picking up the phone—"But what if he comes back?" she asked out of the blue, as if her aunt had said something she hadn't.

Gininha, on the other end, sounding surprised, cutting to the chase—"Well, the thing is, Uncle Dom's gone out with some Dutch people, and when they meet up, they normally take all night to reach an agreement. Uncle Dom won't be home until the early hours . . ." Milene, suspicious—"What if he comes back sooner and finds me there?" Her aunt on the other end, full of patience—"You do exaggerate sometimes. If that happens, you tell the truth. You say you were missing the baby and you just had to come and see her. Really, Milene, there's no need to worry. Come over. Imagine the two of us, all cozy, having dinner together on the terrace, the way your grandma always liked to . . ." Her aunt talking as if we were still in the middle of the *best summer of our lives.*

Then Milene sped off down the road and arrived in no time.

She had gone straight up to see Artemisa, a baby born rather late in the day, a deliberate plan on the part of her uncle, who every now and then thought about his legacy. Grandma Regina had said it was just to keep Aunt Gininha fully occupied, with no time left for anything else. But whatever the reason, or for no reason at all, the baby existed. Milene peered down at the little creature, who had grown so quickly that she couldn't keep still. That restlessness had begun in Gran Canaria, in the days when the catastrophe with Grandma Regina was unfolding. Aunt Gininha had tried in vain to soothe that bundle of human turbulence. The baby moved, rolled over, as if wanting to hurl herself into space, until suddenly, in the midst of all that thrashing around, she fell asleep. A sweaty, defeated little thing, lying limp at the foot of the bed. Milene and Aunt Gininha, arm in arm, wandering calmly through the house, pausing here and there, in the middle of the rooms. No sign of her uncle—"See? See, Milene?"

Dom Silvestre's house wasn't just beautiful. Every decoration and ornament had an entry price and an exit price, the paraphernalia of Aunt Gininha's life accruing value inside that house like gold coins in an invisible bank vault. Paintings, vases, delicate porcelain figurines, modern sculptures that looked more like smooth, weathered rocks, paintings with signatures her aunt deciphered from a distance, Buffet and Vieira da Silva, hanging on the wall above some ivory tusks—"Look, this one's worth a fortune . . ." Her aunt explained that all those pieces had come from people who owed Uncle Dom huge sums of money and weren't paying him back, and that it was very difficult, sometimes, to assess the exact value of such objects, since it was an area her uncle knew nothing about. They had a consultant, someone else who owed her uncle money. Her aunt hovering close, leaning in, drawing her niece toward her, turning away from the treasures and heading out through the garden to the covered terrace. Her aunt saying—"You won't believe what's happened to us. Do you know what Uncle Dom says? That if it weren't for that terrible business with Grandma Regina, we would have stayed in Las Palmas and been none the wiser. Because the awful thing is that while we were away, some people were plotting to liquidate Dom's company . . ."

Plotting against her aunt? Who was plotting? Who?

Aunt and niece, on either side of the table, having dinner on the terrace, the night peaceful, the beech tree lit up. Glasses of prawn mousse, the way Milene liked it. Her aunt confiding in her as if she were a valid confidante. Her aunt telling Milene she wouldn't believe what these people wanted to do—"When we came back, we were facing fines for outrageous amounts, all long overdue. Fines from the state, fines from the council, all at once, and your uncle knew nothing about it. Two more days, and it would have been too late. It's been dreadful, just dreadful . . ."

"Help yourself . . ."—Aunt Gininha had said, chattier now, recovered from the first onset of grief.

"Uncle Dom won't be back anytime soon. Like I say, he's with those Dutchmen. And if it wasn't them, it would be someone else. Last night, for example, your uncle didn't get home until four in the morning. With everything sorted, thank God. By then, those damn papers were kaput . . ." Her aunt explaining in words that seemed to belong to Uncle Dom Silvestre rather than her. It was as if her aunt were distancing herself from her husband, and as if, at the same time, the densest part of him were rising and expanding within her. Milene understood that. Her uncle speaking from her aunt's lips—"No, you'll never really understand, Milene. You see, as far as the inspectors are concerned, the situation is still illegal, so they fine you as much as they can, but if half the fine ends up in their pockets, everything's legal again. The law is shaped like these men's back pockets. Do you understand what I'm saying, Milene?"

Milene understood that someone was plotting against her aunt, and that was quite enough. They both looked out at the garden, where golden reflections glittered on the lawn. Inside the house, the baby, tired out and asleep in the white cot. Bruno José playing with the children next door. Her aunt saying—"Just think, Milene, Uncle Dom only got wind of the setup because we came back early from vacation. Poor, poor Grandma Regina . . ." Aunt Gininha letting her long hair brush against her plate, wondering at those enigmatic laws, laws that regulate wild exchanges between life and death, laws with their parcel of horror and their pinch of utility, which we sometimes benefit from without knowing how. Now her aunt, grown emotional, struggling to swallow the prawn mousse. Aunt Gininha, with two tears landing in her elegant glass. Oh, poor Aunt Gininha . . .

"I'm so glad you came. Do you remember the Lentiscal Quarry?"

The Lentiscal Quarry was no longer a pit of terraced earth resembling an amphitheater, as required by law, but rather a cliff face sloping smoothly down like the inside of a bowl, and yet still an excellent quarry, full of gray limestone, all of it usable and ready for extraction, from the finest grit to the coarsest gravel. Even so, there was no point in her uncle buying more land around it, because they were already up to the backyards of the houses. Milene wouldn't believe the trouble this caused her uncle. Every day there were complaints from private individuals because of the blasts. Papers and more papers. Nor would she believe what it had cost him to make sure those papers went straight into the trash. Even now, her uncle still managed to blast far above the permitted vibration level, because he was the one who owned the seismometer that measured the blasts; the inspectors didn't have one, and they even used to ask him for the readings, for themselves and for other people, when necessary. Yes, Uncle Dom had the device. Which wasn't certified. But which almost was. Certified-ish—"I know, I know, you don't understand. I'm just telling you all this, Milene, so you know we're in a bad way . . ."

Gininha sounding like an extension of her husband. Milene even wished she could say—*Half of Aunt Gininha is Dom Silvestre now, my aunt is speaking out of his mouth. I'm looking at her lips and they're his, not hers, moving up and down . . .* But she couldn't say that. Meanwhile, her aunt was sighing deeply. Why was she sighing? He was the one who answered. Because all it would take to put the kibosh on the Lentiscal Quarry was for someone to certify the seismometer, or some nitpicking bureaucrat to come along and start some tangled legal proceedings. And then what would Uncle Dom do with his life? With our life? Her aunt looking out at the luminous lawn, her aunt wanting her to eat more, much more—"How long can we keep everything going? Just in case, Uncle Dom is extracting as much as possible, getting out everything he can, working night and day. He's spent more than I can tell you on floodlighting, so the machines can work twenty-four seven. But who knows what's going to happen, the situation could change at any moment. Do you see what I'm saying? It's because things are so uncertain that Uncle Dom went to talk to those Dutchmen tonight. We don't know how much longer we'll be able to use the Lentiscal Quarry . . ."

"And then what, Aunt Gininha?"

"Yes, Milene. This is what I've been coming to. We need to think of other options, Milene. Now that poor Grandma Regina has died, we have the necessary conditions. I don't know if you follow me, Milene. It's so difficult to explain . . ."—Aunt Gininha in mourning, in black and white, her white blouse covered by her very long, dark chestnut hair tumbling down over her collar, as if she were a young girl. Aunt Gininha telling her to help herself to more, much more, and saying—"The conditions are there, Milene, and you can even help us. It's about the problem with the Old Factory. But when our *roulement*, our rotation, begins, every three days we'll talk about how you can help if the quarry does close. But now let's change the subject.

"Tell me, Milene, what have you been up to? How are you spending your days? Have you been back to Praia Pequena? Don't you go much to Mar de Prainhas anymore? Wasn't it wonderful when the beach there was all wild . . . I still remember, back in '85. You were as tall as you are now, but for some reason I remember you as much smaller. You three were so funny, coming out of the water and calling to me . . . Are you sure you don't want anything else? I had the fruit salad made just for you. You should really cut your hair too, it's all sticking up. And maybe a dress. Don't you ever wear dresses?" When her aunt stopped talking about the quarry, that pit carved out of the earth, that gaping crater by the ocean from which her uncle had raked in all the money he could want, the part of Uncle Dom that lived inside her disappeared. Once again, Gininha was her beautiful aunt who made you want to hug her, just like the Gininha of the *best summer of our lives*, when she had walked along the shore hand in hand with her two boyfriends.

And there they both were, nearly ten years later, sitting close together, enjoying the warm summer evening. Their arms around each other.

Chatting, sighing. Her aunt completing Milene's syncopated sentences, feeding her fruit salad with the dessert spoon. The murmur of Bruno José's games with the children next door floating over the fence. Milene remembered the sound of the water on the day the gardener had told her that her aunt wasn't at home. But she wasn't going to talk about that. The two of them discussing future beaches, and future summers they would share. Too engrossed to notice anyone arriving, whoever it might be. And yet right there, unmistakable, was the living, breathing opposite of what they were expecting. Someone was walking toward them. But who?

Striding down the path, across the lawn, was Dom Silvestre.

————

Gininha got to her feet.

Yes, it was him, Aunt Gininha's husband, in the flesh, walking toward them with rhythmic, regular steps. Treading now on the paving stones, now on the lawn, advancing toward the terrace. No doubt about it—those were his pale trousers, his almost short legs, his slight paunch, squeezed tight by his belt, yes, this was Uncle Dom in his entirety, lit up by the spherical lamps in the grass, moving in their direction. Aunt Gininha staring, hypnotized, not moving, not saying a word, as if a taut nylon thread had attached her eyes to the toes of Uncle Dom's shoes, which were making their way down the stepping-stones scattered among the long grass. Like a partially visible avalanche. He drew nearer. Her aunt fell back into her chair. The remaining food in the terrine in suspense, the magnificent house in suspense, honor itself in suspense. Aunt Gininha's gentle eyes bulging, covered by a thin layer of ice. *Aunt Gininha? Aunt Gininha?* Then Milene stood up, grabbed her bag, and ran around the side of the house. She raced across the opposite lawn, past a peaceful blue swimming pool where a little peacock often slept beside an artificial waterfall. And then, slipping through the still-open gate, Milene vanished from the scene.

VIII

MILENE LEAPT INTO HER CAR WITHOUT A BACKWARD GLANCE. She flew down the road, and only stopped when she saw the phone waiting for her on Grandma Regina's coffee table. Her heart was racing. She dialed. She heard—*If you want to leave a message for Lavinia or João Paulo, please do so after the tone. Thanks. 'Bye . . .* Her heartbeat slowed. "No, he's still not there"—But she needed him to be there at the other end of the line, so that she could talk to him about a particularly sad thought that had assailed her while her Clio was speeding down the road. With her car taking the bends perilously fast, as she somehow managed to keep control of the wheel, she had come to the conclusion that the good were not strong and the strong were not good, and while there were many horrible weak people, she had yet to come across many strong good people. Why? What did goodness have to do with strength? Were the two qualities mutually repellent? Even in João Paulo? Could a good person not be good and impose his goodness on others? And if he did impose his goodness, would he be using the same methods used by bad people? It was just a thought she'd had, but she found it deeply troubling. She even knew of cases that exemplified the different categories, but could think of no example of someone who was both very good and very strong. That's what she wanted to say to João Paulo, if he was there. But he was still not in his wooden house with the tin roof on the other side of the Atlantic. He had still not returned from Miami or some other such place, accompanied by Lavinia. But perhaps he would come back that very night and call her. She would sit and wait. She wouldn't even listen to music, just so that she could pick up the phone at the first ring—*João Paulo? Goodness, I've been thinking and thinking. The good are very weak, the bad are very strong, and the others are a little of everything. That's all I have to say to you today . . .*

We would find out two years later.

Also on Grandma Regina's coffee table was Milene's address book, with, on the cover, Lord Snowdon's photograph of a very young Meryl Streep perched in a tree. Next to the words *Personal Addresses*. It was a small tome, filled with writing in Milene's round hand. While she waited for the phone to ring, Milene was reading through the names and numbers and crossing them out. The agony she had felt after what had happened in Aunt Gininha's garden was gradually ebbing away as she selected addresses to deselect. She needed to forget about the moment she'd caught sight of Dom walking across the lawn toward the house. She even imagined he'd been there all along, frozen, waiting for the right time to appear. In order to catch them out and destroy them. Milene had her pen between her fingers—*Right, there's a name that can disappear*—ANABELA. Anabela was the same age as her but had married years ago and devoted her days to her children, as if her one role in the world were to ferry children back and forth to school. Her life was a form of enslavement, it really was. She crossed her out. And Isabel?—She crossed out ISABEL and crossed out JAIME, people who were of no interest to her anymore either, being too deeply involved in their very serious jobs.

Working from morning to night in offices, like machines. She would sometimes drop by and wait for hours, but they were always heads down, hands occupied, every minute of the day filled. Cross them out. And then there was her old friend LUÍSA. Luísa used to work in a record shop with a window facing the Marina. It was a lovely window, with reflections of the yachts superimposed on the records. That's where she'd bought the albums chosen by *Blitz* as the very best. Ever since they closed the shop, though, she'd heard no more from Luísa. She probably had a new boyfriend and was working in some other record store; she hadn't been in touch. Cross her out. And on it went, crossing-out after crossing-out. JOANA, PAULA, SARA, VERINHA, brief friendships all crossed out. What she should really do is cross out the names of her aunts and uncles. So as to forget them and their proposed rotation. The only reason she didn't was because she felt she ought to wait until the days shortened, and see what happened with that perpetual calendar of theirs. She didn't believe it would happen, and she didn't want it to. But she was curious. Then Milene flipped through her address book several times and found what she was looking for. On one of the last pages, in a slanting hand, was the name Violante.

VIOLANTE.

And no, she wasn't going to cross this name out.

Violante was not yet sixteen, but it was as if they'd been born on the same day of the month and were exactly the same age. They liked the same music and talked about the same things. Violante, like Milene, loved the water, and while she swam, she would talk to the sea. They held the same conversations with the sea—"Come on . . . That's it . . . See that one over there, let's hold hands and head for that big one . . ." They would talk to the waves, when the warm wind was blowing from the southeast and when, for two or three days, the sea turned white and seemed genuinely threatening. They would hold hands, raise their arms, and, clinging bravely to each other, confront the waves. The waves would force them apart and knock them over. Violante would shout—"Ooh, you bastard, I got a real mouthful then . . ." The two of them laughing and spluttering. The two of them holding hands again and wading back into the sea—"Come on, let's piss in it . . ." Then, worn out, they would lie down on the sand, no need for towels. Milene had owned her car for three years, and their friendship dated from around then, when Violante had accepted a lift from her. At the time, Violante was only thirteen. Milene was more than twice her age, but during the summer, it was as if they were twin sisters. They hated the same things. They loved the same things. They even looked rather alike. And if, during the winter, they saw less of each other, this was only because Violante spent every evening, every endless Saturday, Sunday, and holiday studying, and so she wasn't often free. And unfortunately, during that last summer, they had scarcely spoken.

There was a bar on Praia Pequena where Violante worked serving coffee and soft drinks, and so she was only free either far too early in the morning, or in the evening after sunset. Milene would arrive about eleven o'clock, go for a swim and a run, then sit at the bar, waiting for Violante to have a free moment, which never happened. Even so, it had become her favorite beach, so much so that Milene had entirely abandoned the beach at Mar de Prainhas. She just never went there. And she had gone straight to Praia Pequena on that Monday, the eighteenth of August, when it had occurred to her to look for proof that her grandmother had passed that way en route from the gas station to the Diamond, and she had, quite fruitlessly, ended up questioning the people who lived there, with all the ensuing hullaballoo. Now it was already halfway through September, but since the phone still hadn't rung and her thoughts about the division between good people and bad people had returned to where they came from, Milene had decided to go find Violante.

Why not? Violante might still be at Praia Pequena, and, if so, the two of them could once again join hands and do battle with the waves, plunging into them, almost losing their swim-suits in the process, with the waves bearing down on them and the two of them shrieking with delight. Perhaps. Sitting by the phone, Milene promised herself that, yes, she would go and see Violante again, and the very next day she did just that, but as soon as she got near the beach, she realized that nothing would happen as she expected it to.

Not a soul to be seen. Even the swirling sand seemed weary. The waves stood up beneath the effect of the east wind, and then, as if they'd already done their bit for humanity, returned to their solitary watery existence. The waves rose up, revealed themselves, then fell back, in obedience to some undulatory law, absolute and totalitarian. They disappeared, became nothing, only water, then were reborn as if they were the throats of living beings impris-oned in the horizontal. Breaking free from that identity, they rose, curled, and fell, stretching out like a sheet of foam, and when that wall of water collapsed onto the water beneath, which had only that moment ceased to be a wave, along came another. And another and another. Irresistible, loud. In previous years, when no one else was around, the two of them used to go out together and face those waves. On that day too the beach was deserted. Every-thing seemed set and ready for them to hurl themselves into the water now. Milene could already feel the waves tugging at them. Violante was there. The bar was open. Milene walked over. *Vio-lante?* Violante wasn't there.

She must be somewhere close by. A few bottles were lined up on the wooden counter. The coffee machine was on, and there was a pool of spilled coffee around the container for the grounds. On the boardwalk white napkins were flying about as if they had deliberately been released into the air by the dispensers on the tables. Inside she saw Violante's bag and a beach hat identical to her own. They'd bought their hats at the same time. A sweater was hanging from a hook. Yes, she must be somewhere close by.

Still calling Violante's name, Milene went around the bar and saw her friend.

No, at first she didn't see her.

She saw only Violante's back merged with some larger object, her face invisible, and on her head a hand not her own. What's more, Violante wasn't sitting on the bench itself, but on a pair of knees sticking out from the bench, two long legs wearing ripped jeans. And her head wasn't raised, but resting on another person's shoulder and covered by the hand holding it up. Violante's arms were hidden, as if she didn't have any of her own, and was enfolded instead by the arms of someone else. Both Violante's face and the face of the person holding her were hidden. Two invisible faces. It felt to Milene as if Violante were disappearing into that other unknown figure. She wanted to say—*Violante?* And it was as if she had.

The person holding her friend finally looked up and revealed himself. A boy. His eyes fixed briefly on Milene's face, then looked down again at Violante, who couldn't see her. And Milene called again, this time more loudly. But the boy looked up and gestured to her to be quiet. It was as if he were saying—*Now that you've found us, go away, shut up* . . . The boy's face once more disappeared behind Violante's hair, which he kept moving around with

powerful, circular motions of his fingers. Milene thought he might
be about to kill her.

"Hey!"

What was he doing? She crouched down and picked up a couple of pebbles. She wanted to throw them at the couple, to separate them. The boy covered part of Violante's face, either her
mouth or eyes, and stared at Milene. He didn't speak or move or
ask anything, he simply looked, as if his very immobility should
be enough to maintain silence on that bench and frighten off
anyone who approached. He waved his free arm, indicating to
Milene that she should go away. Far away, away from the wooden
bench, the bar, the beach, from the warm waves that continued
to rise and fall. Far, far away so that they could be alone. That's
what the boy's arm was saying.

Milene let the pebbles fall to the ground.

The pebbles made a dull *plaf.* Retreating across the sand into
which her feet were sinking, and seeing, first, the couple disappear, then the bar, then the beach, Milene was returning to her
place in the world—Villa Regina. While she was driving, she was
gripping her pen between her fingers, ready to cross out the name
VIOLANTE from her address book.

Because they had both agreed that they would never ever kiss a
man, even if the man looked like Schwarzenegger. And Violante
had always said she felt the same, that she wasn't in the least bit
interested in boys. She certainly didn't want to go out with them
or sleep with them. Her plan for when she was older was to adopt
dozens of children, just like Mia Farrow, and Milene thought this
sounded good. They were free spirits, going to matinees of war
movies at the Cinema Metropolitano. They both hated rom-
coms, which they called sloppy-soppies.

Now, though, because of Violante's job and all the fuss surrounding Grandma Regina, they had grown apart, and now, when Milene, on her own initiative, had gone back so that they could once again, hand in hand, plunge into the waves, she had found Violante sitting on a boy's lap allowing herself to be kissed. While the boy held on to Violante with one arm and with the other ordered Milene very firmly to get lost. She wanted no more to do with Violante. She crossed out her name and number.

That was that.

But it wouldn't be as simple as that. Some crossings-out make only the lightest of marks, others leave permanent scars.

Either way, for the next few days, Milene lived her life close to the phone. The following evening, the person who called was Ângela Margarida. It was as if Milene were running from stage curtain to stage curtain, and whichever one she drew aside offered her a scene from someone else's play, one in which she would never have a part. Aunt Ângela Margarida was very direct—"Are you aware of what's been happening?" And without commenting on her own abrupt departure in a taxi, mid-mourning, she explained why she was phoning—she had been busy following Uncle Rui Ludovice's every step. Had Milene not heard the news? Ah, no, of course not. She was forgetting that Milene only read *Blitz* magazine and listened to American music. The world could split in two and half of it be lost in space and Milene wouldn't notice. This was Aunt Ângela Margarida's attempt at irony as she strode down a corridor at the clinic where she worked. So Milene still had no idea what was happening to Uncle Rui Ludovice?

After the reports about Grandma Regina's sad disappearance, reports in which they had all been vilified, it seemed that life had begun to collapse around Uncle Rui. Every day nightmarish stories appeared in the newspapers, all involving her uncle. Her uncle had been too upset even to sleep, and he needed Aunt Ângela Margarida with him day and night. That's why she hadn't been to Villa Regina. That's why she was phoning, because they simply must get together. Very briefly, Milene would have to describe exactly where she had been and with whom, who had attended Grandma Regina's funeral, and other such details. So said Aunt Ângela Margarida, on the other end of the phone, at around six o'clock in the evening, from outside the clinic—"Are you listening? Your uncle's going to have to talk to you soon, because something very strange indeed is happening. Tell me: Who spoke to you? Who approached you at the time? Who did you meet on the morning you walked along that path to the railway track? Think, Milene, think back to those dreadful days. Rack your brains . . ."

No, she wouldn't rack her brains any longer.

That was it. Milene, our cousin Milene, filled up her car with gas, checked the tire pressure, washed the windshield, and, jumping into the driver's seat, headed in the direction signposted *Spain*. She felt confident, perfectly capable of reconstructing the journey as if she had done it only the day before.

And she did just that. On the day when Antonino had been so determined to hand her over to someone, anyone, they had left Aunt Gininha's house, Quinta da Amurada, with him in front and her behind, driving down the highway as far as the exit for Santa Maria de Valmares, and there, instead of going straight on, he'd set off along a dirt road, past some sparse stone pines, through open countryside, to a point where a rope was looped along a hedge of parched rockroses, indicating a fast-growing area of human habitation. Then a plastic billboard had appeared and, after that, the foundations of a resort, with rows of huts surrounding the resort-to-be, but which was, as yet, just an enormous hole.

Or, rather, *part* of a resort-to-be, with a printed sign that said *VILA CAMARGA*. That's where she'd stood waiting in the sun, so that the foreman would see her, until Antonino came scrambling back up the slope of the excavation where it was all happening and said something like—*They're not just going to pay me, they've given me the afternoon off as well* . . . And that was the first time she had seen Antonino Mata actually look pleased. Perhaps the only time, because on the night when he'd taken her home, it was so dark she could only just make out his face. She remembered only the shiny fabric of his shirt, while he kept asking her awkward questions about that perpetual calendar. Anyway, the only really good moment had been when he'd said something like—*The devil must be taking a very long siesta. The man wrote the word* bereavement *on my work slip and suddenly I have the whole afternoon free* . . . And while she was recalling all this, Milene had closed the car door and was walking over to the edge of the pit from the bottom of which rose concrete platforms held together with steel rods.

However, instead of standing there, as she had that first time, Milene sat down on the edge of the crater, swinging her legs, and watching the diggers standing motionless while other machines, busily pounding the earth with electrical hammerings, trembled and shook. She enjoyed watching and listening. Cement mixers turning, sputtering engines rending the air. A lot of young men in yellow helmets. Beneath one of those helmets must be the gangly figure of Antonino, his shirt unbuttoned and flapping in the wind. As she bit into the sandwich she'd brought with her, she began studying each of the more than thirty men working there. At first glance, it seemed that none of them was Antonino, who was always agitation personified. Besides, while the gray mass of the foundations had grown considerably, everything else seemed to be happening very slowly. There was something lackadaisical about the men, as they stood around, hands on hips, waiting for someone else to do something, or as if they were all each other's foreman. Only the machines seemed to rouse them into action, as if the electric current jumped from the machines into their veins. The cranes moved very slowly too, either not moving at all or moving like drunken birds, depositing buttresses and girders at the feet of those very slow, waiting workers. But none of those present looked like Antonino. Even if he wasn't doing anything, he'd be sure to be pacing up and down, waving his arms about. From what she could see, though, there was no one like that there. Meanwhile, one of those tall machines reaching out over the crater had begun to move its jib back and forth, and she remembered then that Antonino had said something else apart from—*The devil must be sleeping* . . . He'd also said—*If it wasn't for you, I'd be up there today* . . . Could he be inside that glass cabin?

Milene had stood up and begun walking along the edge of the crater, until she could confirm that it really was him making that crane turn. Yes, it was! And given that the jib was turning so very slowly, surely he would see her. And if he saw her, wouldn't he realize how glad she was to see him? Not just because he was up there, but because he would remember saying to her—*If it wasn't for you, I'd be up there today* . . . What she found strange was how such a very agitated person could possibly enjoy operating such a ponderous machine. Milene stuffed what was left of her sandwich, still wrapped in a napkin, into a gap in the fence. She wasn't going to take her eyes off that cabin until something happened.

She then sat back down on the edge, determined not to leave until that pulley-like machine stopped, not once taking her eyes off it, and with no idea how the driver could possibly descend from that suspended box. She had gone to that site, still at the hole-in-the-ground stage, hoping to see him moving around below, but she'd never thought he would be up in that machine called *Lieb-*

herr which resembled an arm tied to a leg. She sat until past mid-day, watching him perched at the top of that contraption, and finally she noticed him wriggling around inside the glass cabin and beginning to descend, a foot here, a hand there, hanging by his fingers, by his arms, approaching the ground at formidable speed. Milene felt like calling out—*Hey, you! Look up here. I've been watching you . . .*

Had he really not noticed her?

No, he hadn't. Instead of clambering up the steep slope to where she was sitting, Antonino had climbed up the opposite side, where there was a kind of path cut into the cliff, and he hadn't even gone over to his van. A small group of young men were standing around a big yellow vehicle, an old American car, a Pontiac or something, and as soon as Antonino was in and had shut one of its curved doors, the young men had sped off, as if taking part in a rally, swerving left and right, bumping over pot-holes, and throwing up dust. Gone. Milene thought that if he *had* seen her, he would at least have waved, since he wasn't doing the driving. She was sure of that. He obviously hadn't seen her from his lofty perch.

"He must be blind as a bat," she said to herself, watching him jolting off into the distance. "That stupid guy just vanished and didn't even look over here. He didn't see me . . ."

But he had seen her.

Milene had proof of this as it was getting dark that same evening. She was listening to music and had turned the volume down. Antonino Mata's Mitsubishi van had appeared at the cross-roads, then turned and driven up to the front of Villa Regina, where it remained for some time, as if intending to stay there, but then, instead, the van had glided off down the road, its wheels churning up sand, and bearing away with it the driver's dark face. Milene didn't turn the volume back up, hoping to hear the sound of those wheels again. What was that all about? What would you call such behavior?

A game without rules had begun. A tenuous thing, hanging by a thread, with no losers and no winners.

For an indefinite number of days, Milene, of her own accord, would go and sit on the edge of the crater overlooking Vila Camarga, to watch Antonino working the crane. He would head off for lunch in that dented yellow Pontiac, along with four or five other men, the car making a terrible racket and kicking up dust, and yet Antonino never so much as glanced in her direction. As night fell, the roles were reversed. He would drive past Villa Regina, as if he were keeping watch on the house. Entrenched on the first-floor landing, Milene would pretend not to have seen him. She knew he drove past, could see him through the windows, but she didn't show herself, as if she had no idea whose van it was. Perfect. To use an expression popular with certain members of our family, they could have carried on like that until the end of days.

IX

AND WHILE THAT WAS GOING ON, INSIDE THE *FÁBRICA DE Conservas Leandro 1908*, Ana Mata had crouched down by her riverbeds, just where they came together in a single dense stream. Each day, perched on her chair, she watched the movement of the water, from the first morning floods, which ebbed and flowed and spilled over the banks, to the evaporation of the small islands that formed at low tide, as the torrent sank back between the paving stones.

They were predictable, Ana Mata's rivers. They smelled best when everyone was washing in the morning, and she could tell who was in the shower by the scent of the soap in the rushing water. Yes, she always knew. Her rivers ran with Palmolive, Lux, Nivea, Musgo Real, and each aroma was different, although it was impossible to say which flowers gave them their smell. Violets? Roses? Cinnamon? Blends, grasses, hybrid fragrances, truly wonderful scents. But when someone poured a substance they shouldn't down the sink, instead of carrying it in a bucket far away from the kitchen, over to what used to be the compost heap, then Ana Mata's rivers could smell very bad indeed, and suddenly, what was usually a stream of water, gliding smoothly along under the open sky, would be reduced, just like that, to a foul trickle, for which the only word she could find, among her very saddest thoughts, was *sewage*. At these times, the stench of Ana Mata's rivers could be really acrid, like rancid lard, or poisonously sweet, like a decomposing ox. And that was precisely what she feared would happen that afternoon, because one of her daughters had tipped a bucket of fat into the stream after washing some meat, and now no one was owning up. She didn't say this aloud out of respect for her daughters, but inwardly, with a heavy heart, she labeled them liars. Liars, traders in untruths.

But no, she thought in her own language, she wouldn't say anything.

Ana Mata knew full well that her daughters were distracted. All three of them, all very tough, very fat, had chosen that Saturday to cook up a big *cachupa* stew and throw a party for their friends from Bairro dos Espelhos. They were celebrating the TV show that would feature Janina Mata, who had inherited the voice of all the men in her family. And this was the right thing to do. Always, even since before leaving Ribeirinho da Praia and making that journey along the African coast, she had known that a person has to share all the good that comes her way, or she'll deserve all the evil that follows. She'd always said this to her daughters, and they'd always listened. But now, instead of offering around the happiness that had landed in their laps, along with some simple food, and saving any money left over, they had decided to prepare a great banquet, so everyone could see they were the mothers of a singer. And this was all wrong.

The *cachupa* that her daughter Felícia had been cooking since morning contained pork, beef, chicken, bacon, ham, galantine, smoked meats, and every kind of Portuguese sausage, which was a really shameful waste. In her hands, those same ingredients would have been enough for five ordinary *cachupas*, and filled the stomachs of a hundred people rather than twenty. However, her daughters, in their eagerness to seem important by putting everything in the pot, were not only taking sustenance from the needy, but also cooking up a horrible hodgepodge that no one would be able to eat. She, Ana Mata, who had known real rivers, like the Cacheu and the Mansôa—she certainly wouldn't eat it. *Tushp, tushp* . . . She spat. Swearing, in the name of God and her three little rivers, that she would only eat the corn she had ground herself. Fortunately, her grandson Domingos was very good to her. Three years ago, he had made her a mortar from eucalyptus wood so special that there wasn't another like it. Think of her poor friends who didn't have wooden mortars, whose children and grandchildren gave them mortars made of stone and expected them to make do. A stone mortar lacked the necessary softness of touch, it chopped the corn in half, split it into pieces. Not her, she ground and ground, *tumtum, tamtam*, and all that came off each seed was the husk and the bran, just the way it should be. At the bottom of the mortar, each grain remained intact, round and tender as a gleaming pearl. A proper mortar. That's why her corn was always in demand. She had ground it right there, next to her rivers, with her own assiduous hands. And to think, again, that those daughters of hers, as thick as thieves, had bought a whole bagful of meat, dumped it all in a single pot, and then, as if that weren't enough, tipped all the fat from it down the sink, and now none of them would own up. Not Germana or Dilecta. And certainly not Felícia. *Liars*, thought Ana Mata again, saying nothing. Because the more her daughters cooked with fancy ingredients, the more they seemed to lie. And if that was so, what good did rich food do anyone? *Tell me that*—thought Ana Mata in her own language, crouched by her rivers. Her hair wound into a bun high on her head. And at that moment, she had looked up.

"Domingos! Bring me a stick, boy, I want to push this stinking fat out of the way . . ."

She had asked a second time. But there was no point, because Domingos wouldn't answer. Domingos and Antonino were on the factory roof, aiming a satellite dish at the sky. But Ana Mata didn't know what it was, and tried again—"Antonino! Bring me a stick, would you, or a piece of reed, to see if I can get rid of this . . ."

Ana Mata hadn't seen what was going on. She was too intent on the situation at her feet to notice that everyone had gathered by the kitchen and was looking up at the roof, where her two grandsons, helped by a third person, were holding on to a big white disk, the corolla of a giant flower with plastic petals. The satellite dish still wasn't fully attached, but to the people waiting it was as if the whole World had already arrived there, simply because it was angled toward the endless expanse of space. No, Ana Mata hadn't noticed a thing, engrossed as she was in the grease clogging her river, thinking all afternoon of the twig she would use to dislodge that slimy yellow broth. Nothing at all.— Can't you see they're not listening, *senhora*? Can't you see, don't you know? Aren't you part of this world?

Then her daughter Felícia explained very loudly, so her mother could hear. Felícia, annoyed—"Get your backside out of that *cautcha*, Ma, and come and watch what's going on. Can't you see they're connecting our house to the satellites up there in the atmosphere? Can't you see? Now we're going to have three tele-vision sets, and the biggest will reach more than three hundred channels at a time. Do you know how many three hundred chan-nels is? A hundred, plus a hundred, plus a hundred . . . Did you hear what I said?"

Ana Mata turned her head and saw—under the lean-to there was a new screen, as big as a door lying on its side. It didn't seem possible. Three televisions, three hundred channels. She knew perfectly well how many three hundred was. But since each person was just one person, however many three hundred was, it was more than anyone needed. *Three hundred?*—she thought, feeling rather unnecessary herself, as she stood there, thinking, watching the rivers. Meanwhile, Ana Mata's grandsons, along with the satellite engineer, were climbing down from the roof, where the wheel the size of a beach umbrella was now pointing up at the afternoon sky. Three hundred. And would that thing help them see Janina better? And help them hear his beautiful voice better? Ana Mata would have to wait for answers to these questions, because the satellite dish wouldn't start working for a while. It wasn't yet time for the satellites' opening night. That would come later that evening. No, there was no need to say much more, Ana Mata understood everything. She understood that her daughter Felícia just wanted the people from Bairro dos Espelhos to notice the satellite dish fixed to the roof, announcing how they'd gone up in the world. And meanwhile Ana Mata didn't have so much as a twig or a reed to send that fatty water on its way, any more than she had the power to expose the hidden intentions lurking in that courtyard. No power at all. That was it, her daughters, those fat, conceited liars, had given in to vanity. So she would go herself to get a wooden fork and clear the stagnant waters of her river. She didn't need favors from anyone. It was Domingos and Antonino she had the least trouble with. Her grandsons clambered down from the roof.

"What are you doing, Grandma?"

"Nothing, Domingos, dear, just unblocking a bit of shit that's clogging up my river . . ."

"Oh, really?"

For them, she could still manage a smile. With her back turned, prodding at the trickle of water, dredging, silting, creating rapids and weirs, great fluvial storms, to free the current of that rotten animal stink, she cleaned and purified, and they didn't even mind, although she was taking a bit too long—or so Felícia thought. Yes, Ana Mata could unblock it all she liked, but she had to do as she was told, and more than anything she had to be quick, because people from Bairro dos Espelhos would start arriving at any moment and no one wanted to see a woman rummaging around on the ground, hunched like a mosquito, at the beginning of a party. The tables had been separated out to accommodate more people in the courtyard. The *cachupa* would be served in its own enormous pot. Cars could be heard outside, the two dogs barking with love for the new arrivals. And there were people who came on foot too, carrying their own chairs on their heads. Everyone hurrying. Janina would be on soon, around half past seven, even if his song had already been recorded. Had it or hadn't it? The people on foot pouring in. Felícia Mata would telephone Janina himself and find out.

When she did find out, standing in the middle of the court-yard, the middle of the Diamond, she yelled—"Listen, it's been recorded already and it went really well. All that's left is for us to watch it . . ."

Excited, she called back, more loudly this time—"Janina? Listen, it's me again, your mother. Just to say that a whole bunch of people from Bairro dos Espelhos are going to be here. Your oldest, dearest friends. Never forget, son . . . Even if satellites are beaming you all over the World, even then, never forget you were born three times. Are you listening? The first time was in Ribeirinho, back in Santiago. The second was in Bairro dos Espelhos, when you were eight and a half. And now, listen, son, look, the third and final time was five years ago, when you were thirteen, and you were born again here, at home in the *Fábrica de Conservas Leandro 1908*. Remember that."—Felícia standing poised, in a silk dress with ruffles at the neck, a silver bracelet, the telephone at her ear, and everyone from Bairro dos Espelhos arriving en masse.—"What do you say, Janina? Oh my . . . And now you've been born a thousand times . . . But that's a whole other story. You were born the number of times you needed to be born. Ciao, lots of love. Now everyone's ready to hear you sing . . ."

But before Felícia Mata had put the phone away, she suddenly remembered someone she'd completely forgotten to invite. A real oversight. Her children bustling around the place, all dressed up, the tables laid and Felícia kicking herself. The telephone back in action—"Dona Milene? Yes, it's me, dear. Listen, today's that party for Janina. D'you want to come? Come on, love, and bring us a little of your high spirits. We're waiting for you. You're all that's missing. Don't be embarrassed, come on. All these people know you own a fifth of this house. Come on, what are you wait-ing for . . . ?" And still without greeting the new arrivals, Felícia fixed her eyes on Antonino, who was pacing up and down, and called—"Hey, Antonino, you're used to bringing that funny for-getful girl, go and pick her up, will you, because she's too scared, and she might not come, or she might come late and end up miss-ing Janina. Go on. I know you've got changed already and put your perfume on, but you wouldn't want to be smelly when you pick up the white girl, would you, now . . . ?"

Only then did Felícia Mata throw herself into the kisses and hugs and call for the huge cooking pot to be brought through, with a lit candle underneath to keep it warm. Life might be going very wrong in other parts of the World, but there, at least, all was peace and happiness. She was even convinced that the satellite would one day work in the opposite direction and start transmit-ting the conversations from their courtyard to other people, so that they could see for themselves how to live in peace and hap-piness. Especially through Janina, when Janina came back to rest after all the adventures he had in store.—"Yes, dear, right away, lots of hugs and kisses. Well, Antonino?"

Antonino had no choice. He got into his vehicle.

At the crossroads by the Hotel Miramar, he followed the Estrada das Brisas and then turned off outside Villa Regina. Nothing out of the ordinary. Felícia Mata's son was just doing in the middle of the afternoon what he usually did at nightfall, approaching silently, as if investigating some suspicious goings-on. Again, he'd brought his children. At that moment, Emanuel, Cirino, and Quirino were sitting in the back and playing with a bottle of Havana cologne, spraying it all over each other. Antonino snatched the bottle and slammed it down on the dashboard, irritated. The scent of it filled the van. When Milene came outside, Antonino removed his sunglasses, turned off the music, and said very sternly—"Now, you follow behind in your car. Okay? It'll be too late for me to bring you back. Probably too late for anyone else, as well. Do you understand?" Then he stowed the Havana bottle in the glove compartment, and instead of explaining, politely, why he drove past every day, and instead of mentioning the long hours she spent waiting by the foundations of the Hotel Camarga, to see him going up and down, and instead of telling her how and under what circumstances he went up there, since he didn't always go up, or explaining why he never even looked at her when he was on his way down, it seemed Antonino had come all the way there just to say—*Quick, it's getting late. I don't have all day, you know* . . . He hung out of the window in a white shirt smelling strongly of perfume, without explaining why he pretended not to see her when he was operating the crane, or why, once he got out, he then sped off with his friends in the yellow Pontiac and never said a word to her. Instead of explaining that, which wouldn't have taken a second, Antonino simply said—"Right, let's go . . ." In a great hurry, as if the sight of her touched some muscle in his body that made him race off in another direction. Milene, puzzled. Were there two Antoninos? Could the Antonino who drove so very slowly past Villa Regina every night possibly be the same one who was in such a rush and shouting, *Let's go, let's go,* as if she were just an object to be ordered around?

Yes, off they went, her in front and him behind. When they pulled up next to the palm trees, he made the children get out and announced—"There are loads of people in there. I don't like crowds. And besides, I've heard Janina so many times before that I'm sick of it. I'll just take the kids in and then go. See you . . ."

But the courtyard wasn't as full as all that. Or at least it didn't look it. Everyone was sitting around the little tables as if it were a café, the huge pot of *cachupa* had its candle underneath, and up on the roof, the big plastic flower was signaling like a cosmic switchboard to its listeners in space. Felícia had saved Milene a good spot, right by the three televisions, all tuned to the channel on which Janina would appear. Felícia thrilled because the landlady's granddaughter had come. Yes, there she was, Dona Milene, who was their landlady as well. Who didn't know her? The *cachupa* had been sampled, though it was agreed that as soon as Janina appeared, which would be any second, the forks would all immediately be put down. Now it was happening. Janina was walking onstage. The group froze. Felícia, on her feet, whimpered softly into her hands, then fell silent. Everyone fell silent. And then Janina appeared, multiplied by three.

He appeared and for two and a half minutes he was there on the three televisions in the courtyard. He was all over the walls, the doorways, the washing, the roof tiles, the palm trees, the surrounding landscape, Mar de Prainhas, the coast, even the southeasterly Gulf wind must have borne off snatches of that voice. Every face lifted toward Janina. It was Milene's first time seeing and hearing him, and she was dazzled as well. Even Antonino Mata, who hadn't left after all, seemed to be proud of his brother. When it was over, Felícia said—"Good Lord, sisters, I've gone blind! I saw so much that I couldn't hear a thing . . . How about you?"

It really had all happened so fast that some hadn't managed to see, and others hadn't managed to hear. Others had been watching that performance but seen only the previous one, the one in the Coliseu. But it didn't matter. When the next singer came on, and the three televisions showed three of him as well, singing sickeningly saccharine words, on the same stage where Janina should by rights still have been performing, the people from Bairro dos Espelhos made a beeline for the sumptuous *cachupa*, singing with one voice—*Carpeting the sea, carpeting the sea, with my handkerchief* . . . Switching off the televisions three times. And then they were into Saturday night, the party for Janina in full swing. Inside the Diamond there was nothing but joy. With the exception, still, of Ana Mata.

Sitting in the armchair she herself had dragged over from her riverbeds, Grandma Ana Mata, unlike everyone else, didn't move. Her arms sticking out, mosquito-like. Tears in her tiny eyes. Felícia asked—"Why all this sniffling, Ma? Why aren't you budging from that chair?" Ana Mata didn't respond. Antonino, who was still there after all, with his children in tow, also asked—"Tell me, Grandma. What's wrong?" Some friends from Bairro dos Espelhos who had finished eating went over to her too. The old woman from Ana Mata's island, who had also come carrying her chair on her back, bent down toward her friend, confused—"Are you unhappy, Ana Mata? Tell me . . ."

No one could understand what was making Ana Mata sad, now that the whole country loved her grandson Janina. To cheer Ana Mata up, the sturdy daughter of her fellow islander even began dancing and singing Janina's hit song, as she had months before in Bairro dos Espelhos—*I'm gonna get loud, I'm gonna get tough, if my handkerchief isn't big enough . . . Ooh, ooh!* The sturdy woman imitating Janina's falsetto, that moment when he outdid even Terence Trent D'Arby with his wolf-like howl. Hadn't she heard? So why was Ana Mata sitting there sniffling in the midst of so much joy? Why did she want to go back to her little gray house so early, when it was only eleven p.m. and there was so much laughing, talking, and eating ahead of them? And Domingos's machine was playing at full blast? Felícia's patience wearing thin. "Let her go, she's just crying because the wooden fork she stole from the kitchen wasn't enough to unblock the rivers . . ." And she called to Antonino, who was still there, who still hadn't left, who was still pacing up and down and smoking—"Go on, Antonino, take your grandma home, in case her tears stop her from seeing where she's putting her feet . . ."

Yes, it was a fact. Antonino Mata was still there after all.

Milene had begun saying her goodbyes. Everyone delighted with her, asking about her family, sharing their impressions of the tragedy in August. They all recognized her, Flora most of all. She knew the ins and outs of what had happened, and the stage where it had all played out was still right in front of them. All parceled up, ready to be made into a movie. Yes, Dona Milene really was a Leandro, they'd know those heavy eyelids anywhere. Lots of kisses, lots of hugs. Face-to-face, cheek to cheek. Right, off you go back home, where people say you and your maid live all alone. Is that really true?

But before letting her go, Felícia, in her shiny silk dress, was seized by an urge to explain the repeated kisses she was bestowing on her landlady. Resting one hand on Milene's shoulder, she said that she and Dona Milene could kiss all they wanted, because in the Mata family it was natural for people of all colors to kiss, just as Jamila Mata had taught them. It was very simple. The Matas had been like that for as long as they'd been Matas. Or at least since the scandal of their great-grandmother Jamila, who had been tricked by Normand, leaving some of the family, herself included, with green eyes and freckles ever since. That scandal certainly hadn't been a good thing at all, but misfortune had taught them an important lesson. Jamila's lesson.

What lesson was that?

It was getting late. Felícia Mata stood in the middle of the courtyard, laughing heartily—"Don't any of you know? Haven't you ever heard about my ancestors? Unbelievable . . ."

No, no one knew. And if the people from Bairro dos Espelhos didn't know, Dona Milene had no chance. It was such a beautiful night, and she'd tell them quickly, they just had to say the word. Quickly, then: Well, into their lives, the Matas' lives, had come an enormous Frenchman, with pale eyes and almost-white blond hair, and he'd tricked them. This Frenchman had washed up on the coast all cut to ribbons, after his ship was smashed to bits entering the bay. A cargo ship in pieces, just outside Cidade da Praia, and just one survivor in a terrible state, looking like he was dying. Who could save that sorry specimen washing in and out on the waves? Completely naked. Best give him the last rites and be done with it. Only there happened to be a girl called Jamila walking on the beach, and she had taken him in and nursed him tenderly night and day, bringing him back to life, and he, with the water barely dry on his skin, had given her a child for her troubles. A daughter, a second Jamila, who would grow up to be

Ana Mata's grandmother. Yes, once he was restored to health and Ana Mata's great-grandmother was pregnant, Normand, instead of taking Jamila Mata with him, had hopped onto the deck of a ship bound for the Caribbean, with a bunch of coconuts under his arm and a monkey on his shoulder. Everyone knew what had happened. Jamila Mata, on the quayside in Cidade da Praia, her belly swollen, watching her lover sail away on the brig, taking a monkey with him for company. Their great-grandmother Jamila abandoned, betrayed. "Is there any excuse for that? Is there?"— asked Felícia, her voice very grave.

But it was thanks to that sad scene, of Jamila weeping and Normand waving goodbye, with that monkey perched on his shoulder, that all Jamila's descendants had learned the lesson. A lesson for tough-as-nails Cape Verdean *badios*, as all the Matas were. And it was a good thing that they'd been betrayed by Normand, a really good thing, said Felícia, standing in the middle of the courtyard. The great lesson they'd learned could be summed up in a few simple words, a handy phrase that explained the world like no other. More enlightening even than a page in the Bible. It seemed like a joke but it wasn't. Felícia reciting as if Jamila's lesson were a psalm—"*When it comes to love and money, remember—white with white, black with black, poor with poor, and rich with rich . . . And monkeys? Leave them up a tree all alone.*" Everyone laughing and questioning. Questioning? How then did they explain Janina's success? The success of living in that house, with running water and electricity? The Matas being welcomed by everyone? It could all be explained by Jamila's lesson, which was passed down from mothers to mothers and fathers to sons. The Matas all believed it and lived by it. Wherever the Matas went, they made people feel comfortable. They inspired confidence. Always friendly with everyone, happy with everyone, not trying to climb the ladder. Because if you know your place you don't ruffle any feathers, in your land or other people's. Simple.

That was why she could kiss her landlady all she liked, as everyone could see. She was very fond of her landlady, no one had ever done her nails as well as she had. Without any misunderstandings. A kiss for a kiss. A hug for a hug. All the people from Bairro dos Espelhos laughing and looking. Yes, yes, there you go, you can feel at home with the Matas. No one could accuse us of being proud, we just want to be what we are. In the bedroom, black with black, white with white, brown with brown, and so on. Nothing simpler. Oh, if Mandela had only thought the same, he wouldn't have spent his life in prison. Because why waste so much time there? Did the man solve anything? Had anything changed in the world? asked Felícia Mata, in her shimmering silk dress. But when it's a given that some people will sleep over here, and others will sleep over there, then no one's going to get upset, everyone can be friends, and hug and kiss, no problem at all. They can work together, live together even, like brothers and sisters.

"Antonino, son? Are you still there? Did you take your grandma inside? Did you put her *cautcha* back in its proper place?"—Goodbye, Dona Milene. Right, let's call it a night. Time for you to go home. It's all over now.

Milene had lingered a little longer, then headed toward the mound. The palm trees were casting their dark shadow over the cars from Bairro dos Espelhos. The vans belonging to the factory tenants were lined up against the wall. And inside the gray Mitsubishi, leaning back in his seat and smoking, sat Antonino.

She moved closer. He tossed away his cigarette end and said— "I've been waiting for you. I can escort you again if you like, I'm going that way . . ."

He was wreathed in a muggy mist of smoke and perfume, the perfume too strong, mingling with the smell of the dry earth, and there was nothing more to be said. Moonlight pooled around them, and on the other side of the road, the two steel rails shone bright among the grass. "The thing is, I had something very important to tell you, and I'd forgotten. Let's go . . ."

Milene knew the drill. Her in front again, and him behind, though it could also be the other way around. Yes, every so often they drove like that over that stretch of land, but for no real reason. They didn't pass through Bairro dos Espelhos, instead going via the gas station and around the Hotel Miramar. When they finally left the old side road at the sign for Kilometer 44, the house was all lit up. He got out. No baseball cap this time. And he said—"Look at the moonlight . . ." Because what else was he going to say with that moonlight bathing the earth? Rounding its edges. Shaping it into a vast circular sheet to catch its silver light. Every outline so crisp that even the shadows of the acacias spread out leaf by leaf over the ground, filling the space between them. Leaning against the van, he said—"If I didn't have places to be, we could go to a bar or something. Would you like that?" Still leaning on the van as if it were a wall, he went on—"I'd go in my car and you'd go in yours, so no one could say that a man like me abducted a woman like you and took her to a bar. Just so I can tell you something. Agreed?" And then he added—"Right. We'll go straight, then around the edge of Bairro dos Espelhos, as far as Riacha. There's a place there where we can get some peace, and no one will bother us . . ."

"What do you say, eh?"

Again they drove along the bumpy strip of coast, from this end to that, their path determined by the roads and the sea, which sent them back and forth like a swing. They stopped by the beach in Riacha and, yes, there was a bar. Almost as brightly lit as Villa Regina. "No, not there"—he said. They'd be better off outside, the Moon silver, the sea silver, all the secretive hidden creatures coated in a layer of silver. It didn't seem real. He knew nothing was like that, nothing was silver, it just looked as if it was. He said to her—"Let's go down to the beach." Then, reconsidering—"No, not the beach." She thought to say—"We can sit in my car." He said—"No, not your car." It was as if he were standing on top of something, and all around there was nothing but emptiness, and no way of getting down. Wherever Antonino looked he saw dangers or difficulties. "I know—you lean on your car and I'll lean on mine, and we'll look out over the beach." And that's what they did. They looked. She saw his shirt, almost white, glimmering in the brightness. And suddenly he said—"If my girlfriend found out, she'd kill me . . ."

Milene, leaning against the white Clio, by the roadside, listening to what he was saying, his voice interrupting the soft murmur of the waves. For Janina's big night, Milene had worn dozens of bracelets on her arms. She shook them. "The girlfriend who's dead?"—she asked, not moving her hands now, in case the bracelets jangled and stopped her from understanding what he'd said.

"No"—he answered. "The girlfriend who's alive."

He was leaning against the gray van, where the moonlight beat down as on everything else, but just then the metal was also lighting up the Moon. His shirt too. It was so white, as if a percentage of it were made of phosphorus. The corners of his mouth were sharp as if pulled to a fine point by a pair of tweezers, and his wide nostrils gleamed. Antonino, nervous, awkward, seemed to be squaring up to fight someone as he spoke—"I can't go on like this, alone, I just can't. I need a woman who'll give me children . . ."—he said. "People from my island like to have lots of children. Multiplying your own face onto their faces is a good thing. It's what life's about . . ."—he said.

Milene repeated what he'd said very softly, just to be sure she understood.

And him, very loudly—"Eunice died. Have you heard about Eunice? The mother of my children? I don't want to think about that now. You know . . . you know, our love was something really beautiful. Eunice and I were holding hands practically from the moment we were born. Twenty years later, getting married was the natural thing to do. People said . . ." Then they both fell silent. With Antonino, however, even if he didn't say a word, he was never really silent. He said—"Since you don't know, I'll tell you so you do know. It's like this—everything about you reminds me of her, and I don't know why. And my girlfriend now is black like Eunice and she doesn't remind me of Eunice. You remind me, and you're white. You're just like her. The things you do, the way you walk. The same obsession with kissing objects when you find them. The same thin little voice, just like Eunice, my God . . . You, Milene, remind me of her. And Divina, the woman I'm with now, doesn't remind me of Eunice . . ." He said. The sea and the sky transformed into a spotless silver platter. A night this splendid could only happen once in a person's life. A tightening in her throat, for no reason, but a tightening nonetheless. She had never seen a night like this before, or if she had she didn't remember. *All right, say something, go on, I'm listening. Speak, speak.* At last, he said—"Who would have thought it? Divina will be wondering where I am. We'd better get going, because if someone sees us here, at three in the morning, I don't know what'll happen. I mean, I really don't know what will happen.

"I just know I've got something to tell you"—said Antonino again, getting into the van, which reeked of perfume, perhaps Havana, as if the glove compartment were open and the bot-

tle had overturned. In the moonlight on that warm, still October night, his excessively thick gold chain was glinting as well,
and his belt too. His belt with its metal buckle shining. And his
watch, his big wristwatch, the size of a teacup. All these things
shone in the distant glow from the moonlit sea. Then he looked
at his watch with its luminous hands and said—"Four o'clock. No
one will know where I am. Let's get going . . ."

They set off, the white vehicle behind, the gray one in front,
back down the road, past groups of youths hunting for nightclubs,
the hotels with people still in the lounges, a lone policeman on
the beat. Then they drove down the longer roads, between houses
whose white façades watched them like large flat faces, as if they
had sprung up out of the earth to greet them, to tell them things
as they passed. Eventually they rounded the gas station from the
north, and then they were at Kilometer 44. He climbed out.

"You still leave all the lights on. Why?"—he asked. His lips
shining, his nostrils shining, all of him shining.

No, she wasn't going to say anything. He still had a girlfriend
who was alive.

"Now we don't know when we'll next see each other"—he said.
"So long."

Then he turned around and said—"Yes, I wanted to tell you
something, Milene. I wanted to tell you not to come and watch
me anymore, when I'm up there in the crane. Do you understand?
They're starting to give me grief about it because of Divina. It's
a real drag . . ."—he said, and meanwhile, for the Moon and the
Earth, it was all a matter of complete indifference. The Moon was
still shining silvery bright, the Earth still taking it in with mortal
passivity. "A real drag, okay, Milene? I don't know how to explain.
And at the same time, you're so much like Eunice. Sometimes I
think you have her soul . . ."

He continued—"Go on, then, go inside. Turn off the lights.

You should take better care of yourself. Go on, go on . . ." Retreating, bit by bit, into his old tone, his tone from the day when he was so determined to hand her over to someone, anyone. His voice grating at the end of each word, the way it had that day.

Milene shouting too—"There's no need to shout. Listen, I'm already gone . . ."

And Milene ran inside, her heels catching her skirt. Her bracelets pressed to her body so they didn't jangle. It was bad enough that the gate made that noise. *Dim, dum.* Feeling upset, she raced off through the garden microclimate and up the steps. She climbed up to the first floor, then peered out from her bedroom. There he was. He was waiting for her to turn off the lights. But she wasn't going to. They would stay lit until dawn. All through the morning, or all day, if need be. Now she was sure he had gone. But in fact, outside, between the two houses opposite, amid piles of cement and pyramids of bricks, he was still there. Only later did Antonino's van begin to glide off down the road. The early morning moonlight so pale it was invisible.

In two years' time, the moonlight would still be bright. But the next few days would prove very confusing.

Milene waited for the telephone to say its final words—*Please do so after the tone. Thanks* . . . Only then did she press her lips to the mouthpiece. She was looking at the houses opposite, the people who once lived there long gone, and in their place, as evening set in, cars where construction workers sat lost in thought. The leaves of the walnut tree curling up, losing their vegetable veins— "*João Paulo? Can you hear me? Can you? I'm phoning to talk about the Diamond* . . ." There was a repeated click at the other end, the mechanism ticking as the tape began to roll. Milene, her lips a long way from the mouthpiece now, shouting in its direction—

"Your telephone makes me sick, I wish I could spit in its face. Maybe I won't leave a message after all . . ."

She was sitting on a stool, between Grandma Regina's armchairs. Over the ticking sound, which sometimes seemed very close and sometimes disappeared altogether, she said, as solemnly as she could—*"My life is just so annoying sometimes . . . I went to Mãos Largas to work there, but I didn't stay . . . When Barbosa found out I wanted to work, he phoned Uncle Rui Ludovice, looking very serious . . . Then he handed me a tray, a notebook, and a pencil that I could put in my pocket or behind my ear. I put it behind my ear. He also gave me a very long apron that came halfway down my legs. I looked in the mirror. Sideways on I looked just like a butterfly. The loops sticking out either side of my waist and the strings hanging lower than my skirt . . . I didn't last an hour tied up in that bow, with that pencil or that tray. The only good thing was the smell of the pizzas. I brought three home when I quit. Yes, I quit . . . There I was, rushing around, when I have so much to do here, in Grandma Regina's house. It's always so dirty . . ."* Milene paused. On the other end, the telephone was still making muffled noises, an intermittent buzzing meant to either repel or attract her, she wasn't sure which. Milene peering into the mouthpiece. Insisting—*"What's going on there? Eh? Your telephone makes me sick, your recording makes me sick. And you're never there. You've gone off to some unknown place. And I just wanted to say that I'm back from the Diamond. You wouldn't believe what it's like now. That whole family lives there, with two dogs, two girls, children, builders, a very old man, lots of old women, kids all over the place. And a widower too. They're always phoning one of them who's a singer and they have a satellite dish on the roof. On the roof of the Diamond. They threw an amazing party, because of the singer . . . Inside the Diamond . . . That's why I was there . . . One of them, the widower, has two wives, one dead and one living. He drives a crane. He has a Mitsubishi van. Which doesn't pass by like it used to. It used to pass by every night . . . Are you there?"* Milene suspected the tape was about to run out. She said very quickly, lips pressed to the mouthpiece—*"Anyway, that's about all I had to say. When you call me, I'll tell you what I saw at Praia Pequena. It was horrible, really horrible . . . But the waves are still the same. Bye-bye. Love from your cousin . . .*

"João Paulo? Yes, the lights are all on. People say Grandma Regina's house looks like a Christmas tree."

X

AND THE PERPETUAL CALENDAR? YES, IT DID EXIST.

The days were growing shorter and shorter, with each sunset coming on ever faster and each sunrise taking ever longer. It had been like that since the Earth began to turn, but Milene only noticed it that autumn, and with it the inevitable implications for her timetable. This was because of the perpetual calendar set up by her aunts and uncle, and which they seemed determined to follow, while she wasn't sure whether she wanted them to nor not. The fact is that when the hour changed, her two aunts began to appear on alternate days, and her life became ruled by waiting— "Expect me between nine and eleven . . ." Yet the person phoning wouldn't arrive until one o'clock. "I can't come tonight, but I'll be there tomorrow at around half past eight . . ." That was Aunt Ângela Margarida, who couldn't come because of Uncle Rui and her work at the clinic. And so on and so forth. The calendar had been intended to last for the rest of her life, but this was so patently absurd that it couldn't possibly last even two weeks. And there would be no need for Milene, as she had initially feared, to beg them to cease their self-imposed torments.

And by "them" I mean her aunts, especially Aunt Gininha, who had still not recovered from the night when Uncle Dom,

instead of attending that meeting with the Dutchmen, had suddenly appeared, striding across the lawn.

Aunt Gininha started coming to Villa Regina one Sunday night,
and then, for two weeks, did her best to keep to the rotation. She
would turn up at around one o'clock in the morning, lie down
on the bed she'd slept in as a young woman, take Milene's hand
in hers, and close her eyes. With the arrival of autumn, and as
the days passed, her grief seemed to grow rather than diminish,
because she would lie there muttering to herself, often returning
to the fact that only three of the five siblings had survived, and
those three had fallen out. She would make particular mention
of the loss of her two older brothers, who had been almost like
fathers to her, because she had been born when Grandma Regina
was well into middle age. She was clearly looking back over her
life and would sometimes ask Milene if she remembered one or
the other of her many boyfriends, or trips they'd made together,
or movies, parties, ethnic necklaces given as gifts in satin-lined
boxes. Milene could remember some things, but not others. She
couldn't remember it all. But sometimes Aunt Gininha was in a
very different mood.

Sometimes she was as bitter as she had been in the past, in the
days when she would arrive unannounced at Villa Regina in floods
of tears, describing, to whoever happened to be there, the deep
divisions opening up between her and her husband. The days when
Grandma Regina would say to her—"Just get a divorce and come
home before it's too late . . ." The days when we all shared her disappointment. Then Gininha had grown more taciturn. By the late
1980s, Gininha would only confide details to one or another member of the family, and they, in turn, would secretly pass these on
so that, in the end, we were all able to discuss them. However,
when Gininha discovered that we all knew about her life, she

clammed up. It was as if she suddenly realized what a fool she had been to marry a man like Dom Silvestre, when she'd had her pick of boyfriends, more than a hundred of them. She was quite right. She withdrew into herself. Nevertheless, at one point, it became known that although she and her husband lived in that beautiful house shaded by a huge beech tree and several plane trees, and even after Bruno José was born, even at the table, in that dining room decorated with Lladró figurines and a pink marble Cutileiro sculpture of a young girl, even there, Uncle Dom would frequently, unabashedly, fart. It was so sad, so very sad. Dona Regina's son-in-law had no sense of propriety. Aunt Gininha was known then to leave the room and go and listen to the classical music she adored, Chopin and Mendelssohn, and she only survived by imagining that she could step out of that house into the company of her former boyfriends, their finest qualities enhanced, and sit among them, combing her long hair and speaking the English of T. S. Eliot, some of whose poems she knew by heart. Yes, sad and bitter. It was then that a great change took place, a change noticed and commented on by everyone—Gininha began to absorb Uncle Dom's logic, as if she were an integral part of her husband. She abandoned tragedy and opted instead for life's more burlesque side. Listening to her daughter talk, Grandma Regina would sometimes think that her real daughter had died, and at others that she was merely hibernating. This was the only possible explanation for the conversation about business that night when Uncle Dom had suddenly appeared on the lawn. That was the only explanation, on those perpetual calendar nights, for her aunt's abrupt changes of mood, the way she suddenly perked up, as if she were dreaming out loud—"You know, Uncle Dom has this amazing project. He wants to build a whole new resort. Nowadays, any entrepreneur worth his salt wants to build a resort. But he has to move fast, because the costs are high. In your uncle's case, he's even had an Italian marketing firm come up with a slogan. It goes—*Here, the Ocean, weary of the waves, lays down its Arms* . . . What do you think?"

It was past midnight, Milene was lying beside her aunt, and her aunt was talking about Uncle Dom's various projects, about the Ocean laying down its arms, about the shape of the quarry-turned-construction site, about the illegal blasting he had done without a seismometer, and about two of her uncle's enemies who had been killed just outside the site, not, of course, that their deaths had anything to do with her uncle. On the contrary, you reap what you sow, and they had, after all, attempted to destroy her uncle's business. True, there had been a few awkward moments in court, but nothing was ever proved. It was hardly her uncle's fault if people chose the biblical backdrop of the quarry for a shoot-out. Wouldn't you agree, Milene? How was your uncle to blame for that? Do you see what I mean, Milene?—Yes, that was the Aunt Gininha to whom the pilot (the one who was always sleepy or who would sleep by day and stay awake all night) would sing a song of the Tonga people, which he called *Ana Latu's lullaby*, and which the two of them would sing, sitting on the sand in Mar de Prainhas—*Oh, the way we walked on the sand* . . . The pilot lying back on the sand, eyes closed. *How our footprints became one.* Her aunt gazing out at the sea—*So precious to me, my dear Ana Latu, oh, so precious* . . . "Do you remember, Milene?" Yes, Milene did sometimes remember that.

If only Aunt Gininha had made that visit to Joseldo's hair salon while she was still going out with the pilot. Or with the biologist and his mother-of-pearl shells. Things would have been so different. As it was, there she was talking about a future resort to be built beside the sea, where the battle-weary Ocean god had lain down his arms in order to rest. A resort of the future, intended by

Uncle Dom as a place for others to rest. What a nice irony. Milene was incapable of irony, but she was perfectly capable of scorn. As they were lying side by side on the same bed, she asked her aunt— "Aunt, can you see where my hands are?"

Her aunt sat up and looked at her—"They're resting on your little boobies . . ."

"No, Aunt, they're covering my ears. Take a good look at my ears—whenever you talk about him and his projects, my hands, whatever I might actually be doing with them, are always covering my ears . . . This finger here is stuck right inside, so that I won't hear a word . . ."

Milene was wiggling two fingers about on her chest.

Her aunt lay down again, rather stiffly now, staring up at the ceiling light.—"Why have these things happened to us? Why, Milene? Tell me . . ." Her aunt was split in two, or, rather, was made up of two people, and she slept very little. The half that belonged only to her, and which always would belong only to her, slept even less and would wake with a start, asking what time it was. She thought it must already be morning, her oblique way of saying that the lights bothered her.

"Would you like me to turn them off, Aunt?" Milene would ask.

"Only if you want to . . ." Her aunt hesitated. "No. If you feel better like that, then why not have all the lights on? Leave them on, sweetheart . . ."

Aunt Gininha slept over five times.

Aunt Ângela Margarida, on the other hand, only came twice. She too arrived late and left early. Accustomed to night shifts at the clinic, she slept badly and fitfully, like a fireman keeping watch over a fire. As soon as she arrived, she headed straight for the buttons on the CD player and the TV, and turned them both off. The lights, all of which were on, seemed to shine even more brightly, but then Aunt Ângela Margarida, wearing high heels and a suit with a very short skirt, visited each and every light switch and turned them off too. The house seemed to sink belowground. They went to bed in adjoining rooms, almost without speaking, although Milene did once say—"Aunt Ângela Margarida?"

"Yes."

"You don't need to come, you know. I'm fine as I am, guarding Grandma Regina's house. To be honest, I don't have anything else to do. You and Aunt Gininha can get on with your lives . . ."

Her aunt did not respond. Milene was peering through the half-open door of what had once been Aunt Ângela Margarida's childhood bedroom, and it felt rather like having a self-flagellating monk living in the house. She didn't say as much, but the presence of that family member lying tensely in the next room kept Milene from her dreams. And her aunt must have sensed this, because on the third day of that lifelong perpetual calendar, she didn't appear. She was then supposed to come on a Sunday, but phoned to say—"It's just impossible. My workload at the clinic has doubled, and then there's Uncle Rui fretting about his life. I spent all last night with him in the living room, trying to calm him down." Then, in a different tone of voice, and walking, as usual, along a corridor, the sound of her footsteps coming down the line—"Tell me, Milene, during those days in August, who did you talk to? Where were you? How did you find out where we were? Because someone has been plotting against your uncle ever since. And the plot won't go away. We need to talk about it. But you go back to bed now, there's no need for you to lose sleep over it . . ."

And that was the end of Aunt Ângela Margarida's perpetual calendar.

———

As for Uncle Afonso, the calendar never even began. That is, he passed his duties on to someone else. Uncle Afonso had acted even before his sisters had, or, rather, he had instructed someone else to take action. That person was his secretary Páscoa.

When it came to Afonso Leandro's turn to keep his niece company, according to that endless lifelong calendar, Páscoa phoned her. As a good, polite secretary, he made no reference to the tense relationship between her and her uncle. He asked if she had slept well, advised her where to go if she needed any shopping or needed to eat out at all. Perfect. Just like a nanny. End of story. Every three days. Until the end of days. However, one Friday in November, Uncle Afonso appeared in person. He arrived with Isabel, at around two o'clock in the afternoon. On a bright sunny day, almost like summer. He parked his convertible under the acacias. Uncle Afonso got out first, and Isabel followed suit. She was your usual bimbo type, and could as easily have been seventeen as thirty-seven. And João Paulo's father, the lawyer and horseman, positioned himself outside the house. Would he ring the bell? Would he use his own key? Neither—he knew she'd be sitting on the first-floor landing. He called out—"Milene, open the door for your uncle!"

Milene, open the door for your uncle? How extraordinary! She ran and opened the door, and Uncle Afonso, in turn, called to Isabel.

"Come on, Isabel . . ."

Her uncle's girlfriend stood hesitating at the front door, before walking cautiously over the red hall carpet to the stairs. In obedience to Uncle Afonso's calls, she then went up the stairs, pausing before each step, as if she were entering a haunted house. "Where are you? Just a bit farther. Here I am. Come on . . ." Isabel continued on up, noiselessly, wordlessly. The couple must have met at the riding club, and they were clearly well suited. He was saying—"I'm here, darling. Another three steps and then to the right . . ." Until Isabel, finally, anxiously, entered the room where Afonso was waiting. It was Grandma Regina's former bedroom, the one she'd used before the stairs became too much for her. And Milene, who had stayed on the landing below to watch this cautious ascent, knew exactly what was on Uncle Afonso's mind. Yes, he may have said, *Milene, open the door for your uncle,* as if they'd made their peace, but the matter in hand was too important for her to feel entirely at ease. She followed them up the stairs. Hearing her approach, they closed the door. She went over to the door and waited. She was right—her uncle was looking at her grandmother's writing desk, which had a drawer for every occasion, little wooden hiding places, small as thimbles, places for keeping paper, dip pens as well as quills, delicate places for storing stamps, and other drawers firmly under lock and key. Her grandmother's bureau made of pale yellow brazilwood. It had been valued by the insurers at one and a half million escudos. Not to mention its Art Nouveau design, which made it an object of solid, elegant beauty. Made for people of a different era, who needed to stand very erect, with their elbows at shoulder-level, whenever they wanted to write anything. A lovely piece. Afonso and Isabel were studying it closely and speaking very quietly. Then he opened the door and, as they went down the stairs, both of them turned back, as if still attached to that object which seemed so firmly fixed to the floor with its eight square feet.

Her uncle had said—*Milene, open the door for your uncle* . . .

What should she do? Afonso passed very close to her, as did Isabel, the two of them talking to each other, but not addressing a single word to her. Then they walked through all the other rooms, her uncle in front, Isabel behind, and sometimes, standing before a particular piece of furniture, they would hold hands. Milene felt like saying—*Please, for God's sake, don't take Grandma Regina's things away, not now, not in a week or a month's time, not ever. Please, Uncle Afonso* . . . But she wouldn't say that. There was that polite phone call from Páscoa every three days, and her uncle was looking at her now with no anger or resentment in his eyes, not even reminding her that she was José Carlos's daughter, and he had, what's more, asked before entering the house—*Milene, open the door for your uncle* . . . which must have been a painful compromise for him to make. Besides, if, on that awful day, she hadn't flown into such a rage when he'd sat down in one of Grandma Regina's armchairs, everything might have been all right, and the three siblings might not even have fallen out like that, or come up with the idea of that perpetual calendar. But Milene wasn't ten or fifteen or even twenty years old, and she knew what they wanted. They were hand-in-hand now before the hatstand that was still covered in Grandma Regina's hats. The marks on the wall left by the photographs and the paintings that had been removed in recent years. Milene plucked up her courage. Her voice emerged as thin as a whistle. Uncle Afonso?

"Uncle Afonso, I've been thinking and thinking, and now I have this to say . . ." She pressed her knees together hard. "If you like, you can take one thing that belonged to Grandma Regina . . ."

Still hand-in-hand, her uncle and Isabel looked at her, surprised.

"Something small. There are a few things over there. I'll show you. You could choose something now . . ."

Her uncle was looking at his niece's face as if studying a mathematical problem written on a blackboard. Milene plunged on— "It's like this, Uncle. You can't take any of Grandma Regina's big pieces of furniture. Imagine if she were to come home now and find it all gone. Imagine . . ."

Afonso Leandro closed his eyes and turned his back. After a

while, he spoke, still with his back turned—"She won't ever be coming home again, Milene. You, better than anyone, should know where she is now." It was as if he couldn't bear to look at the mathematical problem, let alone solve it.

But Milene had placed herself in front of the hatstand and was speaking very loudly, triumphing over her uncle's shaky logic, sharing her certainty with him, because she felt he deserved it—"No, she isn't there in the cemetery, Uncle, that's where you're wrong . . ."

Isabel was standing halfway along the red carpet that led to the stairs, in the bright autumn light flooding into the hallway. The bright light of day shining directly onto Milene's face. Girlfriend and niece face-to-face. Milene knew only that her uncle had said, *Milene, open the door for your uncle . . .* And yet, if he'd wanted, he could have put his hand in his pocket and used his own key. That's why she was speaking like that, making a huge effort to explain what was explainable, out of respect for him, out of recognition and love for him as her uncle, and as João Paulo's father. And her uncle kept looking back and forth between her and Isabel. His bald head beaded with sweat. As if he'd been caught in a rain shower. Uncle Afonso, motionless at the front door. Waiting to see how his girlfriend would react.

"How do you deal with something like this, Isabel? I just don't know. Do you understand it?"

Isabel must have had the ability to enter into Uncle Afonso's very heart, and, although she appeared to be anywhere between seventeen and thirty-seven, she must have been profoundly contemporaneous with him in spirit, in perfect harmony, because she finally took pity on him and, taking his arm, led him out of the house. Her uncle seemingly doomed to be led from his mother's house by a series of women, after confrontations with Milene. This time, though, Milene felt quite happy with herself, because she hadn't said anything offensive, hadn't used vulgar language, far less said anything indecent; on the contrary, she'd merely wanted to explain to her uncle that he couldn't make off with Grandma Regina's furniture, which is why she'd placed a few other objects at his disposal, as long as they were of no particular significance. That's all. But her uncle was leaving, led away by his girlfriend, and saying in devastated tones—"Help me, someone, because I just don't know how to deal with this . . . Let someone else do it . . ." Her uncle being carried off by that bimbo Isabel, through the gate that creaked open, then slammed shut behind them.

Milene feeling perfectly happy with herself, watching them disappear off into the distance in their convertible. Disappearing for good. But for two weeks, Páscoa continued to phone her every three days. Then that was the end of Uncle Afonso's perpetual calendar, until the end of time.

A perpetual calendar, short-lived and yet definitive—as we would find out later.

We would also learn that Juliana continued to start work at three in the afternoon and stay until five. By that time, even the brightest days were pitch-black. Then one day, she was leaving as usual, crash helmet under her arm, heading for her moped, when she ran back in, almost hysterical.

"Miss Milene! Miss Milene! This is the third time I've found that frigging black man outside the house in his van, turning around, then driving off down the road. Oh, it did give me a fright! You just feel how fast my heart's beating."

Milene did.

Yes, beneath her sweater, Juliana's heart really was beating very fast. Juliana was terrified that the man might be hiding somewhere, waiting to attack her. Actually, when she thought about it, this was possibly the fifth time it had happened. He always drove off slowly, looking in his rearview mirror the whole time, and only speeding up when he got close to the Hotel Miramar.

"He might have been there even more times than that . . ."

All of this was part of that perpetual calendar. It's just that Milene didn't know it. Aunt Gininha had phoned her—"Milene? Perhaps you could come over and spend the evening with me and your cousins. He's not here. This time, he really is meeting those Dutchmen. I swear." That's what Aunt Gininha said on the phone.

Aunt Ângela Margarida, on the other hand, did actually arrange a meeting. Uncle Rui had been meaning to talk to Milene for at least two months, but he hadn't had time because, lately, his life had been so full of surprises. As he himself said, every day was as action-packed as a Wagner opera. That's why he was only getting in touch now, in November, when he should already have made public his intention of bringing seven lawsuits against those responsible for what had happened to his mother-in-law, Dona Regina Leandro. Rui Ludovice had finally concluded that getting involved with the law was now inevitable. It was agreed that, on Saturday, Senhor Frutuoso would pick Milene up for a meeting where they would discuss August's tragic events, and then, when Aunt Ângela Margarida got home, the five of them would have lunch out on the terrace.

The five of them, because Milene's cousins would join them after their tennis lesson.

And so, at around midday, the chauffeur duly arrived and whisked her off, driving first along the potholed road, then along the smooth one. At one point, when the pine trees gradually thinned out as they approached the Atrium Condominium, which faced the bay, an ideal spot, neither town nor country, neither forest nor beach, and yet all those things at the same time, in that rainless, windless autumn, he said to her—"This time it's for real. Everyone's there waiting for you." And as if she'd never been to the house before, he added—"The meeting's on the ninth floor, but you can get to it from the tenth floor too. It's a duplex. Don't get out at the wrong floor, though. The roof terrace is now called the penthouse."

Milene had been to the apartment before, but hadn't seen the recent changes, which went far beyond anything she was expecting.

A new maid, almost bursting out of a pair of very tight jeans, ushered her into an office the size of a very large living room. When Milene went in, she saw that the "everyone" Senhor Frutuoso had mentioned was no lie. Whether they were waiting for her was quite another matter. Because they weren't. Nevertheless, she immediately spotted Action in action. There he was, along with various other people, all men, all concentrating hard on something or other, and the whiff of various mingled aftershaves filled the dense air with a smell reminiscent of burnt scrub. Strewn about the floor were papers and open files, with glasses and cups beside them. She sat down, and no one said a word to her, not even Uncle Rui Ludovice, whose long hair, at that moment, was covering most of his face. She couldn't see the other men's faces either.

Why had she come?

Each man was absorbed in consulting his particular bundle of papers and his mobile phone, that transient bit of glass through which they all communicated with each other. Then her uncle raised his head from his papers and said, without actually looking at her, so as not to waste time—"We've nearly finished, but, if you like, you can go outside . . ." Adding—"We haven't really had time to talk yet, but we just need to confirm a few details. I won't be a moment . . ." He looked up at the others. They were all, each in his own way, immersed in whatever it was they were immersed in.

"Stay here if you like."

But given how busy he was, did he mean that? Should she stay?

She stayed. She stayed and studied the faces of those people shuffling papers around on the table, the many heads of Action. She counted—Action times nine. This was how Action happened, led by whatever action Uncle Rui Ludovice set in motion. They were like bright, diligent students doing their homework. She counted nine, nine heads. As it happened, there were also nine whiteboards arranged along the wall of her uncle's office, where his personal staff were gathered. Since she had time on her hands, she pondered this fact. Then she noticed the gold-framed paintings on the wall. Nine heads, nine paintings. How interesting. Most interesting of all was the painting of a horse's head, nostrils flared as if eager to escape. Another one depicted a lamp. An oil lamp held up by a disembodied arm. Another showed a fallen head, eyes askew, like two fish jumping away from each other. There didn't appear to be any connection. Another some kind of cow. There the two fish-shaped eyes stared straight out at you and seemed rather alarmed. She was thinking about the paintings and not listening to what was being said. But at one point, in the midst of that torment—no one spoke to her, they probably didn't even know she was there—Uncle Rui Ludovice began talking more loudly and got to his feet, occupying a central position at the table. He was speaking to the only member of his staff who, at that hour of the day, didn't have the jacket of his business suit draped over the back of his chair. The only one who stood out. Her uncle said—"Look, just don't speak to me, all right? Don't try and lay the blame on someone else. It was your fault . . . Are you or are you not a professional?" The other man trying to say something, leaning across the table, addressing her uncle, and her uncle furiously addressing everyone else in the room.

"You turned up here demanding a big fat fee, saying you'd trained at the Piccolo Teatro di Milano or whatever and you were a crowd choreographer. That's what we paid you to do. You were the person responsible . . ." And Uncle Rui Ludovice pointed his finger at the jacketless man in the collarless shirt who was all dressed in black, his hair caught back in a ponytail, mumbling incoherently.

There must be some connection between the paintings on the wall and the men sitting around the table. The man her uncle was talking to was vaguely like the horse in the picture. Then suddenly her uncle shouted louder still, standing in the middle of the office now—"Don't give me that baloney. You failed to take charge of the thing you were supposed to be in charge of." She thought—*Not the hoof, not the light bulb, not the lamp, not the hands of the woman screaming, not the baby, no, none of those* . . . The man in black sitting opposite her uncle, now showing his teeth in mirthless laughter, resembled the neighing horse. Her uncle said—"A choreographer is supposed to know how to organize people. You arrange a gathering in a square, you get two hundred people to leave their houses, and tell them to head off down the wrong road, and then expect the minister to parade past the populace rather than the populace parading past the minister. Who ever saw such a thing? Don't even talk to me about that whole fiasco . . . In short, there should have been a wall of humanity when he drove by, and there wasn't. Everything planned and paid for. A complete disaster . . ." And then her uncle sat down again and began to grow calmer, although he was still breathing hard, uttering brief angry sighs. Action's personal staff putting on their respective jackets, the new paintings with golden frames nine in number.

And then Milene finally pieced together something that needed piecing together and shouted—"But Uncle Rui, how awful!"

And she covered her eyes so as not to see the awfulness.

Mayor Rui Ludovice looking all around him.

Milene on her feet—"How awful! What you have on your wall is *Guernica* chopped up into pieces! I've seen it, I know it, it was even in *Blitz* once!"

Everyone looked over at the corner next to the door where she was standing. The crowd choreographer stared at her. They all stared at her. Milene stared back at them. Why had she gone there? Now no one could take their eyes off her blouse and her skirt. As if they didn't believe in her existence. She hated this. Milene said—"It's true, Uncle Rui. I recognize it now. If you put all the bits together, it's Picasso's *Guernica*. There are reproductions of it everywhere . . ."

This was such an awkward moment that no one moved. The mayor turned, looked at the newly acquired paintings, and said— "Well, they'll just have to be removed." He sat down again, and the choreographer sat down too. It was as if the whole sweaty lot of them had just been doused by a wave of cold water. Her uncle didn't know where to look. He glanced at her, then spoke to the others.—"We're finished now. We've had quite enough comic episodes for one day. You stay, Inácio, and you too, Idalécio. Now that my niece is here, we can talk a little . . ." And one by one, Action's assistants-in-action, there in the heart of the office, said goodbye. Her uncle examined the paintings. Looking in horror at the paintings that had been foisted on him and which he'd bought as a job lot without even looking at them. A stain, a disappointment. Her aunt wasn't at home, as they all knew, but Uncle Rui shouted up at the tenth floor—"Angelita! Angelita!" Her uncle must have been very upset. "Have those crappy paintings removed at once . . ." That wasn't possible just then, though. They couldn't just remove nine paintings, leaving nine holes. Nine holes in a wall. There were only two staff members present. Plus her and her favorite uncle.

Her uncle was looking at her now, rather bewildered. "How come you just roll up here and immediately spot something no one else has noticed, eh?" And then, turning to face her, he asked her to try to remember the names of the people she'd spoken to during those sad August days.

And she, who already had that series of dispensable facts waiting in line in her memory, once again gazed up at the ceiling, partly as a way of getting to grips with the emotion of the moment, but without letting herself be distracted by her wildly beating heart, because she had prepared herself for this the previous day, and had it all down pat, how to begin and how to end. Yes, she was prepared. She summoned up the words and once more lined the facts up ready for inspection, mentally counting them off on her fingers—first, the policemen, then the people from the undertaker's, then the men at the gas station, and, finally, the priest and the nun. "And no one else"—she said, when she reached the end.

"There's one person missing"—said her uncle. And when she didn't instantly recall the name of that person, he said, to save time—"You were the one who ordered the flowers, weren't you? Tell Inácio what you said to the florist. What did you say, exactly?"

Ah, the florist. Yes, she'd forgotten about her. The flowers were so much a part of the *thing* that it was as if they were also part of the church, the wait, and the journey to the cemetery. But Milene could remember everything and could even respond quite quickly. And as quickly as she could, she began by saying how she'd thought of everyone and had chosen flowers appropriate for each aunt and uncle and each cousin, the details of each wreath, each garland, until she came to the big wreath of blue and white lilies and how she'd asked the florist to add a purple-edged card saying—*Deepest condolences from the Mayor of Santa Maria de Valmares.*

And finally, she said—"I really wanted jasmines, which were Grandma Regina's favorite flower, but they didn't have any."

Then Uncle Rui Ludovice asked rather abruptly, while the other two men were leafing through some papers—"Didn't she ask you why *you* and not your aunts were ordering the flowers and paying for them and dictating what should be written on the cards and so on? Didn't she ask you that?"

"I think she did, yes."

"And?"

"I said my aunts weren't here. And I had to say that I didn't know where they were or when they would be back."

"But that's not true. You did know"—said Uncle Rui Ludovice.

She hesitated. Should she contradict him? Should she or shouldn't she? She said—"No, Uncle, I didn't know."

Her uncle clapped his hands together. The moment of confrontation had arrived, and it was quite different from how she'd imagined it. Her uncle flew into a rage, unfurled his anger, then reeled it back in. Oddly enough, she felt very strong. She pressed heels, toes, and knees together—how could she possibly say she knew what she hadn't known? She was simply giving a clear answer about something that was absolutely clear. "No, Uncle, I didn't know"—she said very loudly. This was her moment to be brave. She remembered her stay at the Diamond, and the powerful words spoken to her there—*Be brave, miss, remember that you're very intelligent, very brave, very remarkable . . . Be brave . . .* Yes, this was the moment—"I didn't know."

"Sir, she really can't be expected to say that she knew something she didn't know. That's very dangerous territory. Is there any point? I don't think so. I really wouldn't pursue it any further," concluded one of the other men, leaning over his notepad and his evanescent phone.

The mayor paused to think.

"Let's leave it, then"—he said during that brief pause. "Leave it." And, leaning wearily back in his chair, breathing in that atmosphere still heavy with the presence of all those other men who had been cluttering up his office with their breath and the sweat of that warm autumn day, with the scent of grasses, savannahs, lemon zest, musk and cinnamon, the smell of burnt scrub, he finally turned to the two remaining men and said—"It must have been her, Lola the florist. Right, we order no more flowers from that tittle-tattler with the Spanish name. No, we cut her dead.

"Dead," demanded Rui Ludovice. "She must have been the one who phoned up the travel agents, who, in turn, phoned the newspaper hacks. No, we'll have nothing to do with either the florist or the travel agents. Now it's your turn"—he said to the young man who was about to question Milene.

The young man leaned toward her and began to speak very clearly, as if she were slightly deaf. They must all have discussed the matter already. Milene clutched her bag closer to her. She was beginning to feel impatient. She would answer any questions quickly. She wanted this moment of confrontation to be over now, before she had to dredge up everything else she had in her soul, *Totus Tuus, Alms Box, Confiteor Deo,* as well as those words from the Book of Wisdom. Yes, as quickly as possible. The young man asked her to concentrate—"Think back to the Old Factory. You went there to seek shelter. Was anyone at home when you arrived?"

"No, only the dogs."

"How can you be so sure?"

"Because after a while I heard them all arrive. I was hiding. The dogs hadn't eaten for days. Their bowls were all overturned. And the sheets had dried to a crisp."

"How do you know?"

"I was hiding behind them. When the family arrived, they found me there and almost died of fright."

Rui Ludovice interrupted—"You could interpret that in two ways. Two contradictory ways."

"Yes, that's true, but the facts aren't contradictory at all"—said the young man, who, like the other man, must have been a lawyer.

And her uncle again paused for thought, just for a moment.

"Leave it, then"—he said.

Uncle Rui Ludovice had gone off to make a phone call. He didn't come back. His footsteps vanished across the exquisite parquet flooring and the equally exquisite rug and never returned. The maid, however, did appear, saying that Senhor Frutuoso had said the mayor had said there would be no lunch. No one had time. Neither he nor her aunt. Nor her cousins, who would have lunch at the tennis club. Could Milene perhaps have lunch with the chauffeur?—Milene was still sitting in the office, with the long table quite empty now, and she glanced again at the wall on which those nine paintings composed of fragments from *Guernica* formed a double frieze of gilt frames. It was because of her comment about those paintings, which she had blurted out rather than waiting for the appropriate moment, that she would be lunching alone with Senhor Frutuoso. It was because the last time her uncle had looked at her, while still seated at the table, his eyes had glinted like the eyes of Rasputin, as João Paulo used to say of Uncle Afonso's eyes when he got angry. Uncle Rui was usually rather kind to her, always ready with a flattering comment about her clothes, even sometimes stroking her hair, but at that moment he had looked at her with genuine fury. Yes, fury. It was understandable, really. If all power is a pyramid, as João Paulo used to say, and her uncle was at the top of the pyramid and she was right at the bottom, why on earth had she taken it upon herself to tell her uncle anything? It was entirely her fault that this change had taken place. She didn't need them to spell it out for her.

But she still didn't know if she would have lunch with Senhor Frutuoso.

And it was then that it happened, the most important moment in that brief perpetual calendar.

XI

AT FIRST SHE DIDN'T KNOW WHAT TO THINK.

Senhor Frutuoso had taken the coastal route. They were driving along a winding road, which curved this way and that, independently of the sea's lace-frilled edge, as if it had once run around some mountains that were later demolished, toppled, and knocked horizontal by an earthquake, leaving their different heights inscribed on the ground. As if the road were being seen from above during a thunderstorm, laid flat by a brilliant flash of lightning. Really, though, it was just following the contours of old estates encircled by country lanes, their outlines still there, speaking of past ways of life. Not only did the road snake back and forth, it was also full of potholes, the camber was uneven, and the grass roadsides resembled twisted green lips. After a particularly sharp bend, the words of Mark Twain came into view, unaccompanied by the name of their author, filling the whole of a large, crooked, rust-covered sign—*BUY LAND, THEY AREN'T MAKING IT ANYMORE.* This sign, the property of a struggling real estate firm that had been successful two years before, must have blown over the previous winter, and now it hung sideways on its post, as if resting an elbow on the ground to take a never-ending nap. The sign—*BUY LAND, THEY AREN'T MAK-*

ING IT ANYMORE—was barely legible, a smattering of letters on a metal rectangle, dull and unassuming, the beauty and even potential astuteness of its message long gone. Now it was nothing but an old sign.

But this wasn't the change Milene was thinking about.

What she found odd, sitting in the backseat, was that she had passed this way just a few months before without noticing that deep bend, or the vast expanse of land stretching down to the sea. Back then she had been focused on the vehicle ahead, the gray van she was tasked with following, in that futile marathon, until she could be handed over to her uncles and aunts. She was thinking about that August morning, and at the same time about Uncle Rui's brisk pacing, the Rasputin-like glint in his eye, and about the gray van and that collapsed slogan which she didn't know had been stolen from Mark Twain, and thinking too about the resplendent two-o'clock sun, when suddenly the road and the low, tangled buildings had begun to feel very familiar indeed, as familiar as the ravine about to appear, the earth almost red against the sea, where the ground began to rise out of its flatness into another formation; not that the change was felt inside the anthracite-gray BMW with Senhor Frutuoso at the wheel, continually asking—"Shall we stop there? Or here? Or would you rather over there?"

They were driving past cafés and restaurants, taverns and drinking holes and all kinds of snack-bars, displayed by the roadside as if they themselves were refreshments to be parceled up for some hungry alien; they drove past tables in doorways, their white cloths pinned in place with upside-down plates, and on they drove, and still she couldn't think of anywhere to have lunch with the chauffeur, instead of the promised meal with Aunt Ângela Margarida, her cousins, and Uncle Rui Ludovice. She couldn't see a single establishment where she might say, *Here*. Instead she was gazing south, toward the sea, thinking only that Senhor Frutuoso was taking her down roads she knew all too well. Then she was seized by an idea, a temptation, that would alter the course of her life.

"Stop"—she said. But no, she didn't know how or how much it was going to alter her life.

Milene brought her fist down hard on the seat. The chauffeur, accustomed to following orders, to starting the engine and setting off whether he wanted to or not, and saving his own desires for when he wasn't working, stopped. Clumsily, in fact, at a bit of an angle. The car leaving the asphalt and skidding on the grit and the stubbly grass, as often happened with that BMW. But he stopped nonetheless. There wasn't so much as a bar in sight. Accustomed to listening, to biting his tongue, to speaking only in the gaps, he eyed her in the rearview mirror.

"What's going on?"

"You can leave"—she said. "There's something I need to do."

And before he could object, the mayor's niece by marriage, her skirt too short, her hair parted in the middle, her bag slung over her shoulder, was hurrying through the dry vegetation and even drier grass, at first downhill, then over the level ground, and the sand that was hard at first and then soft, before making off through the trees, while Senhor Frutuoso, leaving the car doors open, attempted to follow her. A man in a suit and tie, used to an entirely sedentary life, trying to run, calling her name, stumbling over the grass and the fallen chestnuts, flailing around like a fish out of water, at three in the afternoon. "Hey! Listen, come back . . ."—She heard the voice of that man she didn't like, knowing he'd soon give up, that he would probably get stuck somewhere among the thyme bushes, because he didn't know where she was going and she was heading cross-country. She could still hear her name being called as she zigzagged through the shrubs and branches, moving ever farther away, but a second later the sound was gone. Because, as she hastened on, it wasn't what she was leaving behind that interested her, but what lay up ahead.

What interested her was the place near the beach, by the sea. The place where those iron and concrete shapes stood among the metal bars, toward which she was walking as if drawn along by an invisible hand. What they were building was visibly different every day. She remembered the first time she'd come, and the extraordinary circumstances in which she had stood there and waited in the sun. Since then, the crater had changed: three floors had been added on top of the foundations, and the structure was no longer a platform fixed in the sand, but rather a giant piece of honeycomb with jutting walls reaching up to the higher ground. Around what was going to be the Hotel Camarga, six cranes took turns moving their arms. When they moved, it meant there was someone inside, maneuvering from within the glass cabin. She knew all about how the men climbed up and down, encircled by the metal bars, and how they could stay at the top for ages, waiting, doing nothing. She had come there often enough to admire Antonino's skill as a driver to know how it all worked. If he was there, she would call to him, tell him to come down from that leg supporting a great long arm, and then he, perched in the middle, like the head and the engine of the whole contraption, would have to come down. But it was a Saturday, the glass cabins were empty and the metal arms were all still. Milene thought—*So you've escaped again, you cheeky bastard. Things always go your way. . . .*

Yes, everything was going his way, even the fact that it was a Saturday. Should she give up? No, she could at least stay for a bit, to see what that world was like without Antonino. On the platform that formed part of the honeycomb, spread across a few different areas, were the workers, hard hats on their heads, all moving very slowly, as if weary of the iron poles they clung on to as if they were crutches. Others weren't doing a great deal, just standing around among nameless objects, materials so heavy the mere sight of them could strain a man's muscles. But Milene, our cousin Milene, looking more carefully now at the big concrete slab, ended up spotting the person she wanted. Among the twenty workers wandering about on the platform, she recognized Antonino. There he was. She recognized the agitated way he was pacing up and down with some object in his hand, which he then casually snapped into place as if that's what it was made for. She recognized him, with his shirt not off but unbuttoned, the upper part of his body seemingly detached from the lower part, just as it was when he climbed into vans. The same kind of obstinate agitation, the same staccato bursts of energy, as if he were launching himself on a series of immediate, unattainable goals, and this was all communicated to his open shirt and his low-slung trousers that bunched around sneakers as bulky and white as inline skates, and then she thought, yes. She had to do it, she couldn't wait any longer. After all, he had a girlfriend who was alive and whose name was Divina. It had to be done, it would be quite easy. She wouldn't give up. She would get to her feet and wait.

Everything was about to be confirmed yet again.

Yes, there he was, neither looking at her nor seeing her. Even if she stayed exactly where she was, with the dry breeze catching at her skirt, even if she stayed until the end of that Saturday, until the end of the day and the following night, and all the subsequent days and nights, he still, for whatever reason, wouldn't see her. Either because he was so totally absorbed in the task of snapping those objects into place, so fully engaged in it, or because he would soon be setting off with the other guys in the old Pontiac, or because he had a girlfriend who was alive. No, he wouldn't see her. The three o'clock afternoon sun was too blue, and the ground too brown, and the birds soaring in the distance too dark, and the building site too peaceful, not to mention the unbearable calm of the nearby sea, its waves lapping unheard, or even the shadow of Frutuoso left behind somewhere—all this convinced her that she hadn't climbed down that uneven grassy slope just to see the steadily growing concrete platform. All this had come about because Milene wanted to call to him in the afternoon silence, a silence broken, just then, by the sound of muffled hammering. It was the moment she'd been waiting for ever since she made up her mind.

"Antonino?"

She called very loudly, as loudly as she could—"Antonino!" She called again, with a rasping yell. Milene calling several times, fully aware of how bad it looked, a girl in a short skirt, jiggling up and down opposite a group of men in yellow hard hats. But she wasn't doing anything bad. There was no time to lose. "Antoninooooo!"—she shouted with all her might, propelling his name into the low rumble of that warm working day on which no one seemed to be doing any work. She called out, shouting as only she could shout, because he needed to decide. He couldn't keep driving past Villa Regina every evening, and arriving unannounced outside Kilometer 44, only to pretend, now, that he hadn't seen her. He was being stupid. What did Antonino want?

So the time had come.

Milene saw him turn around with something in his hand, a joist or a tool perhaps, and then, as if he had some urgent business on the far side, he disappeared immediately into the honeycomb. She saw him disappear behind those gray holes that reminded her of the alveoli in *Alien 3*. Disappear completely. And another guy, standing on a ledge on the eastern side, between two columns, making sure no one could see him, moved his hand to a questionable place on his body and made an obscene gesture. A gesture that sullied everything. Indecent. *"Indecent"*—she said, separating him from Antonino in her mind. Still, as if not wanting that to be the last mark left by the afternoon, a mark too bound up in bodily indecency, something close to feces and piss, wanting the afternoon to be clean again, she had mustered all her courage, and wildly, joyously, frantically, clutching at her skirt, her knees pressed together, Milene began to call—*"Antonino? Antonino? Antonino . . ."* Not to summon him, or to insult him, but as a kind of parting shot, knowing he wasn't among those men staring at her and laughing. She understood. He had ducked out of sight because she was an embarrassment, but at least now that was clear. She hated feeling sad for very long. In fact, she hated feeling sad at all; she never wanted to feel sad, that's how she'd always been and she wasn't about to change. The story had reached its conclusion. It was over.

Milene turned and began walking back the way she had come.

She began climbing up the other side of the sandy slope, picking her way through the thyme and thistles, the pink ice plants and the creeping vines, all desiccated by that harsh, waterless summer, and, borne along by the thought that she had obeyed some inner need, which made her heart feel both full and ready to bite, or ready to burst on contact with the other organs stuffed higgledy-piggledy inside her, seeking some kind of order, feeling no pain, she clambered back up to the road, intending to walk home along the narrow shoulder. As the cars whipped past her, she staggered airily along, like a drunk serenading an empty street, feeling no weight in her feet or shoes, because she had done something utterly stupid, far more stupid even than insulting Uncle Rui

Ludovice's paintings, since the fact that she had gone there meant the connection between them was broken forever, and Milene was actually glad. A feeling so unexpected that she might never get used to it. She walked like a person who has just committed suicide and has no regrets, thinking instead—*Look, I did it, I did it, I did something stupid that no other girl my age would do, and I feel fine* . . . As if she had appeared in a Clint Eastwood or Schwarzenegger movie, and was all muscle and survival instinct. Now she just had to walk and walk. The whole thing was over, once and for all. And as she walked along, pondering that rather abrupt conclusion, Milene didn't notice the docile purr of the car driven by Senhor Frutuoso drawing up beside her.

XII

SENHOR FRUTUOSO DROVE OFF IN THAT UNMISTAKABLE WAY of his, and silently deposited her outside Kilometer 44. Without a backward glance, like someone delivering a stray package he was keen to be rid of.

"A fellow needs the patience of Job . . ." he'd said when he picked her up.

He did turn around when she got out of the car, but only to make sure the door was properly closed. Firmly locked. To make sure she didn't slip back in through any of the car's electronic cracks and ruin his life. Or the lives of his bosses, or give sleepless nights to Senhor Rui Ludovice, or Senhora Dona Ângela Margarida, or the girls who really shouldn't see her very often anyway, because she was a bad influence. Frankly, it would be better if they never saw her at all and never called her cousin. Better if Milene stayed on her own. His pants were still covered in dust from his cross-country pursuit of her. He even briefly got out of the car and brushed himself down. Only after all that had Senhor Frutuoso vanished, flying off, almost levitating, in the direction of the Frame Store and the Hotel Miramar. On the way, he had received a call—"Yes, she's home now, sir. In the house. Of course, sir, where else would I have left her?"

Like someone who has recaptured an escaped pet.

Not that she cared. Feeling completely clearheaded now, she had gone straight to the living room where Grandma Regina's armchairs stood intact, one in front of the other. There was the cherrywood table, and the shelf full of encyclopedias and world classics. The sepia photos, the black-and-white ones, and the ones in color, the painted portraits, the absent and the purloined, those that had left their visible mark on the wall, the paintings of Swiss cabins and scenes from *Giselle* and *Swan Lake*. It was all there waiting for her. She went over to the phone. She dialed the thirteen numbers. They were waiting for her too—*"You've reached five-seven-three . . ."* Milene listened, fearing that the tape might be broken, but the connection was made seamlessly. Milene almost whispered into the phone—*"João Paulo?"* Again it felt as if there were no distance between them. It was as if someone entirely free and available were waiting at the other end but had chosen not to reveal himself until he received the magic password from this end. *"João Paulo?"*—Milene plucked up courage. *"Listen, I had a boyfriend, but nothing came of it. He wasn't right for me. He had a girlfriend who was alive and another one who was dead. He said I looked just like the dead one, and she's the one he loves most . . . Anyway, I don't want anything more to do with him. I went to the place where he works so as to get him to make a decision. Now I don't want to see him again."* The receiver waiting silently for a response. *"I also wanted to tell you that we haven't had any rain in ages. How is it over there? I saw on the TV that it's snowing there now. The kind of heavy snow we never get . . ."*

Milene continued to wait, the receiver between her ear and her lips. And why not keep waiting, since it was such an important day? Meanwhile, darkness had begun to fall, and Milene thought she should hang up, but only because it was time to open everything that could be opened in Villa Regina, time to reattach the inside of the house to the Universe that was just beginning, and from which it was separated only by the thickness of the window-panes. But she went on—"*I don't know if I said, but my boyfriend's part of the third wave . . . But I won't ever go back to the Diamond, not now . . .*" Only then did she hang up and turn on all the lights, from end to end of the house. Wandering about between the music from the radio and the television. But when she grew tired of the noises she herself was making and turned off the radio and television, she stood in the middle of the room, next to the pale lampshades, thinking, thinking her own thoughts. Then she phoned again—"*João Paulo? It's pitch-black night here. I feel like a tiny speck of nothing in the world. I've fallen from somewhere and I'm heading for somewhere but I don't know where. But I'm very happy. That happens sometimes . . .*"

Milene really did feel that her life had changed forever, but she couldn't have known how much. And she wouldn't find out for a while. She wouldn't go to Mãos Largas because she didn't want to run into Barbosa, and didn't want to work for him, or have to wear an apron and wield a pencil. So she would just go wherever. Some time later, one Sunday afternoon, she was at the Pomodoro staring out at the street, when into the restaurant walked a dark-skinned young woman with two boys as dark as her, all three of them smelling of Havana cologne. The smell didn't come from them, though, it came from Antonino, who was walking behind them with his three small children.

Milene noticed that the young woman and Antonino already made a perfect couple. One of the older boys gave Emanuel, Antonino's oldest boy, a clip around the ear. They were arguing over some battery-controlled toy. Antonino yelled at her son. Perfect. They weren't even bothering to be polite with each other. Perhaps they were already married. So that was Divina, the famous living girlfriend.

"Quiet!" said Antonino Mata in his usual half-brusque, half-blunt way.

As for Milene, he didn't see her, or if he did, he chose not to. Gone were the days when his mother had said to her, *Remember, you're very kind, very intelligent, a real gem,* and the days when she'd been wrapped in other people's words, *Introibo ad Altarem Dei, Totus Tuus, Confiteor Deo,* like the arrow, like the cloud, are you feeling all right? Antonino himself saying to Milene, *Look, if I were you, I wouldn't go to the Town Hall, I'd come back to our house, and think about your life,* and so on, until, in the end, they had all left. Divina looking after her children, who were nearly as tall as her, and him looking after his, still with their milk teeth.

As for the living girlfriend, there she was leaving the Pomodoro, she had legs, thighs, firm breasts pushed together beneath a low-cut top, ankles, lips, nostrils, eyes with rather short lashes, cheeks, fingers with which to grip the plastic-wrapped slices of pizza, and inside she must also have fat, tendons, heart, spleen, and kidneys, like everyone else, and yet her name was Divina. Some people had all the luck. Farewell, good luck. Because she and Antonino would never see each other again, never see each other again.

Then it rained in Valmares.

It all began with a few sparse drops. They fell like noisy footsteps. Some here, others there, causing a potent smell to rise up from the dry earth. The drops were as large as the contents of a bowl, but the earth swallowed them up in a trice. That is what the rain was like. The drops, though, were not just water falling from the sky, because the water itself brought earth with it. How else explain why cars were left spotted with what looked like mud? Many people phoned the Meteorological Office saying that it had rained mud. The meteorologists tried to dispel such ignorance, saying it wasn't true. TV screens filled up with isothermal charts from all over the place, to combat this supposition. The experts said that the drops had simply encountered an atmosphere full of dust. But there was a big difference between clouds raining down pure water that became laden with dust as it fell and the existence of such things as clouds made of mud. For more cultivated, imaginative people, the difference was vast, and they could easily imagine great expanses of dark mud drifting around in the sky above Valmares. That would be the end of human life, at least as conceived of by the usual cosmogonies, according to which the Earth is always separated from the waters. Some even evoked the Apocalypse and the visions of John of Patmos, with all the accompanying drama. One housewife displayed a sheet bearing great brown splotches, resembling the skin of some brindled cow. The effect of the rain on her linen. An expert was brought in to make the necessary reassuring noises on local television. This specialist in rainfall stated with great confidence that this was rain with some mud in it and not mud in the form of rain. But the majority of the population really didn't care when precisely the rain became mud, they just didn't want the rain to fall on their courtyards and clothes once it was all mixed up with the dust. That's what they didn't want. They wanted clear water. They didn't care a jot about what went on up above in the atmosphere. The matter was discussed for three whole days. Then it rained some more.

This time the drops that fell were tiny, transparent, and made a kind of healthy mush of the earth. The garden-cum-microclimate smelled of dung, and the leaves Milene had failed to sweep up began to smell putrid, the good putrid smell of wet earth. A month later than usual, yellow chrysanthemums sprang up in the pots in people's courtyards. Then back came the drought, six months early. The hoopoe bird was so stunned that it sang. Clouds of mosquitoes rose up from ponds and puddles. The cars were all filthy. People had never seen such dirty windshields, where boys used their fingers to trace their first graffiti—*I'M DIRTY, WASH ME.* Milene found an *I'M DIRTY, WASH ME* on her Clio and drove to the car wash at the gas station. A gray van was parked in front of her, facing the other way. Inside were some children wearing striped hats. Then everything happened very fast. Milene recognized the children and the vehicle. Standing with his back to the van, feeling for money in his pocket, was Antonino Mata.

She had nothing to say to him. She had already said everything.

But there he was. He didn't smell of Havana cologne, though. It was the end of the day, and his clothes were dusty and his eyes hard. Like his life. She had no idea why she felt so drawn to him, or what it was made of, this substance that bound her to him. He was still rummaging around in his pocket as if he'd lost his money. Then he saw her and came over. He asked: "What are you doing here at this hour? Where have you come from?" He asked this out of the blue, their two cars pointing in opposite directions.

She really had nothing to say to him. She could, of course, make some banal comment, but what? He asked her—"Where are you going?" Why was he asking her that? She wanted to know the same thing but had no answer. She really didn't. And her own ignorance about where she was going, which she became aware of for the first time, continued to grow inside her as she drove off. But she had only become aware of it because he'd asked her the question. And what right did Felícia Mata's son have to ask her that question, when he wasn't a relative, and meant nothing to her; why did he ask her like that, out of the blue, where she was coming from and where she was going? Just because he'd tried to hand her over to her aunts and uncles on that August day when she'd been in a state of shock? A day when she was full of other people's words, other people's orders, as if she were a marionette.

Was this *Abyssus abyssum invocat* summoning her to the abyss? He had no right to ask her anything. No, he didn't, because she'd gone to the construction site and called out to him, and he hadn't responded. And now he had no right even to speak to her.

That's why, there and then, she was going to double back and catch him up, overtake him so that she could say just that—*Go away, go and ask your living girlfriend instead, go on* . . . And she was already turning the wheel.

There was a turnoff where the Frame Store abutted onto the low roof of a bar, next to the Pomodoro and the Banana, the arrow sign and then the turnoff. The road formed a circle, a kind of arbitrary loop that deposited her on the other side of the road, heading in the other direction. She knew which routes he would take. At that hour, he would be heading home to drop off the kids, before taking a shower in the courtyard, getting dressed, dousing himself in cologne, and going to see Divina. Milene was following him now in order to tell him that he had no right. He really didn't. He should have asked her before. After the turn-off, she sped along the empty road ahead. She accelerated, then decelerated. But she decelerated because coming dangerously fast toward her in the opposite lane was the gray van, whose shape and gleaming metallic snout she knew so well.

Had Antonino had the same thought? That there needed to be a settling of accounts? Had he set off after her in order to catch up with her and for them to have it out? Or was it pure coincidence?—It was just too much.

Milene and Antonino parked on opposite sides of the road, slammed their respective car doors, and strode toward each other very much like two people with an account to settle, as if each were about to unleash a projectile that would inflict a fatal wound on the other, and yet, with both approaching at the same speed, they ended up colliding on the narrow strip separating the houses from the cars, in full view of the three children who were now standing on their seats, watching the two of them locked in an embrace, unable to let go of each other and move their cars. His trembling hand on her back. It was almost dark. They had met in the inhospitable world of the highway shoulder. Love pulsated around the irregular row of houses, which made the highway seem more like a street. He took Milenc's car key from her and drove the Clio to where it could be safely parked. From where she was standing, she could see Antonino's legs running and running, lit up by the passing lightning of the other cars' headlights. When he returned, she was exactly where he had left her. Only then did they get in his van. How futile and ridiculous circumstances are. And how decisive. Someone had written *I'M DIRTY, WASH ME* on his car too. They sat down. Where would they go?

Antonino now had two living girlfriends. That's all that could be said.

XIII

AFTERWARD, PEOPLE SAID THAT THE DINNER AT THE LUXOR
must have been arranged at the last minute, at the precise
moment when it became necessary, as if nothing measured and
premeditated in life could ever seem spontaneous. But it wasn't
like that at all. The dinner was the result of communications
between Dom Silvestre and the Dutchmen prior to the night
when Milene's uncle Dom had suddenly appeared, striding across
the lawn, when his wife was least expecting him. A business dinner like so many others, booked for table thirteen in the top-floor
restaurant. The uncles had a plan, a strategy, and a goal. The roles
had been assigned, the timings calculated. And with the Dutchmen it was the same. An ordinary business dinner preceded only
by a special preparatory meeting, in this case a leisurely helicopter
tour. Only later, if that initial meeting went well, would the dinner be confirmed. At the last minute.

The tour, organized by Uncle Dom, would take place that morning. The day's agenda was set: nothing to disagree with, nothing
to declare.

And so, at around eleven o'clock, the helicopter had begun a
reconnaissance flight along the length of the coast, before curving around to the north and then to the south again, flying in

ever-decreasing spirals until it reached Mar de Prainhas. Only then did the helicopter make the Factory its target, circling it first and then skimming straight over the top of it in a perfect tangent. The helicopter was making a deafening clatter, like a plane in a war zone. And yet when it came to the looping precision of its path, the pilot seemed to have learned from the eagles.

"Beautiful, just beautiful . . ."—one of the Dutchmen couldn't help but exclaim. And then things began to go very well indeed.

Even before that, as they traveled over the dunes, with flocks of birds billowing up on all sides, he had spun around in his seat, delighted. But unfortunately, he couldn't make himself understood over the noise. Still, as they approached the Diamond, and the roof of the Old Factory stretched and shifted as if a slice of the Earth's surface had come loose, and that beautiful patch of lichen-filled green grew larger amid the slurry and the sand, and the eleven palm trees fanned out their leafy fingers as if in greeting, Senhor Van de Berg had raised his voice even louder to address the backseats, where Uncle Dom and Uncle Afonso were sitting. At one point, the Dutchman even had to yell to make himself heard—"What kind of birds are they? Over there, yes, over there . . . Look, look, taking off from the ground . . ." As he spoke, some white birds, rose-tinted in the morning sun, soared up together in a single mass, pirouetting between the sand and the sea, alarmed by the noise from the helicopter. Uncle Dom racked his brains, he knew all the local bird species but he wasn't quite sure, and he didn't want to risk getting it wrong. "Cory's shearwaters, maybe?"—he hollered, amid all the commotion. After which the helicopter swooped down and then up again, performing a complete circuit around the Diamond, and flying over it several times. The Dutchman had begun to point his enormous finger—all of him was very large, his almost-white blond hair brushing against the roof of the helicopter—"Hey! There are people there too, yes, look, right there . . . People . . ." Pointing his big fat finger.

At that moment, the helicopter had sunk lower still, and tilted slightly, and the people on the ground had begun running and waving. Senhor Van de Berg, a Dutchman from Rotterdam, had learned his Portuguese in the south of Brazil and inherited his expressiveness from his father, who had emigrated to southern Italy as a young man, and so, pressed right up against the glass, he waved repeatedly, unlikely as it was that the people down below could see him. The Dutchman, shouting over his shoulder, had asked—"Hey! Are there people living in there?" The deafening noise from the propellers made it very hard to respond.

But Uncle Dom decided to attempt an explanation: it was a loan, an *empréstimo*, a short-term thing, and Senhor Van de Berg needn't worry because they were just third-wave people. Uncle Dom leaning close to the Dutchman, the Dutchman leaning close to Uncle Dom, their heads meeting in the middle of the helicopter. Really, noise was the only problem with helicopter travel. It would be perfect if people could fly like that, the blades slicing the air, but with the silent weightlessness of eagles. Just think of the deals that would be done inside those cabins then. But Uncle Dom didn't say any of that just then, although he mentioned it later on. The people on the ground were still waving.

"A *préstimo*? What's a *préstimo*?"

Hard as he tried, the Dutchman couldn't get the word right. And at that precise moment, the helicopter was performing a wider arc, giving a sense of how the building fit into the landscape, where it stood in relation to the dunes and the sea, and then, as it was curving back around, skirting the Diamond to the north, not only did the steel rails gleam in the sun, but the eleven ancient palms rose into view up ahead, in all their untamed elegance. The people Van de Berg was talking about, meanwhile, had run in the opposite direction and were standing by the southern wall, and now, even if they were to return the greeting, they could only have waved goodbye to the helicopter's tail. Should they fly over one more time? No, the Dutchman had seen all he needed to see. The machine descended and ascended almost vertically above the courtyard, and then, sending new flocks of birds scattering before them, as if the nose of the helicopter had summoned them out of thin air, they had made their way back. Still inside the glass pod, with the propellers spinning, Van de Berg had been very specific—he said that over dinner he would like them to tell him the name of the birds, and the meanings of the word *préstimo* and the expression *third wave*. The Dutchman laughed a lot, as if all he wanted was a Portuguese lesson, but the two uncles, intent on their plans, knew full well what was going on. The first stage was over. That was when Páscoa had been given the green light to confirm the dinner at the Luxor.

"The boss would like table number thirteen . . ."

The table stood waiting for them, right by the window. On the group's arrival, the waiter had hurried to light the candles, which floated in holders full of water. The autumn night had plunged the Ria into total darkness. Beyond the area lit by the hotel lights, nothing could be seen. But this opaque exterior didn't matter. Everyone knew the shadows were hiding a long snaking lake like a Persian carpet, which altered its shape from moment to moment, hour to hour, its wet soupy surface always different, always pulled this way and that by invisible, mysterious force lines. They talked about that as they took their seats. The Dutchmen, who had been waiting for this moment for months, felt quite content. Van de Berg was accompanied now by another Dutchman, marginally shorter and less pink, and by his own lawyer, a Portuguese man almost as burly as they were. Uncle Afonso was still accompanied only by Dom Silvestre. Uncle Rui, as agreed, hadn't joined them. This was a business dinner. No sooner had they sat down, the two candles fluttering in the middle of the table, than Senhor Van de Berg forgot the darkness outside and remembered the birds that morning. Beautiful, just beautiful. It was a table for eight, and there were five of them, all dressed in dark colors as if for some kind of ceremony, with the biggest Dutchman sitting at the center, taking up enough space for three.

"So, were they shearwaters in the end?"—he had asked, spacing out the syllables.

Uncle Afonso had then turned to Dom Silvestre. At this particular business dinner, birds were not his area. Let his brother-in-law talk about birds.

"Yes, what were they called again?"

Dom Silvestre was the one with the bird knowledge, not only because as a hunter he was interested in any creature that moved, but also because he had done some research expressly for that dinner. Dom Silvestre considered it very important to be on top of such material, which could be slipped into the conversation at opportune moments. His success wasn't simply down to luck—it took a lot of work. So if Senhor Van de Berg and his associates wished, he could, naturally, discuss the birds, mollusks, plants, lakes, soils, and various rare species native to the local area. Because Mar de Prainhas, of which his wife was co-owner, was replete with rarities. And since the Dutchman was listening with devout attention, Uncle Dom had begun holding forth about plovers and terns, emphasizing the ornithological significance of the little bittern, a marvelous white creature with a pointy feather cap. Yes, it could fly. To demonstrate how it flew, Uncle Dom spread his arms and began to whoop, right there in the Luxor Restaurant, which made the other men laugh. Raising his hand,

sometimes to his own head, Uncle Dom spoke with particular rel-
ish of the western swamp hen, with its purple feet and a little red
tiara in the middle of its forehead. His hand on his own forehead.
A queen. A beautiful bird. Uncle Dom made a croaking sound
like a swamp hen. Then he mentioned too the presence of turtles,
fiddler crabs, and seahorses, as well as truly excellent shellfish.
And, with his eyes fixed on Van de Berg, Uncle Dom made little
kissing sounds as if he were tasting them—"Marvelous . . ." All
these and much more could be found in the area around the Old
Factory. But the flocks they had seen that morning, flying away
from the helicopter, would have been herring gulls, *Larus argen-
tatus*, said Uncle Dom, who had made sure to have a few Latin
names up his sleeve, in case the occasion called for them. Need
he say more?

The Luxor Restaurant was on the tenth floor, and the five men
were sitting by the window. They looked outside and didn't see a
thing, but between themselves all was crystal clear.

The Dutchman still couldn't hide his enthusiasm for the local
winged wildlife. He had loved seeing those birds, flocks upon
flocks of them. Van de Berg still settling into his seat and asking
urgent-seeming questions. Had anyone there seen *Out of Africa*,
by any chance? When Redford's tiny plane had sent the flocks
scattering into the African skies? Because the similarity between
those two scenes was extraordinary. Beautiful, just beautiful.
There were still paradises left in the world, you just had to spot
the paths that led you to them. And he, a man with a good nose,
could sniff out a paradise a mile off. Beaming as he spoke. Meanwhile, Uncle Dom was still going on about how that whole area
was where the birds heading south and the birds heading north
came together and made their stopovers—"A kind of bird airport,
if you will . . ."

And so, with this description of the migratory fauna of Mar de Prainhas, according to Uncle Dom, the dinner at the Luxor had begun. Only then had the Dutchman wanted to know the story of the *third wave*. And, above all, the meaning of the word *préstimo*.

"*Empréstimo*"—Uncle Dom corrected him. "From *emprestar*, to lend, to give something away temporarily in exchange for nothing or almost nothing. Do you follow me?"

Yes, now the Dutchman understood. His associates did too, especially the lawyer. That is, there were people living inside the Old Factory, but it was only a temporary loan, and so Senhor Dom Silvestre prepared to continue his explanation. They still hadn't even been brought the menu, and now all there was left to clear up was the matter of the third wave.

"So you're interested in the third wave, Senhor Van de Berg?"— Uncle Afonso had said, getting in before Dom Silvestre.

Sitting opposite the big Dutchman, Afonso Leandro seemed on top form, as he was in his finest moments. He cleared his throat, a habit he had learned in court, for when he needed to gain time over his opponent. But at that moment, it wasn't even necessary. Half of his head was cool, and the other half was fired up, exactly how he liked it. Uncle Afonso laughing—"The problem is that there's only a third wave because there was a second, and before that a first . . ."

Van de Berg listening attentively. He was the buyer. The dinner was high-risk. And the matter in question very delicate.

Uncle Afonso had said—"I hope I won't bore you, Senhor Van de Berg, but it would be impossible to understand Mar de Prainhas without an explanation of the first wave. And discussing the first wave means recalling the figure of my grandfather. It would be impossible to understand what's at stake here without knowing that at the beginning of this century, there lived a simple man who sold his whole inheritance and mortgaged everything he had and didn't have, in order to build a factory that fed a whole population for fifty years. Do you see what I'm saying, Senhor Van de Berg? There was no one else like him, and maybe that's why José Joaquim Leandro died the peaceful death he deserved, in the middle of the countryside, leaning against his old Chrysler, like a perfect prince . . ." And as that business dinner began, Uncle Afonso added—"Senhor Van de Berg, forgive me saying so, but I'm convinced that Mar de Prainhas was founded by a man the like of whom no longer exists . . ."

"It's the same the world over, they don't make them like they used to . . ."—said the Dutchman, rather moved.

Unlike their flames, the candles stood erect inside the holders full of water. And apart from the candle holders, the only other things on the table were drinks and appetizers, objects so small they seemed more like fleshy embroidery that had leapt from the tablecloth onto the plates. It was a business dinner, and everything had to be thought through. At that moment, Uncle Afonso, who was sipping his whiskey, blushed slightly. Dom Silvestre, by his side, looked rather solemn too. And when Uncle Dom's eyes became solemn, they stared straight ahead, homing in on some invisible point in the distance. But the Dutchman wanted to put the uncles at ease. *Please, please.* The Dutchman repeated the word, the way people did in these parts. What's more, he quite understood that, in this culture, anything to do with family must be treated with the utmost delicacy. Van de Berg spoke a very measured kind of Portuguese, spacing out the words, almost the way a child speaks, but he managed to express himself perfectly. Flanked by his two associates, and with their approval, the Dutchman had begun to coax Uncle Afonso—"Come on, Senhor Leandro, businesses are living things, like animals. They're born, they live, they disappear, and some have children and others don't. And listen, what you're doing is giving your grandfather's business children. Letting it bear fruit, I think you say. Is that right?"

"Yes, quite right, Senhor Van de Berg . . ."—Dom Silvestre had replied.

"Well, then?"

Uncle Afonso, with his equestrian arms stretched over the table, half of his lawyer's mind neat and tidy and the other half healthily astir, before looking at the menu, thought it would help to mention a few concrete details from the past, such as the sound of the factory siren, or the howl of the poor, as the factory workers called it in the 1930s. Uncle Afonso wanted Senhor Van de Berg and his associates to know how, when their grandfather had passed away, his servants' gratitude had been such that they couldn't all fit in the photographs taken to honor him. And back then people still arranged themselves in proper pyramids in front of box cameras, in public parks. Yes, as of 1908, those people, that loyal multitude, had been the first wave.

The menus open on the table. The Dutchman very interested indeed. He too had photographs like that in his childhood home. The tall Dutchman laughed a lot. But he wasn't just a jolly man; at heart he was also pragmatic. A descendant of merchants and seminomadic emigrants, he wanted to get straight to the point. He asked—"And how did the third wave come about?"

"The first"—said the uncle. "I was talking about the first. Forgive me, sir, but to understand the miracle of Mar de Prainhas, you have to understand what happened to my grandfather's property . . ."

By then, the restaurant on the top floor of the Luxor was almost full, except for the tables around the uncles, which they had reserved as well, in order to be able to speak freely. There were aperitifs. Uncle Afonso didn't drink aperitifs.

"Let me be clear, Senhor Van de Berg. We need to set out our point of view. Imagine unimpeachable factory management—for the time, of course, because we have to remember when this was happening, and what a miserable country this was then, at the beginning of the twentieth century. But, all that considered, imagine, for example, what it meant for my grandfather to employ girls as young as seven, whose productivity would have been less than zero, just to give their families a helping hand. See what I mean? Because my grandfather employed dozens of them. He employed hundreds, and their mothers used to kneel before the image of São Francisco do Mar, on the day their daughters started work, dressed for the first time in their blue pinafores, which my grandfather ordered and paid for himself. Do you see what I'm saying? Under the circumstances, both mothers and daughters had my grandfather as benefactor, and if he happened to appear in the factory buildings, at any hour of the day or night, their tiny fingers would be flying along like a violin bow playing a *pizzicato*. Do you see? These people were the first wave, and it's important to mention them so you understand our point of view. Because we have a very particular point of view, we have for many years . . ."

Then Senhor Van de Berg had dreamily closed his eyes, envisioning it all, thinking out loud. Yes, as it happened, he'd watched movies and read a few books about these things, but seeing the places for real was different—"Very interesting, this business with the girls . . . Very interesting indeed. All those little workers, and your grandfather being so kind . . . That's how it was everywhere back then. Isn't that so?"

"Yes"—said the uncle, handing him the menu. "But there are a few things that set this case apart . . ."

"Yes, I'm sure . . ."

Then it was time to explain to Senhor Van de Berg, so that he could appreciate the difference, that the factory he had seen from the helicopter wasn't just a factory. It was a whole world. When their grandfather had passed away, leaning against his Chrysler, stretched out over the hood, one hand on his heart and the other on the car, the whole community had been deeply shaken. The news of their grandfather's death had been followed by countless heartfelt eulogies, endless expressions of regret for José Joaquim Leandro's departure from his earthly life in Santa Maria de Valmares. And as the months went by, the grief still didn't subside. Just to give Senhor Van de Berg an idea: for a long time afterward, the factory girls would hear the Chrysler approaching, very gingerly, and then hear it turn around, its engine in neutral, and sense it coming to a halt right in front of them. Some factory girls even showed people their feet, coated in the dust churned up by the Chrysler.

By now, Uncle Afonso was beginning to laugh at his own words.

No, thank you, he didn't want any more whiskey. He wasn't just a lawyer, he was a horseman as well, an athlete, so he'd better not. He liked to keep in shape. No, what he wanted was to carry on, to demonstrate how his grandfather had behaved not only generously, but also with considerable honor and integrity.

Because, when it came to personal honor, there too their grandfather had been one hundred percent unimpeachable. Suffice it to say that despite having a hundred or so goddaughters in his day, he never once abused anyone's trust or took advantage of any of the girls. There was never a child in the local area who bore any resemblance to him. And back then, in the 1930s, factory owners everywhere would boast about having fathered fifty children with fifty different women. Some even planted an almond tree in their garden for each one, so they wouldn't forget how many they had when they were too old to remember. But not their grandfather. When the time had come to relax and enjoy his wealth and worldly wisdom, he had begun traveling alone between Mar de Prainhas and Lisbon, sometimes by train and sometimes in the Chrysler, without the slightest hint of a scandal. And nor did he imitate other factory owners, who would stroll into the Maxime cabaret with thousand-escudo notes wrapped around their Cuban cigars, and headily confess that the smoke produced by burning money was one of their greatest pleasures. Greater even than absinthe.

The Dutchman, seated between the two tall candles, was appalled—"Did they really smoke money? I've never heard anything so . . ."

"Yes, Senhor Van de Berg, they did . . ."

At that point, Uncle Afonso thought the time had come to go still further in setting out his point of view, which was identical to that of his brothers-in-law. He thought he should point out Mar de Prainhas' clean record when it came to the Second World War.

The two Dutchmen had sat up straighter in their seats and leaned in toward the center of the table. They had also chosen a starter of spider crab, but at that moment all they wanted to hear was how the place fit in with the great destinies of the World. Oh, Senhor Van de Berg would be amazed. Uncle Afonso had also leaned in closer, as he emphasized, even in this respect, the uniqueness of the *Fábrica de Conservas Leandro 1908*. Allow him to explain—You see, during World War Two that industry had really taken off, as everyone knew, and neither he, Afonso Leandro, nor his brothers-in-law would deny that their grandfather had made a fortune. But José Joaquim Leandro had never once had a swastika printed on the lid of any of his tins. Unlike some of his business partners.

What's more, other factory owners had not only doctored the labels on their containers in order to sell directly to the Germans, they had also falsified the contents, filling their tins not with the pink flesh of *Thunnus thynnus*, but with waste products, bones and innards, and even seaweed and bits of grit, which he, Afonso Leandro, as a lawyer, considered a crime against humanity. But their grandfather never did anything like that. He always stood firm. Yes, he had done deals with traders who sent shipments out of the country labeled *Surplus from Portugal*, which was a lie. Their lie. Because what was surplus in Portugal, where so many were going hungry?—asked Uncle Afonso, making the candle flames flicker with the force of his words. But then, when he did those deals— and done them he had—their grandfather hadn't known where his products would end up. What's more, their grandfather didn't care about the nationality of a starving mouth. He didn't mind what language a person spoke if they needed food, just as long as he wasn't sending it straight to Hitler's troops. That was all. Yes, he had made money, but with José Joaquim Leandro, everything had been aboveboard, everything had been fair, a far cry from the murky dealings others dabbled in. In fact, Uncle Afonso didn't think his grandfather's independence and integrity had received the recognition they deserved. But that was by the by. He was only going back over all this in order to explain the survival of Mar de Prainhas. How the factory had kept going, and how it came to be inhabited, at present, by the third wave. This was why he considered the dinner so important. Because it would allow those present, on both sides, to appreciate what was at stake.

"I'm finding all this fascinating"—said the Dutchman, refilling his glass.

And he was.

The meal at the Luxor included spider crabs with open shells, the flesh subtly seasoned, and they had to be eaten slowly. This gave Afonso Leandro time to discuss the second wave. He was feeling in fine form. Setting his spider crab aside, and guided by the cool half of his head, Uncle Afonso explained how in the mid-seventies people had written hackneyed slogans on the walls, like, *The factories for the workers*, and *Down with the exploiters*, and how this had led to a second wave, a second invading horde. "Do you see what I'm saying?"—Uncle Afonso had asked, mentioning too that by then the person in charge of that whole burdensome business had been his mother, who, incidentally, had recently passed away. At this point, Uncle Afonso glanced at the dark night closing off the world outside the window. No, he wouldn't say what he was thinking then. He wouldn't tell Senhor Van de Berg that his mother had managed the factory for twenty years because her husband, José Joaquim Leandro's only son, a doctor in his spare time, had never been especially interested. Or rather, that Luís Leandro, Afonso's father, not only hated the smell of canned fish, but also loathed each and every person who had anything to do with it. And so his mother had taken over. But there was no need to go into all that, so he wouldn't.

Uncle Dom, listening closely, came to his brother-in-law's aid.

"A woman, running a factory, in the 1950s and '60s! Think of that!"

Then Uncle Afonso added—"For twenty years, it was our mother who attempted to steady the ship, while everything else was falling apart. And it was our mother who, against our wishes, poured all we had into keeping Mar de Prainhas going, just the way our grandfather left it, so the workers didn't lose their jobs. But nonetheless, the second wave emerged out of the first—a most unfortunate birth . . ." Uncle Afonso held his head very erect, as if an extraordinary historical event were marching toward him. The fiery half of his head ablaze. The Dutchman looked startled.

"They rebelled?" But before Uncle Afonso could respond, he added—"That's what happened the world over, from Asia to Latin

America. Yes, industrial relations is a dog-eat-dog business . . ." At which the two Dutchmen and their Portuguese lawyer, sensitive people, had put down their knives and forks.

"Yes, one thing led to another . . ."

Uncle Afonso felt rather emotional. It was as if this were the last time he would be able to recall those events, as if he were slipping them into the pocket of someone setting off on a long journey, never to return. As if he were selling them, or giving them away, and they would never belong to him again, or as if he were grinding them up, in sadness and in rage, so as to be rid of them forever. Afonso felt a pang. Then, to get the thing over with, he said it had happened like this—On a day when tensions were running high, and when someone had scrawled, *Every boss is a crook*, on one of the factory walls, his mother had decided there was only so much injustice a person could take and passed the factory on to her oldest son, Uncle Afonso's brother José Carlos. And this brother, in turn, had thought the matter through and concluded that if his grandfather had been alive, he would have done the very thing that he was about to do. In other words, this brother had concluded that it was futile battling against the winds of History, and so one September morning in 1975 he decided to hand the keys to the factory over to new management. And not only that. His brother José Carlos had acquired some notion that he must do the thing properly, handing the keys to the workers on a velvet cushion embroidered with the name *LEANDRO*. And when he remembered this, Afonso felt shocked all over again. Feeling an urge to curse loudly and only stopping himself because this was, after all, a business dinner. Meanwhile, the Luxor Restaurant had filled up, and even the nearby tables, which were supposed to have been kept free, were busy. Van de Berg had long since emptied the shell of his spider crab, looking all the while at Uncle

Afonso, but now he asked him to repeat certain parts of the story that he wasn't sure he'd understood. He was stunned.

"He handed over the keys on a cushion? Like a king to his vassal?"

Dom Silvestre translated into English for the second Dutchman—"A velvet cushion. The keys on a little velvet cushion . . ."

"Precisely."

And Uncle Afonso, neither eating nor drinking, his pale bald head beaded with sweat, described how that act of collaboration with History had put them in a terribly weak position. Yes, at the time there had been articles in newspapers of every stripe, saying that amid all the turmoil and social problems, there were still some people who remained pure, who kept faith with great moral principles. But that gesture, which had been so highly praised, had brought them nothing but huge losses. As far as they knew, there hadn't been another case like it. However, he was only talking about it now so that they would understand the importance of Mar de Prainhas, which, as they had seen, remained intact to this day.

"Extraordinary, just extraordinary . . ."—the Dutchman enthused.

The Luxor Restaurant was still packed, and at every table people were conversing in low voices, but suddenly Uncle Afonso didn't care how loudly he spoke, as if he were no longer a lawyer but simply a scandalized heir. At that moment, he wanted the Dutchmen to know how the Old Factory's management had changed hands. How the siren they remembered so well had ceased to be heard in the surrounding area. By that time—he was still talking about 1975—everyone had a perfectly good wristwatch for telling the time, so there was no need to be summoned to work by that moaning sound that went straight into your ears and skewered your brain. Silencing Grandpa Leandro's siren had been the first modern act of the second wave. But unfortunately it had also been the last.

"It's the same everywhere, Senhor Leandro. In that respect, the world's the same all over. And then there's still this widespread illusion that changing details will change the fundamentals . . . Does that make sense?"

"Yes, perfect sense . . ."

"But did they get your grandfather's business back on track?"

No, not at all. How could they have? The industry was collapsing anyway; the crisis had nothing to do with who was in charge or what equipment they used. José Carlos, like all the other members of the family, had known this for a long time, but unfortunately the new managers didn't. They got everything wrong. They confused the situation at the time with individual actors. They thought what happened in the sea was up to the fish, when, of course, the fishermen were in charge. So it was no surprise that the second wave had been marked throughout by violence. The second wave, that ragtag bunch left over from the first, had to finish with tears and sighs what the first wave had rushed into with shouts of joy, Uncle Afonso explained. Before long, the new management were even selling off the canning machines. They were wheeled out through the factory gates, two and then three at a time, on little dollies, and although they were huge and heavy and made of iron, no one was ever sure where they ended up. A bloodbath. Night after night, out went metal basins, stones, fittings, files full of numbers and figures, out went everything that could raise a little money, regardless of its origin or destination. But they weren't all stupid. One day, someone wrote on one of the factory walls— *Animal Farm. Napoleon the pig takes over.* Whoever wrote that had read books, and not just any books either. They were immediately found out and forced to apologize and leave the factory forever.

"So it was chaos?"

"Total chaos. How else to describe it?"

Then one day, the last day, there had been a serious accident. The thing was, no one was quite sure who had given the order to sell everything off, or who had received the proceeds from the sale. In a heated exchange involving several people, a committee member had pulled out a gun and shot a fellow worker who was just coming in through the factory gates, shot him through the heart. Senhor Van de Berg should know that the gunshot made only a tiny hole, far smaller than a shirt button, but a syrupy red liquid had still come trickling out and formed a pool on the ground, in which the man, first, sat down, then lay down as if taking a rest. The man died without realizing what was happening to him, lying in a bloody bed of his body's own making on top of the grassy mound. And since the employee who had fired the shot was higher up the hierarchy than the one who was dying, and since he was still holding the gun, no one picked the dying man up. The two men just looking at each other. The next day, when the first man had been taken to the undertaker and the second to the examining magistrate, a third individual put the keys back on the velvet cushion, consulted the other five people still left after that decade-long adventure, and decided to return them to the legitimate owners.

"The keys again? And did they hand them back to the same owner?"

"No, sadly they weren't returned to the person who had given them away, Senhor Van de Berg. By then, José Carlos was no longer around. My brother, my eldest brother, had also ended his days laid out in a bed of blood. Less dramatically, though: by the side of the road, a victim of nothing more serious than speeding. Better to die for a slogan on a wall . . ."—said Afonso, with the fiery half of his head. Wishing he could swap those words for the right ones, the foulmouthed ones.

Anyway, the key was returned to his mother one morning in May, and the next day the grass on the mound had been mown and the factory swept clean, the crates piled up, the rubbish burned, and the walls left tall and bare, and in no time the smell of canned fish had been replaced by the salty sea air and the slippery sounds of the birds. A perfumed silence had settled over the factory. It was a pleasure to wander around inside taking photos, said Uncle Afonso. The family had spent an unforgettable summer there, going for endless walks among the deserted buildings and along the white sands of Mar de Prainhas. Oh, those were the days. And so the second wave had come to an end. But then the Old Factory had been invaded by the third lot, a third batch or wave, a few members of which Senhor Van de Berg had already seen running after the helicopter that morning. Just like in Africa.

"Oh yes! The birds, on their way to Africa. An extraordinary story, the story of an extraordinary family . . ."

Afonso wouldn't, however, describe how it had taken them a whole year to decide the future of Mar de Prainhas. He wouldn't explain how the law at the time had meant that the factory couldn't be touched or turned into anything that might have made a decent profit. It wasn't worth it. In fact, the moment the building was listed as an example of industrial archaeology, it became no more than a paralyzed body, condemned to oblivion. A strange object sitting on land that could have had a different fate, if the factory hadn't been there. And the factory was there doing nothing, gradually falling apart among the birds. He, Afonso Leandro, had even come to think they had made a mistake in taking back that cumbersome ghost train that had caused them all so much grief. By then, no one was sure what to do with those walls, which grew darker with every morning that passed.

But why tell Senhor Van de Berg all these distressing stories? What was the point? Senhor Van de Berg would surely agree that omission is the best rhetorical strategy, especially in conversation. It can save a great deal of effort. And so Uncle Afonso's account, if the Dutch gentlemen didn't object, would move straight from the return of the keys to the day when his mother had come across some people having lunch outside the factory gates.

The main course had arrived now. The beef was thinly sliced, well done, served with julienned vegetables. The wine was a beautiful, ruby-red Porca de Murça. The rhythm of the conversation, as it jumped from topic to topic, fit well with the pauses imposed by the slices of meat on the plates. Uncle Afonso was still hesitating. Dom Silvestre's face was quite unreadable. But Senhor Van de Berg asked—"And then?"

"Then came our mother, God rest her soul, if God exists, and if he doesn't exist then let's hope he starts existing soon, because we badly need to think he does. I'll tell you what happened, and Dom, my brother-in-law, will back me up. Our mother couldn't bear seeing that place, once so full of life, all locked up and with no one inside. Visiting it was like stepping into the silence of an Egyptian tomb . . ."

Then Uncle Afonso, sipping a little of the Porca de Murça and taking no notice of the people at the nearby tables, explained how, one Sunday afternoon, his mother, Regina Leandro, had called a taxi as usual, and, on driving past the Old Factory, had noticed that the building wasn't deserted after all: instead, sitting on the mound in the shade of the factory wall, a group of black people were eating lunch out of some big baskets. And since the taxi was virtually creeping past, one of them stood up to offer her some food. The taxi driver said something like—"They're Cape Verdeans, madam, from Bairro dos Espelhos . . ." And with that, he thought the topic was closed. Unless Dona Regina wanted to turn around and eject them from the shade of her wall. Or, if she preferred, he, the taxi driver, could tell them himself not to come stinking the place up again. But that wasn't what happened—Did Senhor Van de Berg understand?

The following Sunday, at the same time, his mother had again driven down the factory road. The same group of people was there again. One of the women had realized that this was the factory owner, turned to face the taxi, and, as a sign of peace, plucked a white handkerchief from her breast and waved it in the air. Then she approached the taxi and explained that they loved it there because of the palm trees and how close it was to the water. She said it reminded them of their own country, that much-missed distant island. That there was nowhere else nearby where they felt so happy. The woman added that they had their lunch there whenever they came to the beach. That they had a van for transporting the food, the children and their elderly mother, who was a mother to them all. That if the owner came back at one o'clock, she'd find the place perfectly clean. They even used to pick up the litter that didn't belong to them, just so people wouldn't say they left rubbish wherever they went. Then the taxi driver had said— "A likely story . . ." And began driving on down the road.

But Uncle Afonso's mother, sitting in the taxi, looking back at the horizon, had begun to wonder. What exactly was the world? The Earth? What were houses? And where were her two dead sons, José Carlos killed on the side of the road and José Eduardo stabbed in Angola? Where were they now? Where was her husband? And her father-in-law, José Joaquim Leandro, whom she had so respected and loved? Were any of them still around? What was she holding out for? She was keeping all this going, but for whom? Until when? It should at least be used by someone who was still alive. Someone who was asking the same questions and hadn't found the answers. At least that. Nothing else seemed right. And so, seized by a generous impulse and without consulting anyone, his mother had made up her mind. The car had turned back. The black people were still on the mound, and Uncle Afonso's mother asked them who was in charge. She was already dying her hair lilac in those days. She had been introduced to the oldest woman, and the two had agreed on the spot that the family would move into the factory.

And that had been the beginning of the third wave.

Senhor Van de Berg, sitting very upright by the large window. Fork hovering—"Beautiful, just beautiful! The third wave . . ."

In fact, the word *wave* had only appeared with that group of occupiers. He, Afonso Leandro, had invented it, he confessed, as a way of linking those new arrivals from Africa with migrating birds, the spread of cholera, and plagues of locusts. Which was, admittedly, rather dramatic, but it hadn't been a popular decision, at a time when no one was sure what to do with the factory, to hand such an important space over to what the taxi driver had described as a bunch of half-wits, insular people with no sense of clock time or calendar days. People from another world, another age. People who knew nothing beyond piling concrete on concrete and brick upon brick, primitive acts that predated civilization. They reserved the night for dancing and making babies. That was the theory he had developed at the time, predicting serious problems ahead. Besides, even now, he, Afonso Leandro, didn't understand why his mother had made such an inexplicable decision alone. It was then, in that context, that he had begun to use the expressions *those people*, *that batch*, *that wave*. In his outraged, defiant state. *The third wave*. As he remembered it, they had named the first and second waves when they looked back over the century, simply because a third had suddenly appeared. A third wave.

"Are you with me?"

And Uncle Afonso, a horseman and respected lawyer, who had appeared in plays as a student and prided himself on his practicality, a man who now and then picked up some floozy lover from the legal disputes he took on between wives and their husbands, was telling them all this, becoming quite emotional, without touching his cold beef or his thinly sliced vegetables, the green spinach rolled up like reels of sewing thread. He couldn't eat a thing, and yet it was only a business deal. Unbelievable. By then, Uncle Afonso was beginning to wonder if it had been wise to tip such a full chapter of their intimate family history out onto the table like that. But when he exchanged glances with his brother-in-law Dom Silvestre, he felt reassured. He trusted his brother-in-law's commercial instincts. In the middle of that suntanned face, there glittered the eyes of the sly fox.

"Forgive me . . ."

"Not at all. I'm glad you told us. An extraordinary tale, extraordinary people . . . I'm fascinated by all that history. A velvet cushion . . . Now, let's see . . ."

The Dutchman, transported—"I'm imagining a beautiful restoration job, with everything respected, everything returned to its original state, okay? Except the siren. The siren can't come back because of the birds. It's too loud and it'll scare them away. But as for the rest, we can have it all exactly as you remember it. Yes, we'll even take the tiles off the roof one by one and keep them safe, all in order, as if they were made of glass. Are you with me?"

The Dutchman caught up in this vision, and his business partner too—"As for the rest, you'll hardly hear a thing. Nature won't suffer in the slightest. Not one tiny bird will disappear. We've done dozens of projects like this, all over the world. It won't come to any harm, not at all. Nature, I mean. Just yesterday we were discussing it with your brother-in-law. We won't disturb so much as the root of a palm tree. Quite the contrary. The palm trees will actually like what we do, they'll be grateful. Isn't that right? Oh, the palm trees will love it, the whole area will turn green . . ." Very much the visionary now—"Even the train tracks can stay where they are. They can go on running along the ground, the way your grandfather had them laid . . ."

Van de Berg reached for his coffee cup, then a small glass of whiskey, promising to keep Mar de Prainhas exactly as it was, so that plenty of people could enjoy the climate, the birds. If the deal went ahead. He would make sure. It had been very good of Senhor Silvestre to take the initiative and get in touch. Yes, it had been most opportune, and both of them, he and his business partner sitting there beside him, were very pleased. As Senhor Van de Berg spoke, Afonso began to look tired. He had slumped back in his seat and his bald head suddenly seemed to have been worn smooth, in contrast to his brother-in-law's thick black thatch of glossy hair, almost Asian in appearance. Their eyes met, however, in mutual understanding.

What are you waiting for?

It was the moment for Uncle Afonso to wrap things up.

"Well, now you understand why it's still there, unspoiled, that jewel in the middle of Mar de Prainhas. A miracle, when you consider the wilderness all around. But I'm not sure if my brother-in-law has mentioned the big problem . . ."

"Oh, there are always problems. That's why we're all here now: so we can solve them"—Van de Berg beaming at his two associates.

"The thing is, we could have the third-wave people out of there tomorrow, only our sisters won't agree. We don't see eye to eye on this. You won't have heard, by the way, that our mother had gone there just before she died last August . . ." The Dutchmen and the lawyer silent, moved. What did they mean?—"And on top of all that, a niece of ours went looking for our grandmother and stayed there for a few days. Two obstacles. Our sisters, typical women, respect that kind of thing, and lots of other things too. And we respect them. Which is why, personally, I don't want anything to do with those people. If I ever have to go there myself, I always keep it short and sweet."

Afonso Leandro spoke like someone trying to simplify a very complicated issue while leaving all the complexities in full view. The Dutchmen, slightly worried, laughing less now, speaking less about the birds and more about the legalities, the Dutchmen's Portuguese lawyer unsheathing his legal expertise, the discussion operating on different levels. First, questions relating to coastal planning laws; second, the matter of getting permission to occupy a listed building, in exchange for services and ten thousand escudos per month; and finally there was the question of the soul. The human soul, that complicated, indefinable thing, that direction-less breeze, imprisoned in the vessel of the body. They were there until two in the morning. The restaurant needing to close and the conversation still going on. Uncle Dom painting a mental picture of a resort called *Palm City*, whose slogan would be, *Where the Ocean lays down its Arms*. The Dutchmen studying the connotations of these terms in various languages. In Dutch, at least, it all seemed rather convoluted. It wasn't clear how the sea could have weapons. What kind of weapons? Eventually, they said they had a flight to Miami the next day, and would then be returning to Tunisia. And since Tunisia was close by, they'd be back in a fortnight, a month. And then they'd like to fly over the whole coast again and, if possible, go in person to see the industrial ruin they found so fascinating; yes, more than anything they wanted to set foot in the place itself. Just a quick visit, with no contact with the residents, so as not to cause any upsets. And then they'd see.

On the tablecloth, the two candles had burned out. Theirs was the last occupied table. Only one waiter was left at the back of the room. They said their goodbyes; it really was very late. And then they headed down to the ground floor.

The brothers-in-law got into Dom Silvestre's Jeep.

Dom Silvestre wasn't saying anything. Had something gone wrong? Silence. No, nothing had gone wrong. Silence. It's important to convey the sentimental value of what you're selling so the client can properly appreciate what's at stake. That was all. Silence. Uncle Afonso, tired and stupidly emotional after that rapid recap of his family history, silent. He had taken off his jacket, his limbs almost too heavy to lift. When he sat down, his whole body felt heavy and soft, like a bag of flour. Exhausted, exhausted. But Uncle Dom wasn't tired in the least, he could have set off on another marathon right away. Outside, there was the noise of the engine, and inside, the two men didn't speak.

Uncle Dom didn't speak until he dropped Uncle Afonso outside his house in Bairro Castro, in Santa Maria, where Isabel was waiting with the lights on, devoted as she was. It was three a.m.—"Now, listen: From here on in we need to drop this business with the birds, the siren, the Chrysler, that whole absurd pantomime you people can't get enough of. You've given them enough sob stories tonight. Don't go through it all again. Don't lay it on too thick. It's time we got things moving, no matter what the women say. Push on, push on, sort out the papers, finalize the terms. Nothing can go on forever. The Diamond's all polished and up there for the taking. From now on, it can only lose its shine. The whole thing will start to go bad on us if we're not careful. Okay?"

Diamond—of all the uncles and aunts, it was Dom Silvestre who used that term the most. The others knew it and employed it as well, but only he, who had invented it, was able to draw out, from the latent metaphor, the profound meaning of all its possible implications. Domitílio Silvestre had spoken of urgency. Urgency when it came to the Diamond. And with that threat, the dinner at the Luxor had ended. With the voice of Uncle Dom, who didn't even say good night to his brother-in-law.

Milene had played an integral role in that dinner, though she would never know it. And other people would only find out later.

XIV

MILENE AND ANTONINO DROVE TO THE RIA IN THEIR RESPEC-
tive cars. They parked in the shade of the wooden canopy, then
walked to the dunes.—Could this really be happening?

It was a Sunday in November. The glare from the sand bounced
back up at the sun. The beach bar appeared to have only recently
alighted on the ground and had not as yet settled down properly.
Its boards were as precarious as the interweaving reeds. As if it
were made of matchsticks, and only an optical illusion had made
it grow to the height of an average man. Antonino had to bend
down to go in through the door. She followed. In the afternoon
sun, he looked straight at her. Who was she? Where had she come
from? Why was she the way she was? He asked the same questions
that his nieces Sissi and Belisa had asked, only in a different way.
Milene was surprised—Why was Antonino Mata asking her those
things as he sat beside her at the bar? Staring across at the high
dunes between the Ria and the sea. Why was he asking about her
mother and her father? Antonino sitting so close, interrogating
her. She could have told him. But she wasn't going to. Why, when
the dunes were the color of gold, and the bar they were sitting at
had the frail consistency of a fishing net, and he, Antonino Mata,
had his hand in hers, before he headed off as usual and gave that

same hand to Divina, why spoil something good with something bad? The dune was offering its back to the birds. The blue tit was already calling to next year's eggs.

She said this while they were sitting at the bar. She didn't want to spoil something so very good with something bad, something evil, she said.

"What do you mean?"—he asked.

Milene casually blew her nose, filled with a growing awareness that she existed and was someone in the world, there among the grains of sand. Each grain of sand, just for a moment, in its right and proper place. If she spoke of pain, some vital thing might die. Don't talk about pain. "Oh, please don't talk about pain . . ."—she said.

Antonino was drinking his beer straight from the bottle. The light passed through the bottle and set off toward the sand, barring the way to the advancing darkness. He wiped his mouth on his sleeve. Birds were dropping from the sky into the water. The woman who owned the bar came over to say—"You know, I was almost dying before I came here. You might not believe it, but this place saved me . . ." Antonino laughing, revealing his gappy teeth. If Milene could, she wouldn't ask anything of anyone, wouldn't say anything to anyone, she would only do what had not yet been done in nature and in life. A whole world to complete, a life to build, clean, tidy, preserve and serve. If she could. But she couldn't, she felt she wasn't resourceful enough. On the other hand, she could at least avoid adding more evil or darkness where she knew both already existed. She could refuse to collaborate with anything that caused pain. She didn't know what evil was, but she knew the pain evil could bring. She knew the effects of evil, but not its roots. Even if she couldn't put it into words. It was something you felt and for which there were no words. If she did have the right words, she'd be thinking about something else, rather than feeling this. What she wanted was to be lucid, for her head to be illuminated from end to end, plugged firmly into clarity and intelligence, but she knew it couldn't be like that. The inside of her head was like a bumper car track, where the neon lights kept flashing on and off, concealing whole areas, creating craters of nothingness. When one area was lit up, others were immediately plunged into darkness. Her brain was incapable of embracing the whole. How to put that into words?

Antonino laughing in the golden sun—"You're quite right, let's not talk about pain . . ."

Milene laughing too—"Let's never talk about pain. Why should we? Let's leave it like that, *you* won't talk about pain, and *I* won't talk about pain, then it will be just as if the stinky thing didn't even exist . . ." she said, again noisily blowing her nose, feeling like someone living in the middle of a terrestrial world in which there was no pain to be seen. Pain must exist in some damp hidey-hole or behind a wrinkle in the sand, but you couldn't see it. And if you couldn't see it or touch it, it didn't exist. Correct? He had finished his beer now. Inside him, the beer transmuted into more relaxed gestures, shinier skin. And he laughed more too, looking away, so as not to show his gappy teeth, his laughter simultaneously shrill and deep—"That's just crazy. If we do that, there'll be some days when we can't say anything . . ." He wiped the bottle's yellow throat with one hand, just to do something. "Okay, agreed, we won't talk about pain." He lit a cigarette, then threw it away.

At that moment, the bar could have risen up above the reeds and flown off somewhere else for a while before coming back, making an unhurried landing, and with them still inside. The birds could have left, carrying off the crests of the waves in their beaks. The sea could have been lifted into the air by the wingbeats of the birds. With the depths of the Ocean unoccupied, people who had been waiting in exile in another world could have come and sought shelter there and founded a new colony. People, that is, who refused to speak about pain, about anything bad, anything evil. That is, people who were innocent not out of innocence, but out of choice. Would that be possible? "Let's see. Never talk about pain. Now, just how would that work?"—he said, amused, lowering his head again to go out through the doorway. Making himself lighter so as not to disturb that fragile tracery of planks erected on the sand. Leading her by the arm along the wooden bridge, the very long wooden bridge, when he would have had endless opportunities to kiss her. But no, she thought, he was saving his kisses for Divina. He merely drew her to him, then pushed her away, making her dance across that carpet of planks in her short skirt. For all his gangly physique, he was a good dancer. He was wearing white sneakers with thick soles, like skates, and he was dancing along the boards of that boardwalk. Just dancing.

It was the beginning of an ordinary love. That is to say, the evenings were as if on pause, but not the days that followed.

The fact is that Antonino had resumed the normal trajectory of his life. And yet, they had come to an understanding. If, when evening fell, the gray van did not appear outside the bright lights of Villa Regina, this was because Antonino would be going to spend the long autumn night at Divina's. She who, like everyone else, had feet, ankles, thighs, armpits, belly and tits, kidneys and liver, and whose name was, for some reason, Divina. When he didn't do that, however, he would drive the van miles away, through the new housing developments, not because he liked neat built-up areas, but because he was keeping well away from any streets where he might encounter Divina. "If she found out, she'd kill me . . ."—Antonino would say, staring out the window.

If my mother found out. If the people at home found out. If

Domingos found out, if my grandmother found out. If Eunice found out. That was one of the reasons why he drove her through the wealthier areas where he could drive at a more leisurely speed without attracting any attention. A perfect meeting of lantana bushes and lawns. Not a soul in sight. No smoke, no radio, no bicycles. And yet there were large cars parked outside the garages and nearby. Streets that were either too well guarded or completely deserted, who could say? Whatever they were, he would park the van between two perfectly laid-out streets and run his fingers through her hair. But he didn't kiss her. He never kissed her. He merely cupped her face in his hands and gazed into her eyes, studying her eyes, her hair, from far too close, as if he needed a magnifying glass to be able to see her more clearly. But he didn't kiss her.—"What's to become of me? What's to become of you?" And sometimes he would say—"What's to become of us?"

Gradually they began to lose in gravity what they gained in joy. Each driving their own car to make the return home simpler. She would only get into his van once they had parked up at the nearest dunes, so that he would then have more freedom of movement. Milene soon realized that he didn't even leave himself time for supper. He would have to go straight from wherever they met to Divina's door. Or so she thought, because they would sit in the van until eight or nine o'clock at night, at which point he would start looking at his watch, like someone waiting for some cruel sorcerer to give him the signal to go home. Antonino would ask—"But why? Why?"—as he squeezed her arms, only her arms and shoulders, never repeating the close embrace they had shared during their encounter on the highway. Sometimes he would say in a voice full of regret—"It would be so much easier just to be with Divina, so much more convenient . . . With her expecting me and me arriving on time . . . But then you turned up . . ." His words, though, didn't match the tone in which he said them. Antonino Mata seemed almost to be mocking himself when he spoke like that—"Yes, my life would be so much easier. We really ought to stop . . ." But these words only fanned the flames. The fire would flare up again. He would clap one hand to his head and say—"Let me think, think properly . . ." Milene sitting in her own car now. Antonino standing by her car window—"Why did you have to go to the site that day and call out to me? If I'd been inside the crane then, I wouldn't have heard you, your cries wouldn't have touched my heart. Why? Why?" Him delaying leaving. "Because I wanted to . . ." she would say, tapping her chest. Her bracelets jingling. Before they left the parking lot, their two vehicles would trace circles around each other, reluctant to leave. Then, one behind the other, they would head back. Attached by an invisible cord.

Love cannot be explained or described, not without seeming laughable. Because no love is laughable, especially not ordinary love.

"Kiss me"—Milene would say.

They were sitting in his van outside the Hotel Cálamo, the dark green pittosporums forming a hedge around them. He was removing all the bracelets from her arms as well as the one from around her ankle, then placing all twenty-one of them on the dashboard, before running his hands up and down her arms, although he still wouldn't kiss her.—"If we were invisible . . ." Yes, if we were invisible, we could go to Mãos Largas right now and have supper. We would park the van out front and no one would see us, we'd go in, sit down at a table, and no one would see us. Not my family or yours or anyone at all, not even Divina. If we were invisible. He would give her a kind of back massage then, his two hands probing her shoulder blades, pressing down hard, as if searching for some rare, hidden bone. He would make her lean against him, but he wouldn't kiss her. The glow from the streetlamp bounced off the green of the hedge onto her face. Milene closed her eyes. When she opened them, he was looking positively terrified. He was the one who had made her open her eyes—"This is really dangerous, Milene, it's really dangerous for us to be here like this. I'm not exaggerating. I've seen loads of movies about situations like this. They always end badly. We ought to stop." He then again grabbed her arms, almost as if he were about to break them, and put her bracelets back on, one by one. Then he grabbed her leg and clipped the final bracelet around her ankle. Before they left, he blurted out—"Oh fuck, why can't we be invisible?"—Then he sped off. And she knew he was speeding off to be with Divina.

It was normal love, wordless love.

"Aren't you ever going to kiss me?"—she would ask, her eyes wide open.

At that point in the year, after the rain of mud, midday was still full of bright needles of light, but the evenings grew dark much too early, as if the tropics had slipped down a few degrees. During the week, they only saw each other when pitch-black night had fallen. Antonino sometimes came straight from work and brought his children with him. They would only go for a short drive then, because the children, tired out after kindergarten, would be getting rather grizzly. The oldest one would keep blowing up empty plastic bags and popping them. On days like that, Antonino would talk very fast about practical things. He would follow her back to Villa Regina—"Do you know how much you spend a month by having the lights permanently on in your spaceship? Who pays for your spaceship, by the way? Good grief! In just three months, that would be enough to buy Divina's oldest boy a motorbike . . ." They would fall out then. It was a normal love.

A normal courtship.

"If we were invisible, I'm not saying we'd go to Mãos Largas or to the Pomodoro, but we'd go somewhere, to a snack bar on the coast road!"—He was starving. One night, they ended up going to the Restaurante do Inglês, a place known to be very private. It was owned by a Welshman whose partner was a Jamaican woman who made spicy bean stews. They didn't go there for the food, though, but because they knew they would be made welcome. Safe. The booths had very high backs, like the seats in old-fashioned train compartments, and no one saw them. Unfortunately, eating in one of those high-backed booths proved too expensive. After that, Milene had started bringing sandwiches they could share in the car, before he shot off to Divina's house.

"Tonight, I'll stay here"—he said. "I'll stay here with you." At the end of that day, the van dragging its wheels past the perfect gardens, the perfect trees, the manicured lawns sown with lamps trained on hedges so dense that they promptly swallowed the light. They would stop outside immaculate vacation homes with lacework walls and toy-town chimneys, houses that seemed to come down the streets to meet them. "I'll stay here, I'll stay with you . . ." The villas advancing toward them. "I don't want anyone to see us . . . If only we were transparent, if only we were invisible . . ."

See you tomorrow.

Milene, our cousin Milene, returned home and immediately ran to the phone. She bent right over it. She listened to the recorded message, then, with one hand almost covering the mouthpiece, left her own message in a very quiet voice—"*Listen, me and my boyfriend need to be transparent and invisible . . . If we were, I'm sure he'd hold me in his arms, sit me on his knees, and kiss me . . . The days pass, and he goes off to spend time with her and not with me, simply because we're not invisible. When you can, tell me what you think about that . . .*" In a very quiet voice—"*The days pass and he won't kiss me and you won't answer . . . Why won't you answer? I wanted to tell you that I've never ever felt this happy. I can only compare it to the time when the three of us used to go out on our skateboards and Grandma Regina would let us race down the road. Sometimes, when he puts his hands on my waist, picks me up, and puts me back down, it feels as if I were on that skateboard again . . . I'm never going to tell him that, though, because he might take it the wrong way. But that's what I'm thinking when he picks me up.*" In a very quiet voice—"*I want to be kissed and kissed . . . What do you think of that? Don't ever tell Lavinia, will you? . . . But all you give me is silence, silence . . . Is the tape in your machine eternal? Never-ending? My aunts' tapes seem to run out nearly every day. Love from your cousin Milene . . . 'Bye. Wait, there's something else . . . It's night here . . . Is it snowing there? Speaking of our aunts and uncles, and your father, I forgot to tell you that Antonino and I have agreed never to talk about evil, never . . . What do you think of that? Love from your cousin. 'Bye . . .*"

"*I've been listening to your answer machine grinding away for more than a minute now, but not a peep out of you . . . Bye-bye . . . It's not cold here at all. They say the world is getting warmer. Some people are already badly affected . . .*"

XV

YES, DECEMBER IN VALMARES WAS SO HOT THAT NO ONE could tell if those muggy early mornings were left over from September, or if they were paving the way for the following June. So it was no surprise that people's dreams were also off-kilter.

The dogs slept at night and howled at the Moon by day, their faces turned to the sky. Felícia took siestas as if it were summer, and after dinner she dozed off and dreamed she was someone else. Indeed, in the early hours of that particular morning she had dreamed she was a very strong man who'd been betrayed by his wife, a very skinny adulteress whom he nonetheless loved very much, and because of whom he had climbed into a boat and sailed off to the high seas to die. In the dream, death would be a relief to him, to the man who was really her, Felícia, and it had been a nasty surprise when she, he, saw the guilt-stricken wife walking over the water behind the boat, asking for forgiveness, begging him, begging her, not to die, and to come back home. In the dream, however, honor prevailed, and he, she, unmoved, didn't turn back, not even caring if the wife drowned, instead sailing on over the waves toward that seductive place where everything would end. As for the wife, she really was very skinny and she did drown. He, she, still in the boat, rowing and rowing. Felícia woke up in a very bad mood, with her body, her real body, drenched in sweat, still feeling one hand grasping an oar, as if her inner world were indeed completely off-kilter.

She had described her dream over breakfast. Her children were there and they all thought that what their mother wanted, when all was said and done, was to be even more in charge than she already was, and that was why she'd imagined herself as a man. Or at least, this was what Domingos said. Claudina's view was that, given her age, her aunt's head was full of thoughts of love and revenge. Only old Heitor piled dream upon dream—"Listen, what you dreamed is nothing new, it's what happened to the telegraph operator in Praia. Remember? Monteiro the telegraph operator. He was the one who set off in a boat to die because his wife had betrayed him; he sailed off into the ocean and just let himself drift. And she, regretting what she'd done, hired a boat and a whole battalion of sailors, then sailed after him, and they lived happily ever after. Dreams never show you the truth, just something like it . . ."

No, Felícia didn't recall the story of the telegraph operator from Cidade da Praia. She really didn't, but that beautiful story must have been buried deep in her memory. What a pity that in her dream, he, she, hadn't forgiven the wife. That's the problem: no one can ever choose how dreams end. Ana Mata, however, who had been sitting by her rivers since early that morning, sorting through the grains of corn, was of the view that while a person cannot control their dreams, they can control how they remember them. So if she were in her daughter Felícia's shoes, from now on whenever she remembered that dream, she'd imagine the man still drifting along, out at sea, not making peace with his adulterous wife, because she didn't deserve it, but saving the things that can be saved in this World. Ana Mata said her daughter could even imagine the man, the man she had been early that morning, taking on a shark, for example, and saving his entire family in the process. It was simply a question of swapping things around. And Ana Mata explained, in her language, how a good mother, if she wanted to, could give her own body for the salvation of her loved ones.

Felícia felt rattled.

What was going on? All she'd done was dream about being a man with a boat, and now her mother wanted her to be greater than Jonah? Jesus Christ! She was seriously losing patience with her mother. All that tragic carrying-on over some stupid little dream.

"Dream it yourself if you want to, Ma. You can dream about putting yourself at the mercy of a shark if you like . . . Yes, you dream that, why don't you? At least Jonah went into the whale's belly and then returned to life to the great acclaim of the people. But you want me to dream about the body of a fish so big that no one could get out of it alive. And to save who, exactly? Yes, tell me that . . . Is someone in danger?" Felícia was beginning to wonder if her mother even loved her own daughter. What a lousy morning. And all because of the December heat.

Felícia made up her mind—She had to forget the man, the sea, the boat, the adulterous wife, Monteiro the telegraph operator from Cidade da Praia, the shark, the whale and Jonah. Forget it all, right away, and go and wash the dishes. Lose herself in the peace she found in dealing with the dishes. Thank heavens for the washing-up.

Now let's get on with our day.

It was around ten in the morning. The plates had long since been washed up and stacked on the plastic tables. Their surfaces, slick and almost luminescent with dish soap, glinted in the sweltering sun. Now only the older people were left in the courtyard. The phone rang and Felícia answered. It was Janina, asking her not to call him because he was only just going to bed. The hard life of a pop-folk singer. Was his mother listening? He'd been invited to Germany. He wasn't going to Toronto after all, he was going to Berlin instead, not to Toronto or Montreal. He could go to Canada afterward. But at that moment, what he needed was sleep. Felícia, indignant—"So you think you can swap day for night just like that? And the people who come to your shows, how do they get any work done? Do your audiences go about their lives in the daytime or at night? And what about your band? Fine, fine . . . Take care of yourself. Sleep as long as you need to. Sleep, sleep, and I won't wake you up. Onward, son, onward and upward . . . *Ciao*, lots of love . . ."

After the disagreement about the dream, Ana Mata, sitting on her own private perch, wearing her glasses, went on picking over the corn. With fingers as bony as bird claws, she picked out a grain here, a grain there, and tossed them over her shoulder. Heitor Senior poking the dogs with his two crutches, trying unsuccessfully to provoke them. Felícia and her sister Dilecta beginning to chop up a fish in a bowl. The fishy water would be carried out behind the factory and tipped away, so that it didn't run into Ana Mata's rivers. Bad smells and flies couldn't be allowed anywhere near the house. The corn husks too had to be discarded a long way from where the three rivers met. Ana Mata had dragged her armchair right into the middle of the courtyard, so she could happily pick over the corn and drop the debris as far as possible from her streams. And from there, where she sat engrossed in her labors, she heard a noise. It sounded like cars. Stopping outside. People were coming.

"Cars outside the gates"—Ana Mata announced in her own language. "Felícia!"

With her hands dripping fishy water, holding them out so they didn't drip all over her body, two fleshy fins sending spray and scales in all directions, Felícia approached the main gates, followed by the poodle, and saw four men arriving in two Jeeps, swinging the vehicle doors open like police officers, and then, once they were all out, turning to look at the factory. All four staring at it with measuring eyes, eyes that can travel in a second from top to bottom and side to side, calculating, adding and dividing. She saw them and she wasn't wrong. Those four people were interested in the factory. But Felícia didn't know who they were. With her hands still covered in fishy juices, she decided to take charge of the situation. She shook her hands dry, giving them a cursory wipe on her rubber apron, and said—"Good morning. Can I help you?"

The four men, who made rather an odd bunch, carried on talking among themselves as if they hadn't heard her. The balding one, in suit and tie, was speaking Brazilian Portuguese to an enormous red-faced man with blond hair. The smaller one, in jeans, his eyes alive and glittering like a rat's, was speaking English to the final member of the group, who was only slightly less gigantic than the first and didn't seem at all English, and had his thumbs hooked into his wide leather belt. This man had brown eyes, and he was the one who looked most often in the direction of the factory, from bottom to top and side to side.

"Good morning, gentlemen. Can I help you with anything?"

None of them answered. Instead, the four men, their eyes moving as one, had begun to walk along the mound, beneath the palm trees, with their backs to her, looking up as they went, as if the factory roof were far higher than it was, and down too, as if the walls extended deep into the ground. Quick. Felícia ran inside, wiped her hands on the first bit of cloth she could find in the hallway, and headed to her kitchen-bedroom, groaning, breathless, hunting through the piles of papers. Quick. She found what she was looking for. The fish scales were faster than her hands, and she had barely touched the papers before there were scales all over them. Sticking to them. Never mind. The crucial, urgent thing was to chase after those people. Dilecta could saw up the spine of the fish by herself.

"Where are you rushing off to?"

In her flustered state, she couldn't answer.

"Where are you going?"

"No time to talk—there are some English people outside."

Ana Mata had left her perch and made her way to the gates to have a look at these English people. But she didn't even catch a glimpse. All she saw was her daughter Felícia running after them, struggling to free herself from the rubber apron she wore for preparing fish.

Yes, Felícia Mata was running after the visitors, the papers in her hand—"Excuse me! Excuse me!" She thought she heard one of them saying *gude*, or *gute*, so she asked—"Excuse me, gentlemen! . . . English?"

But they were walking away, apparently intending to examine the state of the wall on the eastern side. Felícia shouting, running and shouting, hampered by her flip-flops. Running and shouting after them, waving the pieces of paper. There they were. The Englishmen had walked around the east-facing wall, where the compost shed had stood in days gone by, and which, had the Matas not installed a very neat wooden gate, would now have been an entrance that was open day and night, so that anyone could get in. But the shortest of the visitors, the one in jeans, with dark hair and glittering eyes, had given the gate a shove with his shoulder and hip, forcing it open. The structure held at first, but then gave way and the men stepped inside, still looking up at the roof as if searching for something that had escaped them. Then, walking a little farther, and without turning around, the four of them went into the Old Factory, right into the middle of the courtyard. In other words, they had entered the Matas' house. Ana Mata, who had been peering out of the main gates, where her daughter Felícia had disappeared from view, turned back to the courtyard, realizing there was nothing more to see out there. Yes, they were entering Mata territory, sneaking in the back way, and Felícia could do nothing but chase after them, brandishing some pieces of paper. All three—Dilecta with her fish cut in half, Heitor with his two dogs, which had sat down and didn't bark once, and Ana Mata, holding her bowl of corn—all three of them frozen, while Felícia hurried after the four visitors, waving the papers in the air.

"See, gentlemen, it's all legal. All up-to-date, all in order. The contract signed, everything agreed . . ."

She said this from behind them. By then, she had removed her rubber apron and was carrying it over her arm. The four men speaking, two speaking and two listening, walking across the courtyard where, at that time of the day, Ana Mata's three rivers were just a pair of whitish furrows that flowed into a third furrow of slime. As if those furrows were of no importance, the four men strode straight over them and out of the gates, past the pots of flourishing geraniums. Only one, the one with the bald patch, had turned around and said with a nod, as if concluding that surprise intrusion—"And a very good day to you . . ." In very good Portuguese.

Felícia watched them go. The two who had been talking—the one who had said good day and the blond-haired giant—in the first Jeep. The other, darker man, and the smaller giant, in the second. The first two waved at her as the vehicle pulled away. Then she turned to the second Jeep driven by the dark-haired man, who must have been Portuguese as well, and waved the sheaf of papers at him, still all shiny with scales. The darker man started the engine, and as he did so, as he began to reverse, he looked very pleased. Laughing, perhaps. Smiling. She couldn't be sure if he was laughing, but she had definitely seen happiness in his face, especially when she held up the sheets of white paper and said—"Look. Copies of everything, letters to the landlady . . ." In the space the men had so hastily vacated, the shadows of the eleven palm trees lay very still.

"What was all that about?"—asked Dilecta, the fish knife in her right hand still poised in midair.

"They must be buyers"—Felícia replied. "I thought I'd better act fast and show them proof of our rights, so they didn't get the wrong idea . . ." Gazing out over the flat, bare landscape, where the potholed road, beyond the train tracks, curled in on itself and disappeared. "Now they know the factory isn't just a house, with walls and roofs. It's us as well . . ."

But Ana Mata, just inside the main gates, by the pots of geraniums that marked the spot where Dona Regina died, didn't think all four of those men were buyers. No: one of them, at least, was a seller. And if someone was interested in selling the place, well, that changed everything. She thought and thought, but didn't say what she was thinking. Ana Mata just said to her daughter, in her own language—"Watch out, because in the voice of the one who said good day, I heard the voice of my landlady . . ."

"So?"

"So of the four of them, I don't know how many want to buy, but one of them definitely wants to sell . . ."—said Ana Mata, walking back into the courtyard to perch in her armchair and delve once more into the bowl of corn, seeking out damaged grains with her fingers and tossing them over her shoulder, then starting again, resuming her forbidden lament. "If you think it's the dark-haired one who wants to sell, then that means two of them want to sell.

The other one, the bald one, doesn't fool me. He has my landlady's heavy eyelids . . . He's her son. Did you see how they trampled all over my rivers?"—still picking out the damaged grains
from the rest.

"That's right, carry on yakking away, Ma, say whatever comes
into your head. And see where that gets you . . ."

Now, however much their mother spoke and sniveled, she didn't
impress anyone, not even her own daughters. The pair went on
sawing up the big fish, its skin disintegrating into scales that
speckled the courtyard, both of them convinced that the men
had been insolent English buyers, the kind of stuck-up charlatans
who'll stroll into any place they fancy and break down any door
they please, just because they have all those queens and queen
mothers and princesses and speak nothing but English from the
day they're born. But when it came to the Matas' living arrangements, Felícia wasn't worried in the slightest. She had put away
the papers showing that everything was legal, having first taken
care to clean off the scales. Only then did she go back to preparing the fish. She was growing tired of her mother's cowardly ways.
It was hard to believe how she had changed. "Stop harping on,
senhora. Every buyer in the world can turn up, for all I care. Or
have you forgotten that this is the house of Janina Mata King?
That's our trump card . . ."—she said, full of herself now, with
victory in her voice.

"Did you see the numbers on the cars?"—asked Heitor Senior.

"No, I didn't. Now, just look at this crappy fish. Small as a sea
bass, tough as a shark . . ."

Dilecta carried the guts and red-tinged water to the part of the
old factory where, in years gone by, the workers used to make fer-
tilizer out of fish scraps. Felícia washed her hands very carefully,

shook them dry and sniffed them, then picked up the phone and stopped fighting with her mother, who even meddled in people's dreams and made them seem far worse than they were. Enough, enough! With the phone pressed to her ear, she made a very loud call to Janina Mata King—"Are you there, son? Sorry to disturb you. Are you still sleeping or are you awake? Eh? What's going on? I thought you were going to bed. Did you go to bed? You've got a new manager? Someone who takes care of everything for you . . . Yes, yes, I know what a manager is. How about Gaby, is he there? Why does he never come to the phone? Listen, son, on the night, your big night, everyone here will be rooting for you. That's what I forgot to say. I forgot because I had a bad dream. Yes, a horrible dream. I'm glad you're awake, though. Keep talking, yes, talk to your mother. You're going to Berlin and then to Canada. Onward and upward, son, give it your all. Yes, yes . . . *Ciao, ciao.* Lots of love . . ."

Felícia Mata ended the call, and her soul landed back in the courtyard. She would say no more about those Englishmen. It wasn't worth wasting her precious time. And this was how the morning after her dream had ended. A morning so hot that the only thing to do was lie on the sun lounger without saying a word. Everyone coming and going without saying a word. Especially Antonino.

Antonino Mata, more than anyone, came and went in silence— "Nothing to say, son? Is it because of this awful heat? I mean, it's December, for God's sake!

"Antonino, son, are you listening to me?"

He strode out through the gates.—*If only we were invisible, if only we were transparent, if only we could walk down the street like shadows without anyone seeing us, we wouldn't need to go out in separate cars or hide along quiet roads. If only we were invisible. This* was Antonino Mata's life. Every other day, he climbed up the tall-est crane, the Liebherr 145, K series.

"I'm fine, Ma. Now, don't you worry, and I won't worry either . . ."

Other than that, it was an ordinary love, a normal love.

It would happen on the Dunas Machas, when there wasn't a soul on the beach. It was a winter beach now. The lifeguards' huts in the distance and a row of sun umbrellas were the only indi-cations that summer had been there just a few months before. And yet the previous day had seen an extravagant crimson sun-set, and now, to remove all doubt, a dry breeze was blowing in from Africa. Another warm breeze, at that time on a Saturday evening. Some white birds were bobbing around on the water's surface. And there were the two of them hand in hand, walking together. That day they weren't in a rush. If the phone did finally ring in Villa Regina, it would be João Paulo. As for Divina, she wasn't expecting Antonino until later that evening. And so they had gone to the dunes again, and it was there, before that softly undulating landscape, that they met.

To reach the dunes, they had again crossed the narrow wooden bridge held up by stilts. Deep in the water, the silt rose and swirled to form mutant gardens, following the whims of the currents. But the layer of sediment, thick at that time of day, made it impos-sible to see very far down. From the surface, the mud-dwelling creatures were loudly audible, as if the water were full of crickets. And everything else was an infinite mirror. "Can you hear that?" Feeling as if they were at the center of everything, they walked on together, hearing their footsteps rattling the wooden slats, which trembled and announced their presence in that inhabited silence, redoubling the inexplicable thrill, the elation they felt at being out in the open, sometimes with their arms around each other, sometimes just holding hands. A sign to one side informed them that they were walking over *The Longest Wooden Bridge*.

The plan was to have a drink in the beach bar before they reached the closest dune, just like the first time they had come. To sit on opposite stools, separated by a wooden table, watching the evening go by, together, along with a few solitary foreigners too busy ruminating on their own lives to take notice of anyone else's. But the bar, which from a distance looked insubstantial, like an abandoned matchstick model, had its surprisingly solid doors locked. Luckily, they weren't hungry or thirsty, so there was no need to turn back. They walked up the slope toward the dunes, then over the dunes to the beach, quite alone apart from those white birds sitting on the waves. In the middle distance, a pleasure boat full of people sailed by, heading for Sagres. It was the only thing moving. Then he had the idea of lying down in the winter sunshine.

The breeze was warm, almost hot, but it still whipped at the skin around their necks and faces. Milene's bare legs covered in goose pimples. Antonino undid his jacket and used it to make a kind of shelter. There they lay on the sand, their eyes almost closed. With his head slightly raised, Antonino smoked and kept one eye on the beach. The birds still bobbing on the gently rolling sea. A flock of sleeping seagulls, he thought. Were they sleeping or hunting? Sleeping. The birds didn't budge, didn't move their wings, didn't change position; they simply did whatever the sea did, and the sea was doing very little, apart from raising its broad back, stretching out, then subsiding again. Without the birds even moving. They did nothing, those birds.

"Wait here"—he said, tossing away his cigarette and handing her the jacket.

"What about me?"

"Wait here."

Antonino got to his feet and made his way to the water's edge, to look at the motionless seagulls. Then, turning around, he saw that on the sand behind him, Milene had sat up and was waving his jacket, beckoning him back. But he wanted to get closer to the seagulls. He signaled to her, making it clear that he wouldn't be long, that he was just going over there, to where the sun's rays glanced off the water and the birds floated as if they weren't even alive. Antonino walked farther away, making for the light that was turning the sea a kind of colorless color beneath those motionless creatures. He was trying to find a good stone or two to throw at the water, wanting to see if they were asleep or awake, and how they'd react to a well-aimed pebble, that was all. But when he turned around, he saw that, where he had left Milene with the jacket, there was now someone else, a white girl taking off her clothes. He didn't recognize her at first. Then, when he realized who it was, he thought someone else must be removing her clothes. Only then did he understand that it was Milene herself, undressing herself, and he went racing back over the sand.

He sprinted over to her, bewildered and embarrassed and incredulous, while she removed the final item and placed it on the sand. And then, awkward, looking around wildly as if a spring had come loose in his neck, swaying back and forth on those white shoes that sank into the soft sand, shouting at her and at the same time apologizing, as if he were both participant and disapproving observer, he moved closer, attempting to untangle the clothes, which lay in a shapeless heap on the ground, picking them up piece by piece, shaking them out, then trying to pull them over her arms and head, while she wriggled away, skipping over the sand, resisting the clothes, her arms folded over her chest and crotch, determined and amused. He looked around in a state of shock—the boat was still visible in the distance—pleading with her to stop—"No, no, for God's sake . . ." Meanwhile, the naked Milene, wearing only her socks, jumped around in front of him. Her hair, whirled this way and that by the hot-and-cold breeze, was the only thing moving on the shore. *Yes, yes*—she said, shivering in the wind.

But Antonino had covered his face with his hands—"Can't you see how serious this is?" His voice had turned shrill, its natural tone replaced by something high-pitched and rasping. It was hard to make out the words—"Hey! Listen! That's enough . . ." Facing away from her—"Come on, get dressed . . . This has nothing to do with me . . ." Again wanting to make her take back her clothes, her little shoes and her bag, thrusting them toward her. "Because you may not know this, but I know it only too well . . . A black man on the beach with a naked white woman . . . This is how it will end"—and he raised an invisible gun to his left eye, took aim, and fired. Stepping away, not wanting to look at her, trying to hand her back her clothes, then giving in and flinging them down on the sand. Kicking the bundle of clothes over to where his jacket lay and making as if to leave. Milene laughing, between the dune and the beach—"Go on, then, you can put my clothes on, I'll let you . . ."—she shouted.

"I should think so"—he shouted back.

And then, furious, spurred on by some indomitable inner force, he began tugging the clothes over her body, fastening them, angrily shaking them. But once Milene was dressed, as if he had abandoned some goal he had set himself, Antonino clasped her tight and kissed her several times. He kissed her desperately, then wiped his mouth on his sleeve, stepped back, and began to yell— "Sometimes that's all it takes to get a person killed . . . Do you understand what I'm saying? Do you understand or not?" Shaking out her bag and her shoes. Shaking out his own jacket. Shaking the sand off his feet on the planks of the boardwalk that led to the wooden bar. Do you understand? Do you?

"No, you don't understand a thing . . .

"What *do* you understand? This is like some very tired old movie. The kind where everything's fuzzy and you can see the joins in the tape. I'm telling you, I know how all this ends . . ."

And as if there were two separate men inside him, with two different heads and contradictory limbs that were working toward different goals, now that she was dressed, he called her over again, and, shifting her bag around so that it was on her back, so there was almost nothing between them, he kissed her again and again, clinging to her with a force that, though not brutal, was certainly excessive, as if her body might escape, or as if it contained something intangible yet utterly necessary to him, running his large hands all over her, his ten fingers becoming many more hands, their light touch almost burning her skin. Again and again. Eventually, his head aching so badly that he forgot where the bridge was and where they had left their cars, he said—"Let's go . . ."

But she didn't want to walk.

Milene said—"Now carry me over the bridge, I'll bend my knees like this and you can carry me, and I'll kick and kick . . ." And to show him she meant it, she crossed her arms and pressed her knees together—"Go on, see if you can do it . . ."

There wasn't a soul to be seen. The pleasure boat, packed full of people, had become a vague shape vanishing into the distance.

"You said you could carry me, but I bet you can't . . . Go on, pick me up . . ."

He picked her up. As we would only find out later on. Milene's loud guffaws bouncing off the Ria's watery expanse, her body swaying in his arms, him walking on, carrying her, and her shrieking with laughter, and now asking him to do the exact opposite—

"Hey, put me down, put me down, please . . ." Asking him as he crossed the narrow bridge, the one that said *The Longest Wooden Bridge*, crossing it solemnly, definitively, the slats echoing under his feet, as if it were a victory march over uncertain terrain. But a victory march nonetheless. Him carrying her, and her silent now, bundled up in his arms, until his arms began to ache, and him thinking—*It was nothing, nothing happened, and yet this has decided the rest of my life* . . . They walked like that all the way to the parking lot, where neither could remember where they had parked their cars. They had forgotten.

At the time, Milene and Antonino were still invisible.

XVI

MEANWHILE, FELÍCIA MATA HAD AGAIN DREAMED SHE WAS a man and that she, he, was bobbing about on the water. The circumstances may have been different, but now she could see that she really was dreaming about the telegraph opera-tor, and she felt angry with herself for having told the others about her earlier dream. Why dream about people who had long since died? In her guise as a man, she had rejected a skinny woman who, in the dream, just kept walking on the spot, get-ting nowhere, whereas, in real life, the telegraph operator from Cidade da Praia had been rescued by the sailors who his wife had brought along with her, after he'd won back her love by his sacrificial behavior. Why? Then again, the events in her dream were *so* different that she doubted they had anything to do with the telegraph operator's story at all. It was just a bad dream in which she, he, played the part of a really horrible man. Her head ached, and just thinking about the dream made her feel ill. It was lucky they hadn't invited anyone else to watch Janina's show that night.

The poster had advertised Janina as the closing act on *Show Bizz*, promising two new songs. His photo dominated the poster, and in a magazine that had come out on Thursday, they even referred to the program on Saturday night as the *Janina Mata King*

Show. There would be no noisy party in the courtyard, though, no visitors, just the family.

No *cachupa*, no caramel dessert, no sangria.

And so, as evening fell, everything was in its place. The satellite dish ready on the roof. The three televisions linked to the three video recorders by their respective cables, and they'd had several practice runs during the day. Everything was working. The equipment for making three simultaneous recordings had been installed in the shed, making it a proper little studio. It was unlikely the machines would pick up any extraneous noises, but, just in case, children and adolescents were warned to remain quiet. Germana and Dilecta would keep an eye on the youngest. If there was so much as a peep out of anyone, they would be sent straight to bed. Even the dogs had been dragged outside and tethered at the foot of the palm trees, so that there would be no barking on the recordings. They couldn't have dogs barking during Janina's show. Only absolute silence. The Matas were now adding to the joy of Janina's triumph the unspoken responsibility that comes with success. They must act responsibly.

But Felícia felt quite ill.

What if, instead of Janina, they brought on someone else at the last moment? What if he forgot the words? What if he had a sudden blank? What if Gaby slipped up and gave him an iced drink, which would affect his throat, and then no one would understand a word of the new songs? As his mother, she needed a tranquilizer. And then she'd had that weird dream? Who ever heard of such a thing? She, a woman-turned-man, letting a skinny wife walk barefoot over the waves and then drown? In the courtyard, during the day, there had been more talk about the telegraph operator and his story. If those poor creatures, living peacefully now in the next world, ever learned that they would survive merely as material for dreams that turned their stories completely on their heads, they would die all over again. In the courtyard, there was a sense of foreboding, a feeling that something might go wrong.

All silently waiting. The whole family rather subdued, infected by Felícia's sense of foreboding.

And to begin with, *Show Bizz* did prove very tedious. For a whole hour and a half, the program bumbled along, with commercial breaks, jokes, and other people singing, all of whom made the Matas want to either tell them to shut up or smash the TV to smithereens. Until finally, *finally*, Janina Mata King appeared, and it had all been worth it. Offering the three television screens the most beautiful images imaginable of Janina. Everyone sprang to their feet. They were all there, except for Antonino.

The show was just fantastic. Janina against a backdrop of musical instruments. All working as one.

Completely forgetting that she'd forbidden everyone to speak, Felícia was so carried away that she shouted out—"Will you look at that? The sax is blocking our view of Janina!" Just because, for a moment, the saxophone spoke more loudly, and even fleetingly took center stage. That little piece of curved metal soon vanished, however, and Janina reemerged triumphant, driving away the sax, the clarinets and the double bass, and all the other instruments. Janina alone on the three screens, playing with the microphone, pulling it closer, attacking it, mastering it. Filling the whole screen. Janina moving his entire body or just his arms, his face, Janina's various faces, everything moving and shifting, then coming back to form a whole. Eyes closed, lips focused on the words. Fabulous. Standing up now, the Matas could barely hear. Sometimes that wretched saxophone would block him out again. But Janina would immediately return to the screens with his bushy mane of hair, his armbands, his muscles exploding with energy and strength, and all this was happening to a boy of only nineteen. The future of a nineteen-year-old singer shining out from those three screens like a glittering star in the frozen silence of the courtyard. A life divided into two. Before and after. The Matas standing up, holding their breath. And it was only toward the end, when the performance was reaching its climax, when action was giving way to emotion, when he was nothing but pure voice, and his wolfish howl lasted every bit as long as Terence Trent D'Arby's, when the performance was drawing to a close and the current of sound began breaking up and cracking, and he had soared to an even greater height and they could all heave a sigh of relief as the names of the whole army of people behind the making of *Show Bizz* began to snake up the screen over Janina's body like a fat cobra—even the sax had completely disappeared—only then did it suddenly occur to Felícia Mata that she hadn't seen her other son Gabriel on the screen.

"Where was Gaby? Did anyone see him?"

It was true, no one had seen him.

No, no one had seen Gaby, but it didn't matter. They were all savoring that proud, thrilling moment of triumph, as the final glimmerings of *Show Bizz* passed over Janina's face and chest, over his heels, legs, and knees. A televisual apotheosis. The Matas, arms around each other in the courtyard, forming a chain. Yet Ana Mata was missing. Why wasn't she joining in? Then Felícia took pity on her mother, who probably didn't realize what was happening—"Ma, think of this as Jamila Mata's revenge on that traitor Normand. Do you remember your grandmother, Jamila Mata? Do you?"

Well, she ought to. Because what they'd been seeing there in the courtyard was justice arriving a hundred years late. Justice for the Matas and for other families like theirs. They were the incarcerated from those Third World islands, emerging from hunger and thirst directly onto TV screens. Their life being broadcast to the ends of the Earth and the universe, thank God. Yes, thank God. So be glad, Ma. We, the poor, the marginalized, the rootless, the disinherited, are being honored there on the television and soon on every satellite dish. Us, Ma. So why aren't you happy? You're not laughing, not drinking passion fruit juice with your children, your grandchildren, and your great-grandchildren. Why not? Are you going to say yet again that you couldn't hear Janina's voice, that you couldn't understand a word he said? Surely you know that no one understands a song when they first hear it. Especially songs written in English. How else do you think Janina is going to reach all those satellite dishes? Oh, Ma, wait, don't go back to your little house like you did last time, not when everyone's still here, because we can't possibly go to sleep now. We're all here and happy, and with nothing to reproach ourselves for, thank God. What they had seen was almost unbelievable. Janina the Great. Ah, if only that sax hadn't been given so much room, the show would have been perfect. It almost made you feel like turning back the clock and forgiving that traitor Normand. With Janina's success, suddenly everything took on a different meaning.

But had anyone seen Gaby?

No, no one had seen him.

Then Felícia went straight to the phone—"Janina, is anyone there? Is Gaby there?"

How could anyone answer? How? Janina would be utterly drained after his success, so how could he possibly come to the phone? At that moment, he would be far from any phone, with the audience all around him, along with his brother Gabriel. Nevertheless, she called—"Are you there, love?" Then she put the phone down—"No, you're not." The lights in the courtyard trembled in the gusty wind that wafted in as it grew late. Any real coolness would only come at dawn, when all the equipment had been turned off and the courtyard was plunged in darkness.

Before that could happen, though, in the midst of that tangle of cables, near the spot where Ana Mata's rivers met, Domingos and Heitor had sat down, each with one foot propped on a chair, guitars at the ready, and had started to compose. Into the small hours they navigated their way through chords and sequences, fields of sounds and words, always looking for the most beautiful flowers. However clumsily their cracked and callused brick-layers' hands moved over the strings, however badly they played, they still had an inkling of what perfection must sound like. They knew. They were performing little exercises that allowed them a glimpse of greatness, of real skill. Hunched over their instruments, they were gaining a better idea of the heights reached by Janina and his band. Fingering the strings. Until Domingos, overcome by emotion, began to talk like a drunkard, even though he'd had nothing to drink, addressing his guitar—"Oh, Janina, my brother, can I really be your brother? I don't deserve to be, dammit . . ."

Only when dawn was breaking did they go to sleep. Their beds beneath the open windows, as if it were still summer, and despite the breeze coming in off the sea. The whole family sleeping. Ana Mata's three daughters sleeping. Her sons, with the exception of Antonino, all in bed. Her grandchildren and her great-grandchildren had dropped off the moment their heads hit the pillow. When they were all settled, Ana Mata got up.

Very early in the morning.

Everyone was asleep in the Diamond, and with one hand Ana Mata was feeling along the top of the box that served as her headboard, looking for a piece of cloth that served as a hand-kerchief. Looking for the clothes placed on the crate that served as a trunk, sensing in the gloom of that small gray house, the one with the tiniest window, the size of the trap she felt sure was awaiting them all. Her bony hand feeling for her belongings. Her handkerchief, her matches, her comb full of strands of hair, her clothes. She hadn't slept a wink. She finally found her clothes. She pulled the first item over her head, and as it fell loosely to her feet, she drew the second item around her like a blanket on that suddenly chilly winter morning. When she went outside, she was wearing, draped over her shoulders, two overlapping dresses, with two sleeves hanging down on the left-hand side, so that when she reached her plastic armchair and turned around, it looked as if she had three left arms. One right hand and three left hands. The three arms of her dresses. And why not? No one could see what she was seeing. Ana Mata took up her place in the middle of the courtyard, the sleeves brushing the ground, her hands forming a shape like a suspension bridge, her feet resting on the spot where her three rivers met, although, at that hour, they were completely dry. She was prepared to wait. She *would* wait, she thought in her own language.

She would wait a long time.

The sun was already high in the sky, creeping over the paving stones, and no one else was awake. The Matas still had Janina's show playing in their heads and would sleep until late. No one would stop them. It was Sunday too, but no one was going to mass. Felícia had once been very devout, but even she didn't go to mass now. Ana Mata didn't go either, but she would have been pleased to see her children and grandchildren go and pray to God. It wasn't so much praying to God as adding their voices to other people's voices, forming a group, each person an individual as well as being part of a group. Part of a whole. But they thought their lives belonged to them alone, that they weren't linked to other

people. How little they knew. They didn't even know what someone like her knew.

Oh, the things she knew!

She knew, for example, that a war, however far away, wasn't
entirely unrelated to her family's lives. Everything was bound up
in everything else. Men's wars, with men killing other men all
over the place, were connected to what went on around the Mata
family table. She was quite sure of this. The war happening out
there wasn't just happening out in the world, that wasn't where
it started, it began right there, in the eyes of her family. She had
learned this just by looking. On the days when Domingos glared
at his wife, there was more shooting on the TV. She was sure of
this. On the days when they all looked fondly at each other, there
were fewer deaths, fewer starving and disabled people on the
news. On days like that, the American president would say that
peace must prevail, and would appear behind a large table, seated
alongside the warmongers, and looking very pleased with himself.
The opposite was also true. Because everything was bound up
in everything else, which is why she was there, waiting for the
moment when they woke up.

She would wait.

She hadn't slept, and she would wait. She was prepared to do
so because she knew there was a problem. When Dona Regina
Leandro had died outside their gates, she, Ana Mata, had realized
at once that there was a serious problem. But at the time, no one
had believed her. Her family were perfectly aware that the lease
hadn't been renewed and that the Leandro family hadn't sent
anyone to discuss the matter. They hadn't even come to thank
them for looking after their niece. Nothing. No answer, no letter,
no signature. A wall of silence, of indifference, and even then her
family failed to see the problem. She was thinking in her own
language. It was obvious there was a problem.

She would wait until they woke up.

It wasn't her fault her family were so stubborn, their heads so full of clutter that they couldn't see. She, on the other hand, had a slender head and neck, and inside such heads as hers ideas could run free. Anything that wasn't fat was pure intelligence, leaving the veins clear and the spirit free to think. That's why it was best to eat very little. So that you could think. It was because none of her family could think properly that they were unable to see that Janina wasn't Janina. It was such a pity. His voice no longer contained his father's voice or the voices of his brothers, or even his own voice. Janina's voice was now a lie. It wasn't the voice of any of them. Janina Mata King's voice might not have completely abandoned him yet, but it had been transformed into something else. The band no longer accompanied Janina, Janina was just a small, rather discordant part of that band. She was thinking this in her own language. They had all seen and heard him on the television, where it was as clear as clear could be, and yet they had understood nothing. As if they were blind. That's what had made her decide to act. She needed to put a plan in place, urgently. She would set it in motion as soon as they agreed. Ana Mata heard a window opening. She turned around. But it wasn't Domingos.

"Domingos?"

Conceição appeared at the door, leading her two shivering children, João and Aloísio, by the hand. They were naked and had come out to get washed and were surprised to find it so cold. Ana Mata, half unbuttoning her blouse, two sleeves brushing the ground, her hair wild, was finally able to ask—"Conceição, call your husband, will you?"

"Domingos!"

Domingos finally appeared at the door, not yet fully recovered from the previous night. He stumbled out, yawning, with just the hint of a guitar chord in each yawn and stretch. Bare chest, thick hair, so like Janina that he could have passed for another Janina. He stretched and yawned, still half-asleep. Ana Mata waited for this to pass, and when she saw that her grandson was now just scratching himself as he normally did, she said—"Domingos, come over here . . ."

Still stretching, he came over to her.

"Where do you keep your savings books?"

Felícia Mata's eldest son was instantly awake—"What do you want them for?" And, leaving her talking to herself, Domingos walked across the yard in his tracksuit bottoms, on his way to the shower. Ana Mata was unimpressed. She had to allow him time to put down the knife he always brandished, namely his sharp tongue. She let him go. He was still mentally playing his guitar, and she had the whole of Sunday to discuss the matter. She was no fool, she wasn't going to spoil such a well-laid plan by being too precipitate. Domingos was coming back, his hair wet, water dripping down his back. The suggestion of a knife in his words— "Honestly, the things you see in this household you wouldn't see anywhere else in the world . . ." Ana Mata sitting motionless. *Let it go, let it go. Wait until all the blind are awake.* The children came by carrying pails, the two dogs snapping vainly, ineptly at the children's hands. Felícia, from the moment she'd opened her eyes and picked up the phone, was making and receiving calls. She strolled about the yard in a rose-patterned robe, the phone pressed to her ear as she launched into a minor tirade. It was as if she had a third ear pressed to her real ear.

Felícia speaking into the third ear—"Is Gabriel there? Why didn't Gabriel appear on the television? I know it's not up to you, but you do have a contract . . . Well, if it's not in the contract, it should be, whenever you appear, your brother should too, but you appeared without him. I know you're not in charge of what the channel does . . . The problem is I keep having these awful dreams . . ." And she hung up, crossing the courtyard, her breasts bobbing and slack beneath her robe, already receiving another call, which must have been from someone important, because she laughed gaily, ecstatically—"Oh, yes, wasn't it wonderful . . ." said Felícia, her robe only loosely tied, her thick hair and the roses on her robe trailing behind her.

Ana Mata was listening and watching. Waiting. She just had to hope that Domingos would be in a good mood. There he was, fully dressed now, coming toward the table. She was sure he had what she needed in his pockets. She couldn't wait any longer. She asked him—"Have you got all the savings books? Tell me how much money is in them . . ."

Domingos, still with his mouth full, took the books from his pocket and began to read. If anyone was going to read, it would be him, just to please his grandmother. He had to. It was his tribute to her as her grandson, given that everyone had to pay tribute to someone. "In my savings book there's one thousand and twenty and forty thousand escudos . . ." Domingos, who had scant grasp of numbers, read this out very deliberately and entirely inaccurately.

"No, tell me the real amount . . ." said Ana Mata.

"Why would I lie to you? Heitor has much more. He has one thousand five hundred and twenty escudos. As of last week . . . And Antonino? Let's see, let's see . . ." Domingos started laughing—"Antonino has three hundred thousand and twenty-two escudos. The rest must be in Divina's savings book . . ." Domingos laughing in his black tracksuit with blue stripes— "Satisfied, Grandma?"

Ana Mata, concentrating hard—"And what does that come to in total?"

"In total, two thousand five hundred escudos . . ." Domingos, the soul of patience now, and with no knife in his voice, doing the sums, again incorrectly.

Ana Mata was also doing her sums. She thought and thought, with one hand in the air, holding the savings books, so that Domingos wouldn't wander off somewhere. He couldn't go yet because, first, he had to tell her how many new vans, like Antonino's van, you could buy with two million five hundred thousand escudos. Asking fearfully, one hand in the air, afraid her grandson might change his tone.

Domingos Mata, however, was still full of sleepy patience. He told her the truth—"Not a single one, Grandma, or perhaps only half a one."

"Half? What do you mean? You must have money squirreled away in other savings books. That can't be all the money you've saved . . ."

Still on the phone, Felícia walked past her mother and her eldest son. With the phone clamped between ear and shoulder, she was carrying drinks and snacks out to the table, as if it were summer. Now she was saying—"Thank you, my friend, thank you. May God reward you for your kindness, because you being so happy for Janina and his happiness really is an act of kindness, I mean it . . . The phone hasn't stopped ringing since last night, everyone's quite simply over the moon about Janina being such a big hit . . . 'Bye . . ." She finally put the phone down. And once she was free of it, she too went to fetch her savings book so that she could report to her mother. She was there and back in an instant, and in the determined tones of someone who has overcome all of life's difficulties and can now be an example to others, she proclaimed loudly and clearly that there had been nothing in her account for months, zero. "*Zero. Zilch*"—Felícia was saying, ignoring the phone that kept ringing and ringing. She put it away. Everyone in Bairro dos Espelhos was phoning to congratulate her. But she'd had enough. She then went on to explain that she'd given all her savings to Janina and Gabriel. She wanted everyone to know that she'd even paid for Janina's singing lessons. Yes, it was true. And now she had nothing, and that was fine by her. "I'll keep forging ahead. God is great. Our Holy Mother Mary is great. Time will tell, but God never fails us . . ."—she said as if giving a lesson to her mother, who was still clutching the four savings books, none of which belonged to her, and peering at the pages even though she couldn't make out a single letter, and couldn't have even if the letters were the size of an ox. So why are you holding on to those savings books, Ma? She spoke in the same kindly way as she had the previous night. Then the telephone began ringing again, this time ringing and vibrating. Felícia picked it up and shouted—"Yes, thank you, Janina can't come to the phone right now because he's very busy in Lisbon. He'll be doing his exercises so that he's ready to perform onstage. Yes, Gabriel too . . ." Then she turned it off. For good. She put it on voice mail.

She said to her mother—"I, your daughter Felícia, just like my sisters, have absolutely nothing. Germana and Dilecta don't even have savings books. So why are you picking on the boys? None of us has anything and yet we get along just fine."

Ana Mata was waiting. She was moving slowly, but she had a plan.

Prompted by this conversation, the two sisters, Dilecta and Germana, brought their money in notes to show their mother. They both began counting. They counted it out, note by note, sitting on the stackable chairs, beneath a sunshade bearing an image of Pocahontas and her horse in the middle of a field. Slowly, repeatedly licking one finger, they counted out the notes, doing the sums in their heads. But neither of them got to one hundred. This was a familiar scene. Domingos got annoyed then—"God, this could only ever happen here. All we need now is for the kids to bring their piggy banks . . ."

Ana Mata thinking and thinking, stroking the savings books, not wanting to give them back. Her three daughters, their children, her grandsons' wives, and her grandsons, were all there. Belisa and Sissi. Heitor Senior slunk away and stationed himself at the main gates. He didn't have any money either. Everything he possessed was hidden in a boot. Domingos got annoyed again, while Ana Mata continued to think, still clutching the savings books.

Ana Mata handed them back.

"So when we go home, we'll be poor . . ." she said sadly. "Very, very poor. But we must go . . ."

Felícia put her phone down out of the way. Then she faced her mother.

"What do you mean, Ma?"

"Back to our own country, very poor, very poor. But I've decided. We're going back."

"Going back where?"—asked Felícia, noticing for the first time that Ana Mata had a dress wrapped around her with the sleeves dragging on the ground. She suddenly saw her mother as this disheveled woman who had appeared out of nowhere and was bothering everyone. "Have you forgotten how to dress yourself? Anyway, where exactly do you mean to go back to?" The grandchildren started giggling. They were out of their usual routine, having a late breakfast, as they usually did after a party, and they couldn't stop giggling. There was a sense of freedom stirring among the cool shadows in the courtyard, and they couldn't stop laughing. Given the lateness of the hour, the table had been hastily, haphazardly laid.

"We must go back"—said Ana Mata in her own language. "If we stay here, we're all going to disappear, one by one. We must all go back, including Gabriel and Janina. There are lots of places in Praia where Janina can sing. My father sang there, and my grand-father, and all my sons, Janina's uncles. Back in our country, that paradise on Earth." And she began singing softly: *Paraíso di terra, nha gente . . .*

The grandchildren and great-grandchildren started laughing again. Even Antonino's children, sitting on the laps of their old aunts. Even them. It was good to see them laugh. They were all laughing at Ana Mata. Even the two dogs, intently watching people's hands as they passed around food, even their eyes were laughing. Ana Mata sitting in her plastic armchair, her *cautcha*, listening. After the morning showers, three large rivers were flow-ing around her feet. Perfumed rivers. Nivea, Cadum, Musgo Real, Palmolive.

"Not today, not tomorrow, not the day after, but in a few months' time, or a year, we'll go back. Back to our own country. It's a big place, you have to go a long way for water, but it's there. We can fetch it. We'll fetch water every day. What's the point of having so much water? Here we're surrounded by it, and yet we're disappearing. We're all disappearing, no one will escape . . ." Everyone laughing at Ana Mata. The great-grandchildren, among them Antonino's children, were creased up laughing. Even the two dogs, ears twitching, continued to laugh. Conceição felt sorry for Ana Mata.

Bent over the plastic armchair, stroking Ana Mata's shoul-ders and straightening the dress that was draped around her, Conceição explained—"We can't go back to our own country, Grandma Mata, we can't. We're just not in a position to do that. We don't have enough money. Think what it would cost to buy plane tickets for all of us. Think how expensive that would be.

And what would we do there anyway? Where would we work? What would we live on? There's nothing for us to do. Just think about it. Your home there consists of three tiny shacks with a caved-in roof. Don't you remember the photos they sent? No windows and no doors. By now the goats have probably moved in . . . You're living in another world, Grandma."

Ana Mata could feel her plan slipping through her fingers.

She stared very hard at the wall in front of her, the high wall surrounding the courtyard. With her mind left free to think, she thought absolutely everything and saw too much.

This meant that the Matas were trapped. Wherever they went they were in prison. Imprisoned everywhere, here, there, on land and sea. Imprisoned in the house at Ribeirinha da Praia, imprisoned in Bairro dos Espelhos, imprisoned in the Old Factory. *So we're never going back. Is that what you mean?* Ana Mata was thinking. Was that true? Could they be lying to her? Felícia was picking up trays laden with bottles, pressing the edge of each tray against the roses on her robe. Domingos and Heitor were setting off in their tracksuits, mounted on two gleaming bicycles. The children, scattered around the courtyard, were playing with all kinds of objects, objects that squeaked or trotted or ran, and made more of a racket than an old-fashioned water wheel. The granddaughters were drying their hair with blow dryers. And Dilecta had turned on the radio to hear mass. Ana Mata was about to eat her bread and hot milk, but pushed it roughly away. That was the problem—her people were drowning in objects, and meanwhile, far away, the roof on her little house was falling in.

"Felícia?" Ana Mata called.

Her daughter didn't even hear.

———

"Felícia!"

That was the problem. They had no money in their savings books because, she thought in her own language, it had all been spent on the machines and gadgets filling the house and court-yard. Why did they spend money on those useless things? On electric cables. On lamps. On watches and clocks. There were twenty-five of those time-telling things in the house, she knew because she'd counted. On records, magazines, photographs. Shiploads and shiploads of completely useless objects. They had two dogs who neither barked nor bit, and yet who had five muzzles apiece. Ten muzzles in all. And as for dolls, her great-granddaughters had so many that they didn't play at rocking them to sleep or dressing them, they just counted them. And then there were bicycles, every child had their own, as if no bike could pos-sibly be ridden by anyone else. A total waste. Enslaved. Enslaved to places because they were enslaved to objects and machines. They had machines for opening cans, cutting nails, cutting hair, cutting bread, massaging your back, cleaning your teeth. Some made holes in doors, others made holes in walls, still others only made holes in aluminium. A machine for every metal. They had machines for sawing, for mashing, for pressing buttons without you having to get out of your chair, for heating you up, for cooling you down, for freezing, for grinding, for making heat and making wind, for doing away with the old forms of preserving food, cold and salt, they had a machine for everything. They were enslaved by all those things, which meant they were enslaved by the places where those things were to be found. That's what she wanted to say to Felícia, just that. In her own language, she yelled—"Felícia, come here!"

Still feeling on top of the world, Felícia again didn't hear her. She responded from a distance—"You go back, Ma, to your so-called *Paraíso.*' Your sisters-in-law are still there, so you'd have somewhere to stay. Why don't you leave your armchair and go and join your younger sisters? You can go, but I don't want to. I don't know about *my* sisters, but I don't want to. Do you want to go back, sisters?"

Dilecta and Germana said nothing, neither yes nor no. Ana Mata waited for them to speak, but the two dull, tedious creatures said nothing. Her granddaughters said nothing. No one opened their mouth. It was as if she were seeing a lovely flower-strewn road suddenly plunge over the edge of a cliff; Ana Mata kept looking straight ahead, looking for the future, but it wasn't there. Three tiny roofless shacks. It was as if a grave had opened up at her feet and swallowed her plan to take them all back with her.

But Ana Mata had further to fall. The grave she had entered would grow still deeper. The bright day had turned pitch-black. The dress around her shoulders had slipped off.

"Do you mean you lied to me? That none of you are going to go back? Is that right? So what am I going to do? How can I go back to my country alone? I trusted you, I thought we would come here and then go back. But now you want to die in a country that isn't ours. And it's not a good place for my bones, it's not good for the bones of the Matas, their bones are over there, in our earth . . ."

"Who says it isn't good?"—asked the unflappable Felícia, pacing up and down. "No, Ma, when it comes to the dead person we all carry through life, what matters isn't other people who are long dead and buried, but the future of the living person inside us. Why ruin the lives of the people we love because of the dead person we all carry around? Forget it, Ma, there's no such thing as a safe place or a good place. The only safe place is our body. What else do we have? Perhaps we don't even have that . . ."—

Felícia Mata eating bread, picking her teeth, speaking as if she were immortal. Answering the phone.

And, sitting with hands clasped, glass of milk overturned and bread discarded, the sleeves of her dress dragging on the ground, Ana Mata began to cry. They could scarcely understand what she was saying in her own language—"We should make the most of the fact that we're still alive and still honest. Yes, at least we're all still honest. We should take advantage of that and leave . . ." Ana Mata getting up from her plastic armchair, wandering off into the courtyard, then coming back, letting her crumpled dress drag along the ground, and pushing her chair slowly, slowly along, pushing her chair ahead of her.

"What are you doing, Mama?"

Sighing and sobbing and plodding across the courtyard, taking her chair away from its usual position, away from where the three rivers met, taking herself away, bidding farewell to the rivers, since she would never go back, but would always hereafter sit somewhere else. Propelling the chair along with her two bony, mosquito-thin wrists, pushing one world away from the other, separating the two worlds, setting off on a long journey on her bent, skinny legs, across a considerable swath of the world. No, she didn't need anyone's help, she was fine. This was a matter for her alone. She would reach some other place in the courtyard under her own steam. Some other place on the Earth. Pushing her chair, her *cautcha*, toward the open door of her small gray house, with its one window the size of a schoolbook. Turning her back forever on the region inhabited by those who had betrayed and abandoned her.

Forever and ever.

With the phone pressed to her ear, Felícia was bellowing from a distance—"Oh yes, our mother's being very annoying. She thinks she knows everything. She speaks directly to God, but always hears much more than He actually says. Well, that's life. God says one, and she hears two, or even three. She just makes everything bigger. Oh yes, Janina's fine. God is setting us on the right path . . . Janina will be in Lisbon now, fast asleep. Yes, lots of love to you too. I'll pass on your congratulations to Janina . . ." Felícia far away, far, far away.

All of them far, far away, and in the Diamond everything that was far away was also near. Later it was said that, without anyone realizing, it was life propelling them along, all jumbled up together, side by side, just as in mud you find both beetles and pearls. Just as in the grave, finger bones and gold teeth are reunited at last.— "No, my friend, don't you worry about us, we're all fine and dandy, in great shape . . ."

XVII

MEANWHILE, MILENE DIALED THE USUAL NUMBERS ON THE old rotary phone, the kind that spun around and made a noise as if it were full of cogs and levers; she wouldn't even listen to the recording, she knew it all by heart. *After the beep. 'Bye* . . . It was early afternoon, which meant it was first thing in the morning in Massachusetts. On Grandma Regina's table she had placed a clock that was five hours behind, so as to keep track of the time. She didn't want to get it wrong. She'd been waiting for ages. She leaned in closer and said—"*João Paulo?*" Her voice quiet, entirely focused on the mouthpiece—"*I've got news, big news* . . ." Her voice very quiet. Her voice a whisper.—"*Yesterday we spent the whole afternoon together, but he only kissed me at night . . . Are you listening? He kissed me loads of times, really hard, and it was so nice. I loved it. First he kissed my hair, then he searched out my mouth and kissed it all over. He had his eyes shut and I had mine open. I saw it all. His tongue was pink. He kissed me and kissed me. I don't care if he has another girlfriend who's alive. It was so nice . . . First we walked and walked, trying to find our cars. We almost walked right past them, we didn't see them. Then came the whole afternoon and the night, and eventually he decided to kiss me. He didn't kiss me till then, like I said. And afterwards he stayed in the van, right outside the house, sleeping . . . He didn't go and see Divina. But I don't even care if he*

324

has another girlfriend who's alive. Like I said. Goodbye, yes, goodbye. When he kisses me I get an electric shock. Ciao. From Milene . . ."

She didn't wait for a response. She hung up. "Bye-bye."

Then things moved very quickly. It happened the following weekend. Antonino told her to stay parked outside the Restaurante do Inglês. He'd be back in half an hour. "Half an hour"—he said. "Keep an eye on the time . . ."

The gray van set off down the road, disappearing around the bend by the Hotel Miramar. He didn't even end up taking that long. When the van stopped, he got out, holding a bag, and showed her what was inside. He told her to have a good look and check out the contents for herself, so she wasn't in any doubt. Three red ties, a wristwatch, an electric clock radio, a radio shaped like an apple, some striped pajamas still in their plastic wrapping, and an enamel crucifix on a gold chain. Plus a fine porcelain plate with a gold border, printed with the words *FOR MY LOVE.*

"What's all this?"

"I'm giving it back."

"Who to?"

"You'll see. Wait for me here, I'll be gone an hour at most."

Milene waited three hours. She listened to Cyndi Lauper singing "What's Going On" more than thirty times. She saw the first customers arrive at the Restaurante do Inglês, and then the last. When she couldn't stand to hear *Mother, mother, brother, brother, brother* yet again, and the restaurant was closing its doors, the van appeared. Antonino was sweating, as if he'd climbed up three Liebherr cranes one on top of the other and hadn't showered afterward. He was again carrying a bag and he showed her what was in it—A china doll, a very small box containing a very thick gold ring set with a little diamond, a white silk scarf, a calendar showing a picture of an Asian landscape, and a Longchamp purse.

"Do you understand what just happened?"—he asked, squeezing her waist. "Divina and I have returned everything we ever gave each other. We've separated. Understood? Now it's just the two of us, forever. My only living girlfriend . . ."

The Restaurante do Inglês had shut. They weren't hungry, they were skinny and didn't need to eat. It was an ordinary love.

XVIII

JULIANA HAD STARTED ARRIVING FOR WORK AT VILLA
Regina at four o'clock in the afternoon and leaving at six, by
which time it was dark. In recent weeks, she and Milene had
rarely crossed paths. When they did, Juliana would declare
loudly—"This won't end well, you mark my words. In this area
alone, there've been five muggings and two rapes in the space of a
month. There are murderers everywhere. To be honest, it fright-
ens me just coming here, what with you having all the lights on
all the time. If I don't turn up one day, don't worry, I'll just have
decided to do something else with my life . . ." Then she would
ask—"Do I really need to clean Dona Regina's room again? The
dust won't have had time to settle since yesterday. Do you expect
me to catch it in the air? I don't cook, I don't do the shopping.
Do you expect me to lick the house clean the way a cat licks her
kittens? And while we're on the subject, why don't you get a pet to
keep you company? A nice little puppy to liven up the place . . ."
But that afternoon, after the night when Antonino had thrown
away all Divina's things, everything changed.

Milene wasn't at her usual post, halfway up the stairs, but was
sitting instead, knees together, in front of the mirror in her bedroom, staring at her own reflection. Studying herself. Scattered
over the bed were bits and pieces of jewelry, and she'd clearly been

327

trying on clothes too, because various items were draped, inside out, over chairs or hung on door handles. Hats and berets were perched on the bed frame, and at that precise moment, Milene was trying on a beanie hat, an orangey red one Juliana hadn't seen before. But it wasn't the objects that betrayed the fact that something new had happened to Milene, it was her entire face, which was quite changed, as if a rare glow were revealing hitherto invisible features. Juliana caught the effect of that glow in the air.

"Has something happened?"

At first Milene said nothing, then blurted out—"You're not going to believe this, but one night, we went to the beach and threw things into the sea. And that's all I'm going to say . . ."

"Threw things into the sea? What things? What beach?"— Juliana asked suspiciously, because she'd known ever since August that, sooner or later, something extraordinary would happen. A sudden flash of insight told her that the long-awaited event was now beginning to take shape. That pile of clothes and sundry baubles was simply a sign. "What beach? What things? Tell me . . ."

Milene couldn't tell her, she could hear Antonino's voice saying—"*If only we were transparent, invisible, if only we could walk about freely without anyone seeing us . . .*" It had in fact been just last night that they'd thrown those things away. The Restaurante do Inglês was closed, and they sat in the van, holding hands, with the Clio parked next to them, neither of them able to summon up the will to go home. Then they'd gone to the Dunas Fêmeas, and, in an act of unusual bravado, Antonino had left the van and started throwing the objects into the sea, one after the other. As if by ridding himself of them he were throwing off a curse—"Here goes that expensive purse, the doll, the white scarf I had to work so hard to buy . . ." Milene had tried to save at least something— "Oh no, not the ring, don't throw away the diamond ring . . ." she begged. But he remained impervious. "No, here goes the ring and the calendar . . ." he announced as he threw object after object into the dark sea. Each object zinging through the air. "Go on, off you go, all the presents I ever gave Divina . . ." This had happened not several days before, but the previous night, and Milene was now getting ready to go out earlier than usual. Antonino had told her they could go and pick up his three kids, Emanuel, Cirino, and Quirino, because going to fetch the children from kinder-garten was something they *could* do together. They couldn't go to other places, but they could eat at the Restaurante do Inglês and pick up the kids afterward. If only they were transparent, if only they were invisible, if only they could go out and about and be seen by no one . . . Milene was in a hurry. Juliana had arrived early. She felt both surprised and troubled, sensing something in the air, while Milene, saying nothing, continued trying on that new hat. Juliana attempting to unpick the thread of what exactly had happened.

"I'm sorry, Miss Milene, I'm going to have to stop working here. I'm sorry, but I've had enough. There's a Belgian lady who lives down the road who pays me almost double. Ever since they built the motorway, this whole area has really gone to pot. There are thieves and murderers everywhere. I might be all alone here one day, and some guy could burst in through the front door, rape me, and steal my wages . . ."—Juliana listening to her own voice. "But what were you saying about throwing things into the sea?"

Still sitting in front of the mirror, Milene laughed—"And someone kissed me!"

Juliana took a step back.

"Who kissed you, Miss Milene? Who?"

A whirlwind swept through Juliana's mind. Suddenly, out of nowhere, from quite where she didn't know, came that knowl-edge, that intuition, that discovery exploding inside her. Quite where those facts had come from or how they'd taken shape inside her head, she had no idea. She took a step forward this time, trembling, pale as pale—"Miss Milene, you're going out with that man in the gray van, aren't you? No, don't lie, don't lie to me . . ."

Sitting now among those piles of clothes, Milene screamed—"If you tell anyone, I'll kill you. I'll kill you if you say so much as a word . . ."

Juliana clapped one hand over her mouth. Unable to remain standing, she sat down next to Milene, head bowed, to stop the rush of blood, which is what tended to happen when she was taken by surprise like that—"Miss Milene, I knew this would end badly, I didn't know how or when, but I knew . . ." A long silence fell. Then she got upset and began to cry. "Oh, you poor things. I mean, I really like black people, especially after seeing that movie *Uncle Tom's Cabin* . . . I totally support them . . ." Juliana was almost beside herself. "And you kissed . . ."

"I'll kill you, I mean it . . ."

Juliana still with her hand covering her mouth. Something really big had happened. She had felt sure something major would happen in that house, but hadn't known what or when. Now she knew. Still with her hand over her mouth—"I won't say a word, Miss Milene. I swear on my father's soul." And, looking at Milene, she squeezed her lips together with two fingers as if she were sewing her lips tight shut, and then, in a gesture as old as female solidarity, she began stroking Milene's hair. That's a very short skirt you're wearing, Miss Milene. You can see every inch of your legs. Put your heels together. And put some earrings on, and a pretty white pendant would go well with your new hat. Advising her, admiring her, her eyes moist with tears. Goodness, so he'd *kissed* her. Milene was being loved and respected and touched by the gift of love. "Don't worry, miss, I'll leave all the lights on and lock all the doors. Off you go, and don't you worry about a thing. But be careful, very careful. You can kiss, but don't let him do anything else. Then we'd be in a right pickle. So be careful . . ." Juliana standing in the doorway where the night had already arrived, in order to watch her leave in her white car. Two headlights in the darkness. A beetle buzzing in the night. Off you go.

"Miss Milene!"—Juliana managed to reach the car just as it was moving away. "It's agreed, then. I won't say a word, and you haven't said a word to me, all right? We're together, but separate . . ." Juliana's heart pounding as she watched Milene leave. It really was very touching. For Juliana, it was as if a love story like the ones you see in movies were appearing over the horizon. And that distant line seemed to be suddenly painted in bright reds and crimsons, with surging music in the background and two people running along the beach toward a deserted shack. But nothing of the sort happened. On this side of the horizon, in real life, everything would turn out to be rather more banal. Regardless of Juliana's fantasies about grand, extraordinary deeds, nothing happened in the days that followed, apart from a mist that descended in the early hours. Two days later, everyone had forgotten about the heat wave that had made summer linger almost into Christmas.

Yes, a mist descended, as silent as the darkness of which it was a part. A mass of fine water covering everything. The mornings hung there in abeyance, as did the afternoons. Even up close, you couldn't make out the walls of the houses. For five whole days, in a region accustomed to brilliant sunshine, that milky stain, which stopped light from entering windows, had various consequences. Radio Valmares issued hourly safety warnings, urging drivers to turn on their headlights. At the airport, no planes landed or took off. On the sea, a ship passed by, sounding its siren, which moaned out for two whole hours, something that hadn't happened for many years. Major events. On one morning alone, there were several car crashes, leaving three dead and eight injured. The two lovers who yearned to be invisible listened to the news bulletins, but paid no attention, that was just other people's lives or, rather, deaths, people behaving foolishly. Nothing to do with them. They were perfectly happy with the mist. At the end of the day, they would sit and kiss in the Mitsubishi van, neither more nor less visible than usual, but believing themselves to be invisible. Antonino more than her.

Around the Old Factory, the feeling was that the mist wasn't just water vapor but something solid and heavy, like a thick blanket wrapped around everything. There was nothing visible between the spot where Ana Mata's rivers met and the place where she now sat in her *cautcha*. You could see nothing from one wall to the other. And then, at this worst of times, they were expecting Janina to arrive.

Yes, Gabriel and Janina would both be coming. They were taking a break from their concerts and from recording their third disc, Janina's first CD, an album with twelve tracks, two of which he'd sung on *Show Bizz*. On the recording, though, just on those two tracks, they were going to add in three more guitars and two clarinets, plus a double bass to accompany the falsetto parts. That way, you'd be able to hear Janina's vibrato to perfection, followed by the wolf howl that he performed far better than even Terence Trent D'Arby in his prime. That's where the deep pulse of the double bass would come in. Like a dialogue, *dumdum, dumdum*, do you see? Yes, dear, yes. Felícia knew all their plans, and approved of them all, because the only thing she hadn't liked was seeing too much of that sax player. And what about the *reco-reco* as percussion? Were they including that? When? Where? On just one of the tracks. Oh good. Then stop your recording, sweetheart, and come home.

Yes, they would come. But how?

Janina had said on the phone that they'd be coming with a friend of Gabriel's. Gabriel had said they'd be coming with Janina's manager. A mother's heart always fears the worst. Somewhere there exists a bay of blood in which, in a mother's worst nightmares, children drown. In this instance, though, everything was fine, for it turned out that friend and manager were one and the same, and that he was happy to drive the more than one hundred and eighty miles, at his own expense, so that Janina and Gabriel could visit their mother, their old aunts, their grandmother, their brothers, sisters-in-law, and the children that Janina so adored. "They're being driven down by their friend and manager"—Felícia explained, rather disappointed by what she considered to be the annoying presence of the mist, in a place that was normally wall-to-wall sunshine. As a proud mother, she had imagined her son arriving in an open-top car, like Elvis in his prime, besieged by fans, arriving in the warm light of day, so that all his friends from Bairro dos Espelhos could be there in person. She knew that in their hearts all the locals nurtured the dream of one day receiving Janina the singer with a banner on which would be painted the words—REMEMBER, JANINA MATA KING BELONGS TO BAIRRO DOS ESPELHOS. When that happened, who knows how far that banner would reach, how far his fame would reach? It was certain to reach right around the world, until everyone knew someone who was aware of the link between Bairro dos Espelhos and Janina Mata King, the singer.

Dreams, the glimmers of a dream of fame and glory in a mother's heart.

"At least they're coming . . ." said Felícia with a sigh.

Some dreams would have to be postponed. That triumphal encounter between the small world of the neighborhood and the wider world beyond it would have to wait until Janina had finished recording that CD and making the accompanying music video, which would involve endless walks up and down the seashore and at least ten changes of clothes. They were only going to be there for forty-eight hours, to visit the family incognito, and, as luck would have it, this was the third consecutive day of mist, in a region where mist was almost unknown. A thick mist, meaning that Janina's return to Valmares would go unnoticed. *At least they're coming*, thought Felícia Mata, aglow with life. The world was rolling slowly toward their gates, to the gates of the Diamond.

The Matas had opened the main gates to the factory and waited outside. It was as if all the trees had up and left. Even the tops of the eleven palm trees had vanished into nothingness. Vague silhouettes in that entirely unexpected mist. What was taking the boys so long? Why didn't they phone? Would they be able to find the factory, plunged as it was in that stupid mist, which made them feel as if they were part of the sea? The Matas were waiting both internally and externally, waiting and suffering. Except there was no use succumbing to despair. Hard though it was to believe, the boys were finally on their way.

And there they were.

On the road, steeped in the white blur of mist, two yellow headlights appeared, piercing the dense afternoon air. Behind those slowly approaching lights, which seemed to be searching for something they had lost, was a magnificent car, a maroon Alfa Romeo. Its glittering chrome traced lines in the mist. There they were. Felícia's heart skipped a beat—had Janina not come? However, her feeling of alarm lasted only a second. The person driving was a young man with milk-white skin, as if he'd become the human face of the mist. Pale eyes, staring straight ahead, looking for the place to park his car. Beside him, sitting very upright, was Gabriel, his very dark dark glasses glinting. Even before they had stopped, he put one finger to his lips, because on the back-seat, curled up beneath a black-and-white-checkered blanket, like a small, insignificant parcel, was Janina, fast asleep. Felí-cia shooed away the children and peered in, and with her face pressed against the window, she couldn't help but cry out—"Oh, poor boy, you're so thin."

This wasn't at all how she'd imagined it would be. Besides, they'd been waiting so long, and time had passed so slowly, but now that the moment was here, everything was happening very fast. Too fast, because Gabriel got out and, before greeting anyone—as if he were a complete stranger, an officer of the law or something, or a stony-faced bodyguard—he sternly held back the crowd of familiar faces surrounding the car. The windows of the maroon Alfa Romeo were too narrow to contain so many faces, and they all dispersed in response to Gabriel's imposing gesture, as he positioned himself between the car and the mist, looking very tall in his thick-soled cowboy boots.

"Sorry to have to do that," he said, "but Janina's sleeping."

"Sleeping, you say?"

Yes, Felícia was surprised, the whole family was genuinely sur-prised, but it was a fact, no one could deny it: he was fast asleep. The proof was there for all to see. Gabriel placed one hand on the car door, as precisely, confidently, and suspensefully as some-one about to open a window onto Hollywood, or the door of a cage at the circus, and yet, after this theatrical gesture, all they saw was a shape, Janina curled up on the backseat. But the shape was moving. Janina was waking up. First, he uncurled, pushing back the blanket, then he yawned and stretched. He was taking his time. Gabriel and the manager, the milk-white driver, were still both guarding the doors, while inside, finally, the drowsy one was disentangling himself from the blanket and getting out of the maroon car in order to surrender himself to the family melee. The tribe were waiting for him just two steps away, and despite the rather chilly atmosphere created by Gabriel, they held out their arms to him, embraced him. It was Janina Mata King in the flesh. And he laughed. Surrendered. But nothing would be as Felícia had imagined.

It was nothing like the moment she'd been preparing for in her head and for which she'd asked her other children to leave work early. And Domingos, Heitor, and Antonino were all there. When Felícia at last managed to get near Janina, she held out her arms to him, almost toppling over—"You made it, son . . . But you're so thin . . ." Her arms tight about Janina's neck, summing up in those few words various contradictory thoughts—*You made it, my dear, but you've paid a high price . . . We didn't realize just how high a price . . . And maybe the fact that you've grown so thin might mean that, in the future, you won't be able to do it again . . . You need to take very good care of yourself* . . . And other such thoughts, all strung together one after the other, inside her head at the moment of his arrival. She must drive away such thoughts. *You made it, my boy.*

"You made it!" she said triumphantly.

A mother grateful for the fact that he *was* her son, thanking God for such happiness. And Janina with his family around him, standing next to the red car, next to the milk-white young man, all of them gathered together to celebrate Janina's great success, and yet it was a much quieter affair than they'd envisaged. Even the children were quiet. Felícia Mata then folded both visiting sons in a long, respectful, pitying look—"But you're both so thin, so skinny, especially Janina. Let's go into the house and have something to eat, eh?"

But Gabriel, very tall in those boots-cum-stilts, intervened once again. Gabriel decisive and in charge—"Please, don't get him too wide awake. Last night we were working into the small hours, and now what Janina needs is to rest. Don't get him too excited with all this fuss. We've already eaten and drunk, but we've had no sleep at all . . ."

Felícia thought this rather excessive. True, the manager was there and they'd never met him before, but she couldn't help but wonder at Gabriel telling *her*, Janina's mother, that her son needed to sleep. Of course he did, they weren't fools. So why was Gaby saying that? They weren't blind. They were perfectly capable of seeing the state Janina was in and didn't need to have it explained. That's what Felícia said. But Gabriel turned sternly to his white friend, the manager and driver of the red car, as if he were the only person there.

"Didn't I tell you? We should have gone straight to the hotel. Our mother just doesn't understand . . ."

The manager said nothing. They were standing in the middle of the mist-filled courtyard. The washing line, from which dangled a solitary item of clothing, was completely invisible even though it was only about a foot away. Their faces were immersed in that sticky liquid, as if the Earth's absence of wind, energy, and emotion wouldn't allow the clouds to move. As if, like the mist, they too had descended wearily onto the streets, the waves, the ports. And the Matas were gripped by the strange sense that everything was very different from how they'd imagined. Janina, who on the television appeared to be all sinew and rippling muscles, really did seem to have lost a lot of weight. There were dark shadows under eyes grown small and bleary with sleep. He didn't even look like Janina. "What did I tell you?"—Gabriel said, his hands on his hips and with a haste that bordered on arrogance or some other feeling so surprising it didn't yet have a name. A very serious word surfaced in Felícia's mind, but she immediately rejected it. No, it was just that, haste. Gabriel had removed his dark glasses, which he'd kept on until then to protect his face, and, addressing his older brothers and the other people standing around, he said—"The thing is, we only have two hours . . ."

Felícia couldn't believe it. Rooted to the spot in the middle of the mist-enveloped courtyard. The satellite dish invisible, the piles of plastic chairs all steeped in that water vapor—"Two hours, Gaby? You drove one hundred and eighty miles in that exhausted state just to spend two hours here?"

"It was either two hours or nothing"—said Gabriel tensely, his dark glasses hooked over the opening of his leather jacket. The other man, the friend, the manager, stood by, silent and shy, his pale eyes seemingly devoid of emotion or doubt. He must be the architect of other people's success. There are individuals like that, who only want success for others, never demanding anything in return. Felícia had heard tell of such altruistic folk. But what mattered was Janina, marooned in the mist, his long hair tied back and looking so thin, and apparently chilled to the bone. This isn't how they had imagined him. Surprised and offended, she said—"Two hours? What can we do in two hours? We prepared a nice, cozy room for the three of you. We even swapped the beds around. You've got three big beds in there now with the softest eiderdowns, with blankets, heating, water, electricity, toilet, everything, everything you need for a good night's sleep, but now you're leaving." Felícia distraught, the children distraught.

"Didn't I tell you she wouldn't understand?"—Gabriel said again, walking past his other brothers as if he were the spokesperson, and as if he held the key to everything and now had to give a detailed explanation of something that could not be communicated by mere mental osmosis. There they were, the whole family, and not one of them understood. Gabriel was quite clear—Yes, two hours, because Janina needed to rest, which is why their friend, Janina's manager, had reserved rooms for them at the

Hotel Continental. That's all. They had to think of Janina. It would be a major mistake for the family to wear him out when he was in the middle of recording a CD.

"Well, if it was such a big sacrifice, why did you come at all?" asked Domingos, leading his wife and children over to their house in the courtyard.

"Because of Ma, because she kept going on and on at us to come . . ."

"And now we haven't even got *two* hours, because half an hour has already gone. We've only got an hour and a half now, and by the time we've finished arguing, we won't even have that . . ." said Antonino. The children were all looking rather alarmed to see how very different life was from what they'd seen on TV.

In the midst of the general exodus, Felícia managed to say— "Just a moment, let's think about this calmly. I can see he's lost a lot of weight, but he's not at death's door. And with only two hours, or less than two hours, I can't imagine anything bad will happen. Look, people, let's go inside . . ."

"Inside where? Whose house?" asked Gabriel.

"Look, just come inside . . ." said Felícia Mata, hoping to salvage something. "There's no point arguing. Anyway, at least Janina can sleep here, since that's what he came here to do and what he needs. And the rest of us can go about our own business . . ." Felícia's voice had lost its impetus. It was like her usual triumphal voice, loud and imposing, but somehow broken, fractured. And then they all went to their usual places in the old buildings that once, many years before, had housed the canning factory, and Janina, who appeared to have taken a strong sleeping pill, Xanax or Valium 10 or something, went to lie down in the music room.

"If you've only got two hours, then there's only about one hour left . . . !"

Gabriel said in a low voice—"Do you have the key to Janina's van?"

An offended Felícia emptied the contents of an old jug onto the table and, without a word, handed him the key. Gabriel and the milk-white young man left. The manager in the maroon car, and Gabriel in Janina's van. The two red vehicles, one behind the other, setting off together. Felícia watched them go. She glanced at her watch. She wasn't usually a clock-watcher, but that frustrated visit had taken three-quarters of an hour. She had little more than an hour to enjoy having her son Janina sleeping in a bed in her house. It hardly seemed possible. When she went back into the courtyard, it was empty, because everyone had retreated to their own house, feeling at odds with life, and yet they would have loved to show Antonino and Gabriel the recordings they'd made in triplicate. Or at least ask a few questions. They didn't even know what Janina's new CD would be called. Felícia walked past the door to the music room and felt like crying. What *was* going on? They would be back in an hour to collect Janina, and meanwhile she couldn't even wake him up.

Felícia took a deep breath, went over to the door, knocked gently, and went in. Janina stirred on the bed. She sat down very quietly and said softly—"Forgive me for coming in, Janina, but it's only me here and I won't say a word. You go to sleep . . ."

Janina wasn't yet quite asleep. He reached out to take Felícia's hand and squeezed it. Felícia said, again very softly—"We made three recordings of the whole show. And we made you a whole new bookshelf all to yourself here. When you wake up, I'd love you to see it. But you go to sleep. Pretend I'm not here."

Janina again squeezed his mother's hand. He really was exhausted and deeply regretted having come at all. He spoke and breathed as if he weren't fully asleep.

"Your grandmother's aged a lot. The poor thing keeps saying

your voice isn't *your* voice anymore. And we don't even know yet what your new CD will be called."

"*Solar Disk*"—said the sleeper in his half-broken sleep. Outside, night was falling fast, mingling with the mist, as if it were another world entirely.

"Oh, lovely. *Solar Disk*. It will be wonderful. Fabulous name. It sounds like the sun sinking into the sea. Who chose the name?"

Janina didn't answer. Immersed in the dark red gloom of the music room.

"Who chose it?"

When he still didn't respond, she fell silent and sat there for a while, not moving. Then she left. At least she had spoken to him. When the two hours were up, the three men would all go and sleep at the Hotel Continental. She didn't even know where the hotel was. Where was that ideal place where they would all be able to rest and relax? What would it be like?

Then night fell. And there was no sign of Gabriel and the manager. Janina was sound asleep in the music room. Gabriel had his phone switched off, as he had earlier in the day. They could talk later, yes, later. Felícia sat at the gates. All night. A terrible night. At daybreak, the two cars arrived, and the two men parked them very quietly and entered the courtyard equally quietly, and Gabriel said to his mother—"We spent the night in Bairro dos Espelhos. We're going to make Janina's music video there. We spent the night discussing it. We're not going to film him just by the sea after all, we're mainly going to film him in Bairro dos Espelhos . . ."

"In Bairro dos Espelhos?"

"That's what I said, isn't it?"

Ah, so that's how it was, now she was beginning to under-stand, the life of a singer was very hard, so was being the singer's companion and manager. She'd had no idea it was like that, she'd imagined it would be more like one long party, as it had been until recently, with Gabriel and Janina traveling from town to town and venue to venue in their van. Sometimes with a band and sometimes without. She couldn't have known that, not being particularly well educated and perhaps even rather ignorant. And maybe the exhaustion of one brother and the exasperation of the other were just a necessary part of what it took to make a record, and she, of course, didn't know that. Whatever the truth of the matter, and however uneducated and ignorant Felícia might be as regards the making of records, when she saw her two sons head off the next day, she had the strange feeling that something, some emotion that would have been perfectly understandable to find in Janina, was, instead, alive and well in her other son. As if a sub-stance of some kind had transferred from one to the other, and, in doing so, had made things go slightly off-kilter. That idiotic mist, like an unpleasant gift sent from afar, persisted, and although she couldn't *see* clearly, she could still feel clearly enough. The vanity, pride, and impatience, the feeling of triumph, which could and should, quite rightly, exist in Janina's heart, were now there in the eyes of his brother. The success of the former was rattling around in the head of the latter. Wrapped in a blanket, Janina continued to be a sweet, fragile boy. A fragile sweetness combined with great willpower. A kind of miracle. Doubtless God was watching over him. Whenever Janina needed it, God presumably gave him the strength he seemed to lack. She found some of what was happen-ing quite simply unfathomable, a kind of present mystery. And that enigma left her with a sense of unease, a strange feeling of nausea, a desire to vomit up some bothersome object. Plump, strong Felícia wasn't feeling at all well, she was trembling inside. And she didn't know if this malaise was physical or mental, the product of the surprise that had come to meet her along with Janina's arrival. That morning, Felícia had gone into the house, stumbling slightly, only slightly, before going to lie down. Lately, she hadn't even had any bad dreams. Neither the telegraph operator nor his skinny wife had returned to haunt her, they were submerged somewhere in her past life and were now leaving her in peace. And yet, that lightning visit by her sons seemed more like a fantasy, a dream. There must be certain events that, regardless of whether they were good or bad, were neither dreamt nor real, and for which there was no name. "Oh dear!" Felícia said with a sigh, flopping down on the bed, in her kitchen, which doubled as her bedroom.

That was when the episode with the maroon car occurred.

For soon the mist lifted its veil from the gritty, yellowish earth, and the sand reappeared, besieged by the sea, the waves beating upon it with a certain arrogance, as if a stronger hand than usual were hurling them against the line of dunes where Antonino Mata and our cousin Milene would lie, side by side, on Saturday afternoons. They would lie there for two whole hours, opening and closing their eyes, and not talking about the future. Although he would sometimes ask—"And now what are we going to do? I'm looking for the path, and I know it's there, but which one is it?" Then he would fall silent. Milene had the answer, she wanted him to make love to her. "Make love to me"—she would say.

Sometimes Antonino would burst out laughing, as if she'd just cracked a joke. She saw him shaking his head and laughing, his eyes closed, his throat rippling as if it were full of individual vertebrae. At other times, though, he would say nothing, but would look very serious and thoughtful. Sitting very upright, very still, he would say—"No, we can't. We're not married. You're not Divina. She'd already had husbands. That was different. No, not with you. We're not savages. The men from the island where I come from, *badios* with bare, cracked feet, they always have loads of wives, but

I don't like that, I was brought up differently, I respected Eunice, and I respect you. Let's not talk about it . . ."

"Oh, let's"—she would say.

"No. We're not savages."

Milene would sit up then too: *Savages?* What did he mean? It wouldn't be like that for her. When she lay down on the sand, on his jacket, it was as if those encounters were the logical, irreversible consequence of the afternoon when she'd left Senhor Frutuoso sitting in the BMW, while she set off toward the cranes that, in the distance, seemed to be beckoning to her, drawing her toward some urgent decision, and she had obeyed, walking straight ahead, no turning back. That, for her, had been the decisive day. Milene thought Antonino was wrong. In response to his silence, she would ask again—"Why savages? Why?"

"Let's not talk about it now"—Antonino would say.

It was as if they'd not only agreed never to talk about pain, but had also put a ban on any talk of plans. Whenever they approached the door to the future, the conversation seemed to suffer a kind of short-circuit. He would remove her rust-red beanie hat then and kiss her. They would go on kissing as they lay on his jacket. Their heads cold, almost damp. They would only stop as evening came on, and they went in search of the gray van parked behind the dunes, ready to drive back. The breeze rose up from the sand, and the sand found its way into their clothes and their shoes, as they walked along, arms around each other, in the direction of the van.

However, that day, Antonino's vehicle was not alone. There were other vehicles too.

To be precise, there were three cars and two vans parked next to his Mitsubishi. There, where the sandy path emerged onto the empty space behind the dunes. Tire tracks crisscrossed the sand.

As they were walking back, the cars had all begun to move. Perhaps the occupants were feeling the cold too and, having abandoned the idea of walking across the dunes to the sea, were now returning to their homes. Perhaps. There were several men and one woman. The gray van had to stop and wait for the others to leave. Milene and Antonino stayed inside, waiting for the other cars to move off. Whoever was in them, those cars formed a kind of caravan, and one of them, the one hanging slightly back from the others, was the same as the car that had brought Janina, the same maroon Alfa Romeo in which he'd been sleeping when he arrived and left. That car stopped and waited until there was a distance between it and the others. Only then did it set off, turning very fast, and as it did, the profile of the driver was finally revealed, and Antonino thought he recognized the face of the manager.

"That's Janina's car"—Antonino said. "What are they doing here?"

The maroon car was driving quite fast, and Antonino raced off after it.

"Are we chasing them?"—asked Milene, not understanding why he was in such a hurry.

But Antonino had already changed his mind.

No, regardless of whoever was in the car, it wasn't worth pursuing them. He didn't want to bother anyone. They must have come looking for images for the music video and were doubtless staying at the Hotel Continental so as to avoid the domestic strife in that dreadful household where everyone was vying to be the one in charge. Nevertheless, they continued on in the same direction, the maroon car in front, the gray van behind, the other cars already out of sight. Antonino was right on all counts. Indeed, when they reached the turnoff to the Hotel Miramar, the maroon car immediately headed in the direction of Bairro dos Espelhos, which explained everything. The music video was clearly being put together there.

Early one morning, days later, when Milene wasn't with him, Antonino was driving to work and, as he passed the road connecting with the dirt track leading inland, he suddenly saw a maroon car identical to the manager's appear and then overtake him. He again sensed that the driver was the milk-white manager, although he couldn't be sure. When the car reached the crossroads, though, it turned off toward Bairro dos Espelhos. He saw it in his rearview mirror. Yes, they must be making Janina's music video there. Or perhaps not. There must be loads of cars the same color and the same make, not that he'd ever noticed any maroon Alfa Romeos, all gleaming chrome. He would from now on. It was the same car that had brought his two brothers, Gaby and Janina, on that misty day.

A week later, Antonino was driving along that same road with the children in the back. Emanuel suddenly stood up on the backseat, shouting excitedly—"It's Janina's car, Janina's car . . ." There in the rearview mirror was the maroon car just as it was turning off toward Bairro dos Espelhos. Antonino made a U-turn and followed. In that area, there were only two streets suitable for traffic, and as for a main square, there was really only one worthy of the name. This time Antonino was determined to find out who was driving that car. He accelerated. The children were thrown about as the van bumped over the potholes. A hundred or so yards before the square, he saw the car disappear, a dark red shape merging in among the concrete walls and tin roofs. When he reached the square, there were plenty of people standing in doorways, but no one had seen the maroon car.

Leaning out the window, Antonino described the make and color of the car.

"No, we didn't see anything. If it did come this way, it must have just vanished . . ." said a rather dim boy, retreating into his house.

"If it came down here, it must have been going like the wind, because no one saw it . . ."—said another, slightly brighter boy, stepping out to scan the horizon blocked by gray houses. For the first time, Antonino felt he didn't know these people. Where were the kids he'd thrown Pringles to just last summer? Where? They all seemed quite different. They formed a tight-knit group, but none of them, young or old, had seen the car he had been chasing—a beautiful dark red car bumping down the Bairro dos Espelhos road, with a milk-white face at the wheel.

"Okay, fine . . ." he said.

And he abandoned the chase.

Ribeirinho da Praia in Cape Verde was full of stories about motorbikes and cars being driven by headless men. Other stories claimed that vehicles had been seen speeding past with no one in the driver's seat. But Antonino wasn't prepared to be diverted, he wasn't going to start imagining phantom cars traveling back and forth between the dunes and Bairro dos Espelhos whose sole purpose was to make him doubt his sanity. He had too many other things to think about. He had left Divina, he had fallen in love with Milene, a white woman from a rich family. What was he going to do with his life? Where would he go, madly in love as he was with that woman slightly older than him, and who was the very image and soul of Eunice, and who was a constant presence in his heart, had even crept beneath his skin? Who he wanted to spend the days and nights with, making love until dawn? Who he thought about obsessively, almost neurotically, and who he was going to meet now, as soon as he had dropped off his kids? No, he wouldn't let his soul be cluttered up by thoughts of that elusive car, which kept appearing and disappearing like the cars in those Ribeirinho da Praia legends.

Antonino had turned around in the only square, in that place where he suddenly appeared to know no one, and where no one seemed to recognize him either, and so, leaving behind those vigilant figures leaning in their doorways, he sped off down the dirt track, heading for the Old Factory, to sort out his own life.

XIX

THE FOLLOWING SUNDAY MORNING, MILENE GOT INTO THE
backseat of the BMW and let Senhor Frutuoso drive her to Uncle
Ludovice's house. Outside, the trees sped by as if their roots were
electrified, the sky as if it were inhuman and illusory, and the
sea, distant and unreachable. At that time in the morning, people and houses seemed to be tumbling along, like the lumbering
limbs of flightless birds.

But that moment had nothing to do with the aftermath of
the fifteenth of August, when she had been in a state of shock—
*Because this time I won't be in a state of shock. Even if they know
everything, I'll answer their questions like a strong person would,
someone much stronger than them. And since I'll be telling the truth,
nothing bad will happen to me . . .* Milene settled back into her
seat and faced reality. Reality meant the sky's wide-open expanse,
which stretched out high above her and seemed barely to leave
room for the earth. The shoulders on either side of the road were
like narrow paths running past the houses, which were protected
from the traffic by security fences. And if she, inside the car,
was trying to disappear into her seat, it was only while she mustered the courage to face them in a few minutes' time—*You old
fuddy-duddies, you idiots, you bunch of losers, go away and leave me
alone . . .* Milene knew that, but she didn't know anything else.

———

Milene didn't know that police officers had been patrolling the main roads in Valmares since the previous night, or that the traffic had been diverted since seven that morning. That day marked the opening of a new sports complex, with gyms, running tracks, tennis courts, an Olympic-sized swimming pool, two natural lakes right in the middle of the lawn, and a bird-watching station, and construction was also beginning on a day-care center for orphans and the elderly. But what was really being launched was a new urban development, a term that had slipped away from its old meaning and now denoted this great slew of housing, almost a thousand tiny houses all slotted together and looking as if they might slide down the cliff. And it was this—this new row of miniature dwellings, exposed to the sun like gregarious mollusks yet to reveal their soft insides—that needed to be celebrated in style, starting with an international marathon.

By then—around half past eight in the morning—the marathon runners were already on the move, the starting pistol having been fired and the ground having been shaken by that human throng. The route was marked out with white banners that said *Welcome* and *Benevenuto*, and more banners saying the same thing in different languages had been hung up all over the place. Here and there, by the sides of the roads-turned-marathon course, groups of people waited to see the runners, who, at the time, were still a single mass moving at a leisurely pace. The TV cameras and press vans whipped the crowd into a frenzy, and meanwhile the police went about their business quite normally. Behaving with all the brusque ferocity the occasion required, the officers directed the traffic very sternly indeed, giving orders with stiff, awkward arms. Seen from a distance, they could have been making obscene gestures rather than telling people whether to drive on or stop. With their frowning, inscrutable faces, they wielded an authority that has probably remained unchanged since the beginning of time, and which therefore, through a kind of ancestral memory, brought as much pleasure to those who wielded it as to those who willingly obeyed. Even the few who disobeyed and rebelled seemed to be having a good time. People who wouldn't generally set eyes on a policeman for months on end now had a rare opportunity to gesticulate and shout at several, simultaneously and at the top of their lungs, about all the ways life had wronged them. They swore loudly and colorfully, yelling out profanities more commonly used in drunken brawls, or, long ago, when berating a stubborn beast of burden. And so Milene heard insults being hurled at them, at her and Frutuoso, as if, inside the car, the pair were two sides of the same coin—*You slave, you pathetic lowlife . . . And as for you, you cosseted little bitch, get screwed, go to hell . . .* And she heard plenty more than that before the anthracite-gray BMW passed through the security barriers and began driving down the route reserved for the marathon runners, waved on by policemen whose constant gesturing this way and that seemed nonsensical and absurd. But Milene wasn't aware of any of this. She just knew that she had been picked up at eight-thirty, and that now, hunkering down in her seat, she was going to think about her aunts and uncles and plan how to confront them.

Meanwhile, Senhor Frutuoso, who had driven at breakneck speed down the nine or so miles of highway that formed part of the marathon route, still hadn't said a word to her. Only when they turned down the side road to the Atrium Condominium did he comment—"Senhor Ludovice wasn't feeling very well at the opening ceremony for the marathon . . ." The chauffeur hadn't spoken to her since the day she ran away from him through the bushes, and yet he had dragged her out of bed half an hour before, furiously ringing the bell outside Villa Regina, and then, when she appeared on the veranda, saying—"I've been sent to collect Senhora Dona Ângela Margarida's niece . . ." As if he were addressing somebody else.

Milene's first thought was that her relationship with Antonino had been discovered. That Antonino was right—if only we were transparent, if only we were invisible. And she had mentally prepared herself, trying to overcome the lingering effects of that state of shock. Meaning that if Aunt Ângela Margarida and Uncle Ludovice asked her if it was true, she would stand up and say the worst thing she could think of, to stop any argument in its tracks. She would say—*You idiots, you old fuddy-duddies, you bunch of losers, mind your own business. I adore him. He's already kissed me thousands of times. And I'm planning to make love with him, as soon as he agrees. So go away and leave me alone* . . . And since she certainly wouldn't be given a lift home, she had imagined walking all the way back to let off steam. But as they approached the orderly surroundings of the Atrium Condominium, with the triangular pediment above the entrance featuring a Triton with a curly tail, the chauffeur had unexpectedly offered that new detail. And when he opened the door for her, Frutuoso had even said— "Anything could happen, if you ask me. The boss was in a very bad way . . ."

So this wasn't about Antonino after all? It was about something else instead?

But Milene couldn't be sure until she took the elevator up to her aunt and uncle Ludovice's duplex. She stepped into the living room, and nothing about the scene that greeted her bore any relation to Antonino. Her uncle's belongings were strewn all over the room's vast expanse—his brown jacket was hanging over one chair, his shirt and belt over another, and on the floor by one of the doors, as if they'd had enough and were making a break for freedom, were his two shoes. His socks had clearly also been hastily removed, because they were lying crumpled on the floor a long way apart from each other. Meanwhile, her uncle himself was stretched out on a low-backed Spanish sofa from which the cushions had been removed. An extra heater had been placed nearby, and his two bare feet were poking out of his trousers, thin and exposed, like two miniature ironing boards. Her uncle wasn't dead. And next to him was her aunt.

What's more, Aunt Ângela Margarida had a bowl of some sort of liquid beside her with a white cloth floating on the surface, as well as various tubes of ointment arranged on a stool. Her aunt was squeezing some gel out of one of them, which she then rubbed into Uncle Ludovice's shoulders and chest. It looked like a kind of liniment, and Milene guessed that Rui Ludovice was just very tired. He was always saying that every day of his life was like a romantic opera, and that local government itself was like a painting by Bruegel the Elder, where the most innocent realities were always accompanied by huge fish and serpent eggs, thwarting any dreams of a peaceful life. Tired out, and rightly so, by that great array of responsibilities, from looking after musicians, with their fifes and *bombo* drums, to the treatment of human and animal waste, by way of gaining city status for towns and transforming deserted beaches into blue-flag tourist resorts. Exhausting. Yes, Uncle Rui Ludovice must be suffering from exhaustion. And Milene had stood watching her aunt and uncle, in the middle of the duplex's large living room, with the big bay window looking out on an Ocean as still and silent as an empty thoroughfare, and she didn't know what to think. The more Aunt Ângela Margarida massaged him, the frailer her uncle seemed. But he wasn't dying. His graying chest hair rose and fell at what looked like a normal rate. Milene had said hello, and no one had responded. So why had they asked to see her? What did they want? But then her uncle realized she was there and opened his eyes.

And all became clear.

It was as if, from the day Milene had last seen Uncle Rui Ludovice, when he lost his temper with her over that fragmented *Guernica*, to the present moment, no time whatsoever had passed. The second her uncle opened his eyes, she could see that the same rage was still there. The fizzing rage that made his pupils and eyelids twitch, as if his eyes were on fire. She realized that the full force of Action within her uncle was now entirely concentrated in those eyes. In the look in those eyes, to be precise. Milene was afraid— "Oh, Jesus!"—she said, taking a step back.

But her aunt beckoned to her.

"Please, come and have a word with your uncle . . ."

Her uncle made as if to get up, but Aunt Ângela Margarida wouldn't let him, her authority as his wife reinforced by her authority as his nurse. And Uncle Rui Ludovice was obviously dependent on both. Aunt Ângela Margarida, authority personified, said very quickly—"Yes, come and have a word. He's so tired and he has to go out in half an hour because of the marathon; he has to be there when they cross the finish line, and he still hasn't left. Your uncle has a hunch and he wants you to tell him if he's right . . ."

Milene felt the duplex start to spin. She was prepared for questions about the situation with Antonino and knew what she was going to say about that, but only that, and nothing else. Her uncle sitting up slightly on the sofa and looking at her with that gleam in his eye. His rage on display. And just like that, he asked—"So, do you or don't you remember what happened on the day of your grandmother's funeral?" And then, lying back down and surrendering once more to Aunt Ângela Margarida's greasy hands, he closed his eyes. He was all ears.

Yes, it was Uncle Rui Ludovice's head that was in turmoil. His ears were open and waiting beneath his thick hair, which tufted out in a kind of pigtail. She fixed her gaze on his ears, stalling for time. Inside her own head, things were taking a while to settle. Because here they were, back on that topic which they had never really ironed out, and which she couldn't now remember at all, or only with a huge effort, so huge that at this time in the morning, when she hadn't even had breakfast, it made her feel nauseous. Milene said to Aunt Ângela Margarida—"I'm sorry . . ." Her aunt replied, "Just remember the things you can remember. And don't worry about the ones you can't. You see, your uncle has decided he needs to get this straight before the end of the marathon, because of the people he'll see there, whose hands he will or won't shake, in just half an hour's time. So please, answer your uncle's question. What happened that day?"

"I've already told you . . ."—Milene began, but she couldn't go on.

Then she concentrated. Her uncle with his eyes closed, her aunt waiting. She was still feeling nauseous, but she said—"Okay, here goes—I was alone for a few hours in the Church of São Francisco. I was with my grandma and the flowers and that was it. No one came. Eventually a woman with square calf muscles arrived, and a man, and the priest all dressed up and ready. Then I went in the funeral car, in the middle of all the flowers, along with my grandma's body. My grandma wasn't there by then . . . We went to the cemetery and there was nothing but graves and cypresses and gravestones, and I was there with them, alone. No one said anything to me. My grandma's body went into the ground, but, by then, she wasn't there . . ."

Milene had stopped feeling quite so ill. Now she could remember everything. She hadn't had any breakfast but she could remember it all. João Paulo used to tell her to speak quickly, to think only about what she had to say and not the effect her words would have. And thankfully Uncle Rui kept his eyes shut, which meant she just had to look at the outer folds of his ears and his recently trimmed ear hair. She wasn't thinking about her uncle, just about his hairless ears. But her uncle was following what she was saying, she was sure of it, because he had sat up a little straighter. Milene tried extra-hard to focus only on the parts of her uncle's face where his rage wasn't visible.

"Wait, rewind a bit. What happened in the church? What did the priest do?"—His eyes lowered.

"He crossed himself and then spoke . . ."

"What did he talk about? What did he say?"

"Things a priest usually says . . ."

"And then what?"

"Then he started preaching. It was as if there was a whole crowd there. He must have really liked Grandma Regina. He was defending her, but she wasn't there anymore . . ."—Her uncle's ears at her disposal, one on each side, and Milene spoke straight into them, without letting his eyes put her off, or his glossy hair. "The priest talked and talked, by then it was about three in the afternoon, and I wasn't feeling so good. Just like now, I hadn't eaten anything . . ."

"You can eat something soon . . ."—said her aunt. "The marathon's already started, and your uncle's still here. Your uncle wasn't feeling at all well today. Please, tell your uncle what happened . . ."

Her uncle asked—"Tell me, Milene, did he just talk or did he read as well?"

"He read and then he talked about what he'd read . . ."

"And what did he read?"

"I've already told you. And if I haven't, I was going to, but no one would listen. Now I've forgotten lots of things that happened because I was in a state of shock. But I remember this very clearly. He read the Final Judgment."

"Last time you said it was the Book of Wisdom, and now you're saying something different."

Milene, annoyed—"Oh, for heaven's sake. I'm getting really fed up now, Uncle Rui. What I said, or what I would have said, if anyone had listened, was that he said this—Book of Wisdom, Final Judgment . . ."

Rui Ludovice the engineer slumped back onto the sofa, with relief now rather than disappointment. The proof being that he asked Aunt Ângela Margarida, whose hands were still very greasy, to bring him the Bible—"Angelita, go and get the Bible off that shelf. I have a *feeling*." And he used the English word. "Bring it over and open it at that passage. I was just remembering how they all refused to meet my eye and then suddenly I had a *feeling*. It all makes sense now, I just want to check . . ."

Meanwhile, her aunt had wiped the gel off her hands and taken down from the shelf a large, lavishly bound Bible, which looked as if it had never been opened, its ribbon bookmarks apparently untouched. Her aunt couldn't find the right place. Uncle Rui said to her—"It's like a dictionary or a telephone directory. You look for the part within the whole, and within the part, the heading or words you need. With the Bible, you also look for the verse . . ." But her aunt still couldn't find the book she was after and handed the Bible to Uncle Rui. Her aunt was saying—"You'll miss them crossing the finish line because of this obsession of yours, you'll miss . . ." Uncle Rui leafed through the Bible from beginning to end. It was extraordinarily heavy. Then from the end back to the beginning. Finally, he located the Book of Wisdom. He had to put on his glasses to find the Final Judgment. There it was. He lay back, passing the huge volume to his wife, open more or less in the middle. Her uncle closed his eyes, relieved to have at least found the source. And he said, turning to Milene, our cousin Milene—"Would you recognize the bit you say he read?"

Milene didn't want to commit herself.

This new test was making her nauseous again. She felt trapped inside a web, in the middle of a furious force field that she couldn't control or even see. When she didn't answer, Uncle Rui said to his wife—"Read it out, and she can say yes or no . . ." Aunt Ângela Margarida, before picking up the enormous book and beginning to read, added—"Milene, you don't need to say anything. When you recognize a word, or a phrase, just raise your hand. That's what I do with my patients at the clinic. Nothing could be easier . . ." And she started to read—*Then the righteous will stand with great confidence in the presence of those who have oppressed them and those who make light of their labors* . . . Do you remember that?" Milene wasn't sure. Her aunt reading and reading, her uncle waiting wide-eyed for her to raise her hand, and still she didn't do it. When her aunt read, *And we journeyed through trackless deserts, but the way of the Lord we have not known,* she raised her hand. But she wasn't sure. She only raised it with real confidence when her aunt began to read—"*All those things have vanished like a shadow, and like a rumor that passes by; like a ship that sails* . . ." At that point, Milene sprang to her feet.

"Yes, that's what he read, and then he talked about it . . ."

Uncle Rui Ludovice took the Bible from his wife—"I knew it, and now she's confirmed it . . ." Her uncle read aloud, hurriedly, skipping over the lines. Her uncle read—"*Shafts of lightning will fly with true aim, and will leap from the clouds to the target, as from a well-drawn bow* . . ."

Milene on her feet.

"That's what the sermon was about, Uncle Rui. I was the only one there, along with the flowers and the closed wooden box, and the sun was shining in so it was warm too, and he talked about the lightning bolts that would fall on anyone who ruined the lives of good and just people, if not in this world, then in the next. But he said it should really be in this world, so people have time to discover the meaning of their lives and be saved . . . *Shafts of lightning will fly with true aim* . . . I'm sure of it."

Milene hadn't had breakfast and she was speaking, for the most part, straight into her uncle's ears, clinging to the forgotten scene that had come back to her. But then she saw her aunt and her uncle staring at her as if backing her into a corner.

"Are you sure?"

Yes, she was sure. She wasn't sure where her grandma had ended up, but she was sure about the priest's sermon.

Uncle Rui asked Aunt Ângela Margarida to go and get the file on that event in August, which was clearly of central importance in their lives, because a bunch of newspaper cuttings was soon produced from inside a nearby drawer. Her aunt passed the bundle to Uncle Rui, who read a few of the underlined passages under his breath. And then he read part of one piece out loud. Enraged, he read—"It's somewhere around here—*All her relatives were spending the holidays not only outside the Country, but a long way from Europe, with her niece stating that she wasn't sure whether they were in Japan or China* . . . etc., etc.—*Close colleagues of the mayor have strongly condemned his actions, though they closed the council offices as a mark of respect . . . There is much talk of the shocking cruelty and general lack of respect shown to Regina Leandro, who was such a well-known figure in local industry . . .* Here we go—*Well-aimed arrows fired at those who abandon their loved ones . . . If he abandons his loved ones, what would stop him from abandoning people he doesn't even know? In the middle of August, news of the events struck like lightning bolts at the hearts of all those who still, until yesterday, had faith in his administration . . . It is said . . .*" Her uncle repeated those lines in a frenzy of emotion—"There's the proof, I knew it, that convoluted prose, with its twists and turns, was written by them all along . . . They were the ones who planned it, right from the start . . ."

Uncle Rui read the passage about arrows and lightning bolts, as stirred up as if he had discovered some revolutionary theory. As if he had proved beyond doubt that the World is one big conspiracy, with no mystery to it at all. Uncle Rui Ludovice, mayor, engineer, sitting on the Spanish sofa, discovering the root of all evil in the World. As horrified as someone who makes an incision in the flesh and finds a malignant tumor. Uncle Rui had a stack of that day's newspapers beside him, and he flicked these lightly with his finger and thumb, though not lightly enough, because the pile collapsed and the dailies and weeklies, diligently read and underlined by the press officer, slid in all directions. And yet the light in her uncle's eyes seemed softer now. His voice too. Uncle Rui addressed Milene.

"And later, at the cemetery, did anyone speak to you?"

Milene concentrated again. Yes, she remembered being asked a question that she hadn't answered out loud, but if she repeated what she'd thought without being able to recall what the priest and the woman with square calf muscles had said, it wouldn't go down very well. Milene said—"No, I don't remember anything else."

Meanwhile, her aunt was keeping a close eye on the time, but her uncle had fallen back onto the sofa, his bare feet looking colder and colder. He spoke with his eyes closed, seeming quite fond of Milene now, even calling her by her name. The unfortunate thing was what he was saying—"Angelita, you know as well as I do, there are a thousand ways to murder someone. And these guys are murdering me. On a day like this, with an event on this scale, a marathon with competitors from some thirty countries, with everything perfectly organized, they completely ignore me. I mean, just to open the sports center this afternoon, we're expecting no less than three government ministers. I worked on that directly and personally, I laid the groundwork, I sent the invites, I took the risks, but my name and face don't appear anywhere. It's like I don't exist. They want to wipe me off the map . . ."

Aunt Ângela Margarida was putting the newspapers back into their pile, folding them one by one, without saying a word.

"I'm telling you, they're behind it all. I knew even before our niece confirmed it. The auxiliary bishop didn't say a word to me this morning. He pretended he hadn't seen me, did the rounds and then slipped away as soon as he could. And other people did the same. But why wouldn't he speak to me, when he's usually so polite? Because they're in cahoots. Very soon, when the runners cross the finish line and the medals are given out, the bishop will be there in person. But I won't be the one who speaks to him. At the end of the day, they want me out. They want me out and they're hiding behind other people, or other people are hiding behind *them*. I don't know. They're going after me now and they're using your mother as a pretext, the fact that she died in the middle of August and I wasn't here. Which is utterly stupid, by the way, and has nothing to do with the real reason, of course, which goes way back. But anyway, the fact is, they want me out."

Uncle Rui's feet were pointing at the bay window, which framed a March sea so calm and luminous that something like *Restful Waters* could have been written beneath it, and his head was pointing toward the opposite wall, the back of the room, where a floor-to-ceiling bookcase was full of thick tomes and compact discs. Aunt Ângela Margarida went over to put the Bible back, climbing on a little camphor-wood stepladder. Uncle Rui, meanwhile, should have been getting dressed. By that time, the marathon runners had spread out, with the strong ones in front, the weak ones behind, the crap ones even farther behind, and the really crap ones having given up. And Uncle Rui needed to get a move on. To get dressed, to fold his overcoat over his arm, put a little gel in his hair, apply a little cologne to wrists and armpits, and set off as soon as possible, because after all, some of the roads were closed. But instead of springing into action, Uncle Rui had flopped back down on the sofa, unable to get up. His eyes had lost their fire and grown dull, with barely a glimmer of life in them. He was imagining the marathon. He could see a few runners out in the lead, still fresh and energetic, ready for the final stretch, and the others, the crap ones, already a long way behind. The really crap ones, so far behind that they must have given up. And he felt like one of them. There was about half an hour to go, he guessed, and he felt too powerless to face a group of people all plotting to wipe him off the map. No, he wasn't going to put his socks on, or his shoes, or his shirt, all he wanted was to go on lying there, feeling like a washed-up piece of crap.

"It's over"—he said.

Milene had started to cry. The whole situation was just so horrible. Intelligent people like Uncle Ludovice had the ability to make alarming connections, an ability that made them so unhappy that they'd be far better off without it. She, for example, had no idea how the priest's words, spoken in support of Grandma Regina that August Sunday, related to her uncle's frightening state of collapse. Let alone what bishops and marathons had to do with it all. But they saw those possibly inevitable connections and suffered terribly as a result. Their world was a tangled and mysterious web, like the situations that sometimes pursued her in nightmares. Dogs running after her, ready to attack, chasing her into fields that stretched as far as the eye could see. Or just their jaws snapping at her heels, and her unable to fight back. That's what her uncle's nightmare must have been like. She had pulled her rust-red hat down over her eyes and covered her face with her hands. Refusing, refusing to look at her uncle in that state. She was crying, muffling the sound with her fingers, trying and failing to choke back her loud sobs. Now she was weeping openly. But she had to be quiet because her aunt, by her side, needed to think. In that fraught situation, someone needed to keep a cool head. And that someone was her aunt. Her aunt took charge, just like Geena Davis in *Cutthroat Island*. Exactly like that. Her aunt glanced at her wristwatch and then at Uncle Rui, giving no outward sign of impatience or angst, steadying the ship. At the helm. The example of her aunt's strength made Milene stop crying. Yes, she could see that if she wanted to be even slightly helpful, that great outpouring of pity for her uncle wasn't the way to do it. Her uncle said—"Angelita, it's over . . ."

Her coolheaded aunt tried to reassure him.

"It's not over, not at all . . . You just have to walk onto the stage and hold out your hand to the bishop, kiss his ring, greet him, and even if he doesn't say anything back, you make sure he hears something along the lines of—*Your Grace, we have some very important business in hand, which has unfortunately been delayed. And we're going to make progress with a number of difficult situations as soon as possible. I have plenty of ideas, Your Grace. And so on . . .*" Her aunt said decisively, sensing Uncle Ludovice's hesitation— "You can't back down now, Rui. This won't go on forever. You win some, you lose some, you know that. What do you say?"

Uncle Rui couldn't move, the massage seeming to have paralyzed rather than energized him, and now he felt like one of those runners who had given up. But his wife's words made him nostalgic for Action, as if giving up for an hour had branded him a quitter for all eternity. Action returning to Uncle Rui. Action, ever so softly, starting up again—"And do you have any specific idea that might help?"

"I do"—said Aunt Ângela Margarida, helping her husband sit up. And she had begun passing him his shirt, his belt, his tie, before crouching at his feet to put on his socks, and then his shoes. His jacket. He had to wear his jacket. He put it on. Action receiving the power of action. *Do you have an idea?*—My God, could Rui really not see what needed to be done? Her uncle on his feet. Handsome, tall. Her aunt, still in her bathrobe, spraying cologne on Uncle Rui. Her uncle standing before her aunt, eyes closed. Still in that position, her uncle asked again, without opening his eyes—"Angelita, what is your mother's ghost doing mixed up in all this?"

It was as if her aunt had been slapped in the face. She burst out—"Ghost? What do you mean, ghost? Pah, you're so spineless, you're pathetic . . ." Her aunt even turned her back on him— "People like you find it easier to imagine doing battle against the dead than against the living when they're skulking in corners. It's simpler that way, isn't it, Rui?" Her aunt outraged, livid—"Now, get a move on, quick . . . Your soul can settle things with God once you've got your public life in order . . ."

By now they were in the hallway, by the door.

"But you do have an idea?"

"I do, I've told you"—And then, over the intercom, she asked Senhor Frutuoso if he was ready. He was. "Take Senhor Ludovice straight to the stage. And quickly, because Senhor Ludovice needs to be there in time to see them cross the finish line, and if at all possible, quite a bit before . . ." The elevator on its way up—"So you've got a good idea?" Ângela Margarida opened the elevator door for Uncle Rui and said—"Yes, I do. Offer them a nice donation, a big donation, and then you'll see . . ." Inside the elevator, Uncle Rui felt as if he'd been tricked, and didn't know if he really ought to go down, but Aunt Ângela Margarida closed the door and said—"The chauffeur's outside with the car all ready. What are you waiting for?" And she stood with her ear pressed against the elevator door to be sure Rui Ludovice was going to the ground floor. He was. She couldn't believe it. She ran over to the bay window, and down below she saw her husband getting into the car. It wasn't at all cold, but he was carrying his overcoat so as to look good, in case he had to speak to the cameras. Aunt Ângela Margarida was utterly exhausted. None of what happened to her husband really mattered, it was all just a wrinkle in the human warp and weft that would sooner or later be smoothed out. But for her, personally, it took an immense amount of work.

Uncle Rui was on his way.

Meanwhile, Milene had been brought to a table laid with the remains of breakfast. She was still choking back sobs. Unable to touch a thing at first, too upset by the whole situation, but then, when the television was switched on, she had helped herself to a thick slice of bread and an enormous mug of milk, because all the anxiety and tears had made her extremely hungry. Not her aunt, though. Ângela Margarida was still preoccupied with her husband. Her niece wouldn't understand, but the problem was this: given his goals, an executive like him couldn't go wasting his time on doubts and uncertainties. Her aunt didn't take her eyes off the television. Her aunt, attentive. Everyone was there, except Uncle Rui. There was no sign of the bishop either. Meanwhile, the cameras kept switching back and forth between two scenes—the marathon runners in the lead and the stage with the waiting officials. In both cases, the camera only showed the people in front. Suddenly, in the foreground, her aunt saw a very well-turned-out Uncle Rui, and she could hardly believe her eyes.

"There he is, and he actually looks really good. My God! It's a miracle . . ."—her aunt said, sighing deeply, feeling the calm of duty done and the peace of difficulties overcome. By then, as it happened, her eyelids weren't even swollen.

"Would you like some more? Help yourself."

Ângela Margarida, the perfect hostess, attending to her niece's breakfast, which was a rather leisurely affair, and managing the time very well, dealing it out in at least two different directions. When Uncle Ludovice was out of shot, Aunt Ângela Margarida hurriedly talking to her niece, explaining how every day of her life was an endless struggle. How the whole thing, of which Milene had glimpsed only a tiny part, made her anxious and kept her from sleeping. And so, for example, how could she possibly find the time to be useful to Milene? And yet Milene, that morning, had been very useful indeed to her uncle and aunt.

"Me?"

Yes, her remembering about the arrows and lightning bolts had made all the difference. It had confirmed her uncle's *feeling*. Aunt Ângela Margarida smiling, saying that Milene deserved top marks. Her aunt, fresh-faced, almost blond, moderately pretty, completely shattered, and yet so coolheaded, so strong, that in little more than half an hour, through reasoning alone, she had turned a man sitting slumped on a sofa into that self-possessed figure now standing on the stage, where, by now, the bishop was also to be seen. Milene felt respect for her aunt. Love for her aunt, wanting to put down the bread and the milk jug and say to her— *Now, Aunt Ângela Margarida, I'm going to tell you a secret about me and someone else . . .* And at that moment, her aunt was looking at her and laughing. Explaining that Milene's cousins would have stopped by the kitchen for a chat, but they always slept late on Sundays to recover from their grueling class schedule. They had a hard life, those girls. All Milene could say was—*Listen,*

Aunt Ângela Margarida, one day I want to tell you about something really good in my life. When you have time. I have something really important to tell you. In fact, I thought you already knew. I was prepared. But I'll tell you later . . . Postponing the conversation but announcing the topic. And her aunt actually looking pleased now, explaining that the best thing to do would be to ask Frutuoso to come and collect her and take her home, while Uncle Rui was tied up with the rest of the marathon. In other words, it wasn't Milene speaking at all but Ângela Margarida.

"Are you still hungry? When did you last eat?"

In those final moments, her aunt wanted to clarify a few more things, explaining to Milene, for example, that what had happened that day had nothing to do with the court cases. Milene, as she knew, wouldn't have to go and testify. Besides, now that her uncle's *feeling* had been confirmed, what was the point of court cases? They'd need to take another approach. And now she was going downstairs, because it was eleven o'clock and she still wasn't dressed. Yes, Aunt Ângela Margarida. But what Milene really wanted was to be able to say—*You wouldn't believe what's happening to me, Aunt Ângela Margarida, you really wouldn't* . . . If she said this, maybe her aunt would ask—*Why, what is it?* For the simple reason that there are two sides to every conversation. A conversation, at the very least, requires two people. And so Milene took off her woolly hat and said her part.

"You wouldn't believe what's happening to me, Aunt . . ."

Milene waited, hat in hand. She had said her part. But her aunt, still in her nightclothes, didn't say hers. She didn't ask— *What is it?* Just eight letters, just three syllables, and she didn't say it. Instead her aunt got up and headed for the door. Okay, fine, then Milene wouldn't say anything else either. So much for her dream of saying something important about her life to Aunt Ângela Margarida.

———

Milene thought about the simplicity of those three syllables as they drove along, past what was left of the roadblocks. The police officers were still around, giving orders, arms flailing as if they had springs in their elbows. As they pointed out the alternative routes, they seemed to be aiming punches at the air. At the cross-roads, the banners were still on display, with their multilingual welcomes—*Bienvenidos! Bienvenidos!* But inside the car, neither of them spoke. The driver's only words had been directed at the dry landscape outside, when he announced that the winner of the Valmares Marathon had been an African from Kenya. *"He barely speaks English, just his own language . . ."* The radio had said so. And Milene's one thought was that her aunt could so easily have said those three syllables in response to what she, at the perfect moment, had said to her—*Aunt Ângela Margarida? You'll never guess what's happening in my life . . .*

Her aunt wouldn't even have had to say those three syllables, she could simply have looked her in the eye, as if she had heard the most important words in the sentence—*What's happening . . .* And then, even if her aunt hadn't said anything, the mere fact of looking at her would have allowed Milene to add—*Next time, I'll tell you everything that's happening to me. Not now, because you're in a hurry . . .* And even that would have been just fine. At least then she wouldn't be returning to the same old places, feeling a dark light hovering somewhere above her, in contrast to the brightness of the day. A light that made everything look paler, even the red roof of the Frame Store with its garish sign. And this was all entirely her fault, because she hadn't had the courage to say—*Listen, Aunt Ângela Margarida, this is what's happening. Listen, it's like this . . .* Because not only had she missed her one chance to tell her the news, she had also created that dark light inside her, like the dark light reflected by her surroundings. A dull light that she wanted to send on its way, as if it were a creature with ears and could stay or go, depending on what you shouted at it. That day, with that light turning everything pale, she wouldn't even want to be kissed. Why hadn't her aunt said those three syllables? Why hadn't she uttered those three brief sounds, far briefer even than the clickety-clack of the gate as she let herself in?

Milene returned to Villa Regina just as she had left it.

But the afternoon would prove to be totally different from the morning, as if they weren't even part of the same day. Life was following its own zigzag course, preparing its surprise.

At first, she didn't even notice. Antonino drove past the Miramar and took the road to the Ria in total silence, without explaining why. He still didn't speak when the gray van stopped at the Dunas Fêmeas and the afternoon wind blew in through the window. He just kissed her. Then they shut the windows and sat silently watching the soft, fluffy sand drift this way and that. Up ahead, a beach flag flapped insistently, like a wing. Even when they weren't kissing, the daylight was fighting back against the gloom of those three unspoken syllables. "What are we going to do?"—she asked, without telling him what had happened. Then Antonino looked at her, declaring solemnly that they would have to emigrate to a country where they didn't need to be transparent. A far-off country. A rich country. But where? He began listing places—France, Germany, Holland, America, Australia. Now that he went up in the Liebherr every day, the possibility of running off to some distant place was always on his mind. There was just one problem—he couldn't be sure that, in order to be happy in those distant places, they wouldn't still have to be transparent and invisible. Yes, was there anywhere in the World where they wouldn't have to be invisible? A country that was an extension of the Restaurante do Inglês? Where could it be?—Then Antonino had an unexpected idea.

"Fancy going to the Pomodoro?"

Yes, they could go to the Pomodoro and see what happened. The place where he used to have lunch with Divina, and where, one Sunday afternoon, they had all crossed paths and not said a word to each other. He still didn't really like going there, but all of a sudden he wanted to. Antonino took a deep breath. The flag ahead still fluttering—"Okay, let's go to the Pomodoro . . ." So it was decided. Antonino closed his mouth. The sculpted corners of his lips drawn together. As they left the dunes, he was looking ahead, straight ahead. In they went. Not holding hands or anything, as if they were just a couple of friends who had arranged to meet in a restaurant to catch up. They chose a table. They sat down. He was sweating. Everything around them seemed quite normal, and no one said a word to them. A waiter had come over with some bread and an antipasto, his long white apron brushing his feet. Neapolitan music played in the background. Antonino kept his mouth closed and barely spoke. He was looking around, waiting. Nothing happened. A man at the next table was telling a hilarious story in a very loud voice. Explaining how he had been given someone else's passport by mistake, and for six months had had to live part of someone else's life, in between Brazil and Canada. There was nothing more comical than suddenly being married to another woman, having another mother, other children, and having studied other subjects as a young man. A life transformed into a fancy-dress party. Milene said softly—"See, Antonino? Does anyone care about us? Everyone's telling their own story, and that's that . . ." Milene feeling compensated for those three syllables that had never been spoken. Yes, the restaurant was full, and nobody cared that they were there, let alone that Divina had once been there too. Because who on earth cared about her, about him, about Divina? Who on earth cared about anyone? That was what freedom meant. Milene was beginning to cheer up, to laugh, to pull her rust-red hat down over her forehead. Antonino looked around, waiting, and nothing happened. He even liberated Milene's hair, which had been too hidden for his liking, and let his hand linger there, on her cheek, in the packed restaurant, and all around them nothing happened. And when their rubber-soled shoes touched under the table, it was as if they were touching for the first time. They were trembling. They laughed quietly. Then they laughed out loud. Nothing happened. No one at the Pomodoro cared about them after all. It was as if they were transparent, as if they were invisible.

"Didn't I tell you? Didn't I tell you?"

Another young man with a shorter apron came over then, to explain the more unusual things on the menu. Would they like juice? Would they like wine? Everyone was talking very loudly. Him waiting, and nothing happening. By the end of their supper, they had drunk red wine and eaten *pizza romana*. And never before had a piece of dough covered in melted cheese served as a boat to sail through so many centuries.

That was when he decided. His mind was made up.

Antonino drove down the roads that were no longer blocked, taking the shortcut through Bairro dos Espelhos; he was in an extraordinary hurry. He reached the potholed road in no time, then the railway tracks, the mound, the palm trees, the open gates, and stepped into the empty courtyard. Empty of televisions, empty of his brothers and sisters, each in their own home with their own electrical appliances. The dogs must be curled up at somebody's feet, perhaps sleeping beside his children. But he didn't want to think about his children just then. He really was in an extraordinary hurry. Antonino made for the kitchen, which was also his mother's bedroom, and stopped just outside. The time had come, he couldn't put it off any longer. Felícia, at that late hour, was still washing the dishes. Her son flung open the door.

"Haven't you noticed anything, Ma?"

Felícia gripped the plates more tightly, holding them up to the light like shields. Things were showing their inner selves. Revealing their true natures. Antonino was in a terrible hurry.

"Dona Milene and I are getting married, *senhora*. We're almost sleeping together as it is."

Antonino, one hand on the doorframe, as if he had burst through a pirouetting saloon door, as if he had wrestled with something superhuman and still come out on top. In front of him, Felícia was sliding slowly, slowly downward until her heavy body hit the kitchen chair. Sliding down the sloping seat. There was no crash. It was just like her dream about the telegraph operator, in which she, he, was never fully alive and yet never actually drowned.

XX

THE FOLLOWING NIGHT, WHEN ANTONINO ARRIVED AT THE Old Factory, the knocker on the main gates wouldn't stop banging, even though no one was there. His cigarette kept threatening to burn out, and his lighter produced only a fractious flame that licked at the tobacco but failed to ignite it. That night, however, he was so focused on his own trajectory that he didn't even stop to wonder why the knocker was banging without the aid of a human hand. It was, of course, the wind announcing rain. The only reason the noise bothered him was because he had hoped to make a discreet entrance, to cross the courtyard without making a sound, so that no one would be aware of his presence. He didn't so much as glance at the kitchen as he passed. He had turned off his Walkman, and his cigarette had gone out once and for all. Felícia Mata was standing in the kitchen doorway. An impassable obstacle. Antonino had turned his Walkman back on again as if to pretend he wasn't there—"Hi, Ma," he said very abruptly so as not to encourage conversation, but the door to the kitchen-bedroom seemed to open of its own accord.

"So you've left Divina and are out until the small hours with Dona Regina's granddaughter, eh? I didn't believe the kids when they told me. So it's true . . ."

Antonino had ended up in precisely the place he'd been hoping to avoid. This was turning out to be a very tedious night. In the kitchen, even the edge of the tablecloth was moving of its own free will. The curtain was moving too. In the glow of the fluorescent light, Felícia held out one plump hand to Antonino. A strong hand, the palm cracked and chapped, chipped red varnish on the fingernails. Felícia's chubby hand clasping the large, bony hand of her widowed son eager to be gone. You could see it in his face. *Come on, come on.* His hand, equally eager to be gone, now resting on his knee. All that was left was for him to look at his watch and ask—*Can I go now?* Felícia Mata waiting. Her son Antonino had gone mad. Mad?—Yes, that was the right word. And he chose that precise moment to tell his mother that he loved the girl. Yes, loved her. That he thought of her day and night. That he wanted to kiss her, dress her, undress her, sleep with her, have the children he hadn't yet had. His mother didn't really know her, because if she did, she would see how closely she resembled his lost Eunice.

"All right, Antonino, all right, but wait . . ."

Felícia was looking at the saucepans, surveying the pots and frying pans and the life they contained, the towels hanging from their hooks, the orderly world surrounding her, objects that seemed immobile, but weren't, for they moved and looked at people as knowingly as servants. Then she ran her hand over her forehead and eyes, rubbing them hard, as if wanting to expel through her nose whatever was weighing on her.

"Wait for what?"

"I just think you shouldn't decide right now. Wait a little."

This really was proving to be a very tedious night. Felícia had gone over to the door. It was pitch-black outside, with any untethered objects moving of their own accord. She picked up a flashlight and said to Antonino—"Listen. Come with me. There are things that need to be cleared up . . . now . . ." And she flicked on the

flashlight, pointing it down at the flagstones in the courtyard—
"Come and see . . ."

Yes, this was turning out to be a very tedious night indeed.

Felícia Mata directed the beam of the flashlight at the main gates
and led the way outside. They walked along with the stripe of
light going ahead of them on the ground, passing under the palm
trees, around the old building to the east of the factory, where they
were met by the swampy air of the Ria and the sudden sound of
crashing waves. The dry wind summoning the rain. Felícia going
first, her feet tramping heavily over the sand, the flashlight showing the way, and Antonino following behind, not knowing what
to think about this strange excursion. Felícia walked past the gate
that the English visitors had broken, then reached another, which
opened onto an area full of weeds and tin cans, rotten planks
from the hulls of ships, a place inhabited solely by detritus and
where no one ever came. Walking behind his mother, Antonino
saw her jump down a level, and given the confident way in which
she did this, he realized that she must have come this way not just
once or twice, but several times. Antonino asked—"Where are
we going?"

Instead of responding, Felícia handed him the flashlight, and he
watched her crouch down and start pushing her shoulder against
one of the gates. This must have once been home to an old tank
for depositing fish guts or salt or firewood or water or oil, not that
this mattered now. What mattered was that he could hear his
mother breathing hard as she pushed against the gate. When he
allowed the beam from the flashlight to wander, she shouted—
"Keep the light trained on me." Because he had jumped down
too, and now they were both inside that low, indefinable space, a
kind of open cellar turned trash dump, and Antonino could see

his mother struggling with something or other, her hair, liberated from its hair tie, falling forward over her face. He watched her thrust a stick through an opening in the side of what looked like a cistern for decanting water, and begin removing plastic bags. Then she beckoned him over and indicated that he should shine the flashlight into the opening from which she was extracting those crumpled bags. At one point, she drew back, walked toward him over the plastic bags, and said—"Come and take a look inside. Here."

He bent over and peered in. At first he saw what he assumed were bundles of white bricks, then thought perhaps it was plaster or sugar or detergent. Only after some time did he realize that it was something quite different. And gradually, peering right inside now, the wire from his Walkman brushing the plastic bags, he began to understand the true nature of those packages, with their sticky wrapping, which someone had deliberately deposited there, and then finally he emerged as if from beneath the hood of a car that had slammed shut on his head. He stood still, the beam of the flashlight pointing at the wall.

Dumbstruck.

"You see? Our house is sitting on a powder keg . . ." said Felícia. "That stuff in there is a time bomb . . ." Felícia was pacing up and down between the flashlight and the wall where Antonino was directing the beam, pacing up and down, kicking the plastic bags aside. Her face as pinched and wan as if she'd just removed the body of a loved one from his grave and seen his face. Yet the energetic way in which she spoke was at odds with her face. Felícia was again walking over the plastic bags—"Now do you understand? They buy it, sell it, and take it away. After all I've done for them, they deserve to be shot. Do you see? Now, though, they're going to find out that we're made of sterner stuff. I'm going to take action . . ." said Felícia firmly, filled with an urgency even greater than the swiftly passing hours, for it must have been two o'clock in the morning by then. Antonino was once again training the flashlight beam on the pile of carefully, industrially wrapped bundles, doubtless come from afar, by arrangement with the couriers who brought them there, and he too knew it was time to act.

"I think we should wake up Domingos."

But Felícia Mata must have already imagined various possible scenarios; she dismissed the idea of asking anyone else for help. According to her, they could take care of this on their own. That consignment of goods was probably worth a fortune, just how much she had no idea, but certainly a sum as large as the disaster such a ticking time bomb could mean for their family. Yes, they had to get rid of it as soon as possible, that very night. Perhaps that very moment. You never knew who might turn up—A *time bomb underneath our house* . . . Unlike his mother, Antonino still hadn't had time to put two and two together, but Felícia helped him, indeed, she did nothing else—"As far as I can make out, this is the fourth load I've found here since your brothers have been around. Someone delivers it at night. Someone else comes and fetches it in the early hours. That friend of your brothers is behind it all, that white-faced wuss who was driving the car when Janina came here to sleep. That, of course, wasn't the real reason he came, but I didn't see it at the time. Since then, though, I've watched that red car come and go. How did I not see this, when it was happening right under my nose?"

Felícia Mata was talking in that dark, waterlogged cellar, while Antonino kept pointing the flashlight down at the floor, trying at least to show his mother where she was putting her feet, but she kept pacing back and forth in front of those strange refractory bricks, taking no notice of what she might be stepping in. She said threateningly—"They're not going to make our house a roost for their carrier pigeons. That's all over. Help me, Antonino. In times of trouble, only you can help me . . ." The whole lot must have weighed between seventy and eighty pounds, but Felícia was again leaning into the cistern, tugging at the bundles, and it was as if she herself were part of the time bomb, as if she were the detonator that could either trigger or prevent the explosion, and she couldn't risk losing concentration for a second. It was as if she'd lost all fear, even fear of that place full of fetid, brackish water and who knows what other putrid things. She was determined. She didn't even want the flashlight. He must be quick and bring a spade or even a pole to get the stuff out of there—quickly.

Still shaken, Antonino did as his mother asked and left her there, guarding that poisonous hoard. He returned with a spade, a big burlap sack, and a kitchen knife. Only now was he beginning to grasp that there really was a time bomb sitting under their house, a bomb with a detonator right there among the briny weeds, in that foul-smelling place where his mother was waiting for him at the entrance. Together, using the spade, they managed to remove the slippery packages from the cistern, and Antonino put them in the sack, which he then carried on his back to where the cars were parked. He was ready to speed away as fast as possible, but Felícia wanted to see with her own eyes where that stuff would end up, knowing as she did that her two youngest sons were involved. She wanted to go with him. She wanted to see for herself that they were completely free of that cache of goods. She desperately wanted whoever came looking for the stuff to find it gone. For him to die of frustration, or quite simply to die, especially if it was that white man with the wan face.

"So where are we going?"

Antonino had slung the sack in the back of the van, and, driving past the road that circled Bairro dos Espelhos, he took the coastal route, full of twists and turns, and where the coast grew more rugged, with steep cliffs gnawed at by the sea; he turned off down the sandy tracks. Felícia, her feet and clothes still wet, sat silently in the passenger seat, waiting for the moment when her son could empty the contents of that sack. "Why not dump it here? What are you waiting for?" But Antonino drove on.

They had passed a few buildings, which suggested they were close to the beach, and were now driving down a kind of ravine until the car could go no farther. "Leave it here"—said Felícia. Antonino had already left the car and was carrying the sack on his back. All around was utter darkness. Felícia followed him, shining the flashlight beam at his feet. Obviously, there was a risk they might be seen, but now Felícia's accumulated sense of urgency was growing. "Leave it here . . ." Antonino stopped. A stupid, dry, obscure wind was whistling around them.

"What's wrong?"

Antonino was thinking it through, feeling as idiotic as the situation itself. Should he and his mother be taking on that role? Would they avoid the time bomb ticking away in those packages by throwing them down the ravine for the waves to carry them off, as they thought? Or, on the contrary, would the bomb explode even more violently when, the following day, the packages were found bobbing about near the shore? And how would the people who had lost that whole fortune react? He could see things more clearly now. Standing on the edge of the ravine with the sack on his back, Antonino was thinking that evil and its creatures were everywhere, so intermingled with goodness that it was sometimes impossible to disentangle their roots or, indeed, their actions. Would they get rid of the evil threatening them by simply getting rid of the tangible evil itself? No, it wasn't like that. You shouldn't stoke the fire in the hearth when the flames are coming in through the door. They'd better go home, go down into the bowels of the Old Factory, remove the lid, and put the hoard back just as they had found it. No, not quite, but in such a way that the people who had put it there would see it had been touched, but not tampered with, so as not to anger them. Just to show them they were being watched, that they were in the hands of someone who had not yet reported them. That's how they should proceed, for the sake of Gabriel and Janina. In order to defuse the time bomb they were carrying with them.

They had to go back.

Felícia couldn't comprehend such a complete change of plan and protested all the way home. In a rash moment, she even suggested they stop at the police station and formally, solemnly, hand the stuff over, so that the police would know that none of their family were involved. No one, either present or absent. *Absent?* Only then did Felícia see sense again. Why revisit arguments she'd already silently rejected? Why? Later, back in that muddy cellar, as Antonino crammed the packages willy-nilly into the cistern, Felícia didn't want to go back to the house without leaving her mark. She wanted to take off her shoes and leave them on top of those plastic bags. Two sodden, muddy shoes that would say—*I, Felícia Mata, mother of my two youngest sons, was here and I know who you are. I know* . . . Then she wanted to leave her sweater. Or perhaps the sack. Yes, the sack would be a good marker, so they would know it was the Matas who had been there. It was the sack in which they usually stored the ground-up corn Ana Mata used to make, before, that is, she had fallen into a complete sulk. But Antonino would only allow his mother to leave an entirely anonymous mark. They had to act quickly. Felícia thought and said— "How about making a cross out of two pieces of wood and putting a brick on top?" Yes, that was perfectly possible, since there happened to be two sticks and a brick lying nearby. Just so his mother could believe she was actively battling against the fire from the stars and that the battle would bear her signature. Yes, why not?

In other words, the Matas were enclosed in a circle, each in his or her own way. But not all of them knew it. Some didn't even suspect. And we would only find out later.

Domingos, for example, had always considered himself the guardian of the whole family, but he knew nothing about the time bomb.

Two evenings later, he entered the house covered in white, as if he'd been building walls by plunging bodily into a whole drum of brick dust. Floury white dust on his hair, on his shoes, on his clothes. Unlike most evenings, though, he didn't head straight for the shower. First, he went to the mound where they usually parked the cars, then strode into the courtyard and demanded—"Where are the keys to Janina's van? I want to find out if someone's been messing around with it. The keys. Where are they?"

He clearly thought no one would know where to find them, but Felícia went into her kitchen-bedroom, brought out the same jug as before, emptied the contents onto one of the tables, and there was Janina's van key. Domingos, accompanied by his two sons, was eager to prove something. He made a great show of opening the door of the van and getting in. The engine started. Once this experiment was over, he got out and started kicking the side of the van, hard, and the only reason he didn't dent it was because he was wearing rubber-soled shoes. Domingos's children were staring at their father, feeling rather afraid. "What right have you to damage Janina's van? What right?" asked Felícia. Domingos, the son who had missed becoming a singer by a mere whisker, didn't even answer.

He gave his answer the following day, when the scene was repeated—"Look, don't wind me up, all right? I know someone's been driving that van. Someone takes it out at night. You've been plotting something behind my back"—he said, aiming his remarks at Heitor Junior and his brother Antonino. Shouting—"There's something fishy going on here, I know it . . ." And he looked back at where the cars were parked and where, because there had been no rain and the soil was very thin, it was impossible to see any tire marks. The railway tracks lay there like two supine drill bits. This didn't stop Domingos from studying the sparse weeds, as if they were a map. He found nothing.

For a moment, they were all enclosed in a circle.

In the end, the wind that should have brought the rain brought only two clouds. One of them discharged a few plump drops into the morning, then left. Another crept up on them and produced a fine drizzle, but only stayed for one night. Ana Mata, ever since she'd decided to abandon her rivers and retreat to her small gray house, was now less of a presence in the courtyard. That afternoon, though, she was walking about to see what effect the rain had had on her rivers. None whatsoever. The rain hadn't been heavy enough to change anything. There was no point imagining the rivers were real rivers, their banks overflowing with water fallen from the sky. That only happened after six people had taken a shower or when someone had, quite wrongly, emptied a whole basinful of water into one of them. Ana Mata turned and went back to sit in the place she had chosen as the home for her seething resentments.

Meanwhile, her daughter Dilecta, in the red-brick house, was serving Antonino's children lunch. All the other children were gathered around Domingos's front door, from which Felícia's oldest son emerged, his hair caught back, and carrying a bundle of knives, which he spread out on the table in the courtyard. Everyone followed him, even Heitor Senior on his crutches, everyone, with the sole exception of Ana Mata, who stayed where she was, perched like a mosquito. And Domingos, hairy and stocky, head down, began examining the knives. He had found some rags and was cleaning the knives as if they were swords. He held each one up to the light, checking the blade, the serrations, running it experimentally over the base of one fingernail. There was a razor and a butterfly knife. There was a katana and a dagger, a curved knife for slicing open coconuts, a switchblade, and, most terrifying of all, a viciously serrated Sandokan-type knife. If you were to stab someone with that knife, it would be sure to cause terrible injuries when you pulled it out. The children standing around. Domingos silently showing them just how frightening that knife was. Passing on the message. And so that they too could understand how to use it, even Emanuel, Cirino, and Quirino ought to be there. Someone went to fetch them. The three children joined the audience. There were some dozen knives on display, arranged by size, from large to small. They were only allowed to look, not touch. Then there was the sawed-off shotgun. This was placed on the table, forming an L-shape with the knives. For the children to see. And learn. So that one day they too would triumph in life. Without saying a word, Domingos picked up the shotgun, raised it to his shoulder, and took aim, choosing as his target a towel hanging on the wall, above the arched gateway. For the children to see. For them to see and learn. No one said a word, everyone and everything seemed to have been struck dumb.

"Has everyone in this household lost the power of speech?" Antonino asked.

"Yes," came the reply.

Claudina and Conceição were walking silently up and down the yard, invisible to the others, carrying clothes, baskets, and other things. Passing each other, with only the flip-flap of their slippers, which they wore in the evening, breaking the silence.

Sissi, Heitor and Claudina's oldest daughter, asked her uncle—"Who are you going to kill?"

"Whoever keeps messing with my brother's van. Doesn't matter if it's a man or a woman, or the Devil himself. Ghosts can die too . . ."

Felícia Mata appeared in the doorway of her room, looking very annoyed.—"What business is it of yours? That van doesn't belong to you. Let Janina sort it out. If someone comes and drives the van now and then, so what . . . ?"

"No"—said Domingos angrily, brandishing the Sandokan knife. He spun around and thrust it into an imaginary body next to him, causing the fantasy body to fall to the ground. That was how you slew the enemy. And, armed with that knife, in broad daylight, he marched off toward the van, announcing that he was going to spend the night there. Felícia followed behind. Her nails, with their faded varnish, gesticulating.

"Don't try and find out more than you should. That's all I'm saying. Whatever happens, happens. Leave it to fate. Leave it . . ."

Domingos was holding the knife as if he were about to stab his own mother.—"Someone's using our van, Ma. You can tell from the odometer. They don't go very far, mind, only about twenty or so miles a night. Someone has a duplicate key and they pick the van up, then bring it back. And they're treating us like a load of idiots. And you're saying to me that what happens, happens. I'm going to sleep next to the van tonight . . ."

"Well, if that's what you want, fine"—said Felícia. "But at least stay this side of the gates. They have knives and sawed-off shotguns too. So sleep there . . ."

"I will. Someone's pimping us and Janina and Gaby, but they've got a surprise in store . . ."—said Domingos.

The Mata tribe gathered around the red van as if it were a UFO. The van still bore the image of Janina with the words *Black Power* underneath. And to think that every night, someone or possibly more than one person made off with the van that had seen Janina's first successes. Drove it off and brought it back, parking it in the exact same spot, while, inside the Old Factory, they were listening to music, reading the sports news, or simply sleeping. Domingos wanted clues, he studied the car windows, sniffed at the dashboard and the seats, but however hard he sniffed, with his nose pressed right up against them, he couldn't smell a thing.

That same night, Domingos dragged a crumbling foam mattress over to the gates. As it moved, the mattress resembled, by turns, a stomach half full and a stomach half empty, and once he'd redistributed the mattress's shifting contents, he picked up a blanket and, like a guard dog, his head transformed into a kind of snout-cum-antenna, he lay down behind the gates, fully clothed, leaving them ajar. Domingos as sentinel. Not that he could close the gates, because the barrel of the gun was sticking out between them. The sawed-off barrel. And tucked in his belt, on the side he wasn't lying on—because he was lying on one side, his beret covering that half of his head—he had two knives. One of them, serrated on both sides of the blade, like a shark fin, was the fearsome Sandokan knife, which he had ordered years before, after seeing an advertisement on TV, and which, up until then, he'd kept in its box, never using it for anything, just as an object to be admired. This time, though, he wanted to use it.

He would have taken far more pleasure in catching whoever it was and plunging a knife into his back or throat than in shooting him from a distance. For that reason, Domingos was furious when Conceição came out to ask him to come home and sleep in his own bed and leave Janina's van in peace, because the clapped-out old thing was pretty useless anyway and really didn't deserve such devotion, given that Janina had other forms of transport, and, besides, it was just stupid to spend a sleepless night out in the open on the damp ground. He looked up from where he lay at the gates and pointed the gun at her. Domingos Mata had become immune to all argument, however logical, if it diverted him from the task he had been presented with by the enigma of the vanishing van. He had taken on the immense task of revealing, putting a bullet in, and destroying whoever it was making shameless use of Janina's van, and right under their noses too.

Domingos then concentrated on keeping watch over the scrap of land and road that the interloper would have to cross in order to reach the red van parked at a slight angle between two palm trees. The parking place was the center of a sparse network of weeds that acted as an anchor to the grains of sand, with the fallen leaves and debris from the palm trees forming a compact rug. Between the parking place and the leprous, potholed road was a creamy yellow strip of ground where the rain ran away. That was where the right rear wheel sloped slightly downward. He knew the miniature geography of that spot down to the last detail, because he had studied it closely. He wasn't training his shotgun on the van, though, but on a point a few feet beyond, on the potholed road, or even slightly farther away, perhaps on the field that the night was gradually annihilating, but which existed nonetheless, and from which someone might just possibly emerge, and, without Domingos noticing, without a key, without a sound, start the van's engine.

Then, just like a guard dog that favors hearing over sight, he cocked his ear, and kept it trained on the ground and on the damp, cold air, his cheek resting on the butt of his gun, and then, all ears, all ears, he closed his eyes and allowed himself to drift off to sleep, curled up like a dog at its post, snout resting on the ground, utterly exhausted. His mother's dogs, the gray poodle and the gentle guard dog, were both asleep under a bed somewhere inside, so that they wouldn't get in his way, so that only he would hear any noises. He was alert to every smell, every sound, reduced to nothing but nose and ears, while every other part of his body slept. Somehow, though, his whole being was suddenly startled awake by the sound of Antonino's voice behind him, shouting—"Quick, there goes the van!"

Domingos sat up on the foam mattress, then leapt to his feet and took aim at the spot where the van ought to have been, firing into empty space. Only then did Domingos realize how pointless his vigil had been. About thirty yards down the road, heading in the direction of the gas station, Janina's van had already reached the traffic lights and was about to disappear. Domingos stood at the side of the road and fired a couple more pointless shots. He even reached for one of the knives at his waist and threw it to the ground. He was furious with himself, as furious as a very angry dog.

"Didn't you hear the engine start?" he yelled at Antonino.

Behind Antonino stood Conceição and Dilecta, Heitor Junior and Claudina, all greatly alarmed by the gunshots. Conceição was barefoot at the gates, shivering in her thin chain-mail-patterned pajamas. And, seeing that Antonino was carrying a flashlight, Domingos snatched it from him, shouting—"Get out of here—now!" And he shone the flashlight at the place where the van had last been seen. "Didn't you hear the engine start?"

"What are you talking about?"—said Antonino. "They pushed it first, of course, and only started the engine when it was farther down the road."

Domingos directed the flashlight beam at the ground. Antonino was right. There were the footprints of the people who had pushed the car. Two kinds. He bent over them, flashlight in hand. The prints overlapped. Prints made by trainers, with their particular design, and among them, other prints made by cowboy boots, with pointed toes and block heels. Domingos looked up at Antonino—"They're Gabriel's footprints . . . But what are they doing here?"

Domingos stayed where he was, crouching down, the flashlight between his legs, dumbstruck, thinking. The beam from the flashlight close to his crotch, as if it could give him a strength he knew he was lacking there and elsewhere. "You knew, didn't you?"—he said to his brother. "Didn't you?"

"I'm not saying anything."

Domingos thinking.

"You knew, you smart-ass, you knew . . ."

Domingos had taken his rage at the enigma so far that now, faced with this blinding revelation, there was no way he could contain himself. He stood up, pushed past his wife and the other family members gathered there—who had all, in turn, realized that Gabriel must be the one stealing the van each night—trampled over the mattress, giving it a kick, to which that flabby belly of a mattress responded by rolling up, then unrolling, as if wanting to show that it too had a life, and then he marched across the courtyard and hammered on the door behind which his mother, Felícia Mata, was sleeping.

"Ma?"

He uttered this word at point-blank range, before Felícia had time to turn on the light on the dressing table beside her bed.— "Ma, it was Gaby who stole the van." Felícia's ten fingers visible on the sheet. "Phone Janina, now." His mother turned on her side, without looking at him. Only then, only then did Domingos realize that, for some time now, ever since Janina's visit on that day of mist, his mother was no longer seen pacing the courtyard and bawling down the phone, saying, *Hang on in there, all right?*

Lots of love. 'Bye. Yes, only now did he notice that his mother had become much quieter. Even her fingernails, which now bore not a trace of red varnish, even they were telling him this. Her fingernails, so pale against her dark hands, were proof of this. He was standing before his mother, holding a sawed-off shotgun in one hand and with two knives stuck in his belt. Ridiculous, eh? Ridiculous. A flashlight in his left hand, a gun in his right hand, two knives in his belt, and all for nothing, standing before his mother, who knew everything. That was the truth of the matter.

Ridiculous.

"Shall we hand him in? Shall we call the police?"

"What do you mean, call the police?"—she asked, getting up, fully clothed. For Felícia Mata had gone to bed like that. Felícia Mata, with no solution to offer. She wished she had one, but she didn't. The only provisional solution would be for Domingos to go out, armed as he was, to show Gaby and company that the entire Mata family knew the house was rife with time bombs exploding in silence and killing their victims who knew where or when. But killing nonetheless. Everyone was now in the courtyard, including old Ana Mata, who dragged her plastic chair along with her. But Domingos, standing alongside the family of which he had thought himself the leader, wanted to be reassured that Janina, at least, wasn't involved. Without any hope of that, there was no point in him lying in wait again.

"And what about Janina?"—he asked. "Why don't you call Janina?"

Felícia Mata didn't want to be the one to do it. Domingos Mata picked up his mother's phone. Janina's number was first on the list. He called. *Are you going to answer or not? Go on, answer! If you don't answer, I won't be responsible for my actions.* Janina answered. Domingos yelled—"It's me, your brother, Domingos. Where are you? Are you working with them or not? Tell me, you thief . . ."

Felícia took the phone from her son's hand.

"Janina? I'm sorry, your brother Domingos has gone completely ballistic because of Gaby coming here every night to steal your van. Along with that white guy, the one who drives around in the red car . . . Where are you? Are you working with them or not? Just tell us and put our minds at rest. Because if you are . . ."

Felícia listened. Her kitchen-bedroom was now crammed with people. All the Matas were there, including Antonino's children. Janina's answer, on the other end of the line, at three o'clock in the morning, seemed never-ending, like the interminable reading of a last will and testament. Then, at last, it did end. Felícia put down the phone. She sighed.—"It's all right. Janina isn't working with them. He's still going full steam ahead. He's flying off to some-place in Germany tomorrow, where everyone wants to hear him sing. No, our Janina's still going strong . . ." Felícia wasn't entirely certain of this, but just then she needed to reassure the whole family. Reassure them all, one by one. Especially her hotheaded son Domingos, bristling with weapons completely out of propor-tion to the circumstances. Felícia, already fully dressed, looking around at her family.—"Let's go outside, so that they know they can't just dump Janina's van at our door, or the vile stuff they use it to transport. So that *he* knows . . . Come on, everyone. When they arrive back, they'll see that we know and that we're building a wall to keep them out . . . Come on, people . . ."

It was freezing outside. At a time when springtime should have been in full flow, winter had come back.

Only toward dawn did the van's headlights appear at the end of the potholed road. Two yellow headlights. Then they vanished. The van swallowed up by the darkness. Where had they gone? Then they saw the two red rear lights. The van had turned around and was driving away again. Janina's van was disappearing off to some murky, criminal place, with Gaby in its belly. Transporting to some unknown place a part of Janina himself.

"Should we call the police?" Domingos asked again.

Knowing deep down that the police were only an extension of his own powerlessness.

Felícia stayed in bed for several days after this, not even emerging to do the cooking.

She understood now. She had just joined the vast band of women who complained that they'd given birth to sweet babies, all frills and lace, who, once they'd passed eighteen, would turn up at the door not as perfect little children, but as hollow-cheeked men with bad teeth, cardboard boxes for houses and handkerchiefs for furniture, asking them to hand over their last penny, and claiming they were their sons. Lies. They weren't their sons. They weren't the children they had borne and raised. Was that the case with Janina and Gaby? Yes, it was. She was inconsolable. Where had she gone wrong? Where had she failed? What black-winged angel had followed them?

Felícia now regretted having phoned them so often, having shouted so much. Having thought that the path to glory was just a hill to climb. Having imagined there even was such a thing as glory. "Only Our Lady tasted glory, and a very bitter thing it was . . ."—she said.

Antonino was waiting for her in the kitchen-bedroom, sitting and listening.—"Oh, I didn't know you were there, Antonino. Have you been listening to your mother? What are *you* thinking about? Dona Milene? Please don't bring her to our house just yet, I'm in such a state, I can't decide. How can I possibly think about two such different things? No, don't bring her here yet . . .

"But then again, if you really want to bring her, go ahead. To be honest, I sometimes rather miss the skinny little thing, and the happy days when we found her hiding behind the washing. We'd just come back from the concert, hadn't we?

"What do you think, Antonino?

"But never tell her about the time bomb ticking away under our house. Besides, that will pass . . ."

XXI

NO, THEY NEVER SPOKE ABOUT THE TIME BOMB.

Because right from the start they had agreed never to talk about pain. It had been Milene's idea.—Why talk about obstacles? Why add to them? Let's only talk about love. And about Simple Minds and U2 lyrics, good lyrics like that, and not any others. Let's talk about *Indiana Jones, Apollo 13*, and even *The French Lieutenant's Woman*, which was really boring but at least had a happy ending. That's what we'll talk about. But we won't talk about pain. Ever . . . —She was the one who'd said it, but now he thought he had suggested the exact same thing. Because why talk about pain? Why add to it? It was out of the question. Antonino would never talk about those poisonous packages they had found in the cistern, or the secret use of Janina's van, or everything that had come before, or what he was afraid would happen next. Or the sadness that had taken hold in the Old Factory when they imagined Gabriel living the rest of his life as a criminal, and Janina Mata King, the singer, jeopardizing his career. No, they would never talk about that pain.

Instead, they met up at the end of each day and said nothing, staring at one another, waiting for a different sort of communication. He removed his headphones, stubbed out his cigarette, and undid two buttons on his shirt. He took off her winter hat and began fluffing up her hair. The two of them happy, not saying a word. Sometimes they'd both start talking in a rush, as if they were running out of time, but it was never about pain. Milene described how Juliana had become her secret accomplice, torn between wanting to know all about them and not wanting to know a thing. He talked about the plans he made when he went up in the Liebherr. Visible or invisible, Antonino wanted to go away with her to some far-off place. Although he still didn't know where. He'd started buying *Travel Now* magazine, but however much he read it, he couldn't make up his mind. Magazines like that only featured cities that were already built and finished, with ancient palaces and people strolling in the streets, as if all the architecture had fallen from the sky, perfectly formed, thousands of centuries ago. In only one of them, Berlin, could a forest of cranes be seen rising above the buildings, but the magazine didn't even mention them. How could anyone decide based on pictures like that? What he wanted was a full-color magazine called *Guaranteed Work and Far Enough Away*, but that didn't seem to exist, or if it did, he couldn't find it.

But was it really so important to be far away?

They had become regular visitors to the Pomodoro, and although Antonino still spent the whole time looking around, expecting something untoward to happen, the whole experience seemed perfectly natural. They didn't need to be invisible. And it would be such a shame if they were. It felt so good to see each other, to recognize each other, to look at each other in the mirror at the Pomodoro, as people were going in and out. People who saw them and said, quite naturally, *Excuse me, could we squeeze past? Thanks very much* . . . They liked to imagine what impression they made based on how everyone looked at them. Holding hands, her nestled under his arm, and him in a leather jacket. They glanced around and nothing happened. They took photos of each other, then went to the Big Market to get them developed, waiting outside until they were ready. Sometimes they asked other people to take their photo, and embraced in front of the camera. By now they had tons of photos that no one would ever see. Photos of them, for their eyes only.

When the children were with them, they went to Tocatinas, a kind of rustic tavern in a converted garage, with live music from early evening on and snacks to eat: couscous, yucca, fried banana. The children were allowed in. There were high chairs for restraining the youngest one, however much he wriggled. The kids could chew on the wood if they were teething, and chase each other around the tables, and no one minded. They went there that day. Inside, people were dancing *coladeira* and *funaná*. Outside it had begun to drizzle. Milene took off her raincoat. "Back again, you two? So you really are an item? Are you going to get married? Are you sleeping together? Maestro Cachopinha, a tune for the happy couple! They need to dance . . ."

Milene removed her hat and swept her curly mop of hair to one side. She said—"Allright, then, let's dance. Come on . . ." Antonino resisting. And then, as Antonino led his future bride toward the stage to dance, where they stood facing one another, Tocatinas, a dark-skinned old man with only one eye, grabbed his own crotch.—"Come on, you goddamn widower, show us what you've got!" Two little guitars giggling in the hands of two strapping young musicians, and the old man, giving the lyrics a suggestive twist, the sultry rhythm going to his head, sang—"*Sinhora di Fátima, angel lips, take my life in your two little hands, oh, let me give it to you, where you need it most . . .*" The half-blind man laughing at his own joke, laughing at himself, laughing at the black-and-white couple. Laughing with delight. A delight that took the edge off the joke and turned his obscene gesture into a natural extension of his joy. Antonino very awkward—"Sorry, Milene . . ." Milene laughing, dancing so well, so freely, with her round knees pressed together, swishing her skirt in front of Antonino. "Sorry, Milene . . ." And the old man edging his way through the little group of dancers, swaying his hips to that unholy musical mixture and shimmying over to them.—"*Sinhora di Fátima, my lips, oh, my liiiiiips . . .*"

Milene dancing, thoroughly enjoying herself.

"What's the problem? I don't see anything wrong . . ."

The dark-skinned old man coming closer—"*Let me give you a kiss, on your crystalline lips, on your little-girl lips, a kiss for my sorrow, a kiss for my loss . . .*" Antonino pulling Milene away, and Milene laughing and laughing because the dark-skinned old man was pretending to steal her away from Antonino and repeating his obscene gesture. Milene euphoric. Lowering her heavy eyelids as she laughed.

"What's the problem? I don't see anything wrong . . ."

"Give her a kiss, go on . . ."—said the old man over the music. "Show us or we won't believe you . . ."

"Who are your father and mother, girl? Eh?"—asked a very young grandmother with her grandson on her lap, watching Milene as she danced. The guitars struggling to be heard over the clamor of voices. The woman saying—"Such a pity, dear, your being so white . . ."

Antonino had gone to release the kicking, fidgeting Quirino from the high chair, and to summon Emanuel and Cirino, who were jumping over some tables at the back of the restaurant, where two enormous pots were bubbling away. Milene, still euphoric, putting on her woolly hat, and Antonino furious at how old Tocatinas had butted in.—"That uneducated pig, that savage, disrespecting my girlfriend, Jesus Christ . . ." All four of them leaving in a hurry, bundled out by Antonino, making for the car. Milene holding Emanuel's hand, still laughing, enjoying herself immensely, remembering the silly old man. "What's so funny, Milene? What's so funny, Miss?"—He called her that in certain situations, either particularly good ones or ones that were very nearly bad.

It was a normal love.

But Antonino had grown very serious as he drove back to Kilometer 44. What was going to happen in the future? Where would they go? How would they live?—Tocatinas, more than anyone else, had shown how intractable the situation was. With his lewd interjections, the man had dragged them out of their heady dreams of love, and now they were stuck halfway between their fantasies and the physical world. Confronted with a humdrum reality that brought them down with a bump to the everyday, to ordinary life. Ordinary things, like dishes, dirty laundry, electricity bills, loans, leaky taps, children's wee-wee and dog poo on pavements. All this had been revealed as inescapable, thanks to Tocatinas's profane blessing. A necessary realignment. They had descended from the lofty heights of birds to the level of humans. They were a couple. But if they were a couple, how would they behave? Who would they talk to? Where would they live? All five of them. Where? Antonino racking his brains. Then, once they had parked outside the brightly lit Villa Regina and the row of slowly metamorphosing houses next door, they made a decision. It was Milene who suggested it—"Listen, like I said, let's tell my family about us. We won't ask for anything, we'll just tell them we get along really well, and even that will be a big step . . ." Since he seemed hesitant, and the children were squabbling in the back-seat, she leaned out of the van and flung her arms wide—"Oh, light of my house! Help him say yes, goddamn it . . ." Taking her hat off, then putting it back on. It was an ordinary love.

So they decided to go together, the following Saturday, unannounced, to visit the Leandro uncles and aunts. Milene thought it was the perfect moment, that everything had fallen into place. She went back into Villa Regina feeling happy. What was going on? Her life no longer contained any great abyss or even gloomy days, let alone fleshy flowers or women with square calf muscles. She didn't even think about that anymore. Nor did she remember what João Paulo used to say whenever his two girl cousins thought everything had fallen into place. *Into place?* He'd ask. *Be very suspicious when things are going too well. Look around and you'll see that everything is paired with its opposite—goodness with envy, laughter with knives, love with blemishes, pleasure with bed-sores. Beauty with manure. And that, with minor variations in quantity and order, is what it means for everything to fall into place. Learn that, and never forget it.* That's what he always used to say. And Milene, back then, had learned some things and not others, but now, in truth, she didn't remember any of it. And we would only remember later on.

This is what happened.

Milene and Antonino, that spring afternoon, drove under the tangles of wires meeting in midair, and past the tumbledown shacks on either side of the road, the chaos and ugliness, and then, leaving it all behind and emerging into the part of town where plane trees grew on immaculate lawns, they came to Quinta da Amurada and began looking for the fairy paths that led to Aunt Gininha's house. Antonino was all too familiar with these horseshoe-shaped roads, closed off to the north and open in the south, which had so exasperated him on the first day he tried to return Milene. And surely it was some nameless force, some kind of higher power, that had brought him back now under such utterly different circumstances. Now he'd come to say that he wanted to keep this person whom chance, back in August, had not let him return. He could clearly remember the altercation at the door, where the bronze plaque bore the name of the house— *Vivenda Dom Silvestre*. Outside, everything looked just the same. A panel with lights and an array of buttons suggested that getting in would be a highly complex operation.

But the side gate was open—a stroke of luck, or perhaps a good omen—so there was no need to ring the bell. Throughout the whole journey, they hadn't said a word. Now Milene tugged on Antonino's hand, and in they went. They walked with uneven steps down the garden path to the front door. Her in front, him behind. He was conscious of the risk, but she was thinking only of the surprise. What Milene wanted more than anything else was for Aunt Gininha to be surprised. The last time she'd been here was that summer evening when Uncle Dom's meeting with the Dutchmen had fallen through. But this wasn't the moment to remember her uncle's unexpected appearance. Since everything in her life now seemed fresh and new, she thought that the world, and, by association, the human race, must surely have changed as well, and with them Dom Silvestre, that dealer in the Earth's crust. Milene wasn't afraid in the slightest. They had prepared everything in advance, right down to their outfits. Antonino had on a black leather jacket, belted, and with buckles hanging from the waist. She was wearing a short raincoat, with her bracelets emerging from the sleeves. White earrings glinted on either side of her triangular face. Milene and Antonino, so different, so contrasting, united by their shoes. Both were in white high-top trainers, unmistakably Adidas. Ready to run. Both looking like they were wearing ice skates, ready to lift up their feet and display the soles to the spectators at the rink.

Now there they were, hand in hand, at the door of Vivenda Dom Silvestre. From inside, a boy's voice asked, as if this were any old house—"Who is it?" Milene said nothing, leaning against Antonino, enjoying herself, as if she were playing a practical joke. Playing a trick on her aunt, whom she hadn't spoken to in ages. She didn't need her aunt, and her aunt didn't need her. Milene at the door. The boy was Bruno José; he was ten years old and had now lifted the latch. Right away the door swung open into the hall, and Aunt Gininha, carrying baby Artemisa, who was waving her two tiny arms, was walking toward them between fashionably carpeted walls. *Aunt Gininha? Surprise! I know, it's embarrassing, isn't it?* Milene could tell from her aunt's face—at first Aunt Gininha had seen only the two pairs of giant white shoes on the doorstep, then she glanced up and realized it was her niece standing next to a large, dark-skinned man. Then she glanced down again and noticed they were holding hands. Aunt Gininha froze.

"Look at us . . ."

Poor Aunt Gininha, with the long, straight hair of a young girl, and the complexion of a mature woman, and who was, at that moment, extremely flustered. And oh, such a pity, how different she used to be, going for walks around Mar de Prainhas and having other boyfriends, one of whom would serenade her with that Ana Latu song whenever he wasn't asleep. Yes, poor Aunt Gininha. But during this visit, Milene wouldn't say a word about all that. She was there to say something very different— *Aunt Gininha, take a good look at us. Are you looking? We're going to get married . . .* Her aunt had sat down on a very expensive Burmese chair, between the intercom and a life-sized marble statue of a woman. Terribly expensive. Milene knew the hallway well. There was also a miniature table, too small even for a vase, where Aunt Gininha had leaned her elbow in order to tighten her hold on baby Artemisa, who was trying to jump off her lap, waving her doll-like arms. Milene laughed. Aunt Gininha said to her son Bruno—"Go inside and find someone to come and help me . . ." Then Milene shook her and Antonino's linked hands like a fist, their fingers interlaced between her body and his as if they could never be parted, and explained why she had come.

"Don't worry, Aunt Gininha. No need to call anyone, we just came to say we're getting married . . . Right, Antonino?"

He said yes. Or rather, he stammered a little at first and then said—"It's true. We're going to get married, as soon the papers are ready. We're going to get that sorted soon . . ."

And Milene went on waving that composite fist, those interlaced fingers, between herself and Antonino. Happily. Since Aunt Gininha hadn't moved and no one had come to take the baby, and Bruno José hadn't returned, Milene said—"Right, we're going now. We just wanted you to be the first to know . . ."

Aunt Gininha was slower than Aunt Ângela Margarida in her reactions. She always had been. Perhaps this was why she had stood up and shaken her long hair, as if she needed the dry wind outside to blow into the house and shake her very soul. And perhaps this was why she had turned away, presenting them instead with baby Artemisa's lunar face. With a wave of her hand, she gestured for them to come into the living room. Once inside that white, cushioned space, Aunt Gininha sank down onto the Divani sofa, as if her legs could no longer bear the weight of Artemisa. The baby, settled now, dancing in her mother's lap and flailing her two unswaddled arms, began to sing a kind of nonsense song. Milene burst out laughing, but she didn't go over and stroke the child, much as she wanted to, because she was bound to Antonino Mata by that closed fist. Fingers upon fingers. Inseparable. Forever. Forever. "We're getting married, Aunt Gininha . . ."—she said, sitting down, the two of them facing her aunt.

"And this is who you're engaged to?"—asked Aunt Gininha. Her face still pale.

"Yes, it is."

Antonino thought he ought to step in. He was prepared—"My name's Antonino Mata, and I'm the grandson of Ana Mata, who sometimes used to talk with Dona Regina. In fact, we met, me and her"—and he pointed at Milene—"on the occasion of your mother's death, I mean, your mother's passing . . . My family lives in the Old Factory and we even wrote a letter of condolence. That was when we met, me and her . . ." The pair went on looking at each other, snuggled up close, before turning back to Aunt Gininha—"And now we're getting married."

"Yes, that's right. We've been going out together for months."

Milene fidgeted on the sofa, shifted position, then said to Antonino—"Here, sit back a bit." Aunt Gininha stared at them both, their arms around each other, Milene more energetic than him, more expressive, and Antonino leaning back on the sofa that was as deep as a bed, the toes of his Adidas trainers sticking up in the air. Her cuddling closer, looking at him, all very cozy, presenting Antonino like a valuable trophy, an otherworldly offering to her favorite aunt. Along with his love for her, and vice versa. *Yes, we're not savages, we're planning to get married.* Her aunt so very, very pale.

"You never said anything to us . . ."

At that moment, the baby had begun screeching and thrashing around on her mother's lap, the room filling up with her wails and some really quite extraordinary shrieks. The baby turned and looked at the pair, baring her lunar face to the world. Aunt Gininha, consumed by the child's wailing and trying to calm her down, without once taking her eyes off Milene and Antonino. "Sorry about this . . ."—murmured Aunt Gininha, relieved at the interruption, which gave her a chance to organize her thoughts and words.

"It's fine, Aunt Gininha, don't worry. Antonino's used to it. He has three small children and looks after them himself. They even share a room . . ." Milene glanced at Antonino for confirmation. She seemed almost to be floating, and wisps of her hair, escaping from her hat, blew here and there around her head. "Yes, they share a room. Antonino's a widower. His wife, Eunice, died last year . . ." Milene went on—"He even says he has two girlfriends, one dead and one living, and I'm the living one . . ." She said, resting her head on his shoulder and looking at her aunt. Milene moved by the sight of her aunt's pale face and the baby wrapped in her fleecy clothes. "Yes, he's really used to children . . ." And then, addressing Antonino again, her hair wafting this way and that—"You're used to them, right?"

"Right"—he said, laughing, and then wiggled his fingers experimentally at the baby, who fell silent, buried her face in her mother's shoulder, and cried more quietly. And then she stopped crying altogether. A victory for Antonino. For a moment, a kind of peace had descended over the living room. All three of them, looking at one another without a sound, aside from the baby's muffled hiccups.

"Why didn't you ever say anything?"—Aunt Gininha asked a second time.

Yes, why hadn't she? Again Milene glanced at her boyfriend for help. It was very difficult to explain. How could she explain that at first Antonino had said they should be transparent and invisible, or explain all his other advances and retreats? She looked up at the ceiling, wanting to say that she'd tried to tell Aunt Ângela Margarida on the day of the marathon, but it was very complicated, under the circumstances, to go backward and forward in her memory like that, just to explain something that hadn't happened. So instead she would say something else, which was also true—"Well, Aunt Gininha, I wanted it to be a surprise. A total surprise. I knew you and Aunt Ângela Margarida would be totally stunned . . ."

Milene turning to Antonino and laughing. Then silence fell, briefly, in that living room packed with expensive objects, furniture that increased in value with every twitch of the clock hands, and sometimes even according to the whims of Wall Street, or so people said, and there they were. Milene wanted to reveal how much the carpet under Antonino's feet was worth, but it wasn't the right moment. Partly because three more people were now entering the room. Her cousin Bruno, cautious, as if he'd been attacked by a savage; a maid dressed in lace and a cap like a maid from the past, the distant past; and a puffy-eyed Dom Silvestre, who looked like he'd been woken from a very deep afternoon nap upstairs. Bruno, standing there, doubtless listening for some bloodcurdling cry to come from his imaginary savage. The old-fashioned maid with her lacy apron, picking the baby up. Uncle Dom hovering in the doorway. He didn't come in right away because the two Rottweilers with him needed to be shut outside, where they pressed their snouts hungrily to the gap under the door, whining and scratching as if they'd sniffed out an enemy on the other side. Uncle Dom had sat down next to his wife and was looking at Milene's boyfriend. Never once taking those dark, beady, gleaming eyes off Antonino. Milene didn't care. Let him look. She wasn't afraid of him.

"Whiskey?"

"No, thanks."

"I insist"—Uncle Dom said. "Make yourself comfortable . . ." Though it was clear that Dom Silvestre himself wasn't feeling at all comfortable; he didn't even look at Milene, because his eyes were still fixed on her companion. Fixed. And then her uncle asked—"So, what do you do?" But Antonino could sense the danger, and, pushing down on the fist still connecting them, they got up. Milene, pressed up against her boyfriend, explained that they planned to use the afternoon to visit all her aunts and uncles and surprise them in just the same way. Next up was Aunt Ângela Margarida's house. We'll be off now. And they left. They hadn't even been there fifteen minutes.

Still holding hands, they walked through the greener-than-green garden, where the peacock was resting in the shade of the silver beech tree. And as they turned their backs on Vivenda Dom Silvestre, they both, Milene especially, made a positive assessment of that visit, that surprise, which had certainly left her aunt and uncle totally stunned. Milene was very pleased indeed with the effect they'd had, surprising both aunt and uncle and then sweeping out before they could react. Happy, happy. And as the van traveled down those fairy paths, closed off to the north and open to the sea, she bent over the steering wheel and kissed Antonino's right hand, bringing it to her lips.—"Little black hand, don't be afraid of my uncles and aunts, they won't do you any harm. Don't be afraid . . ." She had seen how his hand shook when he refused the whiskey. "Pretty little hand . . ." They were pleased. Milene bouncing in her seat as they went. Happy, happy. As if in this World, laughter, love, pleasure, and beauty were always served up pure and undiluted. Then the van was driving through the wintry landscape toward the Atrium Condominium. Happy, happy. "Don't be afraid . . ."—she said again. "It'll be easy. I'll ring the bell and say who I am, and then we'll both go up. Aunt Ângela Margarida will be just as stunned. You'll see . . ."

But they didn't see.

At that time on Saturday, only Uncle Rui Ludovice's private

car was parked outside, beneath some rather bare pine trees. Their other cars must have been in the garage. At any rate, the condominium security guard said that no one was home. Milene looked hard at the top floors, the ninth and tenth, where on that gray afternoon the striped awnings were fluttering, and she felt sure they were there. Yes, Milene thought she could see clear signs, such as all the blinds being raised. The two floors gave the impression that the owners were home, everything about them seeming to say that yes, they were, and yet the guard was saying they weren't, pretending to press buttons and use the intercom to speak to people who didn't answer. Milene had been leaning on Antonino Mata but now she stood up straight.—"Let me go up, let me go and see . . ." The man, however, frowned and wouldn't budge. "I don't have permission to let anyone in"—he said. Milene was annoyed.—"This is bullshit, do you hear me? I can tell they're up there. I had a surprise for my aunt and uncle and you're ruining it. Do you understand?" Then a gentleman dressed entirely in white, as if he were about to play golf, passed them on his way out, and she saw her chance to slip inside. The guard yelled—"Stop right there!"

"Do you understand or don't you?"—bellowed Milene.

Antonino took her arm and pulled her away from the argument. The guard, who must have been trained not to rise to such provocations, had picked up a piece of paper and was studiously pretending to read it. Distancing himself from the scene. She shouted at him, as they headed back to the van—"This is bullshit. Do you understand me?

"Do you understand, or don't you?"

And to Antonino—"Hang on a second, I need to think. Why wouldn't they want to open the door? They're in there. I didn't see their cars, and they didn't come to the windows or onto the veranda, or into the penthouse, but they're there. The place is never empty, the maid's always around, even if no one else is. That's it, I'm going back . . ."

They were standing by the wall, the one that began after the garden and ran in front of the houses, keeping them safe. An elegant wall. Newly built and painted, adorned with plants hanging down like hair, and, along the top, stones twinkling with mica and felspar forming an Art Nouveau–inspired lintel, a luxury laid on by Nature. Above it all, a gleaming Triton with curling tail presided over the scene. But Milene saw none of this. Again she asked Antonino to stop. She needed to hear herself think. Because there might, in fact, be something else going on. Why not admit it?—Aunt Gininha may have looked pale, with the Rottweilers barking, the baby crying, and Uncle Dom drinking his whiskey, but she could easily have picked up the phone and called Aunt Ângela Margarida at home. Warned in advance, Aunt Ângela Margarida might not have wanted to look foolish, caught by the surprise they had in store for her; after all, Milene had to remember all that business with the syllables on the morning of the marathon, when she hadn't said anything to her aunt. And when Uncle Rui found out this latest news, he might well have had another funny turn. Or perhaps he'd met another bishop who refused to shake his hand. Poor Uncle Rui, Action in action to the very core, and yet the effects of his Action were so dependent on other people, from the elegant hands of bishops and cardinals to the callused hands of laborers. As her uncle himself sometimes said, the time would come before too long when they would have to reassess democracy. But Milene, feeling disgruntled now, didn't want to think about that anymore. Antonino too was gazing glumly up at the top floors of the condominium.

"What do we do now? Go to the riding club?"

Milene still thinking. No, they wouldn't go to the riding club. Uncle Afonso might not be there. Or he might be there but not want to be. They wouldn't go. They could go to the Dunas Fêmeas instead. Even if they didn't get all the way there, they could head in that direction. Milene feeling slightly cold and talking abstractedly. Saying that the gray sky used to make her ache right there, in her chest and neck, and she'd even had to take pills for it. But that went away when she started loving him. Now the sky could turn any color it liked, for all she cared, and she didn't need to take any pills. One day she'd have to see Violante and tell her all about it. Antonino driving the van in the opposite direction, not saying a word, turning on the radio, turning it off again, playing music that they both liked, and then speeding up, first along the well-maintained highway and then along the road with all the potholes. In the opposite direction.

"Do you know where we're going?"

"No."

"To my house"—said Antonino, nodding in time to the music. Terence Trent D'Arby at the height of his powers, but far inferior to Janina. His brother's voice was so much fuller, whereas Terence's was so much scratchier and coarser, so much smaller, even. Janina was something else. Milene leaning on Antonino. "Your house?"—On the potholed road, her head would have knocked against him if he hadn't cushioned it with his shoulder. His right hand stroking her head whenever he didn't need it to drive. Her drenched in Cacharel, him drenched in Paco Rabanne.—*Do you hear? Let's not talk pain, about that smelly old thing. Let's talk about love instead, about the music we like, about Janina's records, about our life, the good part of our life. My living girlfriend, so like Eunice. Yes, let's talk about that. God placed you in my path, after my days of rage,* Antonino thought.

"The thing is, Milene, it'll be completely different. Your family weren't expecting it. My family knows you really well by now. Correct? Honestly, even my mom, who's going through a lot right now, will get out of bed when we arrive and make dinner for you, just like she did in the summer . . . I'm telling you, Milene, even my grandma, Ana Mata, will be pleased . . ."

And before they reached the mound, Antonino explained how his grandmother had gone on strike against false teeth, glasses, and rivers, and all because no one wanted to go back with her to Cape Verde, to Ribeirinho da Praia, but how even she might join them if he talked her into it, if he told her that Milene was Dona Regina's granddaughter.

He'd even pick Grandma Ana Mata up in her *cautcha* and carry her to the table if need be. In her old age, Grandma Mata saw traps lurking everywhere. Milene shouldn't be surprised if she mistook her for one of them. Antonino amused—"And you know what, Milene? My grandma's the granddaughter of Jamila Mata, and you heard her story that other night. A crazy story, a crazy story of embittered women . . ." Still, he was sure they would all forget their dastardly French great-grandfather Normand's debt to the family the moment they saw them, the two of them, gazing at each other in the middle of the courtyard. "Let's go in holding hands . . ." The Mata women, especially, would have to understand that one original sin was quite enough when it came to making people suffer. So why invent more? Being born with one, which was the same for everyone, okay, fine, but there were lots of different original sins going around, one for this person and another for that, everyone ending up with a few on their plate— that was too many for anyone's liking.

"Are you listening?"

"Hey, catch me!"—Milene cried, before jumping down toward the palm trees and meeting Antonino's arms in midair.

And this was how the pair appeared, her jumping into his arms outside the gates of the Old Factory—as we would find out later.

———

But there were people who said quite the opposite. That the four Mata women had waited at the factory gates, dressed in lamé dresses and beaded shawls and earrings, just to please Milene, as if she were three years old and life were nothing but a circus. And that later, inside the factory, they had eaten roast lamb, and danced and sang to Janina's songs until the early hours of the morning. But that wasn't what really happened. Felícia Mata did indeed dress up in honor of her son Antonino, but only after spending two hours cooking: chicken with rice and tomatoes. While she did that, she wore her usual clothes, including a rather large apron.

She would also end up putting on the snakeskin heels she first wore to the Coliseu dos Recreios, but only because she had them at hand, in a corner of the kitchen she used as a bedroom. And her sisters just wore what they already had on, as did her mother Ana Mata, who did actually deign to put in her false teeth and suck on a chicken wing, sitting opposite Milene. And then the rest of the family turned up, back from a drive along the coast road, and they were very surprised, yes, really quite astonished by what they were seeing, but still, nothing out of the ordinary happened. Contrary to what was said later, they didn't speak much, and no one asked Milene for anything. They all knew that another time bomb might appear at any moment in the muddy waters of the Ria, which seeped into the cellars of the Old Factory. The Matas may have sought refuge in a new world, but they couldn't run away forever from the sadness that shared their days. That eve-ning, Felícia Mata only very occasionally laughed. It wasn't true what people said afterward. And Milene, incidentally, returned very early to Kilometer 44.

Of course, looking back, this may seem unimportant. Drizzle, summer weather, and mist are backdrops, not events, unless they affect goings-on in the human heart. But as regards Milene, it's worth mentioning that the days were getting longer.

That same night, she crept soundlessly to the telephone and spoke in her usual whisper—"*Well, João Paulo . . . I feel more and more convinced that you've moved. Maybe you've even gone to another university to write a different book. Maybe you left this telephone recording by itself and you'll never hear my voice again . . . But I don't really mind. Everyone's got their own life to lead . . . And listen, I've been leading mine . . . It's so nice leading a life, falling in love, and getting married. And meeting each other's family is nice too . . .*" She had just arrived home and was crouching on the floor as she spoke, to avoid sitting in Grandma Regina's armchair. She went on—"*But what's really, really nice is kissing and feeling his hand inside my skirt, and his arm around my waist, squeezing me tight, as if he wanted to split me in half. Sometimes he lifts me up with one hand, as if I were as light as a little bottle, and he spins me around till I get dizzy. When that happens I feel like I'm all his. That's really nice . . . And I know what almost all of his body is like too, because I put my hand inside his shirt. It's all really nice . . . When he squeezes me tight, his thingy's so hard it even hurts. It's all really nice. Sometimes, when he least expects it, I put my hand inside his boxers. That's nice too . . . And it was really nice going to tell our families we're getting married. All of them staring at us as if they'd never seen an engaged couple before, and asking questions as if they didn't have a clue what to ask . . . Like a bunch of idiots. Aunt Gininha was pleased, but she didn't have a clue what to say. And you won't believe it, but out of everyone, the person who behaved the best was Uncle Dom Silvestre. He tried to offer Antonino some whiskey, and it was Antonino who said no, he didn't want any . . . But you could just tell that Uncle Dom was bursting with questions. All he wanted to do was ask and ask . . . We got out just in time. Then we went to see*

Aunt Ângela Margarida and Uncle Ludovice. They weren't at home, or if they were, they must have been having a hard time because of my uncle's public responsibilities, which have left him with a stomach ulcer the size of a bottle top . . . But I don't think they were there. And I wanted to surprise your dad as well. We thought about going to the club to see him ride. I haven't seen him since the perpetual calendar. I was imagining him getting off the horse and us being right there waiting. Us, next to the horse, saying—Uncle Afonso, we're getting married. Like I said, your dad's latest girlfriend is called Isabel. She could even have watched us telling him, I wouldn't have minded . . . I really wanted them to meet Antonino . . . And then I could have asked about you as well, why you haven't picked up the phone all these months. If he didn't want to tell me, he wouldn't have had to, I wasn't going to make him . . . But then it got late and I had to decide between going to the riding club and going to the Diamond. I chose the Diamond because I was really missing it. Inside, it reminds me of movies set in Africa, but only the good ones, because there's no suffering there at all. Everything's peaceful. And when we got to the Diamond, they all made me feel very welcome. They were all shocked, like I said . . . I was so happy. Going to tell your family that you're in love is almost as good as being in love . . ." Milene stretched out on the floor, between Grandma Regina's two sofas.—*"I'm telling you this so you know that I've had enough of phoning you . . . I don't need to hear your voice the way I used to . . . Yes, now I don't even want you to tell me—*We'll never, ever be parted, for as long as we live. *It's not true. There's no point. Now the person I want to tell me things like that is Antonino. What do you say to that?—*He has satiny skin and almost invisible eyebrows. His eyes are brown, but his mother's eyes are blue. His hair is much, much curlier than mine or yours. When he laughs, his teeth are white as chalk. He's missing a few and has two gaps, one on each side, but it looks fine. When he's made enough money operating cranes he's going to buy some new* *teeth. He has a big body and I just fit under his arm, nice and snug, when we walk along together. Now you're only a memory to me, and you will be until you come back and I see you again. But if you don't come, I'll survive. My life is filled up with Antonino. Like yours is with Lavinia . . . I was wondering if Hurricane Andrew passed close to your house. Here we've seen images of the city falling down and a court building flying through the air . . . This is a long phone call, but it's just so you know everything . . . And I don't think this lousy tape recorder is even recording right now. I'll hang up and start again . . . See you . . ."* Milene's back was freezing cold, the living room carpet was as clean as a hospital, but it was cold and damp from so many washes. She sneezed.—*"Well, that's that, I think it really has stopped recording. Goodbye, then, from Milene, at eleven p.m., in Portugal, bye-bye, thirty-two thousand escudos a month in total on international calls, and all for nothing.*

"What do you say to that?"

XXII

THEN MONDAY ARRIVED, THAT WORST OF ALL DAYS FOR Aunt Ângela Margarida. What to do?

Even there in the Clínica das Salinas, where they did everything they could to forget about the body, it was making its presence felt. Usually there were no lines, no cries of pain, no complaints. But now, dangerously, especially on that particular day of the week, the body came and sat in the waiting rooms for what seemed like an eternity. True, none of their patients would utter the kind of obscenities you hear in other clinics, much less in crowded public hospitals. Sad places full of uneasy people, sitting as if lined up for a firing squad, or about to be deported, until a nurse would appear at the door and reduce the identity of one of them to dust by yelling—*Is the person who hasn't yet produced a stool ready to come in now?* And the person, that poor woman over there, now filling the whole room with the awful naked wretchedness of her body, would stand up and hand herself in as if she herself were the specimen container.

No, in the clinic she had set up five years before, with the vital collaboration of Dr. Seabra, it was absolutely forbidden to refer to anyone, for example, as the person with the full bladder or the barium enema, as happened in those other places, where human beings with names *were* treated as if they were mere receptacles for feces. On the contrary, these inevitable physical realities were referred to very tactfully, as if each person were a member of the family and not just a body. You would never shout at a family member, *Go on, have a crap and be quick about it.* Because family ties presuppose that a person has a history and a soul as well as a body. There, in the Clínica das Salinas, people were treated as individuals because they were recognized as having a soul, as being worthy of having their allotted time, their appointment, and being addressed by the name by which they were known at home. Ângela Margarida—or, rather, to give her full name as it appeared on the original deed, Ângela Margarida Soares Leandro Ludovice—knew how much the clinic owed her when it came to kindness and sensitivity.

As the second shareholder, she was part of a team who had developed a very efficient formula, a mathematical balance between the number of patients and the amount of time and kindness expended on each one. A foolproof system. That's why respect and kindness had come to be essential factors in the success of that clinic. Demand, however, had outstripped capacity, and the formula had begun to unravel. It was becoming clear that they were reaching a breaking point. There they were, the people with their names, professions, medical histories, and dates of birth, but on Mondays there were so many of them that the body, that grubby king, was invading the very space from which it had been banned and was now dominating everything. The body was once again making its presence felt. Its flesh, its bones, its fat. And its tumors too, which were merely the body's lush blooms, proliferating hyacinths, their roots deep in the water. There it was, nature unchained, in all its organic abundance, biological chaos, and surplus organic matter. The subtle way in which the patients were treated there was what differentiated the clinic from the public hospitals, where everything seemed to be warning new arrivals to go away, as if there were a neon sign above the entrance saying, *Leave, give up, go and die at home.* Gestures overflowing with respect and kindness took up valuable time. In short, Monday was the day when they had the largest number of patients. Less time, more body, less soul. Less kindness. This only proved what they already knew, namely that kindness and sensitivity depended on how much time was spent on each person. And kindness was time, and time was money, and time was sensitivity, which meant that kindness and sensitivity were also money. They all knew that. The clinic was rather expensive, and if they were to maintain the quality and reduce congestion, especially on Mondays, they would have to start charging even more. From then on, they would only be available to help those with money. Ângela Margarida had already said as much. They needed to check the perverse effect the high number of users was having on their work. A time would come, and quite soon, when they would be forced to make drastic decisions. On that particular morning, she had only just arrived and already she could see a long line curling around the building, as if it were some pop-up health center in India or Pakistan. It had to stop—*Clínica das Salinas, Analyses and Treatments* occupied two buildings right next to each other, two solid three-story edifices built in the sixties, with a view over the saltworks, and a line of casuarina trees in front. Yes, it had to stop.

That day, at eight o'clock in the morning, all these matters seemed particularly urgent for the ironic reason that, ever since the previous day, Ângela Margarida had been feeling nauseous, and her nausea at the sight of that long line of patients was growing, exploding. Her own body seemed to want to make its presence felt, to take precedence over everything else, to rebel. Like all the people lining up at the door to her clinic, she too needed help.

She was driving in the direction of the saltworks, thinking—*Yes, me too, me too . . .* And for the first time in the five years of the clinic's existence, instead of going straight to the entrance, she, the matron, phoned nurse Eulália—"Listen, you're going to have to hold the fort, because I'm not feeling too good . . . It's just a bit of nausea, that's all. As soon as I'm better, I'll be there . . ." And then she leaned back to think, not mentioning that she was almost outside the clinic, parked in front of the saltworks tinged pink in the morning sun. Staring out at the piles of salt and thinking—*We have to do something . . .*

Yes, they had to do something. She was gradually beginning to understand what had happened. Beginning to see everything as clearly as in an X-ray. And that *everything* was the connection she was making between the different parts, as if suddenly, on stage, an actor had kicked open a door and revealed the whole plot, as if someone had said—*That's the nub of the drama. It's what we've been expecting, deep down, since it all began many years ago, we just didn't know it yet.*

Now the thing we were waiting for without our knowing we were waiting for it had finally been revealed, and it really was a surprise. So that's what it was. Suddenly there it was, as clear as the sun rising above the pink horizon of the saltworks in that chilly, cloudless moment. The plot unfolding since yesterday when Frutuoso, without slowing down, had said—"Senhora, there's something I need to tell both you and your husband, but I'd prefer to speak to you about it first . . ." And then he *had* slowed down and turned his face sideways, twisting his mouth so that she could hear him in the back of the car—"Do you know the term 'darkie,' Senhora?"

"Darkie?"

"Exactly . . ."

Then, lowering his eyes, in the time-honored fashion of someone about to share a confidence, identical to the gesture that, since time immemorial, has led two men to take a third man and hang him from a tree and then, together, devour him, a gesture which in itself is neither good nor bad, neither lofty nor base, merely convenient, Frutuoso had said—"You ought to know, senhora, that people are talking quite openly about how your niece, and therefore your husband's niece, is consorting with a darkie . . . And that you're allowing this. And, please, forgive me for using such a term . . ." He had even repeated the same word again, with all the distaste of someone uttering a weighty obscenity. Frutuoso. That was the first connection made by Ângela Margarida's brain. The nub of the drama revealing itself. It had happened the previous day after lunch, when Frutuoso was driving her back from the restaurant to the house in the anthracite-gray BMW. Senhor Frutuoso. But it was only now, as she was driving down the road toward the saltworks, that she saw everything clearly.

She saw her sister Gininha, and the broken compass, the broken reed, that was her sister's will, and saw why Gininha had phoned her on Saturday afternoon to talk about the whirlwind of surprises and unexpected events that had occurred since their mother had passed away. Alas, dancing around inside Gininha's head were many irrational ideas, like those harbored by her own husband, that the dead don't just want things, they want particular things. It was dreadful, she was surrounded by complete nutcases. Yesterday, though, she'd asked Frutuoso to explain himself. And he, as if he were teaching her something, as if he were opening her eyes, had said—"Well, as you know she visited the Old Factory following the death of your mother . . . After all, that's where I went to fetch her when you returned from Cancún. And during the whole month of October, where do you think she went every evening, or almost every evening? Didn't I tell you? Well, I've seen her driving here and there, but always in that same vicinity. I thought you knew . . . Not that you could have known about her and that . . . darkie . . ." And as if Frutuoso had found his employers to be utterly ignorant of what was going on in the world, his voice, in conclusion, had risen in tone—"Yes, senhora. She eats and sleeps with those darkies. Everyone knows, and it won't be long before it's all over the local papers and then all over the national press. Oh yes. And if you'd care to see for yourself, we just need to drive over to the Banana . . . At first they only used to go to the Pomodoro, but then they started going to the Banana and even to Mãos Largas. Oh, they go everywhere . . ."

And so they had driven to the Banana, a roadside restaurant, one of various others, among them the Pomodoro and Mãos Largas, some facing onto the road, others not, the Banana with a large terrace covering the entire sidewalk. Cars and mopeds parked any old how. They had approached stealthily, and Frutuoso, with his spiky Chinese-looking hair, his mustache like a Turk's, his thin face like that of an old Portuguese peasant from the 1950s, but wearing a well-cut, modern suit, drove very slowly and said—"Look, there's his Mitsubishi van and, beside it, her white Clio . . ." Frutuoso had even added—"Would you like me to stop? Would you like me to go in? Would *you* like to go in?" Her astonished silence was saying, *I don't know, I don't know.* But his desire to take the initiative got the better of him, the anthracite-gray BMW stopped, and with perfect timing, as if by prior arrangement, two young men emerged and leapt onto one of those iron horses, which immediately started neighing loudly, then, right behind them, running and jumping, like two children let loose on a beach, came that particular member of the Mata family and Milene, the two of them capering about in the cold, running over to the van. She, Ângela Margarida, saw them, both of them, hand in hand. Milene was much smaller than him, skipping along beside her dark-skinned, gangly companion. He was wearing a voluminous leather jacket, while she had on a very short raincoat. She, she. She waited for him to open the door to the van, then jumped in. She shut the door. They could so easily have spotted the BMW, that's how close they came, but they were obviously oblivious to everything, blind. When the van turned to leave, Ângela Margarida and Frutuoso saw that both were wearing mirrored sunglasses. The Clio remained parked outside the restaurant. Frutuoso had said—"That's really not right, not right at all . . ." Ângela Margarida, though, had turned the situation on its head—"We need to stay calm . . ." Calm, calm, Senhor Frutuoso. Precisely because, at that moment, she wasn't seeing things clearly at all.

Now, however, looking out over the saltworks, with the pink morning light on the wane, to be replaced by the pale April sun, dry and chilly, she could see everything, perhaps thanks to the glow emanating from the quadrangles of water from which the sun was emerging in all its brilliance. Frutuoso had said—"Oh yes, it's fine to stay calm. Meanwhile, though, splashed all over the front pages of those rags, as your husband calls them, will be headlines like *Mayor Ludovice's Niece Going Out with a—*" Just to stop Frutuoso from putting into crude words what she herself feared, Ângela Margarida said—"No, Senhor Frutuoso, people might say that, but they wouldn't print it. Don't you see? Don't you see how dangerous that would be for the person writing it? You don't, do you? Don't you know Portuguese law?"

"No, senhora, I'm afraid I don't know the law . . ."—said Frutuoso, on their way home on that Sunday afternoon.

There lay the crux of the matter, the facts were there for all to see, waiting to be untangled. They had to be. She'd thought of nothing else since, and she'd had a kind of presentiment, to which she hadn't yet been able to put a name, it was only an idea, as vague as it was certain, namely, that something would have to be done.

Yes, something has to be done . . . —she said to herself, as she sat with her back to the clinic, parked opposite the white saltworks. She reached out one hand and groped around for her mobile. The vise-like grip of anxiety about to become still tighter. She phoned—"Gininha?" She needed to have a serious talk with her sister.

"Look, I know all about it. There's no point hiding anything from me. They were there in your house. Well, were they or weren't they? So why didn't you say so? All you said was that she was on her way to our house. Yes, I *was* very busy at the time, but if you'd told me something like that, I'd have reacted very differently . . . No, I'm not blaming you for anything . . . I don't know how all this happened. But now we need to do something . . . I know you have no idea what to do, frankly I'd be astonished if you did . . ." Inside her low-slung Honda, Ângela Margarida was getting angry.—"You're fine with that, are you? But are you fine with it because you think it's all right, or because you don't want to do anything about it?" Sitting motionless in her car, which was like a neat little cabin resting on the salty ground. "Fine, so you're neither for nor against . . . All right, all right. 'Bye, then . . ." Ângela Margarida was beginning to feel hot; she took off her woolen jacket. With a nervous finger, she looked for Afonso's number.

"Afonso?"

Afonso Leandro was on his way to court, and he had a big problem on his hands. He didn't have time just then to worry about José Carlos's daughter. He had a client who was about to lose twenty million escudos over a question of honor. Obviously

Afonso was all in favor of honor, but too much honor made him suspicious. Someone with twenty million escudos' worth of the stuff, for example, might have rather too much. Ângela Margarida, with her jacket off now, was sitting in her Honda.—"Listen, we have to do something . . . Oh, *I* should do something? Why me and not you? You say you're as opposed to it as I am and can see a big disaster looming, but you don't know what to do. As if anyone knows how to face a disaster until they've actually decided to face it. Oh, all right . . . You go and sort out your client's honor, and meanwhile, those two are swanning around hand in hand, your niece skipping along beside him. I saw them myself. But you've got your client to deal with . . ." Anxiety was tightening its grip. Ângela Margarida's reflexes were quickening. Growing quicker and quicker.—"Dom Silvestre? Yes, I've just been talking to your wife."

"Ah. So you saw them at your house and even welcomed them, because you didn't think you had any alternative . . . So the minor obstacle of the Old Factory, which we still haven't sold, has been resolved, has it? What? And you're the one who, for years and years, has been saying we had plenty of time, that we were merely polishing a diamond. Suddenly, though, it all became very urgent, it had to be sold right away, and to those Dutchmen, the very next day. And when it didn't quite go according to plan, then it was up to each of us to sort ourselves out, is that right? From now on, it's each of us with our own racing car, our own piece of land, our own game of golf, our own hunting party, our own stone quarry. Yes, I know you're an expert on how unforgiving the Earth can be. What the Earth doesn't want to give us, it won't. Yes, we can only take from the Earth what it chooses to give us. It's the Earth that's in charge, and you can't force it . . . It's the same with rocks and pebbles . . . But that isn't the example you set for others . . . Milene can go out with whoever she wants as long as that doesn't distract you from your dealings with the Earth's crust. That's what it all comes down to, isn't it? . . ." Dom Silvestre had long since turned off his phone, and Ângela Margarida was talking into the void.

"Dom? Dom?"

She was still staring across at the white saltworks.—How did they manage to extract those pure-white pyramids of salt from that great expanse of dirty water? What force existed in the earth, in the light and the air, that did not exist in the human heart, which, however hard it tried, could never truly transform anything? The poor human heart, a bundle of perfect muscles, tethered to the poor brutish arbiter of the mind. She wasn't sure this was true, but it didn't matter. She was looking out of the car window, thinking, thinking, her eyelids swollen, heavy bags under her tear-filled eyes, her ash-blond hair tinged with yellow. That vise-like grip. Perhaps she should phone her eternally busy husband, Rui.

"Hi, it's me . . . Look, I'm sorry to disturb you, but I just can't bring myself to go into the clinic today. Because of Milene . . . On the day of the marathon, she seemed fine, she could remember everything, could identify those passages we read, was prepared to collaborate. Then, suddenly, comes this bombshell. Don't you think we should do something? . . . What do you think? Yes, we have to do something. To remedy the situation. I'm not sure quite what, but I thought that's what you'd say . . . We need to do something, and not just sit here waiting for the heavens to fall in on us. We need to act. Why wait? For what? For whom? Thank you, thank you, sweetheart . . ." The vise-like grip easing, the feelings of nausea dissipating, her thoughts growing in size, sprouting wings, big wings. Ângela Margarida had turned the key in the ignition, the car began to move. Her husband was quite right,

there was a disease abroad in the world, a disease born of mistakes, Nature's mistakes. Or God's. But how far should we go in
collaborating with Nature's mistakes? Or even with God's? How
far? That's precisely what he'd said to her. Just that, but enough to
give her courage. And in less than a moment, without her jacket
now, in her blouse, there she was walking into the clinic, where
she caught a glimpse through the glass door of the crowded waiting room, and Humanity then seemed to her like an ailing body.
Or one always on the verge of falling sick. As soon as we're born,
we begin to die. A mistake. What was the point of the clinic? To
repair a sick world, the naturally flawed human world. She knew
the clinic had other aims, but at that moment, her troubled mind
saw only the mistake. Nature's great mistake. And the challenge
to human skill to put it right.

She urgently needed to do something.

To find a solution. While she was getting undressed and putting
on her white uniform, and feeling, for the first time ever, incapable of entering the frantic whirl of the clinic, she was thinking
that perhaps the solution would come to her. She sat down in
her small office. She wasn't usually one to linger over memories,
but just then, time flung wide its doors to show her vivid images
of the past.

Especially images of her older brother. It was as if she were seeing
José Carlos during his final years, as well as the circumstances in
which Milene had been born. That subject was never touched
upon, never recalled, it was even forbidden to speak of it. Afonso
was the only one who would occasionally get angry and say
things he shouldn't, in language no decent man ought to use.
Aside from that, there was absolute silence on the subject, just as
their mother had wanted. Now, though, it was unavoidable. Let's

be clear—Ângela Margarida, as well as being the mayor's wife, still felt that she was, above all, a nurse, someone who lived in a world of traumas, illnesses, symptoms, diseases, etiologies, diagnoses, and therapies, and she knew the exact word to describe her niece—*oligophrenic*. It was the word written on the report by the doctor who had examined her in 1977, when Milene was thirteen. He had written *oligo*, and then, in a very painstaking hand, of the sort you might find in nineteenth century love letters, he had written *phrenic*, and explained the Greek origin of those two words to her mother and her, both of them sitting before the desk of that doctor wearing no white coat, who had said—"There's absolutely nothing to be done. You'll simply have to show a great deal of patience for as long as she lives. But don't worry, we're all a little that way inclined . . . either *oligo* or *schizo*. Sometimes it seems we're both things at once. She could easily turn out to be a very happy person. Who knows, she might become an extraordinarily happy person. Otherwise, it'll just be a matter of some appropriate medication now and then, and great patience . . . *Voilà* . . ." The doctor had studied in America, but the word he most often used to conclude any argument was French. He'd already said it several times. A doctor who didn't wear a white coat, who said that we were all mentally ill, who had trained in the United States and kept saying *voilà*, had struck Regina Leandro as someone lacking all credibility. Over a period of two years, she had been to about twenty different clinics. They were unanimous. A similar diagnosis, similar behavioral characterization, with just a few variations, but all certain of one thing—they didn't know the reason. Ângela Margarida, however, did.

It had to do with the child's gestation period.

For Ângela Margarida, the commonly held view that any child born of a grand passion inevitably bore the mark of perfection was a complete lie. As a health worker, her experience had shown that, on the contrary, such children tended to be neurotic and problematic, doomed to failure, as if human beings could not stand too tumultuous an origin. Her experience told her that the children of a tranquil love, or even just a warm, affectionate home, turn out completely differently from those who emerge as the fruit of some wild passion. Passion lives only for itself, and requires no consequences beyond its own actions. Passion needs no progeny. As she saw it, the children of very intense relationships would, instead, be wounded by the memory of their own insignificance, would feel marginalized. That at least is what she suspected, and all her experiences so far had confirmed it. Then along came Milene.

Everyone knew. Her niece had been conceived during José Carlos's violent passion for the air hostess Helena Lino, who was older than he, had the face of Julie Andrews and the temperament of Raquel Welch, a real stunner whom he'd married just six months after they met, dragging everything and everyone along behind him, even to the chapel in Cascais where they were wed. However, after only a couple of weeks, if that, José Carlos had begun to suspect that the blond air hostess, whom he had married in such grand style, didn't belong only to him, but was on general offer to the world. With some justification, he imagined that the entire population, especially the populations of airplanes, wanted to have her or at least touch her, and that she would happily consent. Half the phone calls he made to her, on the stormy weekends when he would return to Villa Regina, were opportunities for him to call her a slut. That's why, immediately after the birth, one memorable Christmas Eve in 1964, José Carlos had taken the child and brought her back with him. The air hostess had never come to reclaim her daughter, as he'd assumed she would. She obviously didn't feel one iota of affection for her. However,

José Carlos did sometimes go and visit the air hostess, and she would occasionally open the door of her apartment to him, her apartment on Avenida do Infante Santo. When she refused, he, an intelligent man, would, like a complete fool, go and sit at the airport, just to watch her strut by with her fellow crew members, before she set off to who knows where. Ângela Margarida was convinced that the only reason José Carlos had given away a perfectly sound, still-functioning factory, an unprecedented act in that part of Portugal, was so that he would be free to pursue the air hostess whenever he wanted.

Why couldn't he have been honest about it? Why dress up his gesture like that, presenting the keys to the workers on a velvet cushion? In Ângela Margarida's opinion, José Carlos hadn't handed the keys to the second wave in response to the winds of History, but so that he wouldn't have the responsibility of remaining tied to Mar de Prainhas. And then came the final journey made by José Carlos and the air hostess in 1976. Only Afonso, when he was in the mood to stir up the past, only he had ever spoken of that journey to Milene. She had never asked about it either, and she'd been twelve years old when it had happened. All that the doctor who'd studied in America had said, as if he were revealing the secret of the World and as if *voilà* were the indelible conclusion to everything, the line drawn under the final sum, was that they shouldn't trouble her with such matters, that she could easily turn out to be a very well balanced person, especially if they didn't burden her with facts about her origins. What was the point? Besides, they couldn't be sure that Milene was the way she was, i.e., unusual, simply because of her father's reckless decision to drive her from Lisbon to Valmares on that Christmas Eve, when she was only one day old. The cause? Her aunt Ângela Margarida could see this perfectly clearly. Unlike the doctor who, despite being told the whole story, had been the first to write that word on Milene's record. He had smiled, declaring himself unable to determine the cause. In his view, Milene could turn out to be very intelligent in her own way, could live a normal life, and, he insisted, when you thought about it, we were all a little like Milene. Yes, all of us—why make a drama out of things? *Voilà.* At the time, this was all that American medical science had to say on the matter, from its headquarters in that very noisy Lisbon street, Avenida Fontes Pereira de Melo.

Yes, something urgently needed to be done.

There was no doubting the facts—at thirteen Milene was like a nine-year-old, and when she was fifteen, she was like a ten-year-old, or a five-year-old, sometimes even a three-year-old, suddenly revealing her true age, speaking in the piping voice of a girl of ten, or lisping as if she were two. When she was twenty, she was about fifteen, and at twenty-five just the same. That is where Ângela Margarida would place her now. Milene was thirty in years and fifteen in age. Given this mismatch, it was understandable that Milene had never shown any interest in love. Her fifteen years were more like a seven-year-old's. A seven-year-old in the body of a thirty-year-old. And that was that. In the way she led her life, managed her affairs, she was just fifteen. Fifteen sober, childish years. And that's why Ângela Margarida and her siblings had slept easily in their beds. Milene wasn't a worry because she seemed quite happy in herself, leading her simple life, following her simple timetable, fulfilling her simple dreams of eating ice creams, drinking fruit juice, and making phone calls, while they, her aunts and uncles, were constantly on the go, caught up in their fast-moving lives. Ângela Margarida had her complicated life at the clinic, her husband had a life so complicated that it wasn't so much a life, more an act of self-immolation on behalf of a vile society that certainly didn't deserve him. Her sister and Dom Silvestre, trapped in their inexplicable existences, with their children, their hideous stone quarries, not to mention various other business deals, fines, death threats, seaside developments, big future metropolises, the ambitions of her brother-in-law Dom, who often didn't even sleep at home, went about with a gun in his pocket, and was the bane of her sister Gininha's life. Her brother Afonso led an equally complicated existence. His law firm, his lawsuits, his interchangeable floozies, his riding outfits, and his horses. All of this had continued and even accelerated since their mother had died in those tragic circumstances.

Even so, they had attempted to keep Milene company, tried to share responsibility for her over the week, but, given the lives they led, this had proved impossible.

In short—on the one hand, there were their complicated lives and, on the other, the ticking time bomb of a mistake that was Milene. Hyacinth roots proliferating underwater. Besides, while the specialist who had kept saying *voilà* during that hour-long consultation had played down the gravity of her condition, he had never actually said there was nothing wrong. The message the doctor had wanted to get across was that we're all part of the same mistake, and those of us with a lesser share of that mistake within us should help those with a larger share, help to free them from that species-wide disease—the fact was that each and every one of us was a variant of that same mistake. It was therefore her duty, as Milene Lino Leandro's aunt, to help her niece.

While initially she had felt something akin to revulsion for the girl, who was blond like her mother and slightly built like her father, thinking her ugly one moment, and merely insignificant the next—a person fated to cause everyone else a lot of trouble—

and who, suddenly, the moment she was left alone, had waded straight into the mud, and while initially this had made Ângela Margarida feel like giving Milene a good shake, slapping her around the face, even imagining her own hand moving back and forth, to punish and to castigate her, and at the same time remove her from danger—she could even hear her own angry words—yes, while this had been her first reaction, now she felt quite different. She was filled with pity and compassion. Affection, even. And, yes, why not? Love. Blood speaking more loudly than her own feelings, now that she'd seen everything, now that she alone held everything in her hands. That much was clear. She must care for Milene, prepare her and protect her, now that she had, for the second time, been abandoned by her family. They couldn't abandon her again. And when Ângela Margarida imagined her niece's future life with that young man, whom her sister and the doorman, the previous night, had described as perfectly normal, but whose gangly, loping figure she had seen leaving the restaurant, then she knew she had to act. Her revulsion was now directed at people like Barbosa of Mãos Largas, who owed their family so much, and who must have known everything, but had said nothing. And what about the cleaning woman? How come she had kept quiet too?—Yes, Ângela Margarida had to take action.

She had to.

Ângela Margarida glanced at the door in front of her and read the name of the director of the clinic—*Dr. Luís Seabra, Director*. It was Monday. Analyses and treatments piling up, and there she was, frozen. She needed a moment to think before she acted. Yes, if the clinic was not to lose its exemplary reputation, she had to stop that flow of people, to divert them, to send them somewhere else. Above the director's desk were written the first words of the Hippocratic oath—*Primum non nocere*. A romantic paint-ing depicted an invalid, wrapped in a cloth, being carried along by two men, with a third, holding up a lantern, lighting their way along a dark path. Doubtless the work of some English artist. It recalled a time when the body was not yet a body, just a bundle of magic and mystery. But then certain ridiculous, outmoded expres-sions did persist over the centuries, the guardians of meaningless principles. *Primum non nocere*.

Yes, she had to act, she had to do something.

First, though, she should try to dissuade Milene. Did she truly love José Carlos's daughter? She did. And when she thought of how helpful Milene had been on the morning of the marathon, and the sensitivity she'd shown to Rui, who had been in an even worse state of despair than usual, and how she had grasped exactly what was going on, Ângela Margarida's heart filled with tenderness. She must protect her, look after her, help her to avoid all the evil of this world.

Throughout that afternoon, there were endless phone calls between Ângela Margarida and Gininha. Gininha totally agreed with her sister, the sensible thing would be to try to dis-suade Milene.

In that, the sisters were united.

One going ahead, the other behind, each in her respective Honda, both heading for Villa Regina, something that hadn't happened since August, after which point they had only gone separately, during the days of the perpetual calendar. The two of them arriving together, as they had on the day of the big bust-up, when they had all just returned from their vacations. The two of them driving up the old road, as night was falling. The two of them seeing from afar the house all lit up, returning to the house where they'd spent their youth, seeing life, briefly, in a lilac-tinted glow. There was Milene's white car, parked under the acacias. The two somnambular aunts, still unable to believe what they were doing, about to enter the house and talk to Milene. And Milene, wearing her beanie hat, about to go out. Annoyed. "Why come and talk to me at this hour?"—It was clear from Milene's tone of voice that "this hour" was the worst possible hour to come and talk to her. Milene standing outside the front door, looking very irritated, telling them she had a boyfriend who was the father of three children, and that she wanted to spend some time with him before it got dark. Looking at her watch. She was late already, Milene said, moving away from the front door. Milene in trainers and a tiny miniskirt, so short that, had it been white, it could have passed for a tennis skirt. A dark leather jacket similar to the one Antonino Mata wore.

"We've come to talk to you. Can't you at least wait a moment?"—*a great deal of patience, for as long as she lives . . .* — "Please, Milene, we want to talk to you . . ."

Milene, in that short skirt, her legs clad in dark diamond-mesh tights. Her bracelets tinkling like bells. With barely a smile for her aunts. Looking at her watch. When had Milene learned to look at her watch like that? When? Milene being decisive—"No, I can't stop. I have my own life to lead, you know." Milene striding over to the Clio, swinging her hips. Without a backward glance.

Gininha, lost for words, caved in.

"Off she goes . . ."

Ângela Margarida feeling that Nature, Nature's mistake, was revealing itself in full force, shaking everything up. As absurd and unfair as an earthquake. And even if it wasn't just Nature's mistake, but God's too, they still had to take action. Because if

God was speaking, he must be a very long way off, for his words had become lost en route, and by the time they reached human ears they were only sighs and whispers. It was necessary, at all times, to invent God's word based on those faint, whispered syllables. Besides, the most consistent image of God relied on the very ambiguity of his words. So thought Ângela Margarida. Then she too caved in. They both agreed on that. They were standing in front of their mother's house. What would *she* have done were she still alive?

She would have caved in as well.

"Listen, Gininha . . ."

And with the sun now vanished, Ângela Margarida convinced her sister to convince their niece that it would be a good idea for her to visit the clinic, now that she'd decided to lead the life of a normal woman. Gininha and Milene were so much closer and got on really well. It was important that Milene should call in at the clinic, because neither of her aunts could recall her ever having any kind of examination apart from psychological ones. It was agreed, decided. If it was up to Gininha Leandro, then Milene would be sure to come.

XXIII

THIS IS THE LAST TIME WE'LL SEE ANTONINO MATA'S VAN. We'll be told about it later, in different circumstances, but as for seeing it in its entirety—the outer shell intact, the cab complete, the paintwork perfect—this is the last time. Right now it's still parked by the acacias, and the outline of the driver, dressed all in black today, is difficult to make out. The children, however, are quite visible. They're wearing light colors and have stripy woolen hats on their heads. The eldest, his thick curly hair escaping from beneath his hat is holding a plastic toy. The middle one is licking the window with his pink tongue. The youngest is asleep in his car seat, underneath a shawl. And for a moment, all four of them are motionless, obscured by the darkness of the branches, with the streetlamp above. But then Antonino opens his window and calls toward the house—"Milene!"

He could shout as loudly as he wanted. There was no one else around. Some of the neighboring houses were still empty, and others were rapidly becoming mere storage spaces. And the main house, shaped like a steam iron, was disappearing beneath the stranglehold of the creeping myrtle. Since the sprawling mass of the walnut tree hid the house where, as usual, all the lights were still on, he called again, insistently—"Hey! Milene!" Milene didn't answer because she was already at the door, already closing it behind her, and now the compact shape of Villa Regina was also plunged into darkness. Milene was about to step into the road. A car came speeding toward her, screeching to a halt on finding its way blocked. "Watch out!"—Antonino hurried over to take her bag. The car turned around, then abruptly pulled away, only just missing Milene, who stood stock-still, her *Blitz* magazines scattered at her feet. "Watch out! You ought to look where you're going . . ." Antonino angry with her. Gesticulating—whatever was she thinking, stepping out into the road without looking? How could she go on living in the middle of nowhere if she refused to take any precautions? he asked, taking her small bag and leading her toward the van, still berating her. Then, feeling its weight, shaking it so that the contents jumped around inside—"Whoa! So much stuff . . . Are you staying the night?"

"No"—said Milene. "It'll be over in no time. I'll be home in three hours."

"Three hours?"—Antonino looked at his oversized wristwatch. "I won't be free then to pick you up." The car whose way had been blocked was now doubling back, passing too close to the van, engine roaring furiously in the early morning. Antonino, who was still clutching Milene's *Blitz* magazines, leapt out of the way, then spun around to get a look at the madman at the wheel, squaring up to the departing car, daring it to come back, waving the magazines above his head. "It's really not safe here, Milene. Not safe at all. How many times do I have to tell you? And now there are thieves all over the place, murderers on the roads . . . How are you planning to get home from the clinic?" Still shaken from having shouted at her, and from the near-miss with that hooligan driver. If the guy had braked any later, he would have hit Milene. Oh well, it was over now.

But as for her getting home, it was all taken care of: her aunt had said she would give her a lift. Instead of just asking Frutuoso to do it, she, Aunt Ângela Margarida, was going to do it herself— Milene informed him.

Aside from that, everything was normal. Milene hopped into the front of the van, and the two children who were awake tried to give her a hug, reaching over the seats. Antonino impatient to get going—"Sit down, you little rascals. You stay awake all night playing games, and then at school you don't learn any-thing because you spend the whole time asleep . . ."—he said, settling them into the back beside their sleeping brother. And off they went, down the road, onto the highway. As they passed the crossroads by the Hotel Miramar, where the road turned off to the Old Factory, Milene said very loudly, over the noise of the engine—"You're going out of your way, and all because of me . . ." Antonino laughed for a moment, pleased. At first he just laughed and said nothing. Then he turned his head, making the van swerve slightly, so that he could look at her when he said—"For you, I'd go all the way to Lisbon and back every morning if I had to. Right? And I'd go even farther too, really I would . . . Anyway, we have no choice." He took her hand, pulling her closer and leaning in. It was a pity the van made so much noise when the radio wasn't on. The Mitsubishi was a solid, powerful vehicle, steady on the road, designed for carrying tools and machinery, and, when necessary, large groups of people. It was quiet too, but every so often it made that guttural growling sound, as if there were a blockage somewhere in the workings. This was why he didn't switch on the radio or play any music—listening to the engine took his full attention. And then the strangeness of the morning, for both of them, made it seem even louder. Neither saying a word. They were driving along the tarmac road now and still had another ten miles to go, another twenty minutes of that

racket. They would drive around the edge of low white crenel-
lated Santa Maria de Valmares and then take the road to the saltworks, following it all the way down, and, at the bottom, where
the air was cool and where, at night, it was lit by the beam from
the lighthouse, there, in isolation, stood two buildings immediately adjacent to each other, in the middle of a grove of trees, and
encircled by spiked metal railings that had recently been painted
green. This was the clinic. Milene had been here before, twice
the previous week. The sun seemed to be coming up more slowly
than usual, as if the northwesterly wind had blown them closer
to Africa. Antonino stopped the van.

"It's still so early. Fancy going over there for some breakfast?
We've got time. It would only take a few minutes."

Milene had picked up her purse.—"I can't, I'm fasting today."
Antonino had climbed out of the car now and was clasping his
jacket to his body. If he let go, the wind would fill it with air, turning him into a Michelin man.

"Fasting? I don't like that word. *Fasting.*"—The word brought
back bad memories, sticking in the pit of his stomach like a bad
omen. He remembered it well, and all that came with it—Eunice,
fasting, septicemia . . . Yes, he remembered. But the two of them
always tried not to let bad things or problems into their conversations, or fears either, like the one that had just gripped him. Still
smarting after that encounter with the hooligan driver, and still
upset because he had shouted at Milene, he tried again—"Come
and eat something, Milene, come on. They won't know either
way . . . Seriously, you have to eat *something.*"

"I can't"—she replied.

Because, while Aunt Ângela Margarida had insisted it would
be over in no time, she had also insisted more than once that
Milene mustn't eat anything beforehand. Milene looked at her
watch. Hers and his said exactly the same: seven-thirty a.m. It was

ridiculous to have set off so early just so they could stand there, half-asleep, staring at one another. Or was it?

He wanted go on talking, to pass the time—"It's clearly not my lucky day. Someone else is going up in the Liebherr instead of me . . . I'll have to move to another country and get a crane license there. It's the only way. Here, people seem determined to ruin my chances. Apart from you, being a crane driver is what I want most in the world . . ." he said, looking grumpy, dressed all in black. "And after that, who knows? . . . Anyway, make sure you look both ways when you leave the clinic. You need to be more careful . . ."

The beginning of the morning was like a piece that had broken free from the natural order of things. They had each set off in a different direction. Milene didn't have far to go. She just had to walk up some steps and she'd be at the door of the clinic. He waved goodbye from inside the van, then disappeared into the blinding light of day. Behind him, she could see the three children with their hoods up, before they too faded from view. And she thought about the emptiness, and about that free-floating early morning, by which time she was sitting on the sofa in the waiting room, between two people who seemed, for some reason, to have spent the night there, while others, neatly dressed and highly perfumed, were also on their way in. They sat down, displaying their shapely legs and reading the books with tiny print they had brought with them. And her simply thinking. Not reading, just flicking through her copies of *Blitz*. Thinking about how she'd have to telephone her cousin when she got home. And as she flicked through her magazines, glancing at the music charts and the photos of singers, she heard herself addressing her cousin, heard her voice speaking those boring opening words. Flicking through the pages. *Are you there? It's me, Milene* . . . But this time it would be different, because she was planning to begin by saying—*News, big news. Just to say that I've been spending a lot of time with Aunt Ângela Margarida . . . And the big news is that she talked about you. She said you're writing a book about human stupidity and you're already on page one thousand . . . Is that really true? Big news . . .* And after telling him her news, she would tell him what he deserved to hear. That she wasn't going to telephone him anymore. Because that was life; everyone had to go their own way. And on thinking this, or perhaps because of the silence filling the large waiting room, or for some other reason entirely, Milene felt the need for some chewing gum.

Somehow, although she was sitting there, in that room full of chairs and silent people, it was as if she were back on the beach at Praia Pequena, and her friend Violante, whom she hadn't really thought about for months, was still sitting in the lap of that guy with the ripped jeans, and had turned around and looked her in the eye, and said—*Why are you so sad? All you have are reasons to be happy . . .* Maybe it was because of the scare with the car that morning. She needed another piece of chewing gum. And possibly another one after that. Milene thought as she waited, flicking through her copies of *Blitz*. Not reading, her mind on other things. Outside, only the pointed railings and the dark, spindly arcs of the casuarina branches, slicing up the view of the saltworks. Outside the door, the flight of steps. Coming up them, Aunt Ângela Margarida. About to arrive. *All you have are reasons to be happy . . .* Milene had arrived early because of Antonino, that man who was so uptight about time, and about everything else. What her aunt had said was—"Eight on the dot, Milene, don't forget . . ."

But her aunt had arrived before eight as well. And the morning breeze had brought color to her cheeks. She was wearing an almost sky-blue skirt suit, in a heavy fabric, with a cape the same color on top. Milene clearly wasn't the only one who thought her aunt looked beautiful, because a tall, brisk man in a jacket, his collar pulled up to his ears, his mere presence sending a couple of people scurrying out of his way, walked past her aunt and asked— "So, all ready for your special day?"

"Of course"—Ângela Margarida replied, following him through the glass door. She reappeared about fifteen minutes later. It was a quarter past eight on the dot.

She was dressed in white now and on her head was a cap with two holes in it, one on each side, through which you could see her hair. Her sleeves were rolled up, as if she no longer felt cold, and she looked ready to face a hard day at work on the human body. The morning breeze was still blowing outside, bending the grasses and lifting stray scraps of paper from the path, but it was as if it were still grazing her cheeks. As if it were flooding her being with unusual benevolence. She had never seen her aunt like that before, walking over to her so placidly, helping her out of her chair, and propelling her gently into a vast, dimly lit area, saying—"Do you want to give me your things?" Her aunt's cheeks pink. Milene handed over what she had with her. It was only half past eight in the morning. "It'll be ever so simple, over in no time. Now, if you could get undressed and put this gown on"—said the nurse who wasn't in charge. Only her aunt was really in charge. "It'll be over in no time"—said a third cap-wearing person, without turning around, while pushing a kind of trolley.

And then, from behind the frosted glass, came a man's voice, the same one that had said—*Ready for your special day?* It was a deep, melodious voice, a voice like the color of her aunt's cheeks. The man must have been a doctor, judging by how at ease he seemed. He sang under his breath—"*Rock-a-bye, baby, in the tree-top . . .*" Then he began singing in earnest. His voice behind the glass had too much vibrato, as if he were sending up the way a real chorister would sing, although he must have been a chorister himself, given how well he projected the notes, filling every nook and cranny of the space. Behind the glass in the semidarkness, he carried on with whatever he was doing, stooping slightly as if he were washing his hands in a sink, though he wasn't actually washing them. Then he straightened up, his voice climbing higher as he himself rose, staring straight ahead—"*Oh! Come and see, my child . . . It's so beautiful to dream . . .*" He came farther into that gloomy space, and the nurse, her back turned, flicked a switch of some kind. The place lit up then and it was a room, not an empty expanse. Milene, by now, was wearing nothing but a hospital gown and she was cold.

"Are you cold? Don't worry, we'll be done in no time."

The doctor's back was still turned and he again sang under his breath—"*Oh! Come and see, my child . . .*" And he kept singing, going up and down the scales, blithely, irrepressibly. Milene found it odd that he should be singing like that and started to laugh. The doctor turned to look at her, holding something up in the air, and sang again—"*Oh, come and see . . .*"

"Please, Dr. Seabra, don't be so sadistic . . ."—said someone else whose back was turned to her, cutting him off. A decisive, despairing voice. It sounded like her aunt. To break the ensuing silence, Milene laughed out loud. She laughed out loud so that they would know she was laughing. Yes, it was Aunt Ângela Margarida's voice. Don't be so sadistic. Her aunt leaned over her. Looking up at her from below, Milene could see her quite clearly, her cheeks fuller from that angle, her hazel eyes, her sleek, shiny blond hair framing her face, and her heavy eyelids, just like Grandma Regina's. Her aunt's eyelashes so very dark, making her eyes seem rounder. Her aunt's eyelashes fluttering, looking at her, her aunt rubbing her hand, her aunt's hand asking if she was cold, and lots of other faces, all peering down at her. But then her aunt's voice mingled with that of the musical doctor, the two becoming a single voice, disappearing into the yellow and then into the dark. And there was still time for the thought, the vague, half-finished thought, that this wasn't why she had come. Yes, it was just a flicker, just a feeling in her body, which was sinking, all of it, down that slippery slope, floating on a pillow of air, on which were written the words—*How strange, this isn't what I came here for.* And after that, she couldn't say—*Hey, I've just plunged into nothingness*, because that was exactly what she had done.

The nothingness continued to be nothing at all.

A long, weightless, spaceless expanse, stretching endlessly ahead and behind.

Except that the nothingness wasn't entirely nothing, the nothingness must have retreated a little, must have turned back, temporarily postponing total nothingness, because it, the nothingness, had begun by being a branch pressed against a window. A branch that came in and out of view, scraping at the glass, then vanishing. As if it wanted to get inside and couldn't, and as if that branch were all that existed, containing each and every possible kind of consciousness, and since it could neither get inside nor give up, it was nothing more than a branch, because nothing, apart from that coming and going, was happening. The branch was the only being that moved, that wanted to be, to exist, right there, over there, close to something that was both her and not her, making her something rather than the nothing that was merging with that powerful piece of tree, that primordial being coming and going so monotonously, scratching nasally at the windowpane, in the form of nothing at all. And only after the branch had moved to and fro outside the window, like a powerful, ancient hand wanting to come in, as ancient and wild as the days when trees were the same as animals, or when, released from their roots, they turned into animals, only then did she think that she existed again, and feel, to her amazement, that she was less than nothing, or maybe more than nothing, but not absolutely nothing, and she was astonished to find herself in that state, winding her way toward wakefulness. And the branch fluttered into full view, then vanished, and she wasn't the branch and she said— "I'm Milene. I'm not the tree trying to reach in at me from outside the window. Maybe I'm even less, maybe I'm dead, but whatever I am, I'm not that . . ." Astonished. "Milene?" she called to herself. And her hand found her chest and her shoulder. Then nothing. It was still only a bodily sort of daze, and hadn't yet reached her consciousness.

In other words, she was still semiconscious when her body said to her—*You and I have set off down an unforeseen path.* Because it was something utterly new and unexpected. Something surprising. But since the surprise didn't reach right into her brain or heart, it didn't turn into fear. Milene couldn't have said, as she felt her head heavy on the pillow, that she was afraid. Maybe it was a kind of fear-before-fear, a fear made of letters, constituent parts so far away from one another that together they couldn't quite become perplexity, though perhaps a hazy hint of it. Not fear, then, but what precedes it, its antechamber or its harbinger. For example, a fragment of that fear drew closer and showed her the window, the top half of which was white and the bottom half black night. Which meant that it was night now, not morning or afternoon. Another fragment of that fear brought her some bare arms and hands, and a cap and all the rest, but they didn't belong to her aunt, they belonged to someone else, someone kind but unknown to her. Another fragment of that fear made this unknown person say—"What a night, eh? Did you hear that?" Yet another fragment heard a rumble. She knew that sound, the sound of lightning out at sea, muffled by the water, scrawling wild lines across the sky. Go to sleep, get some rest. What a night, eh? It's winter bidding us farewell. The other fragment approached in total silence, wearing a blue wool suit and matching cape, and with sleek blond hair, cut level with the earlobes. High heels moving on tiptoe. The figure leaned over her, not making a sound, then vanished behind the bed. The fear did not become fear proper, but took on the bodily form of her aunt. And then, once again, she fell asleep.

XXIV

A CLOUD WAS BEGINNING TO COVER THE AREA BETWEEN THE clinic and Aunt Ângela Margarida's house. To the south, the cloud thickened and grew, and more clouds appeared behind, closing the gap. *Six*—she thought.

Six plates, six sets of cutlery, six trout, six tiramisus, six. Six small glasses, six tall glasses, six linen place mats, six napkins, six coffee cups, six champagne flutes, six chairs, six chair backs, six. Six aperitifs, six digestifs, six green salads with melon and smoked ham as starters. Six right hands to move six knives, six left hands to carry food to the mouth, six mouths, six heads, six foreheads, six opinions, six tongues. Six, six of everything, for that special night. Six of everything to resolve just one problem. Six people brought together to take stock of the situation and together confront the big problem. It remained to be seen who would speak first. "Six"— *Good grief, why am I walking around and around the table when the maid has already laid all six places? I feel utterly exhausted.*

Ângela Margarida removed her blue cape to reveal a suit of the same color and the same fabric, with a nipped-in waist and a short skirt. She brushed the hem of her skirt. Should she change? The wind and the rain had touched the cloth here and there, leaving it damp. And in her hair she carried a little of the thunder and lightning that was still rolling around over the sea. It had been such a pleasant morning and yet, afterward, what an afternoon and a night had descended on her life.

She looked at the clock. Half past eight. She knew Rui would be late. He would, as usual, arrive after everyone else. Poor Rui. However much she stressed the importance of being on time, she knew what always prevented him from keeping his promise to be punctual. Her husband was carrying one hundred and ninety square miles of territory on his back. The permanent challenge of one hundred and ninety square miles of territory, with its past, its future, and its troubled present. It was a lot to carry. Rui, Mayor Rui Ludovice, was a tall, very erect man, who walked down the street with his back ramrod-straight, but if the population to whom he devoted himself could see his soul, they would see that it was often crawling on all fours, like a galley slave. He would reach the top floor of that building with its view over the bay, the lighthouse and the islands, and wouldn't even notice them; he was too weighed down by all the anxieties of a galley slave. She often imagined him as one of the Volga boatmen, except that, in his case, he was dragging a boat along on his own, a boat too heavy for his back and shoulders. Day after day, at around mid-night, he would carry that burden, because that's what it was, up to the top floor, in order to rest for five hours and sleep for only three, despite the sleeping pills and the conscientious back rubs she herself gave him. What would become of him if it weren't for her? If she weren't a dedicated nurse? What would become of him and the other members of the family? Each of them owed her an incalculable debt. All of them, in one way or another, depended on her. The six who would be coming tonight, and their children too. Six. Suddenly she clapped her hand to her head and said— "Six? Good grief, I forgot about me!" There were seven of them. Ângela Margarida felt unwell.

"Now I understand. I must be ill."

Seven? No, not seven. There would be six of them at the table, including her. She was counting herself twice. Six. So she wasn't so ill after all. Just tired. She ought to change her suit to chase away the heavy atmosphere. Still those distant rumbles out at sea. It didn't matter, though, it was the last thunder of the winter they hadn't really had, the last squall, the last storm, the last bout of staphylococcus, the last influenza. And then, possibly even the next day, along would come the sweet summer weather. Perhaps tomorrow. Joana and Sabina, her two daughters, were shut up in their rooms studying, and would then fall asleep, far removed from this whole business. Only six, not seven. She was pretty sure that the first to arrive would be Gininha and Dom Silvestre, separately, each in their own car, then Afonso and the Fairy Isabel, and only long afterward, long, long afterward, Rui would come through the door. Isabel was the problem. What could they talk about if he brought her? How could she ask her to leave the room when the time came to talk? Who was she anyway?—Then, to her surprise, all five arrived simultaneously, and Afonso hadn't brought Isabel, but his first wife, Alda Maria. This was an excellent sign. Afonso had understood the gravity of the situation.

Yes, outside, the spring weather was enjoying its final thunderstorm. Had they even had a first storm that year? Had there been any storms at all? She couldn't remember. The last storm she could recall seemed to have happened many years ago, in ancient times. A distant memory, from before she was born. It was strange how everything seemed to have changed. Whatever the truth of the matter, if summer was about to come, then that night should be the last night of lightning. Indeed, just as Gininha and Dom sat down, there was a flash of lightning, and Gininha let out a yelp. A typical muffled Gininha yelp, hand pressed to mouth, with Dom observing her from the other side of the table. However bound they were by the same interests, not even their baby girl, Artemisa, could bring them together. They were separated by nature until eternity beckoned, and even beyond eternity. How was that possible? *I'm getting confused*, thought Ângela Margarida, and she went over to the big bay window, where she lowered the multiple blinds one by one. Afonso said—"Don't worry, the light-ning bolts aren't aimed at us . . ." Afonso laughing, playful, jokey, easing the tension of that awkward moment, which was the rea-son for their sister inviting them to that impromptu supper. Even Rui had grasped how serious this was, and, abandoning the one hundred and ninety square miles of territory to their fate and to his assistant, he had managed to arrive on time.

"Let's get down to business . . ."

Said Afonso Leandro, aperitif in hand, sitting next to his first wife of some thirty-odd years ago. Alda Maria was the same age as him, but seemed younger, and seated beside him she made him look considerably older. As if, together, they'd not only failed to escape the passage of time, but were both sinking fast. For a moment, Ângela Margarida thought about the communicating vessels linking youth and beauty, thought what a shame it was that Isabel couldn't have been there without actually being there. A deaf-mute presence seated beside Afonso, a bright lantern lend-ing him a youthful glow. However, she had to drive this absurd, pointless idea from her head. There was no way Isabel could have come. It would have been disastrous if Afonso had brought her. Bringing Alda Maria was fine, though. As the mother of João Paulo and Danila, she'd been involved from the start in that complex web of loves, rights, and interests. At decisive moments, Afonso knew who he could rely on. There they all were.

The five of them, and with her, six. They had started eating. No one spoke. Then Afonso Leandro said—"It seems we don't even need to talk. The sole purpose of this supper is simply having us share the silence . . ." No one else spoke. Then Afonso went on— "I'll come straight to the point. The problem is this—José Carlos's daughter has got involved with a member of the Mata family, and, like it or not, we have to face up to that problem. It's a real drag, but . . ."

Dom put down his fork and said—"It's very odd. Without our realizing, we're beginning to be led by them, we're becoming part of the third wave . . ." Dom Silvestre laughing. Ângela Margarida unable to quite hear what was being said around the table—Six green salads, six slices of melon, six portions of smoked ham, a flash of lightning entering the room, a roll of thunder rumbling around outside. Still a big gap between thunder and lightning, so they were in no danger.

"Please, don't get off the point, just say something concrete about the matter . . ."—This was Ângela Margarida, unable to eat a morsel. "What do *you* say, Gininha?"—No green salad and melon. No ham. She couldn't eat a thing either.

Then Aunt Gininha plucked up her courage, shaking back her long, youthful locks—"I think that, given the way things are, there's nothing to be done about it . . ." She again shook back her hair, as if this helped her give voice to her thoughts. "Whether you like it or not, Milene, in her own way, really loves that person. I saw them together at our house, the way she looked at him. What right do we have to interfere in her life? What right do we have to make her change anything? It all happened without our involvement. Why should we think it's up to us to stop anything? What right do we have? *You* might have the right, but I certainly don't . . ." She was addressing her sister, who was sitting across from her.

Ângela Margarida hadn't had time to change her suit, and the blue woolen fabric, her unnaturally yellow hair, her dark eyelashes and puffy eyelids, all combined to make her look utterly exhausted. Like someone on the verge of collapse, having danced too much at a ball. Six fish, six knives, six napkins. Thinking—*I feel bad because I did something good, but I must say nothing, must keep it to myself, tell no one. As if a fish had done it. A fish with no tongue, no voice, no language.* Ângela Margarida's unease was plain for all to see. Afonso, on the other hand, was utterly serene in his three-piece suit. The upper half in perfect harmony with the lower. They all looked at him, it was his turn to speak.

Afonso said—"Right, yes . . ."

Then he went on—"There's nothing better than summing up, that's what the law teaches us. Precision and concision. So this is how it is:—As regards those two, José Carlos's daughter and that fellow Antonino, of whom I have no wish to know any more, there's nothing to be done. You can't accuse him of seduction or abuse, let alone rape or deception, because that's not at all the case. As Gininha said, no one can stop them. End of story. Secondly, as regards the patrimonial situation, he and his family are the tenants of the factory, they have a lease and have kept to its terms. According to that lease, they must be given six months' notice to leave. Signed and sealed. But who's going to put them out in the street? We could do that, assuming we agreed that we *should* intervene in their relationship. How would that look, though, when their relationship is public knowledge? In fact, it was public knowledge long before we knew anything about it. In short—I can see a way of taking legal action, but not how we could deal with the public backlash, unless we all agreed to act as if we knew nothing about the matter. Period . . ."

Six halves of six fish, six fish spines on show, six heads filled with smoked ham, six portions of toasted almonds on top, six champagne flutes full of champagne. At that moment, no one was eating. Should they go forward or turn back? Let the process take its course or try to reverse it?

They looked at each other. The six of them sitting around the table. Six fish heads, six spines, six tails.

Dom Silvestre began to laugh, although who knows why, and, taking a sip of his champagne, he began saying—"Why even talk about reversing the process or letting it take its course? As soon as I saw them curled up together, all snuggled up on our sofa, I could see there was only one way to go, and that's forward . . . I can still see it now. There was your sister, frozen in amazement, and them wriggling around on the sofa . . ." Dom sipping his champagne and laughing. And something within him added—*Sit, sit . . . On the ground . . .*

It was clear that Dom was preparing to intervene in his own sweet way. Six green salads, which contained every possible green thing, even half a dozen pistachios among the leaves, being handed around the table. To be eaten before the trout or with the trout, what would be best? And Dom said—"On another subject, I found out yesterday that some bastard cross-breed Rottweiler had attacked its owner, its trainer. The guy was just putting down food for the dog, and it went berserk. Do you know why?"

"No, why?"

"Because it wasn't a pure breed, it was a cross between a real Rottweiler and an Alsatian. It just flew into a rage, went mad, and bit off its owner's nose. You see what I mean? A guy loses his nose because of some crazy crossbreed dog. Makes you think, eh? A crossbreed loses the sense of smell proper to its breed, and therefore belongs to no breed at all and doesn't even recognize its owner's smell. Avoid crossbreeds like the plague . . ."

"What are you trying to say, Dom?"

Dom Silvestre poured himself some more champagne. Didn't

anyone else want some more? Was no one drinking? Did no one really know what to do about that silly creature Milene? He obviously needed to be more explicit. He knew Africa. Africa had given him everything and almost taken everything from him too. It was pure luck that he'd managed to get on that British Airways plane one night with a load of precious stones wrapped up in a handkerchief. Plus a few more in his socks and shoes. But enough of that. He had a theory:—Humanity was all one, but within humanity not all men were equal and you shouldn't assume they were. He, for example, thought that international sporting events had become the biggest farce in modern times. Why do we humiliate ourselves like that, when we're just not on an equal footing?—Six fish spines, six heads with open jaws, six gleaming plates, and a flash of lightning coming in through the slats of the blinds covering the panoramic windows. A great boom immediately opposite, echoing over the sea. "Jesus! I hope you've got a lightning conductor!"

Dom jumped.

"I don't honestly know, but it goes to show that living in an apartment like this has its downsides, contrary to what the population may think, the ones who are always leaving inane messages for me scrawled on walls . . ."—said Rui Ludovice, getting up and opening the windows, confronting the storm breaking over the sea. "It might feel like it's right above us, but it's actually miles away, almost in Morocco. Forgive me opening the blinds, but I prefer to be able to see what's happening. Anyway, Dom, you were saying . . ."

Dom continued—"It's completely unfair and inadmissible to make a European compete with them in a hundred-meter race. Their coccyx is positioned differently. Their legs fit differently in their joints. But it's the coccyx that counts. One Humanity, but different coccyxes. Different coccyxes, different races, different contests. There's only one Olympic Games because there's only one Humanity, but just as they put on separate contests for men and women, they should have separate contests for them and us. What I mean is, there's one *Homo faber* for various species of *Homo athleticus . . .*"

"Where did you find that out?"

"It's the same with singing, that's another myth. Their oral cavity is different too, their teeth are different, everything inside resonates in another way, it's just not a fair competition. They sing one way, and we sing another. That's why I chose the right moment to escape South Africa, where I have to say I had a very good life, but I could sense mayhem coming. I could smell it. As I said, I left with those precious stones before the great farce arrived. I even put some of those stones in my toothpaste . . ." Dom laughed loudly. Although it wasn't clear what was so funny. Far off, the sky's grumblings were moving westward, in search of the wide-open spaces of the Atlantic. To wander about among the waves. Six tiramisus, six dessert spoons, six. Six thimble-sized glasses. Six, for the liqueur.

Ângela Margarida could stand it no longer.

"Yes, but what are you getting at?"

Dom Silvestre saying that he didn't eat dessert, and could they bring him some fruit. Then concluding—"It's the same mess everywhere, and you, who even had a brother cut to pieces in Angola, you've always disagreed with what sensible people like me have to say, people with actual experience on the ground, well, now you'll have to face the consequences. Too bad. Who would dare put a stop to something like that—in public? Who? Who would dare? That's fine by me. I saw it all, the moment I went into the living room . . . And meanwhile her over there, well, she turned white as a sheet and almost dropped the baby. And I could see right away where it was all leading . . ." Domitílio Silvestre laughing. Small and swarthy, dark eyes glinting. Eyes almost closed, but glinting even more. Around the table, six plates with their respective tiramisus intact, dessert spoons resting on them. And no one could laugh or eat. Should they turn back or carry on?—Oh, let them carry on. He, Dom Silvestre, had put all their discussions about selling the Diamond on standby because Afonso's sisters couldn't make up their minds. Not because of Afonso. He'd like to see just how they were going to dig themselves out of that particular hole. Instead of seizing their chance at the opportune moment, they'd just let things go to pot. They should have acted before tragedy struck. Dom was talking as if some omnipresent lawmaker presided over all commercial wheelings and dealings. As if he'd always been right, both when he'd supported the arrival of the third wave, and later on, when he'd raised the alarm, signaling that the third wave had run its course, and should make way for a new lot, a new wave. They all saw how contradictory this was, but were nevertheless intimidated by his reasoning. So where had they gone wrong? Had it merely been a matter of timing, or was it also a question of principle? The big square table rooted to the floor, no one touching the desserts or the glasses. Hands folded. Twelve hands, twelve arms, six heads, six memories, six plans, but only one decision to make. What are we going to do? *It's very hard to decide, but once a decision has been made, then carrying straight on, all the way, is the easiest thing there is . . .*

And Afonso Leandro was about to speak, when his first wife, the mother of his two legitimate children, his future legitimate heirs, had an idea—"May I say something?"

"I haven't been in on this from the start, but it seems to me that you should evict the Matas as soon as possible"—she said.

She was still a good-looking woman. She wore her hair in a style reminiscent of Mrs Thatcher, stiff, bouffant, plebeian, but as if expecting to be crowned. Everyone looked at her, waiting to hear her commonsense words. Her prim tight lips were carefully painted, and her words emerged from somewhere in the back of her throat—"That's what I'd do, independently of whether they get together or not, Milene and the young man, I mean, I think those people should go back where they came from—to Bairro dos Espelhos."

Everyone waiting to hear those commonsense words.

"There's nothing to stop them from doing that. Here's how it would work: They would go back to Bairro dos Espelhos, and meanwhile apply for social housing, with Rui pulling a few strings, then we could sell the factory and the land, and problem solved; besides, personally, I think the business with Milene will turn out to be rather secondary"—she said. "Because things will never work out between them anyway. Whatever happens, though, first of all we need to sell that albatross of a building as soon as possible. The place is beginning to look as if it's jinxed, when you think of the number of disasters that have happened there . . ." Alda Maria sitting very erect, and now beginning to attack her tiramisu, dividing it in half and putting half to one side. She couldn't possibly eat it all. "And Rui here could, as I say, always pull a few strings. They'd be back in Bairro dos Espelhos in no time. Anyway, that's what I think. Which isn't to say that I agree with Dom's views, because I don't . . ." said Alda Maria. The storm somewhere off in the distance now. What would Rui Ludovice's fellow party members say if they knew about Dom's theories? Silence. The table cleared, the glasses still full. All standing up now, all silent, thinking. Some of what she had said was very sensible.

"What do you think, Rui?"—asked Alda Maria.

On the ground, baby . . .—Dom Silvestre had stood up too, and was pacing the room.

The person who answered, though, was Rui Ludovice himself.

"I'm not even going to bother answering you, Alda Maria. I'm talking to myself here, and do you know what I'm thinking? That every one of you is using me as if I were your own personal snot rag. Listen, if I did as you say, I'd be putting my career on the line for the hundredth time, and all to benefit you. Frankly, dear sister-in-law, you've got your eye on a share of the profits from the sale of that albatross, as you call it, whatever it takes, even if it means your brother-in-law, for the umpteenth time, pulling a few strings . . . If those people do leave the factory, I take the rap. If they move into one of those slums in Bairro dos Espelhos, I take the rap. If they suddenly rise to the top of the list of candidates for one of those concrete rabbit holes by moving from Mar de Prainhas to the new quarter, I take the rap. If they jump the line because one of them has connections with a none-too-bright member of our family, I take the rap. The walls everywhere are daubed with the words *pig, fascist, bastard, thief,* and they're all aimed at me, you understand? I'm your personal latrine, your bidet. I'm . . ." Rui Ludovice was too enraged to say any more, and was pacing so furiously up and down the room that he was almost out the door. Beside himself with rage.

Six sugar lumps, six coffees, six herbal teas, for each person to choose, with, on the side, six dark chocolate truffles the size of marbles. Six people sitting around the glass table. Six glasses of whiskey, for whoever wanted one. No alcohol for Rui Ludovice, who was seething with rage and exasperation, full of stomach ulcers, full of invisible curvatures of the spine and the base of the neck weighed down by those one hundred and ninety square miles of national territory and shedloads of ingratitude—"Rui, your pills, Rui . . ." The mayor lay down on the Spanish sofa, the cushions all in their proper places. True, one August morning

Regina Leandro had been found dead outside the gates of the Old Factory, when they were all away on vacation. No one would ever know why she had gone there. She had found herself in an ambulance with the doors open and had presumably staggered the one-and-a-bit miles to the factory gates, just so that each of them could amuse themselves imagining a reason. That was his mother-in-law's final gift to the world. The fact was, though, that while they had all gained something, why, even Milene had found a boyfriend, only he, the mere son-in-law, had really suffered. And now they were asking him to pull still more strings. Well, he wasn't going to do it. And since everything Rui Ludovice was saying was true, no one uttered a word. Rui was absolutely right. The storm outside appeared to have abated. They had all given their opinion on the matter, but no one could yet see a clear way ahead. Still, they couldn't leave without some concrete decision being made.

But how?

Calm, peace. An herbal tea, a whiskey, a cigarette, or nothing, they didn't need anything. Only to make a decision.

All of them silent, each with his or her own thoughts, his or her own self. Thinking, thinking. They had to decide:—To go ahead, as they had initially thought, or go back?

Aunt Ângela Margarida said—"Let's imagine a bisecting line between the two axes."

"What kind of bisecting line?" asked Dom.

"One that would see the Diamond remaining in our hands, until we decide otherwise, with none of us losing out, as well as allowing Milene to join the Matas, which is what she wants, and thus allowing us to remain true to the humanitarian principles that have always been so important to our family, but without sullying our good name. On the contrary, that bisecting line would be good for both parties, without us violating any of our principles. It would help Rui Ludovice at this difficult moment in his life, as well as act as a safeguard against everything that Dom fears might happen. Finally, to be quite clear, I'm not going to embrace Dom's depressing parable, no, we all have to accept each other just as we are, and Dom is what he is. That's his right. The bisecting line would work there too. It would, above all, be a way of respecting love, as Gininha wants . . ."

Six people, one room, two big bay windows looking out over the bay, various pacings back and forth, each person wondering on which side of the bisecting line their life would end up. Let's see, let's see what happens.

"But my dear sister-in-law"—said Dom, pleased. "How exactly would that work?"

No, she wasn't going to tell them what had happened, what she had plotted, what she had done, with courage and determination and willpower, coupled with an instinctive desire to save her tribe, like her mother up until she reached a certain age. After that, best not think about it. No, she wasn't going to tell them. She would only mention the idea as a hypothesis.

"My dear brothers and sisters"— said Ângela Margarida.

And she went on—"All this happened because we failed to give Milene the attention she needed, we failed to treat her as we should have, we left her to her own devices, thinking only of ourselves and our own lives, when she so richly deserved our affection and our devotion, along with everything else that was her due. Milene is an entirely benign person who loves us dearly. An innocent creature who never did us any harm. Any harm came from her father, not her. All this . . ."

Rui Ludovice, eyes closed, was listening to his wife. *Angelita, Angelita* . . . Action outwardly inactive, but inwardly active, totally focused. All of them totally focused.

———

"Let's suppose, for example, that Milene was unable to have children. Would that not provide the necessary bisecting line?"

Ângela Margarida, in her blue woolen suit, looking at them, seeing them all, seeing each of them considering their own interests and their own points of view, to the left and right of that line. Whether the end result would prove beneficial for each and every one of them.

Alda Maria said—"This isn't really something that concerns me, of course, but I'm sure we wouldn't lose anything by finding out the truth. At first glance, it does seem rather a wild hypothesis, but it's worth a try. Who knows? That would also resolve the problem of Milene's over-fondness for our son João Paulo. Why, only yesterday Lavinia phoned me from Massachusetts. Apparently his voice is still on her answering machine, and Milene, it seems, leaves a message for him every day. A completely crazy fixation. When I think of the trouble we had trying to keep those two apart . . . The proof that João Paulo has now forgotten about her is that he moved nearly a year ago and has never once phoned her. If he had, he would have given her his new number . . . And I'm certainly not going to be the one to give it to her . . ."

"Oh, poor Milene!" shrieked Aunt Gininha.

Her husband looked at her—*Sit down, Buggy! On the ground . . .*

Aunt Gininha didn't hear a thing, but she lowered her eyes, took out a handkerchief, and began to weep copiously. The square piece of cloth stretched between her two hands changed color.—"Poor Milene, making those phone calls, thinking she was talking to João Paulo. That's just too much, too much . . ." She got to her feet. Gininha, still girlishly elegant, still very beautiful. You could understand why even now, twenty-year-old men walked past her and said, "*Wow!*" Gininha was genuinely shocked at the limbo to which they had consigned the young person for whom she, Gininha, felt real respect. Shocked by the deceit they were practicing on Milene. Why hadn't Alda Maria told Milene she was phoning the wrong number? Why? Gininha crumpled up her handkerchief. How perverse of Alda Maria. It really pained her that they should treat Milene like that.

But Dom wanted to know more. He interrupted his wife. He hated sentimentality, hated soggy handkerchiefs pressed to tear-filled eyes.

"Oh, stop it, will you?"—he said to Gininha. Then, addressing the others—"So how would you find out something like that? I mean, whether she is or isn't fertile"—Uncle Dom Silvestre waiting for an answer. Without which there could be no bisecting line. Would Ângela Margarida take her to the clinic? Carry out some examinations? Why was she even mentioning this as a possibility? Generally speaking, it was assumed that women were fertile and black men extremely fecund. The Leandro family would soon have a whole nest of half-breeds. Not that he cared. If it happened, it happened. He had seen precisely where the human race was heading when he decided to escape from Johannesburg. And he'd come back to Portugal with almost nothing, mind, just because he didn't want to be there to see what was about to happen, in a land he had thought perfectly safe. The world was a mess. But what did he care? Anyway, did Ângela Margarida have any basis for such a supposition?

They had all grasped that the "bisecting line" depended on that. Just that. All pacing had stopped. No one moved. Even Uncle Rui Ludovice had sat up now on the Spanish sofa, his eyes fixed on his wife, Ângela Margarida. She was sitting very upright on her Interlübke chair. She wasn't going to say anything. Her lips were sealed. Her herbal tea in its cup, the cup resting on her knees emerging from beneath her blue woolen skirt. Opposite her, Afonso Leandro, the lawyer, in a dark suit and light-colored tie, upper half and lower half perfectly coordinated. Afonso took a step toward her.

"Ângela Margarida, where exactly is our niece right now?"

She felt afraid then of the living room door, so large, so transparent, so impossible to monitor. She stood up and went to check that no one was there—"Lower your voice."

"Ângela Margarida?"

She sat down again. Afonso Leandro, her brother, was standing immediately in front of her; he had a deeply receding hairline, well, he was a ladies' man after all, sickening really that baldness should be so directly related to the hormonal system, there were, after all, treatments for hair loss, but did he bother? Had he ever had an implant? Massages? No. Just women and horses, two sides of the same coin. He was standing in front of her, as brutish and arrogant as an obdurate old patriarch. She sat down. He pointed an accusing finger at her—"Ângela Margarida—you've had her spayed, haven't you?

"You have, haven't you?

"You've had her spayed!"

She leapt up from her chair to confront him—"You've always been so foulmouthed, always the first to resort to crude language. Always the same, always . . ."

"Tell us the truth, Ângela Margarida . . ."

He was insistent, threatening, standing in the middle of the room, strong and erect, chest thrust forward. The possible bisecting line made suddenly impossible. Rui Ludovice closed his eyes. Alda Maria folded her arms. One stray lock from her lacquered helmet of hair came adrift and floated in the air. Dom Silvestre began to laugh, although this was hardly the moment for loud guffaws, however tempting, so instead he leaned back against a sideboard, chuckling to himself. Shaking his head. Now he'd seen everything. He was stunned. Gininha took out her handkerchief again and began to shed yet more tears. She wasn't quite sure she had understood, but she had grasped the general idea. She didn't know if it had already happened or was about to, but it was clearly only a matter of time. As for Milene, the facts seemed irreversible. What would their mother say if she were still alive? Gininha began sobbing. Ângela Margarida waited for that first moment to pass. Afonso Leandro slumped down on the sofa immediately behind him. On the table beside him was a glass of William Lawson's whiskey and a few heavy-bottomed glasses. A bucket of ice, some tongs, fizzy water, and still water. He couldn't decide. A glass? The bottle? Ice? Nothing?—Ângela Margarida went over and poured him a drink. Neat whiskey, given the situation, to burn his lips and clear his head. One day, in the not-too-distant future, he would praise her courage. Now, though, she wanted them to understand that you can't reap the benefits of something if you haven't done your share of the work. It was quite wrong to share in something good without also sharing in its darker side. Anyway, this wasn't quite how she had imagined the supper, but since it was the way things had gone, fine, she wanted them to share the burden of her silence, in exchange for the pain involved in making that decision and carrying it out entirely on her own. She still felt very alone and isolated, a slender palm tree on the beach, battered by the desert wind.

No one spoke. It was raining.

"How many people know about this?" asked Afonso, as if returning very wearily from some faraway place.

"Two nurses and Seabra, the clinic's director. All silent as the grave . . ."—said Ângela Margarida.

It was still difficult, just like that, to grasp the advantages and disadvantages of that bisecting line. Very difficult, even impossible.

The time came for everyone to return to their respective homes, each carrying their own sack of silence, to be viewed from various angles but never untied, in the knowledge that once the knot had been pulled tight, a double knot and two round hitches, that secret would become something precious, of inestimable value. Six arms, six right hands, six heads, six hearts. Six closed mouths. Closed forever. None of them must ever speak of the matter, but if ever they did, they must do so in a whisper so soft that the words would die upon reaching the threshold of their lips. Because the matter had never existed. We were gathered together tonight precisely because nothing had happened or existed. And what had happened, although nonexistent in the light of day, had been for the best. After all, what *had* happened? They had merely improved on God's imperfect handiwork. We, silent as God, correcting, with our own human silence, his all-too-imperfect work. If our mother were alive, in these difficult times, she would be on our side. I'm sure of it.

Good night.

Even Uncle Dom said—"Good night, Angelita."

Outside, the ramp leading up to the condominium was wet and glinting after the only storm of the year, so out of place in the spring. For the moment, the rain had stopped. The four gleaming cars silently leaving the grounds. And standing there, looking out over the vast bay, where the lights from the quay were mere dots bobbing on the water, Rui Ludovice was discovering the immense potential of that delicate situation. On the one hand, delicacy and vulnerability, and on the other, potential. Astonished at his wife, in whom he recognized a rare talent. His debt to her was immeasurable. The whole family's debt was incalculable.

In the dishwasher, six sets of cutlery, six bowls, six dinner plates, six pudding plates, six glasses of every kind, six goblets, six saucers, six cups. Six. In the laundry basket, six linen table mats, six napkins, and a pile of other necessary things that had never made it to the table. Mixed up with them, six surprises, six griefs. In the trash can especially, six fish bones, six boneless heads. Six secrets inside six hearts. Six. Ângela Margarida let out a sigh. Her husband, standing, arms flung wide, between two doors, in the spacious panoramic living room on the tenth floor, asking— "How is she?"

"She's still there. She's fine."

The following morning, the late rain was still singing on the windowpanes.

The Wind Whistling
in the Cranes

Postscriptum

TWO YEARS LATER, THE CEREMONY WOULD BE A DISCREET affair. At that point, I still didn't know anything. They sat me with the white women. The church had room for as many as sixty people, but there were only about forty there. The black women were sitting in the row in front. Their dresses sparkled and they had veils and feathers on their hats. We wore hats with wide brims. Mine formed a kind of cone of shade that protected me down to my knees. And meanwhile I still didn't know anything. I was just delighted because that day, Milene, dressed as a princess, was going to take Antonino Mata as her husband, and our whole family was there, together. Yes, it had all come as a huge surprise to me. What's more, I'd just arrived and hadn't yet had the chance to speak to Milene. Not only had I traveled halfway around the world, but mine would be a lightning visit. As in, flying in one day and leaving three days later. And now there I was, sitting in my appointed seat. I couldn't wait for Milene to appear, but it would be a while before I heard the rustle of her dress. It was Easter. Everything was filled with light: the light streaming in through the high windows making even the walls shine brightly. The flowers were pink roses and canary-yellow carnations. The Church of Santa Maria do Mar was near the bay, and its statue of the Virgin Mary, rather than resembling the usual Lady of Sorrows, was a flamboyant figure with the mouth of a young Venus, rescuing sailors from the waves. The day was blue and white, the vestments were gold, the altar cloths freshly washed, and the cruets glinted in the sunlight. And I knew absolutely nothing.

Glory—I thought.

And even before Uncle Afonso had come into view, with Milene on his arm, I pictured the three of us when we were little, hurtling down the Estrada das Brisas to Kilometer 44 on our skateboards. She was five years older than us. She was taller than us and her feet were two sizes bigger, but she played with us anyway, just as if we were all the same age. Wonderful afternoons.—I was sitting with the white women, immediately behind the black women, and feeling so happy as I remembered us racing down the road. At the time, João Paulo and I must have been about eight, and she would have been twelve or thirteen. Her knees turned inward and she never got the hang of skateboarding. We were always faster than her. Then she'd abandon her skateboard and come sprinting down the road to catch up to us. João Paulo would shout—"*You lose, you lose, you put both feet on the ground . . .*" And Milene, thrilled to have competed in a race she had lost, would shout— "*Yes, I lose, I lose . . .*" We had both realized, by then, how desperately she wanted to be included. We couldn't put it into words, but we sensed it. João Paulo, however, struggled to deal with the feelings it stirred up in him and told her to go away. Then he went after her, tentatively, calling her *sis*, and to our astonishment she came back. She came back to us as if nothing had happened. It was as if she were saying, *Come on, come on, let's do it again, so I can lose again.* Yes, I remembered. How she used to talk to her skateboard—"*Right, behave yourself this time, or I'll kill you . . .*" Even if I'd had to fly in and out on the same day, I would have come to Valmares. Milene had found someone to marry. And I'd already caught a glimpse of him, very upright, very serious, in a dark gray suit with hints of silver.

But I knew absolutely nothing.

I would begin to find out more throughout the day, throughout the afternoon. However, at that moment, as Uncle Afonso was walking down the aisle, arm in arm with Milene, her face covered by a veil, a custom I thought had gone out of fashion, her face no more than a ghostly shadow because someone had applied too much pale makeup, yes, at the same time as all that, I was thinking about the three of us, during *the best summer of our lives,* when we went out in Guinote's boat and spent the mornings exploring the streams, the tiny continents, the islands of mud, João Paulo rooting around in the swampy ground, collecting sea creatures in a bucket, while she and I stretched out, doing nothing at all, at either end of the boat. We were older than her by then. She must have been almost twenty. There was no need to talk. We understood one another. On the way back, João Paulo would say— "This is so good, so good . . . We'll be together forever, never to be parted. For the rest of our days . . ." And she'd shout—"Awesome!" And I'd ask—"How long will that be?" And João Paulo would answer—"For at least as long as we're alive . . ." We were fifteen. Then I'd ask—"So one day we're going to be dead?" No, never. We had seen three tragic losses in our family, but we didn't believe in death. At that age, if we had believed in death, we couldn't have carried on living. Then Milene, who, by then was already younger than us, would say—"Don't talk about that, or I'll jump into the dirty water and go away, I'll go away . . ." João Paulo would move closer to Milene and stroke her hair—"You silly-billy. *Never* means we'll be together forever, for our whole lives, and our lives will never end. *They'll never end . . .*" The three of us said it again and again.

Those were the words I was hearing when a guy sitting at an old and slightly out-of-tune organ began to play very loudly, and the little church filled with white light and music. I looked. Her body was still the same shape—her back too arched, her hips too thin, her neck too long. They had pulled her hair back too tightly and it didn't suit her. I would rather they had left it loose. It was a good thing I'd come. No matter what happened, the three of us knew that we had loved one another. For a long time, we formed an island where not even Grandma Regina could set foot. Now Milene had made her way past us, long skirt trailing on the floor. Behind me, the groom. Yes, there he was. At that moment, I could see Antonino Mata arm in arm with a sturdy woman in dark blue, but I didn't yet know her name was Felícia. I would find out later on.

Yes, they must have practiced the steps, but now there was a hesitation; the groom had stopped in his tracks. He was holding on to a pair of white gloves and didn't know where to put them. It was as if someone had suddenly thrust two anesthetized doves into his hands. I noticed he had on a pale gray silk tie, and a pin set with a red gemstone. If he weren't so skinny he'd be a good-looking guy. Yes, a discreet ceremony. The children were dressed like grown-ups and none of them moved or even opened their mouths. And I was thinking of the days when João Paulo would tell Milene to memorize phrases. João Paulo's theory was that Milene needed to help herself to other people's words and then use them as her own. That she ought to train her memory, otherwise she wouldn't pass a single subject in ninth grade. But João Paulo was having her memorize things that made no sense to her. He'd say—"You have to learn, you have to learn intelligent phrases by heart. For example, if someone asks you to talk about thought and you don't know anything about thought—" And I'd say—"João Paulo, no one's going to ask Milene to talk about thought . . ." We were at university by then and Milene was at secondary school, but she still hadn't finished ninth grade. On those hot sunny days, when the exams were approaching, she used to sleep through her classes. But he insisted—"For example, you can learn from Novalis that the thinking organs are Nature's genitals . . ." Milene learned these and other similar phrases by heart. The maid overheard once and went to tell Grandma Regina, who called for her son Afonso Leandro. The phrases were taken as proof that we cousins were developing an inappropriate relationship. So they all conspired to separate us. No one could understand our understanding. "Together forever, never to be parted, for the rest of our days?"—asked Milene. Yes, for the rest of our days, meaning forever, for all eternity. I was thinking about that as I sat in the church, having come back specially for this important moment in Milene's life.

João Paulo wasn't there.

Glory . . .—I thought.

That was about the only word I knew in the rites of the Catholic Church. But then the ceremony began and I was sitting with the white women, one row behind the black women. At least, I'd been told that this was the arrangement. And I had noticed too that every part of that discreet ceremony had been carefully planned, enough to make me wonder if it really was a wedding ceremony and not a shot from a movie, but, at that point, all

I could think about was João Paulo's voice on the telephone, two weeks before, the same old João Paulo, saying—"Have you heard? There's something strange happening between *your* family and the third-wave people?" No, but I had just found out about a romance between Milene, our cousin Milene, and Antonino Mata, a widower and the brother of someone called Janina Mata King, a singer who was the focus of much enthusiastic discussion in Newark's Portuguese newspapers. And in a few weeks' time they were getting married, the way people used to get married in the past. But that was all. And João Paulo had said—"It can't be true. I know what they're like, they must be forcing Milene to do it. I'm seeing the whole movie play out from a distance:—They're going to marry her off to that guy just for the multiracial wedding photos . . . Yes, I bet that's what they're planning . . . I knew there'd be a crime in that family sooner or later . . . I'm going over there, I want to see for myself what's going on . . . I'll get to the bottom of it . . . Yes, I'll go right now . . ." He was still the same old João Paulo, though now he was studying the role of chance in mathematical calculations, when we had all expected him to specialize in some area of philosophy. Or was it the same thing? A fierce intelligence. Harvard, yes, it would have to be Harvard. He wasn't there yet, but he was on his way. Always, always the same old João Paulo. Exhausting. Calm down, João Paulo. People say you're studying a discipline that isn't even in the dictionary, called stochastic calculus. Is that true? What does it even mean? Stay where you are, don't get worked up.—But at that moment, I could see Milene, her back turned, looking like a highly decorated dove, next to Antonino Mata, who was dressed in dark gray silk with hints of silver, at noon on that luminous Easter Sunday, and I felt a stirring deep in my soul, a feeling I held on to beneath my straw-colored hat, because the organ music was still playing in the air and I knew absolutely nothing.

———

It's true, I saw everything and heard everything, feeling really pleased, without knowing that a dinner had taken place two years before at which Aunt Ângela Margarida, sitting next to her husband, Uncle Rui Ludovice, had mentioned a hypothetical bisecting line that would make everyone in the world much happier. I didn't know about the fish, or the salads, or the chocolate truffles, all thrown in the trash along with the bones, since Aunt Ângela Margarida's revelation had only come after dessert. Although it was less of a revelation and more of a correct guess on the part of Uncle Afonso, whose bronzed bald head was visible during the ceremony, above everyone else's, in the front row. Uncle Afonso wasn't especially tall, but his equestrian posture gave him a straight back and supple limbs. And I didn't know either that on the day after that lightning-filled night, everyone had begun to take action.

Or rather, I didn't know that one person had taken action that very same night. I'm talking about Dom Silvestre. Now there he was, next to Aunt Gininha, who, like me, was discreetly attired, in a wide-brimmed hat the same color as mine. My aunt far taller, far more elegant than me, with her girlish dark hair, and meanwhile Dom, in his handsome mouse-brown suit, seemed to have a tic in his left leg, which wouldn't stop twitching. Sitting between my aunt's long, slender legs and the trembling leg of my uncle, Bruno José seemed to have grown up a lot. And, to return to the subject of that stormy night: of course, I had no idea that Uncle Dom had been the first to act.

I found out later, from a reliable source, that the rain had continued falling all night, as it does after a thunderstorm, washing away all trace of sulfur, and when they arrived home in their separate cars, Dom Silvestre had shouted to Aunt Gininha—"Turn the fax machine on . . ." And then right away, without even sitting at his desk, he had said—"Write this down—*Senhor Van de Berg, the situation has changed. Please get in touch. Dom Silvestre Development and Extractive Industries, Dom Silvestre Construction.*" He was in such a hurry that he demanded the fax be sent right away, wanting the message to fly through the night and land silently before the Dutchman's sleeping eyes, so that the moment he opened them its contents would be revealed. And the moment my uncle opened his own eyes the next morning, the machine had announced an incoming message. He waited. A tongue of paper came spooling out with a response, painstakingly written in Portuguese—"*Wait for me on the telephone. I'm flying to the North of Africa. Maybe we meet in Portugal. It depends on the travel agent. They are very annoying. My best wishes, Piet van de Berg.*"

That day, Uncle Dom wouldn't have gone to the Lentiscal Quarry. He had three eye-watering fines to negotiate, but there was plenty of time for that. And three local councils owed him thousands of millions of escudos, all aboveboard and sure to be repaid. As far as he was concerned, everything was fine, everything was under control. He could wait at home, playing with the Rottweilers. Perfectly content. And at this moment too, here and now, lit up by the pale spring sun flooding into the church to celebrate the glory of the Resurrection, filtering through the rainbow-colored windows, Uncle Dom was perfectly content. Apart from his left leg, which couldn't keep still, as if part of his soul were frantically pedaling and his knee were the visible proof. Just then, I heard a great many voices saying "*Glory, Glory* . . ." but I thought perhaps it was my soul. And then I looked over my shoulder and saw an extremely tall man, a giant compared to us, with very light blond hair and a boyish face, next to another, similar but rather less gigantic man, and the giant's name was Piet van de Berg, only I didn't know who they were or what peo-

ple with such Bavarian complexions were doing at our cousin
Milene's wedding.

I would find out later, once I'd decided against going back to my
student accommodation, to that room with the bushiest fir tree on
the university campus reaching up to its window. Yes, I would find
out that six days after the dinner of trout and flaked almonds, and
as a result of the bisecting line, Uncle Afonso, Uncle Dom, and
the largest of the Dutchmen, Piet van de Berg, had flown over the
Diamond once again. The late rain was falling softly. But despite
the weather, the pilot sped off in that direction, circling Mar de
Prainhas twice in a kind of double embrace. For a few moments,
the Dutchman had felt rather glum. It was the monotony of it
all. There were days when the rain turned the whole World into
a washed-out Flemish landscape. But Uncle Dom had reassured
him about the climate here, saying it only rained the necessary
amount. There were just fifteen rainy days a year in Valmares.
Which meant three hundred and fifty days of unadulterated summer. Yes, flying over the area, they saw the birds all huddled up on
the sand, waiting for the weather to improve so they could take to
the skies in eye-catching flocks. The Dutchman's suspicions had
presumably faded by the evening. After all, they must have faded
if he then went on to attend the ceremony. And there was Felícia
Mata too in the front row, sometimes sitting down, sometimes
standing up, with a blue feather in her blue felt hat, and a navy-
blue satin suit, but on the day the helicopter had swooped down
over the Diamond for a second time, even though it was raining,
she had frozen with fear—What if Ana Mata was right? What if
there really was a trap around the corner, a plot against them all?
What if that was the meaning of her telegraph-operator dream?—
It had been a very anxious time. Now, however, there were no
traps anywhere. God had brought everyone together under the

same vaulted roof. The higher and more distant he was, the closer he brought us together. And there we all were.

In other words, since he was feeling rather melancholy after the helicopter ride, Piet Van de Berg had rented a vehicle so he could visit the factory himself. When he arrived, the afternoon rain was lashing at the eleven palm trees, and the Dutchman, seeing them dance this way and that, had felt a kind of tropical hope in his heart, with none of the tropics' sad complications. There was no sign of any cars or people, and the factory gates were unlocked. The railway lines, which the rain had stripped clean of earth, sketched out a zigzag path that seemed both pointless and the promise of a dream come true. Van de Berg didn't even understand what dream it was that had gripped him. Logic and more logic, calculations and more calculations, and suddenly the decision came down to two steel rails with no possible use, gleaming in the rain. Unbelievable. Yes, thirty acres of land, including just over half a mile of coastline, an area of almost four and a half thousand square feet, from north to south, three-quarters of the total area made up of boggy ground, neither land nor water, with an old factory in the middle, and yet it was those parallel metal lines that decided him. Negotiations would have resumed that very evening. And there were Felícia's sisters in the front row, dressed almost identically, in very simple hats, with no veils or feathers, just pale-green-dyed straw. Their rounded figures squeezed into their suits. On that other day, however, the day of the helicopter, the two women, wearing scruffy old clothes, had looked outside and then hurried into the courtyard—"Felícia, Felícia, the English guy's still there . . . Look at him, he definitely wants to buy the place, you can see it in his eyes. What's going to happen to us?"—Six days after the dinner with the trout and the bisecting line. Just six. Meaning that six days later, my two uncles and the Dutchman had gone for another dinner in the restaurant at the Luxor. At the very last minute.

The Dutchman had come straight to the point—"So, are the problems with your sisters all sorted now?" In the name of *Van de Berg Real Estate, Rotterdam*, he also wanted a guarantee that the site would be uninhabited, that is, with no people inside, eight working days before the contract was signed. Point number one. No people inside. Point number two, *Van de Berg Real Estate* would need a guarantee that another floor could be built on top of the factory roof. No, not a second floor, just a floor on top, which was quite different. If that was possible, then great, *geweldig, geweldig,* to use a Dutch word. The rest had all been in eloquent Portuguese. It was just the three of them at dinner. The rain was streaming down the windowpanes and it had grown dark far too early for a day in the middle of spring. Uncle Dom had said—"Very good, Senhor Van de Berg. No people inside and two floors is what you're saying. But after those two floors, anything else would mean an extra effort on our part. And anything else we can get you, acting in our own personal capacity, on an informal basis, will also need to be rewarded, in a personal capacity . . ."

At this point, the Dutchman had felt rather vulnerable. He didn't always understand the subtleties of the Portuguese language; still, this was what he had gleaned:—He would buy the place for however much, with planning permission for another floor above the roof, and that was all he would need, because there were the birds, the seahorses, the dunes and the prevailing winds, and the lakes with their tall reeds. But if the owners managed, at some future date, to use their influence to extend the planning permission, they would ask for considerably more. On an informal basis. And Uncle Dom would have said, at that dinner two years before, at table thirteen at the Luxor—"Yes, in a nutshell . . . You see, there are ways around these things." And Piet van de Berg had thought for a bit—"We'll need to look at how it might affect the birds, the lakes, and the dunes. I'll have to speak to my advisers . . ." The Dutchman taken aback. So the idea was that if, when it came to signing the contract, approval had been granted, say, for another six floors above the roof, the price would be considerably higher. But how much higher? And informally, and paid in what currency, and by what means? And who to? And where?— Piet van de Berg thinking very hard, moving the food around on his plate and then pushing it aside. He had concluded—"Yes, this is what it's like with Turks and Arabs too . . ." He would have to speak to his business partners and bring his lawyer along to the Luxor. And then there were the birds, they might not want to keep nesting there if they found some tall buildings in their way. Birds are like airplanes in that respect, they like landing with the runway in sight. Yes, they can even nosedive if necessary, but they get uneasy if anything's blocking their view. That's how birds are. But this, Piet van de Berg understood, was just what it was like doing business with Turks, Greeks, and Arabs. The Mediterranean way. Fine. Or not fine at all.

There was a sense of danger approaching, as they sat in the Luxor. Afonso could smell it. He was the galloping, fence-jumping type and he came to the rescue just in time. He said—"That's my brother-in-law's idea, he was imagining a modern city springing up there. But Senhor Van de Berg would prefer a kind of rural retreat for solitary types, nature lovers . . . And I agree, I'd prefer to have just two floors myself, showing total respect for the birds, the coastline, the sandbank, the palm trees, and the high mound where the old-fashioned cars and the Chrysler used to park, and where the carts used to pull in carrying firewood and drinking water. Yes, Senhor Van de Berg, please, go ahead and do just that . . ." And Uncle Dom had been rather alarmed to see the

Diamond being cut in half. Now, however, two years had passed, and everything was decided. There would be six more floors above the roof. Uncle Rui had been very persuasive. Van de Berg had agreed. Yes, the Dutchman had concluded that there were plenty more paradises on Earth, and the money he'd soon make in Mar de Prainhas could be invested in another one. But considering that, why not go all the way and demolish the lot? Nothing could be simpler—It would take two weeks to prepare the blast, and then in fifteen seconds the Old Factory would implode. Since it was a listed building on protected land, this would have to be done secretly by an independent company with no ties to *Van de Berg Real Estate*. The three of them, sitting around the table, shook hands.

And so, on the day of the ceremony, all that remained of the *Fábrica de Conservas Leandro 1908* were the eleven palm trees, which hadn't suffered at all, their shocks of green hair blowing in the wind, standing in a line along the mound, which now ended sharply, vertically, sliced off like a loaf of bread. The buildings, through which those three human waves had passed, not to mention the tragedies of their owners over the course of a century, had been replaced by an enormous crater. Nothing was left. Uncle Dom was a minor partner, but still a partner, and the development was to be called Palm City and bear that Italian slogan. A wet crater stretching as far as the eye could see. The building work hadn't yet started. Inside Santa Maria do Mar, someone said, or many people said, though I thought it was only my soul—"*Glory! Glory! My body lay beneath a stone!*"

Just then Aunt Gininha pressed her elbows very close to her sides, her shapely rear end encased in her skirt. Milene there at the front, not turning around. I pictured her heavy, drooping eyelids. Through the veil I could see that her earlobes were unadorned.

Why wasn't she wearing earrings, when she liked them so much? Didn't she like them anymore? Wouldn't her aunt have advised her? Maybe not.

I didn't even know that, after the dinner at Aunt Ângela Margarida's house, Aunt Gininha had begun neglecting her teaching duties. Ever since that rainy night, she spent all her time in bed. Uncle Dom and Aunt Gininha's bed was so wide that a normal loving couple could have slept in between the two of them. My aunt now curled up in a corner of the bed with her knees sticking out, as if wishing she were somewhere else. Maybe she was with the mother-of-pearl biologist, or perhaps the dozy pilot who sang that Ana Latu lullaby into her ear. Only she and God knew what she was thinking. Her problem was this—Gininha thought her mother's will was missing something. It said that Milene's share was to be kept separate, so that it could be safeguarded. But what share?

It was up to her to enforce the will. And she and her siblings had never reached an agreement, because they thought that all Milene should get was Kilometer 44. My aunt, the executor, thought Milene ought to receive some of the profits from the sale of the Old Factory. But according to her siblings, no profits should go to their nieces, those two symmetrical daughters of their two deceased brothers, José Carlos and José Eduardo, God rest their souls, when they, the two girl cousins, in their own separate ways, had been unwilling or unable to lift a finger. They hadn't even taken an interest. And so Gininha didn't know what to do, torn as she was between her generous heart and her practical head, which agreed with Dom Silvestre's logic. Everyone knew how her voice turned into the voice of her husband when she argued like him, that the secret pleasures of commerce now had their bastion in Aunt Gininha, who never used to take an interest in such things. But at that point, she had stayed in bed for two weeks, wrapped in resignation's sweet embrace, and meanwhile, outside, the month of April seemed to have merged too soon with a very muggy July, the warm rain rotting the hay and giving people terrible colds. Aunt Gininha had stayed at home, pretending to have one of these colds. She moved so little that her legs stopped being elegant and became merely thin. Uncle Dom stood over her and asked—"So, where were we? Are you going to talk to your niece or aren't you? And tell me—did that brainless oaf Ludovice really go around there after your mother died and say, right in front of the girl, that Villa Regina was worth nothing?" Gininha shifted her knees even farther out of bed and thought of what they had done to Milene. She imagined the Clínica das Salinas and saw Dr. Seabra walking toward Milene, putting her to sleep, and then she couldn't bear it any longer. She just said—"Oh, what have we done to her, what have we done to her . . . ?" But, like João Paulo, I was living a long way away. And even when I came back, of my own free will, I still knew absolutely nothing.

I didn't know that Aunt Gininha, at Uncle Dom's request, had set off down the road in the silver Honda. At Villa Regina, the garden-cum-microclimate was bursting with brightly colored hydrangeas and ferns unfurling their croziers. The walnut tree was thick with branches, and the ivy had crept over the wall, covering it from top to bottom. A fragment of a different climate flourishing right there, where mosquitoes the size of birds hovered above the puddles of rainwater. Perhaps this was why Gininha hadn't noticed the gray van parked outside. Gininha rang the bell, someone opened the door, and in she went, but, on entering the living room, she realized that Milene wasn't alone. Once again she was sitting on a sofa, holding hands with Antonino Mata.

Antonino stood up. Milene too. It was impossible to speak to Milene about the will, the house, the factory, the signatures, and all the rest of it, because she and Antonino were holding hands. They weren't even listening to music, which would have been more natural. Milene wasn't wearing her hat, or her sunglasses, or her purse. She had on a very short skirt, white tights, and matching white trainers, reducing her thirty years of age by exactly half. And he was wearing the same shoes as her, the two of them connected by their white trainers. It was a weekday, during working hours, and he was there with her. Their hands clasped. "Sorry, sorry . . ." Aunt Gininha had returned to the Honda. Back at home, she admitted defeat to Dom Silvestre—"Dom, really, I couldn't do it, I knew the moment I saw them. It would be a crime . . ." But what was a crime to Aunt Gininha? Or a crime to Dom Silvestre?—Now, on that Easter Sunday, Aunt Gininha was staring straight ahead, shielded by her yellow wide-brimmed hat, which matched the yellow trim on the Church vestments. Everything seemed fine.

In the pew in front, next to the three black women and various children of the same color, who were all sitting together, was Alda Maria, João Paulo's mother and Uncle Afonso's ex-wife. Isabel the fairy princess wasn't with Uncle Afonso. I would later find out that my uncle had just successfully handled the divorce case of another young woman, who was much prettier than Isabel and also had the advantage of not knowing how to ride, which made her far more appreciative of my uncle's equestrian skills. Marta Débora, that was the name of my uncle's new plaything. Just then, a choir was beginning a divine recitation. Buzzing around my ears, I heard—"*Resurrexit! Resurrexit!*" But I couldn't be sure it wasn't just my soul. Anyway, I found out later that Aunt Alda Maria had telephoned Aunt Ângela Margarida that very same week. Both taking a position vis-à-vis the bisecting line.

Aunt Alda Maria, in the week that followed the trout supper, hadn't so much as tied back her hair. She had let it hang down over her forehead and ears. This aunt was desperately worried that word would get out about what had happened at the clinic. Despite her formal attire, João Paulo's mother was rather out of date when it came to technological advances in medicine, and knew nothing whatsoever about the effects of keyhole surgery. Yes, poor Aunt Alda Maria still believed that a minor procedure like that, which a doctor could merrily sing his way through, would leave visible scarring or aftereffects. So thought my thoroughly out-of-date aunt, who bore a striking resemblance to Margaret Thatcher. The poor lady foresaw an enormous catastrophe if Milene ever figured it out, or the Matas, or the party leaders, or the newspapers, or the population at large. And if her son João Paulo found out as well, then the catastrophe would be complete. In fact, the whole world could find out and the catastrophe would still be bearable. But if João Paulo found out, if he guessed, if he suspected, that would be the end. He, who always used to say, ever since he began to understand human nature, that a crime would one day be committed in the Leandro family. Aunt Alda Maria panicking, and meanwhile two weeks had passed and nothing had happened. Quite the opposite. People were saying they'd seen Antonino Mata and Milene Leandro holding hands, at the Banana and the Pomodoro, and even Mãos Largas, or outside the nursery when they were picking up the children. Then, with one of her sudden flashes of lucidity, my aunt had said over the phone—"Are you listening, Ângela Margarida? If I were you, I'd marry them off right away. I'd marry them off before all this blows up in our faces . . ." And then adding, with a flash of good sense—"You could even film the wedding—it might come in handy, with things looking so bad for Rui . . ." Ângela Margarida had replied—"What an idea . . ." And this was how, two years before, the seed of this ceremony was planted. But now I was sitting among them and quite honestly I never even guessed, unlike João Paulo. A crystalline voice was singing a solo, because there was a choir in the little church. The voice sang—"*Lord, oh my Lord. You were beneath a stone, the stone rolled aside and you were resurrected . . .*" The voice was coming from above, from on high.

I had been seated with the white women, the women like me, with my cousins Joana and Sabina and other people I knew whose names I didn't remember, but at the end of the row was a heavyset man who looked like Antonino Mata. Next to him was his wife. I would later find out that they were Maria da Conceição and Domingos Mata, whose thick, bushy hair must have stopped the people behind from seeing whatever was happening at the altar. That is, I began to realize that the seating plan wasn't so orderly after all. But I didn't look too closely; my hat meant I couldn't turn my head. When you're wearing a wide-brimmed hat, even the slightest head movement can attract attention.

If I could have looked, I'd have seen that the people I later knew as Heitor Junior and his wife Claudina had been placed at the other end of the row. From where I was, I couldn't see Heitor Senior with his crutches on the floor at his feet; I couldn't see where the friends from Bairro dos Espelhos were sitting, or the friends from America or France. What I saw very clearly, right in front of me, were the shoulders of the person with the blue hat, blue feather, and dark blue suit, shaking as if there were an earthquake. This, I knew, was Antonino Mata's mother.

I also found out that two years before, once the rains had disappeared and summer had begun, the postman came by with a letter from a lawyer. Felícia had a bad feeling about it. In her recurring dream, she was a man, who grew stronger and stronger, while the woman who followed her into the Ocean, in Praia, grew skinnier and skinnier. As if there were a kind of rule in the dream, whereby if one of them expanded then the other had to shrink. Only the previous night, in Felícia's dream, he, she, had become so huge that the Ocean waves had risen all the higher, and the woman, who by then was barely there, had disappeared. Felícia had woken up drenched in sweat; because what had he, she, done to that person to make her disappear? Her heart pounding, Felícia Mata had sat up in bed in her kitchen-bedroom and put her glasses on so she could see better. But it was the middle of the night, and the letter hadn't yet arrived. As soon as it came, she had torn open the envelope and started to read. She was right. A lawyer she had never heard of, but whose surname wasn't Leandro, was summoning her to his office, *to discuss a matter that concerns you* . . . Felícia was beginning to understand the situation. In real life and in the dream. She needed to speak to someone.

She spoke to Dilecta.

And together they had decided how to proceed—They wouldn't tell anyone, or ask anyone for a lift, instead getting up at dawn, waiting until everyone had left for work, and then taking a bus to Santa Maria de Valmares, to the address given in the letter. Which is what they did. And they were right. The lawyer was representing the whole Leandro family. The message was simple, like a ray of sunshine through a window:—They had six months to vacate the factory. Felícia had been expecting it. Her two hands heavy on her purse. Her purse pressing down on her lap. Not realizing the weight was all in her hands, she moved her purse aside. "Maybe so, but we wrote a letter . . ." She carried on. What letter? They had six months. It occurred to Dilecta to say—"Sir, now that my sister's son is involved with one of the heirs to the house, are you really going to throw us out? This wouldn't be happening if Dona Regina were alive . . ." And then, mistaking the man for the interests he represented, she had begun squaring up to the lawyer, who was still young and very well dressed. Calling him a thief.

Her sister needed calming down. The lawyer had asked Dilecta to leave the room, and then summed up for Felícia as follows:—It was all within the law. The Matas would quietly vacate the Old Factory buildings, which were about to be sold to a Dutch company, and return to Bairro dos Espelhos, applying immediately for the social housing the authorities were building across the road, and then, after two or three years, the four Mata families would be guaranteed accommodation. Simple as that. Felícia saying less and less. She had been to Hell and back more than once in recent times. Her son Gabriel, whom she had appointed as a kind of guardian, had gone off the rails, and no one even knew where he was. Janina's van had been seized by the police, shown on TV, and then taken to the scrapyard. Janina's singing was going well, though, he was becoming more and more successful, with an ever-larger band, and an ever-deeper wolflike howl, which made people call him a soul singer. He didn't sing in Portuguese anymore. The rhythm was unpredictable; just when she thought it was picking up, it would do the opposite, and vice versa. Even so, she would always say—"*Onward and upward, no holding back*," whenever he telephoned her. And then she would add, lowering her voice— "*'Bye, now, dear, and remember, steer clear of your brother . . .*" Yes, it had been a real blow. And then there was her mother Ana Mata, who didn't love her anymore, and who was getting old, and her son Antonino, who had fallen in love with the white girl, the owner of a fifth of their house, which would only bring more trouble. Yes, by now she'd seen it all, she'd made the trip to Hell and back several times. So Felícia had been brave enough to say— "You see, sir, the problem is that my widowed son is involved with a girl from that family. And the family wants revenge . . ."

The lawyer was a cautious man. He told her that wasn't true.

And he even did something he shouldn't have—he asked Dona Felícia Mata to look him in the eye. His own eyes wide open, so they could say more than his mouth—"What you and your family need to do is go back to the shantytown along with all the others. Then, once you're there, the mayor will sort something out. I'm not saying you'll be the first to be housed, but you'll be the seventh or eighth. Do you understand, Dona Felícia?" Yes, she understood. She had left that stylish office feeling as if she'd been punched in both eyes. She could barely see the pavement. She and her sister had to sit down outside a café to eat their cake. They weren't feeling good at all. Go back to Bairro dos Espelhos? They repeated these words the whole way home. The two sisters holding hands on the bus, to keep themselves from drowning. They had agreed not to say anything until they were ready to explain it all. They let the summer run its course. And only then did the pair set off for Bairro dos Espelhos.

Felícia's clothes were old and shabby. Dilecta's too. They hadn't bothered to change before leaving the house. That day, they would never have imagined that, a year and a half later, they'd be sitting in a dazzling white church, with the priest wearing pale vestments with gold trim, and that all around them would be heard—"*Oh! Oh! My Lord rose into the air, as soon as the stone had rolled aside!*" It was the voice of the soloist. The voice coming from the choir. Felícia, in her blue hat with its blue feather, her shoulders shaking from the sheer gravity of the moment. I was behind her, and that's when I realized I'd been wrong about the seating arrangement. No doubt thanks to my truly massive hat, I had failed to notice that Aunt Ângela Margarida was now sitting next to the mother of the groom, or that at the end of the row in front, in a dark blue suit was none other than her husband, Uncle Rui Ludovice. Even without seeing him from the front, I was sure he was wearing a red tie. *They weren't sitting there before*—I thought. *Where did they come from?* Yes, people were switching seats during that discreet ceremony, so discreet that you didn't even notice them switching. Only later did I begin to understand. My hat meant I couldn't turn my head. But eventually I realized there was a choreographer at work in that house of God.

I turned around.

Yes, there were only forty of us. At the back, like two enormous candles, were the Dutchmen, and both of them were smiling. Smiling happily over our heads. As well they might—two years before, they had said—"*Uninhabited, with no people inside . . .*" By then the problem wasn't the birds, the purple swamp hen, the white-capped heron; those animals were welcome to stay if they could, but otherwise they could go elsewhere, because there were other paradises on Earth. They'd just have to find them. Because the second point, about the number of floors and the secret demolition job, was all arranged. The problem was that the first requirement still hadn't been met, and this urgently needed to change. The urgency underlined by a second letter from the lawyer. And by then Dilecta and Felícia had finally gone to revisit Bairro dos Espelhos, in the same shabby clothes they'd been wearing at home.

The neighborhood women had crowded around them. The stout, the slim, as well as Flora, and the very old woman from Ana Mata's island. The men too. The Matas were moving back. My God, why were they doing that?—It was hard to hear what people were saying. They all took that tale of eviction as a personal slight, as a parable about life, about the struggle between rich and poor, between one race and another, and an attack on the love between Milene and Antonino, that mistreated, late twentieth century Romeo and Juliet. Surely it all came down to jealousy, because the Leandros might be rich, but they didn't have any singers in their family. And surely it would come out on television that Janina Mata King's family was being unfairly evicted. Yes, there were so many conclusions to be drawn that they all got tangled up, leaving no logical place on which to hang any one satisfying conclusion. But it was all arranged. The Matas would move into the houses of the first people who went to live in the social housing. Who would that be? No one knew yet, and there were so many people on the list. Masses of them. But if it was based on the order in which people applied, they could guess where they might end up living. The two sisters spent an October morning visiting the gray houses, which smelled of dead chickens and fried fish, with a few squirts of air freshener to take the edge off, going from door to door, visiting each and every one.

And so, on that October evening, Felícia and Dilecta had gathered everyone around the table to explain the situation. It was such a terrible shock that Conceição, that very night, had tried to kill herself with one of her husband Domingos' knives. The two sons had sat on the ground and wept. All the children had gone running out into the street. Sissi and Belisa had announced that they were leaving, and planned to cut off their braids and paint their nails, because their father, Heitor Junior, couldn't stop them from living their own lives now that this was going on. They refused to go back to those shacks in Bairro dos Espelhos. However temporary Felícia said it was, that it would all be worth it when they finally moved into a nice big house with taps everywhere, no one could imagine going back. They rebelled. They each looked for someone else to blame, and it wasn't long before they found a suitable whipping boy.

The most popular choice was Ana Mata.

Everyone blamed her. Their grandmother had seen the trap coming but had failed to describe it clearly enough. She had claimed to know everything but hadn't been able to stop it from happening. They spoke to her rudely, forgetting everything she had said, or even using her own words as evidence against her. That was in the early days, and then, around December, they had each begun to sort through their possessions. There was so much stuff that they didn't know how to choose. Domingos made three big piles—to sell, to take, and to leave right there, for the Dutchmen to destroy if they wanted. And then, as February drew to a close, Ana Mata made her decision.

It was precisely because of Ana Mata's decision that her daughter Felícia's shoulders couldn't stay still now, nor could her elbows, or her purse, or the handkerchief she was taking out. The choir was singing and the priest had looked over at the bride and groom; very soon, the priest would be able to marry them. The first part was over, and now they were waiting for the priest to decide that the moment had come. They were kneeling. The only one of us missing was João Paulo, who had threatened—"I need to go there, urgently . . ." Thank goodness he hadn't come.

Yes, Felícia had cried out very loudly, in a moment of silence— "*Oh! Yes, he came back to life just like he said he would and I didn't see . . .*" Repeating the celebrant's words in her nasal voice, and the priest all dressed in white and gold, those splendid Easter vestments. That afternoon, I would begin to learn a little about what had happened. Felícia would say, looking back, that this perfect moment was only possible because her mother had acted out the telegraph-operator dream in real life.

In the church, Felícia's shoulders were shaking because of Ana Mata's decision.

It had happened in early March. By then, the two dogs were both sick. A rich and sumptuous *cachupa* had been prepared but it tasted like a poor imitation of the real thing and nobody ate very much. Half of all their belongings had been sold and the satellite dish had been taken down, its giant white corolla laid on the ground. Turned on its head, the satellite dish looked like a bizarre artifact, something vomited up by a UFO. A hole developed in the roof where it used to be. Loose tiles had fallen into Felícia's kitchen-bedroom. Out in the courtyard, countless gadgets were scattered across the paving stones. A sea of objects they were leaving for the Dutchmen. Amid this great sea they were leaving behind, Ana Mata didn't have the courage to ask if her plastic armchair could go with them. "*Nha cautcha forrode di plástico?*" No, no, forget it, I'll find somewhere else to sit when we move . . . Oh! Forget it, forget the whole thing—she said in a different way, because she had said it in her own language.

And so, one chilly early morning, Ana Mata began to walk and walk. Although, of course, in the end she never told anyone about how she began to walk, crossing the field of slurry and the marshland, or following the path all the way to the dunes, where a few rickety little clam-fishing boats used to come in. At first people thought she had wanted to drag one of those boats into the waters of the Ria and sail all the way out to sea. And then came the realization. Ana Mata had wanted to do what the telegraph operator from Cidade da Praia had done, back in the forties or fifties, no one knew exactly when. People thought that must have been her plan, because she'd taken a proper packed lunch with her in a canvas bag. That is, she'd set off intending to return. To call on destiny for guidance, offering herself up, although without being swept away completely. But that wasn't what would happen.

Her daughters and grandchildren were feeling so sorry for themselves that they only realized the next day that the door to the little gray house was still open. The armchair in the usual

place, next to where the three rivers came together as one, perfumed by the morning showers. Then they had begun their search
and, two days later, they found her, half-buried in the boggy
ground, tangled up in a punctured rubber dinghy that had been
floating there for months, down stream after stream. She was still
holding the bag with her packed lunch inside. It was awful. Ana
Mata's crooked, spindly legs were the first thing they saw. Her
glasses were coated in mud, and as for her false teeth, they never
turned up. This was why Felícia Mata's shoulders didn't stop shaking throughout the ceremony, though she took care to muffle the
sound of her sobs. She was convinced that her mother's sacrifice
had paid off. She looked at the life all around her: yes, the results
were there for all to see.

"*Hallelujah, O hallelujah!*"—sang the voices of the choir, in the
Church of Santa Maria do Mar. I couldn't be sure it wasn't really
my soul returning from some faraway place. Back then, I didn't
even know that someone called Ana Mata had offered herself
up to the Ria to save her children from humiliation, as if such
a thing were possible. Had I known, perhaps my shoulders too
would have started to shake, and I would have felt in my purse
for a handkerchief of my own, and perhaps my hat would have
slid off my head. I don't know. But why not stir up a bit of confu-
sion in the mind, if clarity is always out of reach? What I found
out later was that things had changed. It began with Uncle Rui
Ludovice, the mayor, showing up at Ana Mata's funeral, and not
only him. His assistant and even his chauffeur were there as well.
This attracted a great deal of attention and gave the Mata family
some hope, especially the women. That morning, the cemetery
had been full. People were perched on the steps of the little stone
houses. Soon afterward, a message arrived. It turned out that the
Dutchman, Piet van de Berg, not only respected birds, purple
swamp hens, and white herons with feathered crests. He also,

as much as possible, respected human beings. In other words, he would allow the Mata family another two months to make their arrangements. He would sign the contract while there were still people inside. And then, in early summer, came the best news of all. News that would make it very difficult to separate the story of the family's salvation from Ana Mata's final voyage. But at this moment, the ceremony proper still hadn't begun. It was taking a while because every so often that delicate, almost angelic voice could be heard, suspended somewhere between beauty and death, singing on that luminous Easter Sunday—"*Lord! O Lord! You have returned!*"

How could I have known?

Uncle Rui was sitting next to Aunt Ângela Margarida, who was wearing a sky-blue suit and matching hat. Her hair was straight, and white earrings dangled from her earlobes. Then my uncle, a very tall man, turned around, and I could see for myself. His tie was indeed red against his dark blue suit, just like every politician's tie since the invention of television. Meanwhile, the ceremony was extraordinarily staid and economical. With nothing but the choir to fill the time. I thought the singing was coming from my own soul. And I swear to God, it only dawned on me then that there was a choreographer in the church. At that point, I didn't even know that the allocation of social housing had been so controversial. The Mata family were one of the last on the list, and the list of applicants had been made public. My uncle held a meeting with his personal staff, and the advisers had set things out in the following terms—What would be more damaging: for Uncle Rui to respect the law, meaning that the Matas wouldn't be housed for at least another two years, and he, Rui Ludovice, would go down in History as a strict, impartial legalist, or for Uncle Rui to bend the rules and take pity on these people with close ties to his family?

The advisers had gathered on the ninth floor of the Atrium Condominium. They thought and thought, and eventually concluded that it would be far more humane, and far more acceptable to the population of Valmares, the genuinely Portuguese population, to follow the principle that charity begins at home. Charity triumphing over justice, that higher form of charity, which, however hard you work toward it, is always out of reach. Yes, let's be charitable. And that was what happened. The Matas weren't the first, or the second, or the third, but they were the fourth to receive their brick-and-mortar houses, complete with running water and all the amenities, on the other side of the road. The sisters Felícia, Dilecta, and Germana had stepped into the new houses with smiles on their faces. Never again would they think about Ribeirinho da Praia. The telegraph-operator dream had worked, they were sure of it. This was what made Felícia's shoulders, at various points during the ceremony, resume their rhythmical trembling. And Uncle Rui, who was there as well, standing straight as a eucalyptus tree, had so far escaped all criticism.

In fact, things were going much better now than they had two years ago. His ulcer had healed slightly, and was now no larger than a shirt button. A measly little shirt button. But what I saw most of all were the colors and movements, and what I heard were the delicate canticles.

Now there was no one in between the mother of the groom, dressed in dark blue, and Aunt Ângela Margarida, dressed in pale blue. Their arms were touching. And through the gap between their hats, I could see Milene and Antonino Mata. The bright light in the church was unchanged, coming to rest on their heads. The ceremony seemed almost secret. The choreographer giving only the most discreet of signals. The priest, as smiling as the day itself, was talking to the bride and groom, asking them various banal questions. Which they answered so quietly we couldn't even hear them. It was as if they didn't want to say anything there, that they must have said it all elsewhere, and the priest smiling nonetheless, bringing the ceremony to a moment of rare intimacy, as if the Resurrection of Christ had been interrupted, and the priest himself were making love to the couple. The sun streamed in through the window.

In other words, when it came to Milene and Antonino Mata, I wouldn't learn anything for a long time. That would be the most difficult part to fathom. The most secret, the most intimate. But also the most necessary. And this was why I didn't go back to the campus where my twenty-eight-year-old intellect spent its time trying to impress the grown-ups. Just like that, I realized I knew nothing at all about what really mattered. And that I'd never find out if I went back to that campus protected by tall university trees. What mattered, I suddenly felt, was understanding what had happened right there. Because something had happened, I could tell just from looking at Antonino Mata. He was on the right-hand side of the church and I was on the left, so it was his face I could see, not Milene's. All I could see of Milene was her narrow body and full skirt, the veil drawn back from her face. They didn't kiss.

Thank goodness João Paulo hadn't come, that I'd managed to keep him in Massachusetts with the argument that he should stay put and not interfere, since for three years he'd taken no interest whatsoever in the person to whom he used to promise—*We'll be together forever, all three of us, for the rest of our days* . . . Was it just because he was no longer a teenager that his love had become so imperfect? What right did João Paulo have to throw one of his classic tantrums, just as Milene was getting married, when he'd forgotten all about her? And why was he threatening to check into the Hotel Miramar so he could spy on other people's lives? So that he could impose his own order on things? Life in Valmares had an order already, it didn't need his intelligence. If a crime was going to be committed, as he predicted, it wouldn't be stopped by his beloved mathematical deductions chockfull of Latin words— it hadn't been easy to persuade him. The night before I left for Lisbon, João Paulo was like a caged bull, pawing the ground on the other end of the line. He said I was wrong, that he hadn't forgotten her, on the contrary, he loved her so much that he'd kept her preserved in his thoughts all this time, which is an argument so unoriginal that writers have been using it for as long as books have existed. And, that being the case, my busybody cousin could stay exactly where he was. He didn't have the right. Only I would go. And I didn't suspect a thing.

Then came the sermon.

The priest was speaking quietly, to a small, peaceful, well-mannered crowd. He seemed to have practiced his words on the seashore, addressing the Ocean waves. When he raised his right hand, he spoke of the Glorious Resurrection. When he raised his left, he spoke of there being just one Humanity. When he clasped both hands together, he turned to the bride and groom and said—"A single entity, a single soul, a single heart. Rising above all superficial differences . . ." All very abstract. But he spoke in more concrete terms about Regina Leandro, saying very quietly—"Yes, that wise woman, who passed among us in the dark of night, without our knowing, and, while reaching out one hand to death, reached for her granddaughter with the other and gave her over to the power of love . . ." I stared down at the floor in embarrassment, feeling as if those grandiose tropes were coming straight from my soul. But I was safe: it was all very quiet and very quick.

Even then, my aunts' shoulders remained absolutely still, as if they were made of clay. And I swear that when the sermon was over, I still knew absolutely nothing.

For example, I had no way of knowing that things at the Clínica das Salinas hadn't gone entirely according to plan. That Milene had woken up the next day with the rain pounding on the windows and refused to leave the room. That the hours had passed and she stayed sitting on one corner of the bed, clutching her two bags. No matter what they did, they couldn't make her move. The rain coursed down the windows, and the casuarina branch blew from side to side as if it were waving. Why wouldn't she leave the clinic? Why wouldn't she go down those steps? To Eulália, the nurse, Milene had said that she wasn't leaving because she'd lost something. "But what, what have you lost, Miss Milene?" Ângela Margarida would never forget the self-doubt that gripped her when she saw Milene on her hands and knees, looking under the bed, searching for something she couldn't find. "What is it, what is it, Milene?" Milene with her belongings spread out on the bed to see if anything was missing. Then, for a moment, Ângela Margarida had wavered. She thought perhaps she should tell the girl the truth. Out of a kind of respect for her logic-less logic, her knowledgeless wisdom, her intuition, which resided somewhere close to reason, though a long way from its center. But only for a moment. Her niece had seemed so vast to her then, her vulnerability and poverty so great that they spread endlessly ever outward, above and beyond everyone else. For a moment she had seemed to merge with a kind of nameless Humanity, something resistant to understanding and unreachable by human words. Aunt Ângela Margarida felt respect for that thing, which existed beyond proper names and ordinary lives. At that moment, she wanted to tell her niece what had happened, what they had done to her there—the kind of self-destructive impulse that can seize even the bravest of people, at the most unexpected times. But this was all just a suicidal delusion. When she realized what her innermost thoughts were up to, Ângela Margarida hardened her heart, strode over to the bed, and shouted—"Tidy up that mess right now. How stupid can you be? Do you honestly think anyone here is going to steal from you?" And she began hurriedly packing Milene's belongings into the bags, stuffing them in any-old-how.

Fortunately, at the end of the afternoon, a soaking wet Antonino had appeared at the entrance. Ângela Margarida would never forget how Milene had walked into his waiting arms, or how he had held her, hugging her tightly and glaring suspiciously around, before leading her away, supporting her by the elbow, as if transporting her through the air. And Milene following, letting herself be led, glancing over her shoulder and still clutching her bags. Yes, it had certainly been hard. But it had been worth it. And now, two years later, there was Ângela Margarida, dressed in blue, and there was her niece, dressed in white; it hadn't been an easy journey, but they had made it in the end. It was Easter Sunday. Beautiful spring weather in Valmares. Everyone there knew what they knew. I just sensed that something had happened.

The priest alone sang—"*O Lord . . .*"

All the guests repeated the words back to him. A small, tasteful ceremony. The people filming and taking photos were very discreet, their equipment unobtrusive. Their movements almost invisible. I turned to look from beneath my hat. And it was true, there weren't black people on one side and white people on the other. We were all mixed together. Arranged by the hand of an expert choreographer. If João Paulo were here, with his stochastic skills, would he have noticed anything more than that?

Later, I would find out for myself that on the afternoon of Milene's return from the clinic, the lights of Villa Regina were turned off.

Milene and Antonino would have dinner at the Pomodoro and Mãos Largas and coffee at the Banana, they went to Tocatinas on Saturdays, they strolled along the Dunas Fêmeas, and when they had time they'd go all the way to the Dunas Machas. They held hands in the Metropolitano Cinema. People would see them around, sometimes in silence and sometimes whispering together.

One night before the end of that rainy June, the lights at Villa Regina were all on. Antonino would have said to Milene—"Milene? I know what the problem is. Grandma Regina might come at night, wanting to sleep here, and not be able to find it. I can just imagine. You should put some lamps out there, on the wall, where it says KM 44. Then when she's on her way down the road, she'll read the sign and come in. Otherwise how will she recognize it, with all the lights on inside the house, when she's never seen it like that before? She'll think it's just some Christmas decoration, not her own home. She'll be wandering around, completely lost . . ." The conversation was half-serious and half-joking. "Do you think so?"—my cousin Milene had asked. Knowing it was half-true and half-false. That the true part wouldn't work without the false part, and vice versa. Anyway, it was all fine. The plan was that as soon as the June rains were over, the two of them would cut back the ivy and tidy up KM 44. They would buy two big lamps to light up the entrance. They'd need very powerful bulbs. The old houses opposite were growing more disfigured by the day, and now they were being used as makeshift shops and warehouses. Sand, wood, scaffolding, and red cars for transporting meat all accumulated in the space outside. It seemed that for one part of the world to progress, the rest had to be left to rot. Yes, it would make sense to change tack, to start welcoming in the departed who wandered the roads by night, lost and looking for their homes. Death isn't dying, death is disappearing from people's memories. And the room upstairs, Dona Regina's bedroom when she was still a nimble, capable woman, could stay lit up forever. And why shouldn't it, if that was what Milene wanted? If she didn't know for certain where Regina Leandro had ended up? Again the priest sang—"*Here I am with you all!*" And I still knew absolutely nothing.

Only then did Aunt Gininha turn and look behind her. Her eye makeup still impeccable.

I would find out too that on the day when Gininha went, for the third time, to attempt to read Milene the will, a copy of which was kept in the safe, hidden behind the *Great Portuguese and Brazilian Encyclopedia*, she had arrived at the house completely possessed by Uncle Dom Silvestre's mercantile soul. It was as if he had given her a dose of some overpowering stimulant. Wasting no time, my aunt had explained that Milene would be perfectly fine with just Villa Regina. Milene knew it wasn't true. That her aunt was lying. That day, however, at the center of her aunt's large eyes gleamed the tiny eyes of her uncle. "It's okay, Aunt Gininha, don't worry . . ." Milene understood and she didn't mind. Back then, Antonino's grandmother hadn't yet disappeared into the mud, and Milene had had the idea of inviting all the Matas to come and live in Villa Regina, instead of going back to the dust of Bairro dos Espelhos. If she wanted the house to herself, to do whatever she liked with, it would make sense to take Kilometer 44 now. So she said yes. My aunt, with my uncle's eyes inside hers—"And you know you can't change your mind . . ." Yes, Milene had already told her, that was fine. It would mean the Matas could use the entire house, from the microclimate to the bedrooms. Juliana was thrilled. If the Matas moved in, it would be just like *Uncle Tom's Cabin*. Everything was falling into place. On that January afternoon, my aunt had driven away happy.

But as for how much Milene and Antonino knew about what had happened at the Clínica das Salinas, no one was entirely sure. Everyone else's contradictions were hard enough to make sense of, but Antonino and Milene's life existed on a more delicate plane. After a certain point, it was simply impossible to reach.

Sometimes, around noon, Milene would go and watch Antonino climb down from the crane, the pair would have lunch together, and then she would continue sitting across from the nearly completed construction, where the cranes stood among the tall towers, interrupting the line of the sea. They were clos-ing the last roof terrace on the hotel, which was surrounded by the cluster of new houses that would become Vila Camarga. She loved to watch him climb up, like a big clambering cat, before making the long metal arm hoist materials up from the ground onto the highest concrete slab. Milene liked the way he sat there, moving the enormous needle from place to place, lifting and low-ering the weights. But her favorite part was watching him climb up and down. At the end of the following February, the weather turned blustery. The wind shrieked its way through the cranes and it was too dangerous to go up. One day, the tall metal struc-tures began to sway. Antonino was in the cabin of the Liebherr, and he didn't want to climb down. The guys from the yellow Pontiac had started yelling that there could be a problem. All the workers on the ground, shouting and shouting. The foreman calling to the engineer, and everyone calling to Antonino. The foreman berating him through the megaphone. Everyone staring, baffled. Eventually the winds subsided and Antonino climbed down. What had he been waiting for? What the hell was he playing at? Did he want to get the firm into trouble, was that it? And what if the wind hadn't dropped, eh? They'd have been peeling him off the ground, wasn't that right? What a moron, what a total idiot . . . Milene wasn't there that day. She never heard about it. I would find out later on. Yes, they were in love. They still kissed like before, made plans like before. But something, some nameless thing, had left them. Now it must have been the end of the mass, and the choir was singing—"*Here is the Creator . . .*" The voice of the soloist shining through, bright and pure as the day—"*He is both in Heaven and on Earth, the Creator . . .*"

Or perhaps it was only my soul. I had never really believed in João Paulo.

I would come to learn that, a year before, Antonino had walked into the Modelo supermarket and approached one of the tills. It was a quiet time, between four and five in the afternoon. The cashier was chatting loudly with her colleagues. He had gone in to buy razor blades he didn't need. And he had deliberately chosen Divina's till. He looked at her and smiled, and at first she didn't smile back, but then she called out as he was leaving— "Don't go yet. Wait for me outside and I'll give you a piece of my mind. You little bastard. Wait outside . . ." He had enjoyed the threat. Divina came out soon after, though it was long before the end of her shift. "Oh, are you still here? I forgot I'd asked you to wait . . ."—Feigning surprise. "All right, then, fine, out with it. What do you want?"

Divina didn't have a car.

She got into the gray van. They drove quickly, very quickly.

The road itself seemed to be on wheels. Everything was so easy with Divina, so simple, so comfortable. They went into her house, which was in a kind of village on the outskirts, but it would do, he could go inside quickly and it could all happen fast. Everyone there knew everyone else's business, and nobody cared. It was a small place. Divina began undressing, Antonino too. Even in the dark, he'd know his way around this house. "Oh, I've missed you, you bastard . . ."—she sobbed. They embraced fiercely, and then, half an hour later, Divina was pulling on her bra and panties. Divina shouting—"She's put a spell on you, you cheating piece of shit. A Cape Verdean who can't get it up . . . A *badio* born and bred, and now look at you, it's pathetic, you piece of shit . . ." Now Divina was shouting the words from her doorway, for the whole tiny village to hear.

"The less we see Him, the more we recognize Him. O it's really Him, my Lord!"—sang the crystalline voice.

Yes, there they both were. Now they were turning around, and we could see their faces. The video camera moved closer, as if it wanted to take a bite out of them. For a moment, the silence in the little church was so real it seemed alive. Yes, something had happened. It had happened before Ana Mata set off with her packed lunch to look for a boat, inspired by the telegraph operator in Cidade da Praia. Around the end of January, when Milene wanted everyone from the Old Factory to move into Villa Regina, and the Matas were preparing to return to Bairro dos Espelhos. I would never know for sure. That meeting was always a mystery to me. But I would have good reasons for thinking that this is what happened.

For thinking, that is, that Antonino Mata had gone to the Town Hall in Santa Maria de Valmares one morning, at around eleven o'clock. That it was a Monday and the waiting room was full. Antonino Mata, who had never made an appointment to see anyone, wanted to meet with the mayor. The receptionist that morning, a woman in orthopedic shoes and wearing a necklace of freshwater pearls, eyed him as if he were a dog asking to be let into a butcher's shop. "And what exactly do you want?" Antonino was wearing an enormous watch on his wrist and white thick-soled trainers on his feet. His two missing premolars made him look rather hollow-cheeked. What's more, he was pulling on a cigarette. It wasn't a great first impression. But he had insisted—"Please, go in and say that Antonino Mata's here to see the mayor, tell him I'm sitting right here . . ." The woman went through a door and then returned. He settled in to wait. For the first hour, he sat on a bench. For the second, he paced up and down, and for the third he stood still, hands in the pockets of his leather jacket, almost entirely motionless. The receptionist, as if she had forgotten who he was, had asked him vaguely—"What was it you wanted?" He hadn't even answered, simply turning his back on her. By then it was half past two. The door had opened and Rui Ludovice the engineer had left with his assistant and secretary. "What about you, aren't you going to have lunch?"— Antonino Mata had said no, he'd stay there and keep his place. She understood that this man was determined to wait for the mayor, no matter what. Then she said—"Here, write down what you want . . ." He had written—*My name is Antonino Normand Mata. I would like to speak to the Mayor.* After looking at the piece of paper for a while, the woman had decided—"It would have to be later on, in the afternoon . . ." Although of course it was already the afternoon. She added—"Yes, much later on." That was fine. He didn't mind how late. She pretended to remember something. Was it about an old factory? Yes, exactly, he had answered. It was a bit later by then, but not much. The mayor and his small team had returned and begun receiving people again. And then at around four o'clock the receptionist had said, as if she had single-handedly overcome a major setback—"Wait there . . ." Suddenly conspiratorial—"He's going to see you after hours. Oh, whatever will become of us when we no longer have this kindhearted man as mayor?" Antonino Mata would be kept waiting until eight that evening.

By then the Town Hall was deserted. Only the assistant was still working. The mayor had told the receptionist—"You can go, Dona Eulália. It's late. I'll be heading off soon myself. And Frutuoso can leave as well." So there were three people in the building, including Antonino. The mayor had said to his assistant—"Could you go and get that file I mentioned?" The man went back into the office. Only then did the mayor look at Antonino Mata. "What's going on?" And Antonino Mata would have said—"What's going on, sir, is that someone's days are numbered. I'm going to go after them, you see, and I want to know who to go after. I'm talking about what your wife did to my girlfriend at the clinic . . ." Rui Ludovice had been careless. The buildings were deserted, without even a security guard around. He called to his assistant, getting to his feet. "No, stay there. This time I'm only here to tell you what I know and ask if it was you, your wife, or someone else who had that shameful thing done to the girl. Tonight you just need to tell me that. And you can turn my pockets inside out if you like—you won't find anything. But next time will be different . . ." The assistant, hovering nearby, didn't understand the substance of the conversation, and wondered about going to get help, but Rui Ludovice held up his hand and said, in two different directions and with two different meanings—"Now, just keep calm . . ." Aunt Ângela Margarida's husband asked the assistant to leave the room. The real problems would start if the assistant overheard why this man from Cape Verde had come.

And so they were left alone in the building to talk.

What did they talk about?

Antonino would have mentioned all the knives he had at home and all the firearms he knew how to use, and his irresistible thirst for revenge, which had been accumulating in his ancestors since time immemorial, and he would have said that, yes, it had fallen to him, it was time for retribution, and told the mayor to look him in the eye—what he was feeling at that moment was a desire for death, pure and simple. He wanted it more than anything else. An entire life, he knew, could be justified by one moment of revenge. Yes, he was thinking of Milene and he wanted revenge; he didn't want justice, justice was impossible. Antonino's hands had turned white with rage. On the table, the hands of the mayor of Santa Maria de Valmares were trembling slightly. That night, the button-sized ulcer was definitely going to bleed. But Rui Ludovice was a man of action. Sometimes he was Action itself, looking down from on high, reaching down from on high to smooth things over.

This was one of those times. Ludovice had said—"Right, let's think this through . . .

"I don't know precisely what happened. That's a matter for women and doctors, that sorry bunch who like to rummage around in human bodies . . . I don't know what happened. Still, one thing is certain. If you're right about what happened, and you want to get revenge, then be my guest . . . Now, I don't know anything, but what I can say is that if I were you, in your position, first of all I would think very carefully . . . Revenge feels good, of course it does, but it only lasts a minute. And in this case—and because you want, specifically, to take revenge on me—you have two doors in front of you. You have the door of revenge, which you can walk through and feel very pleased with yourself, knowing your hand will never forget how good it felt to get even, and yet, behind that door—well, you open it and there's only the abyss. The abyss. Are you with me? On the other hand, if you hold back, and instead go through the other door, the sensible door, you save your three sons, your mother, your aunts, and all your brothers from falling into the abyss . . . You even save Milene from falling into the abyss. Think carefully . . . If you choose the first door, then all of them, beginning with Milene, who is the reason for all this, will end up down there in the abyss. As I say, you have two doors. If you choose the second, you save them all, maybe even those brothers of yours who the police have their eye on, and most importantly, Antonino, you save yourself. Yes, because at the end of the day, you matter to yourself, Antonino . . ." Aunt Ângela Margarida's husband was on his feet now, pacing up and down in his office, and his rhetorical instincts led him to give a demonstration. He opened one door, acting it out, and said— "Imagine this is the door to salvation. And this other one is the door to the abyss . . . Walking through this one feels good for a second, but then you lose everything. And walking through this one might be difficult, but it means everyone is saved. The choice is yours, Antonino . . ."

Antonino, the palms of his hands white with rage, could barely hear what he was saying. It would be a long night. We know they left at some point. And that Rui Ludovice, with sudden and uncharacteristic daring, might even have said—"I didn't do it, but since it's me you've chosen, then by all means, take revenge on me . . ." They were in my uncle's private car. Antonino's face felt damp. My uncle would have continued—"But if you don't, you'll guarantee all your loved ones a happy life . . . And you

505

know what, Antonino? It's a long time, a very long time indeed, since I came across a real man like you. Sorry to change the subject, but what education do you have? Seven years of school at the São Nicolau Seminary in Cape Verde?—And you didn't finish the eighth. You were only interested in engines and electricity. You want to qualify as a crane operator. You want to move a long way away, with your three children and Milene. Yes, I can understand that too, you like cranes because you like seeing things from above, you like moving weights around. You like climbing quickly up and down, and feeling your heart pounding when you get to the top. You like the feeling of danger when the wind's whistling in the cranes and they might topple over. You like going up even when they might topple over and kill you. Yes, yes, Antonino, I understand. You need help. You see, I didn't know you before . . . You can clearly see the two doors opening, you're standing in between them and you still have time to choose . . ."

And by the look of things, Antonino had chosen. But it would take him another year.

It wouldn't have been an easy choice; he must have gone back and forth from door to door, day after day and night after night, month after month, as demonstrated by his visit to Divina's till at the supermarket, before making up his mind. And now there they were. Milene turned to face the guests before Antonino did. Her veil was drawn back and she was smiling, her eyes bright, her face flushed. She seemed about to hurl herself into the arms of the person who had just flown in on the morning plane. It was Antonino who held her back. He led her over, calm and composed. I had to take my hat off to kiss her. The two of us looking at each other and laughing, just like in the *best summer of our lives*. Only it was a different boy in the boat this time. They had to separate us in the end. Milene and Antonino made their way out of the church. The guests, once again, formed two rows. There, on the ground, there were almost forty of us, and nobody had left yet. To someone looking down from the white vaulted roof, we would all have looked the same. To a bird flying through the sky, all the same. And to the vaults of Heaven itself, did we even exist? The priest waved goodbye, smiling. Standing in a ray of sunlight, which made the gold on his cape gleam. The choir sang on, sending their silvery voices into the skies—"O my Lord! When will we see You?"

Outside, where the group had gathered, endless photographs were being taken.

Lisbon, July 10, 1998

About the Author

Lídia Jorge was born in 1946 in the village of Boliqueime in the Algarve, southern Portugal. After university, she became a schoolteacher and spent six very formative years in Angola and Mozambique. In 1980, she published her first novel, *O Dia dos Prodígios*, to great acclaim, and it was later made into a film by Margarida Cardoso, as was *A Costa dos Murmúrios* (translated as *The Murmuring Coast* by Natália Costa and Ronald W. Sousa). *O Vale da Paixão* (translated as *The Painter of Birds* by Margaret Jull Costa) brought her five prizes, including the prestigious Prix Jean Monnet de littérature européenne. Her other novels have garnered her still more awards both in Portugal and elsewhere, notably the 2006 Albatros Literaturpreis awarded by the Günter Grass Foundation. She has also written short stories, children's books, essays, poems, and a play. Her work has been translated into more than twenty languages. In 2020, she was awarded the Guadalajara International Book Festival Literature Prize for her complete body of work. The jury praised the originality and subtlety of her style and her immense humanity in dealing with such themes as adolescence, decolonization, the role of women, emigration, and so on. Her recent novel *Os Memoráveis* won her the Grande Prémio Luso-Espanhol de Cultura, and *Estuário*, her latest book, was shortlisted for the Prix Médicis.

About the Translators

Margaret Jull Costa has worked as a translator for over thirty years, translating the works of many Spanish, Portuguese, and Brazilian writers, among them the novelists Javier Marías, José Saramago, Eça de Queirós, and Machado de Assis, as well as the poets Fernando Pessoa, Sophia de Mello Breyner Andresen, Mário de Sá-Carneiro, and Ana Luísa Amaral.

Annie McDermott's translations from the Spanish and Portuguese include *Empty Words* and *The Luminous Novel* by Mario Levrero, *Dead Girls* and *Brickmakers* by Selva Almada, *The Rooftop* by Fernanda Trías, and *City of Ulysses* by Teolinda Gersão (cotranslated with Jethro Soutar).